Tilly's Story

Tilly's Story

JUNE FRANCIS

Allison & Busby Limited
13 Charlotte Mews
London W1T 4EJ
www.allisonandbusby.com

Hardcover published in Great Britain in 2008.
This paperback edition published in 2009.

A CIP catalogue record for this book is available from
the British Library.

10 9 8 7 6 5 4 3 2 1

ISBN 978-0-7490-0700-3

Typeset in Sabon by
Terry Shannon

The paper used for this Allison & Busby publication
has been produced from trees that have been legally sourced
from well-managed and credibly certified forests.

PEFC
PEFC/16-33-111
CATG-PEFC-052
www.pefc.org

Printed and bound in the UK by
CPI Bookmarque, Croydon, CR0 4TD

JUNE FRANCIS was born in Blackpool and moved to Liverpool at an early age. She started writing in her forties producing articles for *My Weekly* and has since gone on to have over twenty novels published. Married with three grown-up sons, she enjoys fell-walking, local history and swimming.

To my eldest son, Iain, without whose sterling work as my researcher this book would not have been written. Having the knack of finding fascinating snippets of information is a gift and has provided me with plot ideas and often much amusement.

PART ONE

June–December 1920

CHAPTER ONE

Tilly Moran frowned as she folded the telegram and tapped it against her teeth. Would she be able to make it to Liverpool in time to be there to greet Don Pierce when the liner from New York docked – or would meeting her father as she had promised make her much too late? She had not seen Don since just after Armistice Day. She had considered the American quite crazy when he had said he wanted to marry her and was prepared to wait until she had grown up. At the time she had been grateful to him saving her brother-in-law, Seb's life after finding him half-buried and left for dead on the battlefield after the German spring offensive.

Don was a photojournalist and, having returned to America, he had kept in touch by letter. These were always interesting and often made her laugh out loud. If there was a way that she could meet her father and see Don, as well, then she would do it. She concealed the telegram beneath the white cotton bust bodices in a drawer of her dressing table, along with the invitation to Mrs Black's wedding. Her sister, Alice, would hit the roof if she knew about the latter. She had always despised the widowed medium and healer – just as she did their father.

Tilly closed the drawer and glanced at the clock on the mantelpiece. For a moment she was motionless, knowing that if she were to meet Don it would be a close run thing. Then she reached for the large-brimmed straw hat, trimmed with yellow ribbon and a cluster of artificial daisies, and placed it on her red-gold, curtain-styled hair. She glanced in the mirror as she drew on tan gloves, pulling a wry face at the sprinkling of freckles on her nose and cheeks. She would have dearly loved to have tried one of the remedies advertised in Alice's women's magazine to get rid of freckles, if only she could afford it.

Picking up the shopping bag, she tip-toed across the room. She carefully turned the door knob and stuck her head out, glancing this way and that along the landing. To her relief there was no one in sight but the murmur of voices could be heard coming from below. She closed the door gently behind her and crept along the landing and down the stairs. She prayed that she would be able to leave the house without being seen and had managed to reach the front door, unnoticed, when the telephone rang and the knocker sounded. She groaned inwardly before wrenching open the door.

On the step stood Clara, a dark-haired young woman who had stolen the heart of Freddie Kirk, whom she had married four months' ago. Tilly had been a little in love with Freddie since she was a child but from the moment he'd clapped eyes on Clara, the easygoing relationship of their childhood had vanished. The happy couple now lived a few doors away in an apartment above that of Tilly's half-brother and his family, and when she saw them together she almost envied their newfound intimacy.

'You look nice. You meeting someone special?' asked Clara, smiling.

'Dad! But don't mention it to Alice,' whispered Tilly. Hearing the sound of the sitting room door opening – presumably either Seb or Alice coming to answer the telephone – Tilly added hastily, 'Sorry! I can't stop.'

She brushed past Clara and hurried down the path to the front gate, only to pause when she heard her sister calling her name. But she decided to pretend not to have heard her. It could simply be that Alice wanted her to accompany her nephew and niece to the birthday party they had been invited to that afternoon; any other time Tilly would have done so willingly, but not now. She was through the gate and running along Victoria Crescent in the direction of Queen's Park Road. She needed to catch a tram that would take her to Overleigh Road, where her father would be waiting. She knew he was likely to work himself up into a state if she was late.

As soon as Tilly climbed down from the tram, she could see Mal pacing the ground. He was clutching a bunch of red roses in a large, gnarled hand. He must have heard the tram because suddenly he looked up and she saw the relief in his still handsome, weather-beaten face as he caught sight of her.

For a moment Tilly thought of Don, knowing she would not be able to rush away and meet him as she had hoped, and felt a deep pang of regret. It would have been fun to have spent time with him and been brought up to date with his latest assignment. They could have discussed her writing plans, too.

She let her mind drift towards the possibility of a future with Don Pierce. She was far too young to be tied down, of course, but she thought that if any man would support her in her career choice after marriage it would be Don Pierce. She could not imagine any other man being inclined to allow her to carry on with her writing once that gold band was on her finger.

She sighed and then pinned a smile on her face and waved to her father. Immediately, he came shuffling towards her. As they drew closer she noticed the beads of perspiration on his forehead beneath the brim of his old tweed cap. She was instantly concerned because he had made no concession to the heatwave and was wearing a starched collar and tie and a waistcoat beneath his brown tweed suit. He might end up having a stroke if he wasn't careful. Although he was still very active and physically strong he had, of late, had an air of frailty about him which worried her. Having only come to know him during the past year or so, she really couldn't bear the thought of losing him so quickly.

'I was starting to think yer'd changed yer mind, lass,' he said, reaching out to her.

She clasped his callused hand and pressed it gently. 'I promised I'd come, didn't I?'

'Aye. But I know how difficult it is for yer to get away and meet me. Alice wouldn't like it if she knew.'

Tilly linked her arm through his and said cheerfully, 'Let's not talk about Alice.'

'I can't help it. I think of her every time I set eyes on yer, lass.' Mal sighed heavily. 'She was a pretty girl, just like you. Yer know, I thought she would have forgiven me when I saved her little Flora from that gunman last year. After all, she did invite me to yer sixteenth birthday party. But I was mistaken.'

Tilly realised they were going to cover the same old ground

again. 'I know, so did I. But she still might change her mind. I keep telling her it was the lead-poisoning that made you do those mad things when she was little.'

'I'm getting on, lass, and she might leave it too late,' he muttered. 'That thought grieves me.'

'I know.' Tilly squeezed his arm. 'Anyway, let's just concentrate on finding Mam's grave right now.' The last time she had visited the plot was with Alice and the children and she could only hope that she would remember where it was without her sister leading the way.

'It's a long time since I've been inside this cemetery,' mumbled Mal, swotting a midge that landed on his neck. 'Pesky insects! I've been plagued by them in the garden these last few weeks.'

'It's this heatwave. I hope it keeps fine for Mrs Black's wedding next month.'

'The ground needs the rain. I reckon the garden at her new house in Liverpool is going to keep me busy for months. A right jungle it is.'

'But you enjoy being a gardener, don't you, Dad?'

'Aye.' His face lit up. 'I don't have to make conversation and worry about what people think of me. I like feeding the birds and watching the vegetables and flowers grow. These roses are from Eudora's garden at Eastham.' He held the bunch out to her with a flourish. 'She said I could pick them when I told her where I was going. She was always concerned about yer mother, yer know, despite what Alice believes. If only yer mother would have agreed to consult her as a healer, then our lives might have been different.' He sighed heavily. 'Fatalistic, that was Flora. Her condition was God's will and she believed it was her cross to bear, just like I was.'

'She said that to you?' asked Tilly, disturbed by this information.

'Aye.' His face darkened. 'It drove me mad but I can forgive her now because she was always willing to forgive me. I wasn't an easy man to live with and I still regret that she died the way she did.'

Tilly tried to reassure him but she guessed he would always be racked with guilt about the past. She changed the subject. 'When were you last here, Dad?'

He glanced about him as they strolled along a path. 'Not since yer mother and I visited yer grandmother's grave. I'm glad yer reminded me it was yer mother's birthday today. I used to buy her red roses every birthday before I went off ma head with the lead.' His brow furrowed. 'But yer don't want to hear about all that.'

'I'm interested in anything to do with your past, Dad,' Tilly replied honestly, recognising a marble angel. Thank goodness, they were going the right way.

'I'll tell you how the roses came about then,' he said, sounding pleased. 'I'd been reading Rabbie Burns' poem, 'My Love is Like a Red, Red Rose'. It was Burns' Night and Flora loved poetry.' His lined face grew soft with the reminiscence.

Tilly thought, How romantic, loving the sound of her father rolling his Rs and wondering what Alice would have made of this information.

'I wish there was a way of Flora knowing that I was paying my respects and bringing her red roses again,' muttered Mal.

'Who's to say she doesn't?' said Tilly, slowing her pace to match his shuffling gait. 'Surely you haven't worked for Mrs Black all these years without believing in the possibility of an afterlife?'

Mal's face was sad. 'I can't see me getting into Heaven and being with the women I loved.' His eyes glistened with tears. 'I was wicked. I don't deserve yer affection, lass, and that's the truth. Yer can't know how happy I've been this last year since yer went out of yer way to get to know me. Eudora speaks well of yer, too. She says yer can come and visit me any time after the move to Liverpool.'

'I've been invited to her wedding, too. I must admit I was surprised.'

'She says yer kind and yer've got courage, and it'll give you the chance to see where the house is. Yer do realise that it's going to be a registry office do? Mr Bennett has been divorced, yer see. Although, there's to be a service afterwards at the Spiritualist church.'

Tilly nodded. 'Mr Bennett was once married to Alice's mother-in-law, so I knew he was divorced.'

'I didn't know that, or if I did I'd forgotten.' Mal looked thoughtful and absently swotted another midge. 'Are we near your mother's grave yet?'

Tilly had been keeping her eye out for landmarks and guessed they were nearly there. She was right. While Mal read the words engraved on the pink granite headstone, she removed the dead flowers from the black and chrome container and emptied out the stagnant water. Then from her shopping bag she took a lemonade bottle of fresh water and poured that into the flower container. She asked her father for the roses and he handed them to her. For a moment she sniffed their heady perfume, reminded of the Attar of Roses talcum powder Alice had given her last Christmas. Don had sent her a card and a photograph of himself. Her brow furrowed, wondering whether the liner had docked and he had disembarked. Perhaps he was looking out for her on the landing stage at the Pierhead at this very moment.

'I wish I could have had some words written on her stone,' said Mal loudly, rousing Tilly from her reverie.

She stared at the gravestone and read her grandmother's details and then her mother's name and the dates of her birth and death, and, below, the inscription: Beloved mother of Alice and Tilly, 'The Lord, their God shall be their light, and they shall reign for ever and ever'.

'I suppose it could be done,' she mused. 'But it would cost money. Do you have that kind of money, Dad?'

He looked vague and did not answer, only saying, 'Yer don't think Alice would be angry?'

'I'm sure she would have something to say but you are our dad, so I don't see why you shouldn't have some words on her gravestone.'

'I'd like that but I bet Alice won't want me buried here,' he muttered. 'But that'll suit me because I want to be buried next to my first wife, Janet. God rest her soul.'

Tilly thought, Well, knowing that will save an argument when the time comes. Not that she wanted to dwell on the thought of her father dying. 'Tell me more about your life in Scotland with Janet when Kenny was little.'

Mal smiled. 'She'd laugh and sing and dance with him round the kitchen. I used to laugh a lot myself in those days. She brought me out of myself and made me feel I wasn't useless. Yer grandmother didn't approve of her at all because she hated anyone to be happy. She was a bitter woman. My father left her and she never forgave him. I worry in case Alice is turning into yer grandmother. She has that same conviction that her way is the only way.'

His words made Tilly uncomfortable. 'I wouldn't argue that Alice won't budge from what she believes is right, but she's also caring and wants the best for people.'

'Her best,' said Mal dourly. 'I don't want to criticise yer sister. She has good reason for hating me. I was a violent man in those days, but I wasn't all bad.' He smiled suddenly, 'But you, lass, remind me of Flora. She was a fine woman, forgiving me over and over again.'

'She forgave you far too much,' said a grim voice behind him.

'What are you doing here?' Tilly dropped a rose and her heart began to pound as she looked up into her sister's face, trying not to show her dismay at being caught here with her father.

Alice was a woman in her early thirties, smartly dressed and with a good figure. She had flaming red hair and it could be argued that her temper could be fiery, too. In her hand she carried a bunch of pink carnations.

'D'you really believe I would forget Mum's birthday? Why didn't you stop when I called you? I'm disappointed in you, Tilly, going behind my back and bringing *him* here. This is a sacred place to me. I don't want him desecrating it with his presence.' Her green eyes were as hard as glass.

'That's a bit harsh,' said Tilly, her own temper flaring. 'He's not the devil incarnate, you know.'

'I know exactly what he is,' snapped Alice. 'I've told you but will you listen to me? Will you heck!'

'I have a right to choose whether I see my own father or not,' cried Tilly. 'Anyway, how did you get here so swiftly?'

'I was going to ask you to come with me in the motor after I took the children to the party. That was what the telephone call was about.'

'You left it a bit late mentioning it to me,' said Tilly, picking up the fallen rose and placing it in the container.

'I had other things on my mind,' said Alice. 'The telephone went again just as I was coming out. Seb said it was Don.'

'Don?' Tilly's heart seemed to flip over.

'Yes. Seb's gone off to Liverpool in a hurry to see him in your place.' Alice's face tightened. 'Now, who bought those roses? You or Dad?'

'Neither,' replied Tilly, glad at least that Don would be meeting Seb. Hopefully, her brother-in-law would put in a good word for her.

'What do you mean by that? One of you must have bought them,' said Alice.

Tilly forced herself to concentrate on the matter at hand. 'Mrs Black said Dad could take them from her garden.'

'You mean—' Alice's chest swelled with indignation.

'They're roses, Alice, not deadly nightshade.'

'I don't care what flowers they are. You can damn well take them out of *my* container,' ordered Alice, almost choking on the words.

'No,' said Tilly firmly. 'It isn't just your container. Kenny paid half the cost. I'm sure Mam would be pleased if she knew Dad's roses and your pink carnations nestled together in it.'

'You don't know anything about what pleased Mam! I hope *he* goes to hell for what he did to her.' Alice bent down and her hand fastened on the roses in the container and she wrenched them out. A yelp escaped her and she dropped the flowers. 'See what you've done?' she cried, lifting a bleeding finger to her mouth and sucking it.

'What I did?' protested Tilly, gingerly picking up the scattered roses so as to avoid pricking a finger herself. She plunged them back into the water. 'You did it to yourself with your bad temper. Dad regrets the past and is desperate to make amends.'

'And you think that a few red roses now she's dead can do that? You're an idiot! You're letting him fool you into believing that he's changed his ways but leopards don't change their spots. Now throw those roses away and don't you be meeting him again behind my back.'

Tilly shot to her feet. 'I wish you'd stop speaking to me as if I were a child! I'll be seventeen next month and Dad's not getting any younger. Have some pity instead of being so judgemental.'

Alice clenched her fists. 'Why should I pity him? If only you had been there when Mam died.'

Tilly flinched. 'You're forgetting I was. She died giving me life. Have you ever thought that I might feel guilty about that?'

Alice paled and stretched out a hand to her sister. 'Sorry! I didn't mean for you to feel like that. I —'

'Probably not but it's true,' interrupted Tilly. 'I share the guilt about her death with Dad. It's something that binds us together.' Emotion clogged her throat and tears itched her eyes. She fought them back, lowering her head, hoping the brim of her hat would conceal her face from her sister's gaze. Her tears ran down her face and splashed on her mother's grave.

'Stop it! Don't cry!' Alice's voice cracked. 'You aren't to blame. But you never knew her so how can you miss her the way I do? *He's* to blame that my children don't have a loving grandmother to care for them only Seb's blinking mother, and we don't see much of her now she's moved to Liverpool.'

'That's because you chased her away,' said Tilly, wiping her damp face with the back of her hand.

'No, I didn't,' protested Alice. 'She was fed up of living with us. She wanted to be near that-that police sergeant who kept inviting her to concerts. She wants to try and recapture the old days when she was someone on the stage. She can't accept that she's past it.'

'There you go again!' cried Tilly, glaring at her. 'Why shouldn't Gabrielle have a go at doing what she wants before it's too late? She can belt out a decent song and she's quite attractive for her age.'

'Attractive!' gasped Alice. 'She's mutton dressed as lamb. If she had any morals at all then she'd accept that she's getting old and be a proper grandmother to her grandchildren. She's as bad as Mrs Black, getting married in her dotage.'

'Now you are exaggerating,' said Tilly, deciding it was time to leave. She reached for the lemonade bottle and put in the stopper. 'Mrs Black has all her marbles. And she does care about people.'

'So you say but I don't believe it. It's money she cares about. I can't understand a charming and seemingly sensible man like Mr Bennett marrying her,' said Alice. 'But then he did marry Seb's mother and that was a big mistake, too.'

'Don't be bitchy,' snapped Tilly. 'You really have got it in for the three of them. I'd hate Dad to be right about you turning into a bigot like his mother.'

Alice's face paled and her fists clenched. 'How dare you throw his words in my face! You've been spoilt, that's your problem.'

'Spoilt? How?' Tilly was startled. 'I've acted as nursemaid to your children and been gardener, cook and housemaid, as well. I admit I've had plenty of love and attention but there's a lot I've missed out on, too' she countered. 'I grew up never knowing my parents. I know yours and Kenny's childhood wasn't exactly a bundle of laughs but life hasn't treated you too badly since. You have a good husband, three lovely children and a nice home. What more could you ask for?'

The colour flooded back into Alice's face and she yelled, 'I want my sister to be on my side!'

'I don't want to take sides,' said Tilly heatedly, placing the empty bottle in her shopping bag.

'You might have to,' said Alice forcefully. 'I can't relax while you're seeing him. I worry he might suddenly explode and lash out at you or even turn up at the house and hurt the children.'

Tilly stared at her incredulously. 'I don't know how you can believe that about him these days. You should take a proper look at him.' She glanced to where she had last seen her father, but he was no longer there. Guilt filled her. 'Damn you, Alice! You've frightened him away.'

She looked about her and caught sight of Mal shuffling along the path in the direction of the gates. For a moment she hesitated, thinking that if she let her father go, she might still have a chance of seeing Don, always assuming Seb had left a message at the house for her saying where they were meeting. Then Tilly remembered her father's uncertain mental state and, concerned he might do something foolish, she knew that she had no choice but to go after him.

She left her sister and ran to catch up with her father. Slipping her hand through his arm she said, 'I'm sorry, Dad. I didn't expect her to turn up and spoil everything.'

'She still hates me,' he mumbled. 'She's filled with hate.'

'Let's forget about her,' said Tilly. 'What do you want to do next?'

'What do I want to do, lass? I want to go home. Get back to my garden where it's peaceful and quiet.'

'I'll come with you,' said Tilly, hoping there might still be a chance of her seeing Don later that day. Right now, though, she had to reassure her father that he was her first priority.

CHAPTER TWO

Tilly entered the house, unsure of her welcome after the flaming row with her sister. It was early evening and she made for the stairs, hoping to get to the sanctuary of her bedroom and compose herself before facing Alice. She needed to ask her whether there had been any messages from Seb or Don.

She was halfway up the stairs when she heard the living room door open and footsteps in the hall below. 'Tilly, I want a word with you.' Her heart performed a somersault at the sound of Seb's voice. Was it possible Don was with him?

She hurried back down the stairs. 'What is it? Is Don here?'

'So you haven't forgotten him?' asked Seb tersely.

'Of course not!' She realised that her brother-in-law was far from pleased with her. 'But I'd promised Dad that I'd meet him. I couldn't break a promise.'

Seb stared at her from his good eye; the empty socket of the other was concealed by a black patch. 'Tilly, I understand the importance of keeping a promise, but surely you could have made some excuse? Mrs Black has a telephone, doesn't she?'

'I'm sorry. It was today that Dad and I wanted to visit

Mam's grave because of it being her birthday.' She hesitated. 'So what did Don have to say? Was he angry?'

'He was disappointed,' said Seb, his frown deepening. 'He really believed you'd want to see him.'

Tilly moistened her lips with the tip of her tongue. 'Of course I want to see him. I thought that perhaps if you had the name of his hotel in Liverpool I could go and see him now.'

'You're too late, Tilly. Don has a very tight schedule, that's why he asked you to meet him as soon as he arrived in Liverpool. He didn't come over here purely to see you. He's come to Europe to work.'

The colour flamed in Tilly's cheeks. 'He never mentioned anything about a tight schedule to me.'

'He could hardly say much in a wire, could he?'

'So-so where is he now?' asked Tilly, realising she wanted to see Don much more than she had thought, now that a meeting seemed out of the question.

'On his way to London.'

'London!' Tilly was stunned. 'So soon? Why?'

'The journal he works for wants photographs of how Londoners are coping with the aftermath of the war. After that he's off to Europe.'

Tilly was hurt. 'Why couldn't he have told me this in his last letter? I didn't even know he was coming here until I received his telegram.'

'He planned on surprising you, taking you out for a meal in Liverpool and telling you then. This London commission was something that only came up when he was on the ship. The journal wired him about it. It's a pity it's too late to do anything about seeing him now if that's how you really feel.'

'Yes, it's too late,' said Tilly, a tremor in her voice.

Seb's face softened. 'He thought you didn't care enough about him to want him as a husband in the future.'

Tilly sighed and folded her arms, leaning against the wall. 'Perhaps it's just as well we didn't meet if he couldn't delay his journey for one day. Summoning me out of the blue to be at the Pierhead as if I had nothing better to do. Just because he's so much older he thinks he can treat me like a child.'

'I don't think he thinks that at all,' said Seb patiently. 'Age has nothing to do with it. He needed to see your expression when you saw him again. Not every girl would want to marry a cripple however comfortably off he is even if she was fond of him.'

Tilly's hazel eyes narrowed. 'Did someone say that to him? Or is he remembering what happened when Alice saw your face for the first time, not knowing you had lost an eye? I never mention his foot. He hasn't gone and had it amputated without telling me, has he?'

'No. But it causes him a lot of pain.'

'He never speaks about it in his letters,' said Tilly. 'No doubt he thinks I've forgotten because I don't ask about it. Well, I haven't. Because I'll never forget my first sight of the pair of you. I thought you were both heroes and that's how I still feel about Don and you.'

'I'm touched, Tilly,' said Seb, his voice uneven.

She smiled slightly. 'Perhaps I should have written and told him.'

'He's twenty-seven next January and he doesn't want your pity. Saying, "I think you're a hero the way you cope with the pain" isn't particularly what he wants to hear from you,' said Seb.

'Maybe not. It makes me wonder if he wants to settle down

now rather than wait until I come of age. If that is the case, then maybe he'd be better off forgetting about me and finding a woman nearer his own age,' she said with a catch in her voice. 'He shouldn't have any difficulty. After all, women outnumber men, don't they?'

'And who will you marry when you think you're ready to do so if you don't marry Don?' asked Alice, who had quietly entered the hall from the direction of the kitchen. 'As you say, there's a shortage of men.'

Tilly stared at her sister. 'How long have you been there?'

'Long enough. Don's a good man. He could provide for you and you'd have a decent future with him.'

'I wouldn't argue with that,' said Tilly. 'But I'm not ready to rush into marriage just because you want to get rid of me.'

Alice flushed. 'Who said anything about wanting to get rid of you? And I didn't say anything about rushing into marriage,' she added with an edge to her voice. 'You might be old in the head in some ways but you still need to grow up and take the advice of your elders.'

Tilly tilted her chin. 'That last bit is to do with Dad, isn't it?'

'You take it anyway you want,' said Alice, turning to shoo the children into the sitting room as they crowded behind her.

'I will,' said Tilly, 'and I'll tell you now, big sister, that marriage is the last thing I need for the next few years. I want a career.'

'A career!' Alice raised her eyes and looked up at the ceiling. 'Do you hear her, God?' She lowered her gaze. 'Do you really believe you'll be able to make enough money from your writing to support yourself? The odd piece in the local newspaper or a magazine isn't going to be enough to do that, *little* sister.'

Tilly flushed with anger. 'I'm not daft! I know I need to have another job to keep me going until I write my novel and get it published. But it is possible to make a living from writing. There are several very successful women writers in this country.'

'That's true, Alice,' said Seb.

Alice frowned him down. 'Don't encourage her! I'm not trying to be cruel but Tilly needs to mature before she can write about life and love. She needs to discipline herself and control her emotions. Now, if she'd gone to see Don, we would never have had that terrible argument in the cemetery. If she'd seen Don, she could have become engaged to him and they could have got married when she was twenty-one. By then she'd know more about life and he'd be able to support her, and writing could be a nice little hobby for her.'

Tilly was deeply offended. 'You think I'd marry Don just as a means to support me? I wouldn't do that. Besides, I'd have to live in America and I'm not leaving Dad. Neither do I regard my writing as a hobby!' She produced a cutting from the *Liverpool Echo* and thrust it at her sister. 'Read this!'

Alice brushed it aside. 'Then more fool you, Tilly. Life isn't a bowl of cherries with you getting the pick of the best ones. You're not going to change Dad, you know. He'll hurt you. Just like he hurt me.'

'Enough said, Alice,' warned Seb.

'I wondered when you'd bring Dad into this,' said Tilly in a fierce undertone. 'I've a good mind to leave.'

'The sooner the better,' said Alice.

'Suits me,' said Tilly, making to walk away.

Seb grabbed her arm. 'Neither of you means this,' he said.

'She does,' said Tilly.

'No, she doesn't,' said Seb, seizing hold of Alice's arm and trying to bring the sisters closer together. 'Say you didn't mean it, Alice?'

'No. It's her fault,' said Alice, trying to free herself. 'She just won't listen to me.'

'Enough,' roared Seb. 'Now, both of you say sorry before I really lose my temper.'

Alice stared at him stubbornly. Gently, Tilly removed Seb's hand from her arm. 'I'm sorry that things have come to this. As soon as I can arrange it, I'll be out of here. Until then, I'd appreciate it if you could keep Dad out of any future conversations between us, Alice.'

Alice laughed. 'I suppose you think Kenny and Hanny will take you in? It's the sort of selfish thing you would think.'

Tilly had given no thought to where she would go but now she did and knew that living with her other relatives was out of the question. There were enough people in that house already and she would end up having no privacy and neither would they.

She gazed down at the cutting her sister had refused to look at and read for the umpteenth time: '*Decline of Matrimony as a Profession – Women in the Industrial World*' *by Annie S Swan*. Annie S Swan, Elise Grange, Elinor Glyn, Ethel M Dell had all succeeded as writers. She would show her sister that she did not need her family or a man to support her but would do so by her own efforts. She would find a new job and somewhere else to live. But until the day came when she had secured both she was going to have to steer clear of arguments with her sister.

* * *

'What are you doing?' asked Alice, entering Tilly's bedroom a few weeks later.

'What do you think I'm doing?' asked Tilly, tensing as she met her sister's eyes in the mirror.

'You're wearing my hat,' said Alice, picking up a discarded frock from the floor.

'You can leave that frock, I'll deal with it,' murmured Tilly, not wanting an argument. She twisted a strand of red-gold hair round a finger, hoping the curl would stay in place. 'And if you mean that I'm wearing a hat you made for me, then, yes, I am. Although, I was of the opinion that the hat was mine.'

'Of course it's yours. I just wish you weren't wearing it for *that* woman's wedding.'

Immediately, Tilly removed the hat and flung it on the bed. 'I'll go bareheaded. Satisfied?' Her eyes smouldered as she reached for the lipstick on the cut glass trinket tray. The colour was Oxblood and extremely fashionable with those bright young things that the press were calling flappers.

'I didn't intend for you to go hatless,' said Alice, throwing the dress on the bed beside the hat. 'I just want you to be reasonable and see my point of view. Why do you want to go to this wedding? It's not as if Mrs Black was an aunt or a friend of mine.'

'She's always been nice to me and I don't consider your not liking her a good excuse for me to turn down her invitation. Besides, if the rest of my family have accepted their invitations, I don't see why I shouldn't,' said Tilly, unscrewing the lipstick. 'You could be going, too, if you weren't so stubborn; a little dickybird told me that Mr Bennett had personally invited both you and Seb.'

It was the wrong thing for her to say. Alice was already annoyed because Kenny and his wife, her lifelong friend, Hanny, had accepted an invitation to the wedding. It was the same with Freddie and Clara, who was Seb's cousin. Alice knew that, despite her husband not having said a word against her decision not to go, he was disappointed. She could not understand why when he knew only too well what her feelings were towards Mrs Black. Tilly's defiance was the last straw and Alice's control over her temper snapped.

'You're not going out wearing lipstick. You're only sixteen,' she said in a seething voice.

'Seventeen next week,' murmured Tilly, trembling inwardly as she pursed her lips.

'You're still too young to paint your face.'

'I'm not painting my face, only my lips. Do I have to be a certain age to do that? You thought it was OK for me to become engaged at my age,' said Tilly, applying lipstick to her bottom lip.

'Don't be cheeky!' Alice made a grab for the lipstick.

Tilly yelped as her sister's actions caused the lipstick to paint a sweeping line across her cheek and jaw before breaking. 'Now see what you've done!' she cried, staring at the ruined lipstick. 'Do you know how much this cost me?'

'You shouldn't be wasting your money on lipsticks. It proves that you're being paid too much. Now go and wash it off.' Alice pointed to the door.

Tilly decided that her sister really had gone too far this time. She was not going to stand for Alice bossing her about anymore. She had been kicking her heels since their last quarrel, reluctant to move out despite the atmosphere between them. She had been scanning the pages in the

Liverpool Echo looking for a job that would suit her but so far she'd had no luck. She reached for a soiled handkerchief and wiped the lipstick from her cheek and the line of her jaw. Fortunately she had already filled in her lower lip and now she pressed it against the upper one.

She stood up and the deep green pleats that fell from a band of paler green about her hips flared about her calves. The bodice of the frock was a matching deep green and the collar and cuffs were the same pale green as the hip band. She stared at her sister. 'Could you get out of my bedroom, please? I want to finish getting ready.'

'I'll do no such thing,' said Alice, picking up the broken piece of lipstick from the rug. 'This is my house and I've a good mind to lock you in your bedroom so there'll be no wedding for you.'

'You just try locking me in,' said Tilly, furious that her sister should threaten her with such a punishment. 'I'll climb out of the window and if I fall and break my neck, it'll be your fault.'

'What's going on here?' asked a voice from the doorway. 'Your carriage awaits, Cinderella.'

The sisters turned as one and stared at Seb. He stood with his shoulder resting against the doorjamb, watching them.

'Thanks, Seb. I'm almost ready,' said Tilly, glad to see him, certain he wouldn't allow Alice to prevent her from going to the wedding. 'I've just got to get a clean handkerchief.'

'Fine with me. I'll tell the others you won't be a minute,' he said.

'She's been giving me cheek,' said Alice, her face flushed. 'I don't think she should be allowed to go to this wedding.'

'Try and stop me,' said Tilly, turning on her. 'It would do you good to get out and have some fun. It's what I intend to do.'

'And who would look after the children if I'd decided to go to the wedding?' asked Alice.

Seb interrupted them. 'Didn't you volunteer to look after the twins so you had an excuse not to go? James and Flora are keeping their eye on them right at this moment so you'd best get down there.'

Alice made no move to do what he said but placed the lipstick on the dressing table and went over to the window. She ran a finger along the windowsill as if checking for dust but surreptitiously she glanced out of the window at the automobile parked at the kerb. She could see the tops of the women's heads. Hanny was wearing the hat Alice had made her for Clara's wedding. As for the younger woman, she was wearing the one that Alice had given her for the twins' christening last year. Suddenly it seemed ludicrous that she was not going anywhere but her hats were and she felt like spitting nails.

'Robbie Bennett's nephews and nieces will be at the wedding,' said Seb. 'The eldest one, Wendy, is the same age as Tilly, and is looking forward to meeting her.'

Alice turned and looked at him. 'You've met her?'

Seb nodded. 'She's a good kid. Robbie said she was a great help to his sister, Peggy, after her husband was killed in the war. I met her when I visited Watson's motor showrooms in Renshaw Street. I wanted to know how much they were charging for a Dodge touring car.'

'And what were they?' asked Tilly, interested.

'Six hundred and twenty-five pounds. If we could sell a few of them I'd be a happy man.' Seb picked up the hat from the bed. 'Here, you'll be needing this, Tilly. You can't go to a wedding without a hat.'

Both sisters made to speak but changed their minds. Tilly stood still while Seb placed the eau-de-Nil, high-crowned hat with artificial green flowers lining its narrow brim on her head. It was a perfect fit like every hat that Alice made. Seb kissed Tilly's cheek. 'Enjoy yourself.'

She thanked him, picked up her lipstick and popped it in her handbag and, with a last glance at her sister's set face, hurried from the room. As she went downstairs, she could hear Alice talking. No doubt she was complaining about her all over again, she thought with a grimace. Hopefully Seb would calm her down. She wondered what her sister would say if she was ever to find out that Mrs Black had shares in the family motor business. When the company was in dire straits due to a lack of sales during the war, she had stepped in and helped Kenny and Seb out. Both Alice's brother and husband had known she would rather starve than accept help from Eudora Black. Without any discussion, those in the know had silently accepted to keep it a secret from Alice. Tilly firmly believed that Seb and Kenny had made the right decision.

She left the house and hurried down the path to where the motor was parked. There was just enough room for her to squeeze into the back with Hanny and Clara. Kenny was in the passenger seat and Freddie was driving.

They all smiled at her. 'That's a lovely frock you're wearing,' said Clara, who was wearing a pink skirt and jacket with a white organdie blouse. 'Did Alice make it?'

Tilly shook her head. 'I didn't dare ask her to because of it being for Mrs Black's wedding.'

'I know what you mean,' said Hanny ruefully. 'She's really got a cob on about us all going. I'm glad I had this outfit made for Freddie and Clara's wedding so I had something fairly new to wear. Although,' She sighed. 'I wish I had your figure, Tilly. I put on too much weight with the twins and despite all the running around I've done since they were born, I'm finding it hard to shift it.' She turned to Clara. 'You're going to have to watch that, love, now you're expecting.'

'What's this?' asked Tilly, her ears pricking up.

'We're having a baby,' said Freddie, without looking round.

Tilly's heart sank and she almost blurted out: *You didn't waste any time, did you?* It had been difficult enough for her being Clara's bridesmaid and having to stand in the church, hearing him say, *I do.* She could imagine what it was going to be like now Clara was pregnant. Freddie would treat her as if she was made of porcelain and Hanny and Alice would welcome her into *their* club. It would be Mothers United! They'd have their heads together discussing morning sickness, varicose veins, the actual birth, as well as breast feeding and the best way to keep your nappies white.

'Congratulations!' Tilly managed a bright smile. 'When's the baby due?'

'Christmas!' answered Clara, positively glowing. 'It could be born on the twins' birthday.'

'I hope not! Fancy having to buy three birthday presents on Christmas Eve, as well as Christmas presents.'

'You don't have to buy anything,' said Hanny firmly. 'We know you don't get much of a wage.'

'Alice doesn't believe that and all because I bought a lipstick,' murmured Tilly.

'You do have a birthday next week,' said Hanny. 'I'm sure the company can afford to give you a rise. Isn't that right, Kenny?'

'I'll mention it to Seb,' he said.

Tilly murmured a thank you and found herself dithering again about moving away from Chester.

'I wonder if Don Pierce will send you a card,' said Hanny.

'I like Don,' said Kenny, glancing over his shoulder at the three women. 'He's witty, funny and talented. But I'm not sure if he'd be in favour of you painting your mouth, Tilly.'

Tilly sighed. 'Please, Kenny, don't you have a go at me, too. Alice had enough to say.'

'Doesn't approve of you wearing the new in-colour lipstick, does she?' asked Hanny, her eyes twinkling. 'Trouble with Alice is that she's forgotten what she was like at your age. She was only fifteen when she fell for Seb. Kenny worried himself sick about her because she loved clothes and made the most of herself when she went out with him.'

'She never tells me anything cheerful about when she was young,' said Tilly, slipping an arm through Hanny's and hugging it. 'Just before I came out I had lipstick smeared right across my face because she made a grab for it to stop me putting it on and then she threatened to lock me in my bedroom. I'd move out right now if I had somewhere to go.'

'You're not serious?' asked Hanny, her blue eyes concerned.

Tilly did not answer.

Kenny said, 'I could see this coming. Can't you sort it out between the two of you, Tilly love?'

'I don't think so,' she said with forced cheerfulness. 'She's adamant I stop seeing Dad and I won't.' Kenny glanced at his wife but this time both kept silent. 'I can guess what you're thinking and I don't expect you to take my side,' said Tilly, her voice quivering.

'I suppose you could always come and sleep on our sofa as

a temporary measure,' said Clara. 'Although—'

'No! It wouldn't work,' said Tilly firmly. 'Thanks all the same but I don't want to cause trouble between you and Alice. Besides, I need a room of my own because I'll want to write.'

'Perhaps you could sleep at the yard,' suggested Freddie.

'No, she can't,' said Kenny hastily. 'You're forgetting the new apprentice is going to bunk down in the building; he'll be acting as a caretaker. But I have to admit I don't like the idea of your leaving home, Tilly. You're too young. This matter could be easily be remedied if you were just more discreet about seeing Dad.'

'I tried to be discreet,' said Tilly indignantly. 'But Alice was forever asking me where I was going and whether I was meeting Dad. As it happens, I haven't seen him since Mrs Black moved to Liverpool.'

'So you'll be seeing less of him,' said Kenny. 'You could point that out to Alice.'

Tilly thought, I'm making no promises, and pressed her lips tightly together.

Silence fell as the car motored across the Old Dee Bridge and headed on through the bustling streets of Chester to the road that would take them to Birkenhead. Clara broke the silence by beginning to discuss the coming wedding and how different it would be from her own. Tilly let the conversation wash over her, thinking ruefully that standing on her own two feet was not going to be easy. How could she combine being independent with seeing more of her father? She decided that while she was in Liverpool she would put feelers out and see if anyone she came in contact with knew of any available lodgings, as well as suitable employment. Surely in a city the size of Liverpool she should be able to find something?

CHAPTER THREE

'You must admit Mrs Black is looking good for her age,' whispered Hanny in Tilly's ear, as they stood amongst the milling crowd outside the Spiritualist church on Daulby Street.

'They both look happy, that's the main thing,' said Tilly, gazing at the newly married couple.

'She's looked years younger since they started seeing each other,' said Joy, Hanny's younger sister, who had held the post of Mrs Black's housekeeper for the past few years. A plump, warm-hearted woman in her late twenties, she had a cheerful manner despite having lost the man she loved during the war. 'And her name's Mrs Bennett now, don't forget!'

'It's not going to be easy getting out of the habit of calling her Mrs Black,' said Hanny.

'I like what she's wearing,' said Tilly, her hazel eyes fixed on the bride, who was dressed in a lavender shot silk dress and jacket with a matching hat decorated with artificial violets tucked in the brim. As for the groom, he was looking extremely dapper in a charcoal grey suit and spotless white shirt with a silver coloured bow tie.

'What did you think of the blessing service?' asked Clara.

'Well, they certainly cut out all that about marriage being for the procreation of children,' said Hanny, small dimples appearing at the corners of her mouth.

'Thank goodness! It would hardly have been appropriate,' said Joy.

'Alice would have had a fit if she knew about us being united with the spirits in a circle of love,' said Tilly, her eyes twinkling.

'I liked that part,' said Clara. 'I thought of my parents and gran.'

'I confess my mind wandered off some of the time,' said Hanny absently, looking about her. 'I kept thinking about the twins and hoping they weren't driving Alice round the bend.'

'Are you looking for someone?' asked Joy, noting her sister's behaviour.

'I had thought that Gabrielle might have turned up to watch Eudora and Robbie do the deed,' answered Hanny.

'Actually, Mrs Black did send her an invitation but she declined, saying that she had a previous engagement. I don't suppose you know that she's singing on the stage at the Belmont Picture House,' said Joy. 'It's only about a ten minute walk from the new house. She calls herself the Liverpool Nightingale. Anyway, I'm going to have to toddle off now. I've left a couple of hired maids in charge back at the house, but I want to be there to take the cloths off the buffet and make sure that the champagne is chilled enough to serve to the guests as they arrive.'

'Can I come with you?' asked Tilly. 'I thought I might have seen Dad here, but I suppose I should have realised he'd find the service, and all these people, too much to cope with.'

'Of course,' said Joy, linking her arm through Tilly's. 'Wendy, Mr Bennett's niece, is coming back with me, too. She's a helpful young woman.'

Tilly remembered Seb mentioning this girl and looked forward to meeting her. She excused herself and went with Joy to where Wendy Wright, a mousy-haired, slender girl with wide-apart grey eyes and pleasant features, was standing. She was wearing a dark blue dress with white spots and a white straw hat with a blue ribbon. She stood a little apart from the crowd, watching the antics of two younger boys and a girl who appeared to be performing some kind of dance.

Joy touched her arm. 'Are you ready, Miss Wright?'

Wendy started. 'Yes, Miss Kirk. I'll be glad to get away. I'm seriously thinking of disowning these three. I don't know where Mam's disappeared to but I hope she's not far away and makes sure they keep out of trouble.'

'Are they your brothers and sister?' asked Tilly.

'Yeah. Are you Miss Moran?' Wendy gave her a cool stare.

'Yes. Tilly Moran. I'm glad to meet you,' said Tilly politely, thinking the girl did not sound so friendly. 'My brother-in-law, Seb Bennett, mentioned having met you.'

'He said you were nice looking and he was right,' said Wendy. 'He also said you were a secretary but you look too young to be one of them.'

'Seb flatters me,' said Tilly, taken aback by the other girl's bluntness. 'I'm more your general dogsbody, although I do type invoices and letters and reports, as well as do the filing and make the tea.'

'I wish I could type. Then I could work in an office and earn my own money. As it is, Mam insists on my working in the shop and I feel it's my duty to do so with me being the eldest,' said Wendy, a tiny frown furrowing her pale brow.

'What shop is that?' asked Tilly.

Before Wendy could answer, Joy interrupted them. 'Come on, you two. You can talk in the car. I've no time to waste. The driver has to come back here after he's dropped us off.'

The girls followed her and climbed into the back of the black shiny car waiting at the kerb. They relaxed against the back of the leather seats.

'Wouldn't you just love to marry a man who owned a car like this?' said Wendy, spreading her skirts so they didn't crease. 'I'd like to learn to drive.'

'You would?' said Tilly.

'That's what I said. Imagine how quickly you could get from A to Z and to take to the open road. Whizzing along the country roads away from the dirt and smoke of the city. I could even go up to Cumberland or to Blackpool.'

'Don't you like living in Liverpool?' asked Tilly, surprised.

'Of course, I do! I like the shops and bustle but there are times when I like to get away. At the moment I can only manage to get as far as the park or New Brighton. Uncle Robbie took us all out in his new car the other week and it was a real treat. I told Mr Simpson about it and he was impressed. I don't think he realised we had a rich relation.'

'Who's Mr Simpson?'

Wendy smiled and her face changed utterly, so that Tilly's first opinion of her changed. 'Mr Simpson's a private detective who comes into the shop. Mam says he's not good-looking enough to be handsome but I like the way he looks. She says he doesn't dress smart enough but I don't mind that either. I've told her, as a detective, he sometimes has to disguise himself so that he appears ordinary, so no one would give him a second glance.'

'I've never met a private detective,' said Tilly, feeling a stir of interest, but thought she had better show some interest in the shop. 'So what kind of shop do you have?'

'A newsagent's and sweet shop but we sell cigarettes, as well. The shop used to be two shops next door to one another and were owned by two spinster sisters,' explained Wendy. 'But they died within days of each other and the leases came up for sale. We have Uncle Robbie to thank for loaning Mam the money to buy up the leases. She'd always wanted a shop but used to say that Dad was as useless as a snowball in Hell when it came to him getting her what she wanted.'

'He's dead, isn't he?' said Tilly sympathetically.

'Yeah! According to Mam he wasn't much cop as a husband but he was an OK dad.' Wendy sighed and fiddled with a brooch pinned to her dress. 'He gave me this when I was ten, after me gran died. I really value it because it's all that I have to remember her by. We've no photographs of her but at least I've a couple of me dad. I'll show you them if you ever come round to our shop.'

'So where is your shop?'

'West Derby Road. We'll pass it on the way to Uncle Robbie and Aunt Eudora's house.'

A silence fell.

Tilly glanced out of the window at the passing scene and thought about what Wendy had told her and how such a job as hers was perfect for meeting people and learning about their lives. She wondered what she did in her spare time, not that she could imagine the other girl having much of that between working in the shop and helping her mother in the house.

Tilly turned to Wendy. 'What do you do when you have any free time? Do you read at all?'

'I read the newspapers and magazines in between serving customers. I like to keep abreast with what's going on in the world and up to date with the latest fashions,' said Wendy. Her face took on a dreamy expression. 'I'd love to go to Paris, wouldn't you?'

'I suppose I would,' said Tilly, thinking that Wendy's clothes weren't very fashionable. Probably that was due to her mother keeping her short of money. She thought of Alice, another one who took a great interest in the latest fashions and with her nimble fingers could imitate the patterns of the designers' latest creations. 'Who would you go to Paris with if you had the chance of going there?'

Wendy did not answer immediately but then said in a low voice, 'Mr Simpson, without a doubt, but don't go repeating that to anyone.'

'Of course not!' Tilly dropped her voice, having decided to let her curiosity about this man have its way. 'Tell me more about Mr Simpson.'

Wendy smiled. 'He used to be a policeman but lost his job during the police strike last year. His pension went and everything! I know this because it happened to all those policemen who went on strike for better pay and conditions. It's not that he's complained to me about it. I'm sure you know that there's thousands unemployed and the numbers are growing. I've sensed the anger in him when he talks about the unemployment situation.'

'I know there's a lot of dissatisfaction among the working classes about low wages and conditions, and that it's led to strikes and go-slows,' said Tilly. 'Is Mr Simpson one of those who blames the situation on there being more women in the workforce?'

'Oh no!' Wendy's eyes widened. 'His sister was widowed and she's got a job in Jacob's biscuit factory. He's got an office in town and he's advertised his private detective agency in the *Echo*.'

'Does he get much work?'

Wendy hesitated. 'He doesn't discuss his work with me. I suppose that's why he's called a private detective. But he did tell Mam that there's lots of crimes that the police don't have time to deal with that he could solve.'

Tilly was fascinated. 'So where's his agency?'

'I can't remember the address off-hand but he actually lives not far from us.' She paused. 'Look through the window! This is West Derby Road now. We've just passed the Hippodrome Theatre and will soon be passing Emmanuel's Church. Then we'll come to the Olympia Theatre and not far after that is the Palladium where Uncle Robbie plays. Our shop is on this side of the road after Boundary Lane, where there's a tobacco factory.

Tilly gazed out of the window with interest. 'And Mr Simpson's house?'

'He doesn't have a house,' said Wendy. 'I heard him tell Mam he lives in lodgings with his sister and is lucky to have that. He's only been there a couple of months. I suppose if it had been a month or so later he could have had Uncle Robbie's room.'

Tilly's ears pricked up. 'Your Uncle Robbie's room – is it for rent?'

'I don't think Mam's thought about renting it out.'

To Tilly it suddenly seemed too good an opportunity to

miss and she took a deep breath before saying, 'Do you think she'd consider me as a lodger?'

'You!' Wendy stared at her. 'Are you being funny? Uncle Robbie said you live in a lovely big house over in Chester. What would you want to come and live in Liverpool for?'

Tilly knew it was not the done thing to go telling strangers about the arguments and upsetting things that went on in the family so was wondering how to reply when a thought occurred to her. 'Have you met my dad?'

Wendy flicked back her long hair. 'You mean Uncle Robbie and Aunt Eudora's gardener and general handyman?'

'Yes.'

'I hope you don't mind my saying so but I find it hard to believe that he's your father. I mean you talk posh and live in a big house and he's a gardener.'

'He was an engineer once, I believe, but he got ill after he changed his job and worked with lead.'

Wendy nodded. 'I see. He was a man down on his luck and had to take any old job in the end.'

'It wasn't exactly like that,' said Tilly, grimacing. 'The main thing is that I want to live nearer to my dad. You see I only got to meet him last year.'

'How come?'

Tilly began to tell her as much as she needed to know to rouse her sympathy but made no mention of Alice's attitude to their father. She was hoping that if she could get Wendy on her side then she might be able to persuade her mother to take her on as her lodger.

'I must admit that I thought there was something sad about him. He chunners away to himself and sometimes acts like there's someone else there. I thought he might have been seeing ghosts – what with Auntie Eudora having been a medium, but she says not. Besides, since the war there's plenty of men around who mutter away to themselves and keep shaking their heads as if they can't get rid of the sound of the big guns. It's a real shame.'

Tilly agreed that it was indeed a shame. Both girls fell silent, thinking of all those men mentally scarred by the Great War. The country did not seem to be doing much for them. So much for the land fit for heroes that Lloyd George had promised! thought Tilly.

'He's started work on the garden but it's still a real mess,' said Wendy. 'A right jungle, my brother calls it. He said that he wouldn't be surprised if there were a couple of tigers and snakes in there.'

Tilly smiled. 'So will you introduce me to your mother so I can ask her about renting her spare room?' she asked.

Wendy agreed. 'OK. No doubt she'll be glad of the extra money. What'll you do about getting a job over here? You won't be able to work for your family anymore.'

'No. But I'm bound to be able to find something I can do,' said Tilly confidently.

Wendy nodded. 'Look, there's the Palladium where Uncle Robbie works. See what film's showing? *The Romance of Lady Hamilton*! Love, betrayal, death and adventure! It sounds fun.'

Tilly agreed that it sounded like the film had all the ingredients needed for a good story. She thought of her writing and hoped she would be able to prove to Alice that she had the talent to become a successful novelist. But first, she was going to have to find herself a job to pay rent and feed herself.

A few minutes later Joy slid back the glass partition between her and the driver and the girls in the back. 'We'll be there any minute. I hope you're hungry, there's lots of lovely food to eat!'

Wendy said, 'I suppose it'll be family hold back until the guests have helped themselves?'

Joy smiled. 'I suppose it'll be OK if you're really hungry to snaffle a sandwich but not so it's noticeable.' She closed the partition.

Tilly looked out of the window, impatient to arrive at their destination and see her father before the newly-weds and other guests arrived.

The house overlooking Newsham Park was not as large as Eudora Black's former home in Eastham. It was built of yellow brick and was three storeys high with bay windows on the ground and first floor and also plain rectangular ones on the second floor, as well as smaller dormer ones jutting out of the roof. The house was semi-detached but situated on a corner, so that there was plenty of room to park alongside it. The front garden showed signs of having been tidied up and Tilly presumed her father had begun work here first so as to create a good impression for the wedding guests. The car dropped them off at the kerb before turning round and heading back into town.

Tilly followed Joy and Wendy round the side of the house to the rear of the building. She was hoping she might see her father in the garden but there was no sign of him in the large walled area. But here, too, there was evidence that he had been at work despite former flowerbeds being a tangle of briars, brambles and ground elder. The grass had been cut and some earth cleared and raked over. At the far end of the garden there were fruit trees and an outhouse with windows on the ground floor and upper one. She wondered what purpose the building had served in the previous owner's time.

Suddenly she noticed a face peering over the neighbouring wall with what appeared to be a bird's nest on its head. She turned to Joy. 'There's someone watching us from next door.'

'I know. Ignore her. She's real nosy. Perhaps it goes with the name,' said Joy, sounding exasperated. 'Not that she ever speaks.'

'Who is she?' asked Tilly.

'According to the maid who works in the house the other side of that one, she's some sort of poor relative to the owner. He's a Mr Leonard Parker and is in shipping. Apparently, his father died the other year and he inherited. I've yet to catch sight of Mr Parker but I gather she's acting as his housekeeper and caretaker while he's away on business.'

'The war's left a lot of ship owners in trouble,' said Wendy. 'I heard Mr Simpson talking about it to some other bloke in the shop. A lot of ships were sent to the bottom by the German U-boats and the owners have got to find the money from somewhere to build new ones if they're to remain in business.'

Joy shrugged. 'They're not the only ones to suffer due to the war. Anyway, I've work to do.'

Both girls nodded. 'Have you any idea where Dad could be, Joy?' asked Tilly, as they made their way to a rear door in the house.

'If he hasn't come to see who's in the garden then I reckon he's not in his living quarters down at the bottom of the garden. Most probably he's taken Nanki Poo for a walk in the park. He shouldn't be out too long so it's no use you going to look for him.'

'Is the dog named after a character in *The Mikado*?' asked Tilly, thinking her father would probably be happier living in the outhouse rather than the attic of the main house.

Joy's brown eyes twinkled. 'That's right. Although our Nanki Poo is supposed to be descended from a Chinese lion dog. He's a Pekinese and belongs to Mr Bennett. Apparently, he always wanted a dog but due to his travelling about as a musician in America he never got round to having one.'

'Mam wouldn't let him have one,' said Wendy. 'She says she was bitten by a dog when she was a kid and it put her off them completely. She likes cats, though. We have two and they keep the mice down.'

'You have mice!' exclaimed Tilly.

'They never last long,' said Wendy cheerfully. 'Tabby is a real good mouser.'

'Enough about mice,' said Joy, giving a little shiver. 'I don't have many horrors but mice is one of them. Anyway, Mr and Mrs Bennett will be here soon and I want everything ready by the time they and the guests arrive.'

The two girls said no more but followed her inside the house where there was a faint smell of paint. The maids were in the dining room and Joy gave them orders to remove the cloths. As soon as they did, Tilly's mouth began to water. She had never seen such a spread. What with rationing of basic staples and other shortages, there were some foods her family had gone without during the war and since. She had not expected such a feast, but then Eudora Black had money and money talked. There were hams, several chickens, salmon, plates of pastries and sandwiches, bowls of salads, as well as bread and butter, trifles, apple tarts and chocolate, coffee and fruit cake.

'I never realised she was so rich,' said Wendy.

'The mistress is a clever woman and has been careful with her investments. Your uncle isn't daft with money, either,' said Joy. 'Now, Tilly, you relax and have a look around. It's a nice house now it's been done up.'

Tilly was not of a mind to go wandering far but she took a peep into the drawing room, which was lit by electricity, and she noticed not only was there a piano but the room had been cleared for dancing. She was tempted to lift the piano lid and run her fingers over the keys. Seb had been generous enough to pay for piano lessons for her when she was younger and she loved music, almost as much as she loved writing. But she resisted.

The french windows were ajar but the scent of roses and carnations came not from the garden, but vases set on surfaces around the room. She gazed outside, hoping to see her father returning with Nanki Poo, but there was no sign of him. She felt slightly anxious about him, hoping he would not deliberately stay out longer to avoid the guests.

She returned to the dining room in time to see the maids placing plates of hot sausage rolls and pies on one of the tables. Joy and Wendy were bringing in bottles of champagne in ice buckets and setting them on another table where there were glasses on trays.

'I don't suppose we'll get to sup the champagne,' said Tilly, going over to them.

Joy smiled. 'Oh, I think you'll be allowed one glass as this is a special occasion.' She stilled suddenly. 'Is that the sound of a car? I must go and open the door to them.' She hurried away.

Wendy quickly snaffled a sausage roll. 'Have you ever drunk champagne?' she asked.

'No, only sherry.'

Wendy smiled. 'I have. Me and the kids were allowed a taste when Uncle Robbie and Aunt Eudora got engaged. I'm glad it will be out of a proper glass and not someone's slipper.'

Tilly's eyes twinkled. 'What if it were a glass slipper like 'Cinderella's?'

'Still, wouldn't fancy it,' said Wendy seriously. 'She'll have worn it, won't she?' She stuffed the tiny sausage roll in her mouth, only to spit half of it out onto the palm of her hand. 'Bloothy hell! That's hot! I think I've burnt me tongue,' she added in a muffled voice.

Tilly stifled a laugh. 'Drink of water?'

Wendy nodded and the pair of them left the dining room and headed for the kitchen, narrowly avoiding the bride and groom and the first of the guests as they entered the house.

'That was a close call,' said Wendy, after downing half a glass of water. 'If Mam had been there she would have said it served me right for being greedy.'

'I don't think you're greedy, just hungry like I am. It seems a long time since breakfast,' said Tilly, wishing she'd got Joy to point out Mrs Wright to her earlier. The woman sounded a bit of a tyrant.

'I didn't have breakfast. Mam was arranging for an old crony of hers to look after the shop while I had the job of chivvying the others to get up and get ready. She thinks we've got to keep on the right side of Aunt Eudora.' Wendy looked thoughtful. 'I still find it hard to take in that I've got a rich aunt. You know she's got lots of properties in Liverpool? She was left them by her dead husband.'

'Well, he'd hardly leave it to her if he were still alive,' said Tilly, her lips twitching.

Wendy giggled. 'You know what I mean. They're not houses like this, though,' she said seriously. 'She took me around with her to visit some of her tenants in her motor. Your dad drove us.'

Tilly blinked at her. 'Dad drove? I didn't know he could drive.'

'Uncle Robbie has been giving him lessons. He wants to carry on playing in the orchestra at the Palladium and as Aunt Eudora has her finger in several pies that take her to parts of Liverpool that aren't as nice as here, he said that she needed a man with her.'

'You do surprise me,' said Tilly.

'But it does make some sense. If there's any trouble he's quite strong, isn't he? He could protect her. All that digging and mowing in the garden builds muscle,' said Wendy.

'I suppose you're right. But I wouldn't like him to get hurt,' said Tilly.

'Uncle Robbie is thinking along the lines that he'd be more of a deterrent. Aunt Eudora's planning on making improvements to her properties. I think the work here made her realise it's not only a garden that falls into rack and ruin if it isn't looked after but the buildings, too. Some of her tenants still cook on the fire and don't even have gas light in all the rooms but make do with candles. There are some really poor people in Liverpool, you know. And losing husbands, brothers and fathers has made some families' situations much worse.'

'I'm sure you're right,' said Tilly, moved by Wendy's words. 'I've led a pretty sheltered life – but that's not to say that there weren't times when my family weren't hard up. I remember Hanny telling me that when I was little I lived with her and

Kenny in rooms in a coal merchant's terraced house, near the railway. Things got really bad when Kenny had his foot damaged and couldn't keep both his jobs going. Hanny wanted to go out and get a job but he didn't want that and they had terrible rows.'

'Poverty is a killer,' said Wendy.

Tilly looked at her, thinking she was very perceptive and decided to change the subject. 'What was this house like before they moved in?'

'Dark,' said Wendy, glancing about the kitchen with its newly painted walls of eggshell blue. 'Really dark with brown paintwork and peeling wallpaper and yellowing ceilings. It gave me the shivers when Uncle Robbie brought me and Mam here to have a look at it. The old spinster who lived here hadn't had anything done for years. Poor soul. Anyway, it's looking nice now,' added Wendy on a cheery note. 'There's a lovely bathroom upstairs and two lavatories, one inside and one out. I just love this house.'

'Do you have a bathroom over the shop?' asked Tilly.

'No, just a tin bath we bring in from the yard and fill from the kettle if we want a bath on a Saturday night,' said Wendy. 'Otherwise, we make do with a wash down or go to the public baths.'

Tilly drew in a breath. Wendy stared at her. 'Oh dear, I suppose that's put you off renting our spare room,' she said. 'Even our lavatory is outside.'

With a sinking heart, Tilly hastened to reassure her that it hadn't. 'If I want to be near Dad then I have to live over here.' She did not add that she could not see herself being able to afford anything better and she still had to find herself a job. Of course, she was presuming Mrs Wright would take her on as a lodger and that the rent she asked was within her means.

'Good,' said Wendy, her grey eyes pleased. 'I suppose we'd best get back to the dining room and see whether Mam and the kids have arrived. Besides, we don't want all the other guests to tuck in and eat everything before we have a chance to fill our bellies.'

Tilly agreed and followed her out of the kitchen. She could not help wondering about what the rest of the living quarters were like behind and above Mrs Wright's shop. She thought of all that she took for granted at her home in Chester and almost wished she had kept her mouth shut about leaving home. But there was no going back now.

CHAPTER FOUR

Guests were crowding into the dining room and the champagne was being poured and space had been made for the bride and groom to say a few words. Tilly spotted members of her family but before she could go over and speak to them, Wendy was leading her over to a woman wearing a navy blue costume and plain felt hat trimmed with a white gardenia. What could be seen of her hair was grey and fluffy. She had a long face and cheekbones that jutted out, and she was frowning. Suddenly she must have spotted the two girls, because her heavy-lidded eyes widened.

'I was wondering where you'd gone, girl,' she said, addressing Wendy.

'Didn't Pete tell you? I couldn't find you outside the church, so I left a message with him,' said Wendy.

'That's because I chose not to go inside that place,' said her mother, dropping her voice. 'I don't approve of all this spiritualist nonsense and your Uncle Robbie's the same. You'll see he'll put a stop to your Aunt Eudora's gallop. There'll be no séances held in this house.' She paused and stared at Tilly. 'Who's this?'

'This is Miss Tilly Moran,' said Wendy, urging Tilly forward. 'The other Mr Bennett told me about her. This is me mam, Tilly. You can have a word with her now about renting Uncle Robbie's old room.'

'What's this?' Mrs Wright's sharp eyes washed over Tilly's face, before lingering on her hat and then her dress. 'Very nice. But what are you thinking of, girl, wanting to leave home? Found yourself a fellow in Liverpool, have you? Well, I'll tell you now I'll stand for no hanky panky under my roof.'

'I haven't a boyfriend,' said Tilly, her cheeks reddening. 'I just want to live near my dad.'

Before either could say anymore the best man hushed them and the speeches began. Fortunately, they were soon over. Toasts were drunk and the serious business of eating began. Tilly did not get a chance to grab a plate and pile it high because Wendy's mother took up their previous conversation as if there had been no interruption.

'Why can't you live with your dad?'

'Because my dad works here for Mr and Mrs Bennett,' said Tilly.

Mrs Wright's heavy lids rolled back. 'The gardener! Why would you want to live near him? What help is he going to be to you living in Liverpool?'

'I'm not looking for him to be of a help to me. I just want to see more of him. I only found out he was alive last year,' said Tilly, bristling slightly.

Mrs Wright fixed her with a stare. 'I did hear he'd spent time in an asylum but there's lots of people sick in the head since the war. Anyway, if you want to rent my spare room I'm not against it. If you want breakfast and an evening meal as well, I suppose we can cater for that. It'll cost you fifteen bob a week.'

Tilly mentally reviewed her savings and her heart sank. Was the amount fair? She had no way of knowing because it was as Alice had said: she had been spoilt, never having to hand over much money for her keep. Her savings would be gone in a month if she had to hand over that much every week. Perhaps she should try bargaining.

'Twelve shillings,' she said, managing to keep a tremor out of her voice. 'And I want to see the room first.'

'Yer've got a nerve,' said Mrs Wright in a flat voice. 'I could probably rent it out to someone else for fifteen.'

Tilly shrugged. 'If that's what you want to do, Mrs Wright. But just remember the proverb about a bird in the hand is worth two in the bush.'

'Mam, don't be mean,' said Wendy, linking her arm through her mother's. 'I want Tilly to stay. I think I can learn a lot from her. Besides, she's used to living with kids and won't be complaining about the racket ours make like some others might. And we need someone who's honest and can come recommended. We don't want a lodger rifling the till during the night.'

'Are you honest, girl?' asked Mrs Wright, opening her handbag and taking out a packet of cigarettes and lighting up.

'Yes.'

'Then I'll accept twelve and sixpence and you can give a hand with the chores. That's my last offer, girl. I like it that you dress well and are clever. Perhaps you'll be a good influence on my Wendy and Minnie. Come round after the do and see what you think. You can even spend the night if you want.'

Tilly was astounded by Mrs Wright's sudden capitulation and decided that her offer was fair. 'I'm not sure about staying. I'm here with part of my family.'

'Please yourself but the room will be getting advertised in the shop this week if you don't want it. I reckon in the light of the housing situation being the way it is, it'll be snapped up.'

'I'll take it.'

'Good. Because we kind of know you, I'll just ask for a fortnight's money in advance instead of a month's. Wendy, you take her to see the room after you've had something to eat,' said Mrs Wright.

'Come on, Tilly,' said Wendy. 'Let's go while the going's good. I'll introduce you to the rest of the family, so you know what you're letting yourself in for.'

Wendy hurried her over to where her siblings were filling their plates. First, she introduced Tilly to Minnie, who was thirteen and showing signs of early womanhood. She was stuffing her face with cake. Next came Peter, a lad who had a look of his Uncle Robbie except his hair was jet black instead of pure white. Lastly, there was ten-year-old, fair-haired David.

Tilly experienced a sudden pang of what felt like pain, thinking that once she left home she would see little of her nieces and nephews in Chester.

'Miss Moran is coming to live with us,' said Wendy.

'Why do you want to come and live with us?' asked Minnie, giving her a frank look from deep blue eyes. 'We're a noisy lot, you know. Especially, our Peter. He plays the clarinet.'

'Do you?' asked Tilly, looking at him with fresh interest. 'I play the piano. I don't suppose your mother has a piano?'

'No. Uncle Robbie took his piano with him,' replied Peter. 'Mam doesn't much like music. She only tolerates my practising because Uncle Robbie has told her that I have a future.'

'Well, let's hope he's right. I'm sure he knows what he's talking about because he's a professional musician.' Tilly smiled. 'As for noise. I've nieces and nephews and they're not exactly always quiet and well behaved.'

'How old are they?' asked Peter.

Tilly told them.

'Only babies,' he said, rolling his eyes. 'I'm a scout. I suppose you've heard of Lord Baden-Powell?'

'Yes,' said Tilly. 'The hero of Mafeking and the founder of the scout movement.'

'I'm ten, the same age as one of Miss Moran's nephews,' said David, knuckling his older brother in the side. 'You're always making out that you're all grown up when you're not.'

Peter swiped him across the head. 'Shut up, Shrimp.'

Wendy frowned. 'Enough of that. Miss Moran won't want to come and live with us if you carry on the way you are.'

'What does Miss Moran do?' asked Minnie.

'She works in an office,' said Wendy.

'I also write,' murmured Tilly.

'Write what?' asked Minnie, staring at her.

'Stories.'

'I bet they're for kids,' said Peter, biting into a sandwich. 'I can read my own books,' he added through a mouthful of food.

Minnie laughed. 'Pull the other leg. You hardly ever pick up a book, you'd rather play that stupid clarinet.'

'It's not stupid!' He glared at her.

'Don't you two start,' warned Wendy.

'Not everyone is a reader but they can still enjoy listening to stories,' said Tilly. 'Although, I want to write a novel, a grown-up novel.'

'I read Mam's *Red Letter* magazine,' said Minnie, with a smirk. 'I've always been a good reader.'

'I heard Mam telling you off for reading those stories. She said they're too old for you,' said Peter. 'They're all about lu-uv.'

Tilly was amused by their squabbling. Her brother and sister had been too old for her to have this kind of relationship with them. She was reminded of Alice being shocked and ticking her off for reading Elinor Glyn when she was only a little older than Minnie.

'I like adventures. The bloodthirstier the better,' said David, with relish.

'Enough,' said Wendy. 'I'm getting something to eat. Now scram, you lot.'

While Tilly helped herself to food, she wondered what Kenny and the others would think of her decision to lodge with the Wrights. She was soon to find out when her half-brother, Hanny, Freddie and Clara appeared at her shoulder. Hanny asked her what she had found to talk to the Wrights about.

'You seemed to be in deep conversation with Mrs Wright earlier,' she said.

Tilly realised that her family had been keeping their eye on her, so she told them about what had been said and received the reaction she had dreaded might happen from Kenny. 'I don't think I can let you do this, Tilly,' he said, frowning.

'Why not?' asked Hanny, taking a mouthful of champagne.

'It's not as if Mrs Wright is a stranger.'

Kenny disagreed. 'But she is a stranger. I've never met her before until today.'

'But she's Robbie Bennett's sister and we all know him. I think we can trust her to look after Tilly,' said Hanny.

It was not part of Tilly's plan to have Mrs Wright looking after her and telling her how she should behave, but she guessed that now was not the time to say so. At the moment she had Hanny on her side and had to appear to agree with her.

'She's almost a relative,' said Tilly. 'I'm going to have a look at the room later.'

Hanny drained her champagne glass. 'We'll come with you.'

Inexplicably, Tilly was alarmed by the suggestion. 'No! We're here as guests and we can't all just nip out.'

'And there's the entertainment,' said Clara. 'I'm sure we've all been looking forward to hearing some of the members of the Palladium Orchestra playing and to having a dance.'

'You're right,' said Hanny. 'Besides, we can't stay too late or we'll miss the luggage boat.'

Tilly nodded, wishing she had kept quiet about her plans. She excused herself and, carrying a plate of food, went in search of her father. There was no sign of him downstairs but several musicians were practising in the drawing room. For a moment she listened to them before leaving the house by the french windows, hoping to find Mal outside.

There was a light down near the outbuilding so she walked towards it, only to stop with a start when she heard herself being called. She recognised her father's voice but could not immediately work out where it was coming from. The next moment she felt a damp nose sniffing her ankles and, looking down, she saw a dog. Its peculiar little flattened face was framed by a mane of hair, resembling that of a lion and there was something very attractive about him. She bent down and held out a hand. He sniffed it and allowed her to stroke his head before she realised her plate of food was in danger of receiving his attention.

'Yer look bonnie, lass,' said Mal, coming out from behind a tangle of shrubbery.

'So there you are, Dad. Where've you been?' asked Tilly, straightening up.

'I had to get away,' he answered, placing a trembling hand on her arm. 'Nanki Poo dug something up and I didn't know what to do. Couldn't tell Eudora, it being her wedding day.'

'What is it? Do you want me to have a look? It's not treasure, is it?' she joked.

'Nay, lass.'

'Then perhaps we should eat first. I put extra food on my plate, thinking you mightn't have had anything to eat.'

Mal showed some interest in the plate and, reaching out, took a small pork pie and popped it into his mouth. Tilly ate a ham sandwich and wondered what the dog could have dug up that had Mal in a dither. It was peaceful in the garden, although she could hear the strains of music, the hum of conversation and the sound of laughter coming from the house. Soon there would be dancing but who was there with whom she could dance? She thought of Freddie and then Don and sighed.

Mal took a sandwich from the plate and bit into it. 'These are good. I watched Joy and the lasses making them. Eudora and Mr Bennett are going away, you know. They're going on a liner to foreign parts for their honeymoon. They'll be gone for a few months but she said that Joy would give me my tonic and see I had all I need.'

Tilly thought he sounded much calmer now. 'Do you like Joy?'

'Aye. What's there not to like?' He seemed surprised.

'Couldn't you have told her about what Nanki Poo dug up?'

He shook his head. 'She was busy. You can come and look. See whether yer think the same as me.'

He took another sandwich and gave the dog some ham from inside it. The meat was gone in seconds. Then he led her towards the outbuilding.

'I don't know if I did right bringing it in here,' he muttered, taking her over to a bench on which stood a storm lantern.

By its light Tilly could make out a shoebox on a sheet of newspaper. She put down the plate and stared at the box. She had the oddest feeling when her father removed the lid to reveal a small heap of bones. He took out a tiny skull with careful fingers. 'What d'yer make of this, lass?'

She scrutinised it carefully. Her heartbeat had quickened. The skull looked the wrong shape for a pet rabbit, cat or dog. 'It reminds me of a doll but the head of the one I had was made of wax. This doesn't look like wax. Are you thinking, Dad, that it's a baby's skull?'

She heard him swallow and then nod.

'There was the odd shred of material and a bit of a label with the bones. The box dis-dis—'

'Disintegrated?'

He nodded. 'So I put the skeleton in this box. How d'yer think it came to be there, lassie?'

Tilly was silent for a moment, thinking deeply. 'Perhaps when she was young, the old spinster who lived here got herself into trouble.'

'Aye. She'd have kept it secret.'

'Yes. Perhaps the poor little thing was born dead, so she buried it in the garden at dead of night,' whispered Tilly. Her imagination took flight as she thought about who the father might have been. Perhaps a soldier or maybe a married man?

'What should we do with it?' asked Mal. 'It doesn't seem right just to put the bones back where I found them. Besides, Nanki Poo might dig them up again.'

Tilly agreed with him and was tempted to suggest that they took the bones to the nearest minister of religion so they could have a Christian burial but somehow she doubted that idea would appeal to her father. He'd never had any time for the Church. 'We could bury them again but in a metal box this time,' she suggested, thinking she could say a few words.

'Aye. And I could get a nice rosebush and plant it over the box,' said Mal, sounding more cheerful. 'Then I'd know exactly where the bairn was buried and not dig there.'

'Yes,' said Tilly.

'It would be our secret.'

'Yes.'

Carefully, he placed the tiny skull back in the cardboard box and replaced the lid. 'Yer'd best be getting back to the party now.'

'You're not coming in, Dad?'

'No, lass. I was asked but I don't want to be mixing with a load of strangers. My quarters are upstairs and I'm happy there.'

She would have liked to have seen them but decided that perhaps now was not the right time to suggest it. 'I'll leave you the plate of food,' she said, planting a kiss on his cheek. 'I'm hoping to settle nearby so you can expect another visit from me in a few days.'

'That's great, lass,' he said, beaming at her. 'I'm sure that news would please your mammy.'

Tilly wondered if that was true but had no doubt about how her sister would feel. Alice might miss her help in the house and with the children but she would be glad to get rid of her. Tilly hoped there would be no arguments when she arrived home. It would be much better for the pair of them if they parted on relatively good terms.

Tilly entered the house the way she had left it and stood a moment by the french windows, listening to the music and the hum of conversation. Her eyes scanned the large room, tastefully painted in soft muted colours of pale peach and cream. All the furniture had been pushed against the walls and the carpet rolled up. Due to the confines of the room, the band consisted of just four members of the orchestra: a pianist, a violinist, a flautist and a trumpeter. Together they made quite an interesting sound. Tilly felt the rhythm go through her and she tapped her foot. She watched the swirling couples who had taken to the floor. She knew the names of some dances and had even practised the foxtrot with Alice last Christmas. Tears suddenly clogged her throat. Despite the anger between her and her sister she was going to miss her.

'Where have you been?' asked a voice.

Tilly turned to Wendy. 'I went to see Dad. He's not coming in but I took him some food.'

'Is Nanki Poo with him?'

Tilly nodded. 'I think I'll go and get some food for myself. I didn't eat much.'

'I'll come with you,' said Wendy. 'And when you've finished I'll take you to the shop.'

Within a short space of time Tilly and Wendy were walking past St Margaret's church and across Belmont Road and the pub on the corner. 'There's still plenty of people about,' commented Tilly.

Wendy smiled. 'It's Saturday night. Isn't it like this in Chester, near where you live?'

'In summer, yes. During the light evenings you can watch the day trippers still out on boats on the Dee or listening to a band. Some just enjoy walking along the riverbank. It's really nice,' she murmured.

'You'll miss it.'

'Yes.' Tilly found herself remembering an evening last spring when Clara had come to stay. Tilly had been thinking about leaving Chester even then and had known she would miss the familiar sights and sounds of the city where she had been born. She had thought her loss would be balanced by seeing different places and gaining new experiences but she had imagined that to be in some far off foreign land. Never had she thought that her first taste of living away from home would be across the Mersey in Liverpool.

'Here we are,' said Wendy, stopping outside a shop. She opened the door, causing a bell to tinkle overheard and they went inside.

A middle-aged woman was reading a newspaper spread open on the counter. She was sucking a gobstopper and it fell out of her mouth and onto the newspaper when she looked up. 'Now, see what yer made me do! What are you doing here, Wendy? Is there summit wrong that yer back this early?'

'No. I've just brought Miss Moran here to take a look at

Uncle Robbie's old room. She's moving in as our lodger.'

'Bloomin' hell, I didn't expect yer mam to rent it out that quick. The dust has hardly settled since Mr Bennett left.' She picked up the gobstopper and stuck it back in her mouth.

Wendy sighed. 'You've ruined that newspaper. Tilly, this is Mrs Pain, a neighbour from the street where we used to live.'

'How d'you do?' said Tilly, holding out her hand.

Mrs Pain removed the gobstopper and placed it in the pocket of her pinny. 'Fair to middlin',' she said, shaking Tilly's hand. 'Yous aren't from around here, are yer? Where are yer from?'

'Chester.'

Mrs Pain made a face. 'Posh area, hey! What are yer doing coming over here? Gorra job?'

'Not over here I haven't but hopefully I soon will,' said Tilly.

'Miss Moran works in an office. She types and is going to write a novel,' said Wendy.

Mrs Pain stared at Tilly. 'Should I have seen yer name in the *Echo*?'

'I doubt you'll remember. I wrote about the death of the thief who tried to steal the takings from the Palladium. He disguised himself by wearing different wigs.'

Mrs Pain's eyes widened. 'Bloomin' hell. I remember reading about him. Real nutcase. Fancy that being yous that wrote it. Clever. I can just about write me name but I'll turn me hand to anyfin to earn a crust. Lost me man early in our marriage to consumption.' A shadow crossed her face. 'But life has to go on. If yer make it rich then let me know if yer need a cleaner.'

Tilly could not help grinning. The woman was a real

character and showed courage. 'I've got to get an ordinary job first.'

'That would be an office job,' said Mrs Pain. 'I clean some offices. I'll keep me ears open for yer.'

'Thanks,' said Tilly, delighted to have made such a contact. 'I have typing skills and a reasonably good head for figures.'

'Yer mean yer can add up and take away and balance the books?'

'Hopefully, yes.'

'When you two have finished, we'd best get going upstairs,' said Wendy as she unfastened a small bolt under the counter and lifted the flap. 'Come on, Tilly.'

She led the way into a sitting room and showed Tilly that behind that was a kitchen and then a scullery that opened onto the backyard. 'There's the lavatory down at the bottom,' said Wendy.

Tilly schooled her face to not show what she was feeling. It would be OK in summer skipping down the yard but not in winter. 'Nice big yard,' she said.

'Yeah. Mam had the dividing wall knocked down, that's why it's so big,' said Wendy. 'Here's the bath,' she added, hitting it with her fist where it hung on a whitewashed wall. A clanking, rumbling noise reverberated inside. 'We have to chase the lads out if us girls want a bath in front of the fire. I'll show you upstairs now.'

Tilly was led along a dark short passage and up a flight of stairs. She was hoping the bedroom was big enough to hold a desk for her typewriter. She had not thought to ask whether the room came furnished or not and was soon to find out.

Wendy clicked on the electric light and gazed about the bedroom. 'Not bad, is it?'

Tilly gave a sigh of relief at the sight of the walnut tallboy, the matching dressing table, a cushioned wicker chair and the three-quarter bed. There were also shelves in the alcoves either side of the fireplace and a stand with a bowl and a jug, and still there was plenty of room over by the window for her desk and chair. 'It's great,' she said.

'Minnie and I share and so do the boys. We have the back rooms and Mam has the other front room. I hope you won't be disturbed too much by the traffic.'

'I'll have to get used to it,' said Tilly, unable to imagine finding anywhere as large for the money with two meals a day thrown in, as well. She went over to the window and gazed out at the shops on the other side of West Derby Road. 'I'm really pleased.'

Wendy smiled. 'We'd best get back to the party then.'

Tilly nodded. 'The others will be wanting to go soon because they won't want to miss the luggage boat.'

But it was obvious when they arrived back at the party that Clara and Freddie were enjoying themselves too much to make a move yet. As it was, Tilly was not to get to see Alice that evening to break the news to her because they missed the luggage boat and ended up staying at the Arcadia Hotel on Mount Pleasant. The three woman had to share a double bed in one room and the men in another. Hanny was worried not only about the twins and what Alice might say when they arrived home the following day but also about her elderly mother.

'There's nothing you can do about it,' said Tilly, snuggling up against her back.

'I'm sorry that this happened,' said Clara. 'But it's not often Freddie and I get the chance to dance together and what with the baby we'll soon have even less chance.'

'It's all right, love,' said Hanny. 'I'm sure Seb will realise what's happened and will look in on my mother. Don't you agree, Tilly?'

'Yes,' said Tilly, although she was not so worried about Seb's reaction to their staying out all night as her sister's.

CHAPTER FIVE

'Well, I think you all had a nerve staying out all night,' said Alice, across the dining table to Tilly on Monday morning. She had not spoken to her at all on Sunday.

Tilly looked up from her breakfast plate and swallowed a mouthful of porridge. 'You didn't say that to the others when they dropped me off.'

'I didn't have to because I'm sure they knew how I felt.'

'And you think I didn't?' asked Tilly.

'You're not a mother,' said Alice.

'Neither is Clara yet. Besides, I don't know what being a mother has to do with us missing the luggage boat and staying overnight in Liverpool.'

'Did you see Father?' asked Alice.

Tilly stiffened, wondering what her sister would say if she told her about the tiny baby skeleton he had shown her and how they planned to rebury it.

'That was a question best not asked,' murmured Seb, looking up from the pages of a motor catalogue he was perusing as he had finished his breakfast.

'I don't see why,' said Alice, bristling. 'Whose side are you on, anyway, Seb? I know you've never been able to understand my feelings about Dad.'

James and Flora raised their heads from their plates and looked first at their mother and then their father.

'That's not true,' he said firmly. 'And we've been through this before.'

'I'm not having him come here, trying to make friends with the children,' said Alice.

The last thing Tilly wanted was to come between husband and wife. 'I'm sure I've told you before that he won't be coming here,' she said, glancing at her nephews and niece. 'Although, he's perfectly safe. I'll be moving out this coming weekend. I've found somewhere to stay and I'll be looking for a job once I'm living in Liverpool. I'll be within walking distance of Dad and Joy will be there, keeping her eye on him, as well.'

Alice thumped down the jug of milk she'd just picked up. 'I can't believe it! You mean you've found somewhere already?'

Georgie, the youngest, looked up. 'You're going to break that, Mummy, if you're not careful. You've slopped milk all over the tablecloth. If I'd done that you'd have been cross.'

She frowned him down. 'I am cross with your Auntie Tilly. Obviously, she does not want to spend her birthday with us. After all these years she's found someone she thinks is better to share it with.'

'You mean Granddad,' said James, nodding his head sagely. 'I remember him from last year. I'd like to see him again. There's not many boys at school that have a live granddad.'

'There's children in school that don't have a daddy,' said Flora, sighing.

'Well, you have, so you don't need a granddad,' snapped Alice. She turned on her sister. 'See what you've started?'

'I didn't start anything,' said Tilly indignantly. 'It's you that started it by asking me a question that you already knew the answer to. You were just looking for an argument. I'd rather leave on good terms with you than be arguing.'

Alice's cheeks flamed. 'I'm not looking for an argument. I still think you're too young to live away from home but I'm not going to stand in your way. Hopefully, you'll soon realise you've made a mistake and which side your bread's buttered on. Where are these digs you've found?'

'Over a shop that belongs to the other Mr Bennett's sister, Mrs Wright. She's renting out his old bedroom to me.'

'And how much is that going to cost you?'

'Twelve shillings and sixpence,' said Tilly, 'and well worth the money.'

'You've seen it, then?'

'Yes!'

Alice stared at her. 'You'll soon be out of pocket and begging to come home.'

'No, I won't. I've some savings and I'll soon find a job,' said Tilly.

'I think you're making a mistake, Tilly, but I'm not going to stand in your way,' said Seb, pushing back his chair and getting to his feet. 'We'll miss you at the office.'

Her face softened as she looked up at him. 'But you shouldn't have any trouble finding a replacement.'

'No. But you'll be needing a reference. I'll write one out for you.'

A reference! She had not thought of that. 'Thanks,' she said gratefully.

He smiled faintly. 'I think for the peace of the household you've got to spread your wings. Just be aware that Alice does know your father better than you do.'

'Thanks for that,' muttered Alice, getting up.

'I'd like to know what Grandfather did to make Mummy hate him so,' said Flora.

'Don't you start,' warned Alice. 'I'll not have your grandfather mentioned in this house. Now finish your breakfast.'

'I've had enough,' said Tilly, her expression tight. 'If you'll all excuse me. I'm going to my bedroom to pack.'

'You don't mean you've changed your mind and have decided to go today?' said Seb, startled.

'Yes! Because Alice is going on about Dad again. Although—' Tilly paused. 'I suppose I *should* really work out my notice?'

'That won't be necessary if you want to be off as soon as possible,' said Seb, sighing. 'But it might be sensible if you stay until you find a job in Liverpool.'

'I feel I've a better chance of doing that living over there.'

He nodded. 'If that's how you feel.'

Alice's face quivered. 'We'll need an address,' she said harshly.

Tilly stood, resting her hands on the back of her chair. 'I can't remember the number of the shop but I'm sure if you address it care of Wright's newsagent's and sweetshop, West Derby Road, Liverpool, then any letters will get there. I mean Don might...' Her voice trailed off and without another word she left the dining room.

After she had packed most of her clothes and placed some books in a box, along with another cardboard box containing typing paper, carbon paper and a spare typewriting ribbon inside it, on her desk, she knew that she was going to need help to get it all to Liverpool. She decided to ask her half-brother if he could arrange it, but before doing so she checked how much money she had. She had been paid on Friday and after giving Alice money for her keep, she still had a couple of shillings left, as well as several pounds in loose change in a tin in the bottom of her wardrobe. Hopefully this would see her through the next month.

Ten minutes later she was in Kenny and Hanny's kitchen telling them her plans. She could tell from his expression that her half-brother was still not in favour of her aims.

'I still think you're too young,' he said.

'Alice said I was too old in the head for my age and that's because you and Hanny never treated me like a child. Have some faith in me, Kenny. I'll be seventeen soon. I'm quite sensible, you know. I swear if I get into difficulties I'll be in touch. I'm only crossing the Mersey, not the Atlantic.'

Kenny's expression thawed. 'It's not a matter of not having faith in you, love. I know you can be sensible and you're not going far but Liverpool isn't like Chester. It's a port and has all the glamour and excitement and trouble that's attached to ports. It also has more poverty and social unrest, as well. Not to mention the religious divides.'

'But I won't be living down by the docks. I'll be living with a family,' said Tilly. 'And Joy won't be far away. Surely you can trust Joy to keep her eye on me?'

'I suppose so,' he said grudgingly, glancing at Hanny. 'For a moment I'd forgotten about your sister being over there.' He put an arm about Tilly's shoulders. 'OK. I give you my blessing. But you do realise this will be the first time I won't be seeing you on your birthday.'

'It can't be helped,' said Tilly, thinking of her father. Her sixteenth birthday last year was the first time he had shared in her special day. She was hoping that this year they would be able to spend her seventeenth birthday together but decided to not mention that to Kenny.

'I'll get Freddie to load your stuff in the back of the car and he can drive you to Liverpool.'

'You think he'll manage to get my desk and chair in as well as everything else?' asked Tilly.

'With the hood down?' said Kenny, thoughtfully. 'I'm sure he'll think of someway of getting them in.'

'Of course, he will,' said Hanny, glancing up from her knitting. 'He's very resourceful, my brother. We are going to miss you, though, Tilly.'

'I'll miss you, too.' Tilly bent and kissed her. 'I will be back to see you.'

Hanny touched her cheek. 'You make sure you are. If you need help at any time get in touch.'

On the way out of the house, Kenny slipped an envelope into Tilly's pocket. She looked at him. 'Birthday card,' he said.

Tilly thanked him and walked down the path to her sister's home.

A few hours later during lunchtime, Alice, Seb and the children stood at the gate, watching Tilly climb into the front passenger seat. 'So you're off,' said Alice, her expression taut.

'It looks like it,' said Tilly, smiling brightly despite the tightness in her chest and the prickle of tears behind her eyes.

'You will be coming back, Auntie Tilly, won't you?' called Flora.

'Of course,' said Tilly, blowing her a kiss. 'You're all my favourites.'

'Will you be bringing us a present?' asked Georgie, skipping over to the car and climbing on the running board.

'You don't ask questions like that,' said Alice, following him over and dragging him down. 'Now say goodbye to Auntie Tilly.'

'Goodbye, Auntie Tilly,' said Georgie, and he blew her several kisses.

Tilly mimed catching them. 'I'll keep these close to my heart,' she said.

Alice made a noise in her throat as if to say *Don't be silly.*

'I'll see you then,' said Tilly.

'OK! Get going,' said Alice, sounding impatient. 'Father will be waiting.'

Tilly had been about to say *I'm going to miss you, Alice,* but her sister's words so annoyed her that instead all she said was a bright sounding 'Bye, everyone!' She waved.

Freddie had already started the engine and now sat a moment, gazing sidelong at her, his elbows resting on the steering wheel. 'You all right?'

'Why shouldn't I be?' she said in a tight little voice.

'I remember the first time I went to sea, I wanted to howl but I had to get over it and I did. At least you're not going far and there's no war about to break out.'

'Thank God,' she muttered.

'Yes, indeedy,' said Freddie, and with a toot on the horn, he drove off along the familiar crescent towards the Old Dee Bridge and Tilly's new life.

She was in no mood to talk. She felt a little scared despite all the reassurances she had given her brother that she was grown-up now, sensible and able to cope out there in the big wide world. After all, it was true that she was not going far, but she was going to have to watch her money, so would not be able to visit Chester as often as she might like. Of course, if she didn't find a job pretty soon then she might have to slink back home like a dog with its tail between its legs. She tilted her chin. No! Whatever happened she was not going back until she made a success of this move and proved to her family that she could truly survive independently of them. She thought of Don and wondered if he had lived close by how different her life might have been. But then, with his profession, he would still have left her for weeks or months on end. She sighed. No. She had to make a life for herself, as well as spend as much time as she could with her father. After all, she did not know how many more years he had left to live.

'You'll be able to phone the office if you need to chat,' said Freddie, rousing Tilly from her musings.

'Of course,' she responded. 'But I don't plan on making a habit of it. I have to stand on my own two feet. If I phone it'll be questions, questions, questions. Besides, it'll cost money and I'm going to need every penny I have.'

'You'll be applying for jobs.'

'I'll have to, I can't live on air,' she said crossly.

'No. None of us can. I was just making conversation but perhaps I'd be best concentrating on the traffic and leaving you in peace.'

Yes, do that, thought Tilly, gazing about her. They had passed the Falcon Inn on a corner of Lower Bridge Street. How long had it been there? Probably as long as the ancient cross and the medieval cathedral. She was not so sure about the covered shopping rows but parts of the city walls went further back than the cathedral to Roman times. If she closed her eyes she could picture them in her mind and would carry their images over the water to Liverpool, where, most likely, her future landlady had been up hours ago and might be expecting her.

Several hours earlier Mrs Wright had woken her daughters by banging on the girls' bedroom door.

'What time is it?' groaned Wendy, rubbing her eyes.

The mattress sagged in the middle as Minnie rolled against her. 'Why d'you have to bang so loud, Mam?' moaned Minnie. 'I don't have to get up yet.'

'The sooner you're up the quicker you can get every thing done. You haven't got much longer at school and will need to look for a job, girl,' said Mrs Wright.

Wendy glanced at the alarm clock, which was getting temperamental and had failed to rouse her. 'Goodness, Mam, it's half-six! Far too early for our Minnie. She'll only get in the way.'

'The newspapers are here and the delivery boy won't be long after them. I've put the kettle on,' said Mrs Wright. 'Our Minnie can make the tea and some toast. I'll get started sorting out the papers. Besides, our new lodger might make an appearance today and one of us should give her room a going over.'

'OK!' Wendy kicked off the bedcovers and tumbled out of bed.

Minnie scrabbled for the covers and drew them back over her. 'I'm going back to sleep. I don't want any tea and toast.

I'm never going to work in a shop, the hours are too long. A nice job in an office will suit me.'

'You'll be lucky. Tilly Moran has got a better chance of getting an office job than you.'

'Sez you,' murmured Minnie sleepily.

Wendy gave up on her and sat on the edge of the bed, dragging the well-worn cotton nightgown over her head. She reached for the garments hanging over the bottom of the bed and began to dress in camisole, drawers, black stockings and a plain blue dress that was six inches from the ground. She pondered on whether she could get away with taking up the hem another inch without her mother noticing but decided it was unlikely. She reached for her shoes and fastened the laces, before hurrying downstairs to the outside toilet.

Afterwards, she washed her face and hands in the scullery sink before entering the kitchen, where a kettle was steaming away on the gas stove. She made a pot of tea and a couple of rounds of toast before carrying the tray through into the shop, where her mother was at work.

'Here yer are, Mam,' said Wendy, placing tea and toast on a shelf safely away from the danger of being knocked over. 'Our Min has dozed off again.'

The shop bell jangled and a man entered, followed by the paper boy. Wendy smiled as she recognised Mr Simpson. He needed a shave and his clothes were looking rather rumpled but she still considered him an attractive man.

'Good morning! You're early. Your usual paper?' she said.

'That's right, Miss Wright, the *Daily Post*.' His eyelids drooped and his hazel eyes turned into slits as he yawned.

Mrs Wright looked up from her counting and writing numbers of houses on corners of newspapers and magazines.

Home delivery was a new service they were offering their customers and it was proving a success. 'You look tired, Mr Simpson. Were you out all night?'

'Aye. But what you told me clinched the business.' He brought his head close to Mrs Wright's and lowered his voice. 'I saw my quarry coming out of the address you gave me, so I can wind up the case.'

Wendy tried to appear as if she were not listening but she was all ears. In what way had her mother helped the great detective?

Mrs Wright's mouth pursed disapprovingly. 'I don't hold with bigamy. Disgusting! Although, no doubt there's plenty of it about due to couples rushing into marriage during the war and then realising their mistake. Moral standards have dropped shockingly and I intend keeping a tight rein on my girls.'

Oh no! Not that old chestnut, thought Wendy. Her mother was always going on about the dreadful moral standards of the day.

'There's nothing new under the sun, Mrs Wright,' said Mr Simpson, digging into his pocket and bringing out a handful of change. 'People are just more honest about sin these days. The war's caused people to question the beliefs of the older generation.' He slapped the money down on the counter. 'I'll have a bar of Bournville dark chocolate, too, Miss Wright, if you please?'

Mrs Wright fixed him with a hard stare. 'Sugar is still on ration, you know.'

'I know, Mrs Wright, but surely you don't begrudge a hard-working man his bar of chocolate. I'll make it last me the week,' said Mr Simpson.

A question in her eyes, Wendy glanced at her mother. She turned her back on them and reached for her cup of tea. Her mother's behaviour frequently didn't make sense to Wendy because she often said one thing and did another. Wendy knew this and that's why she took a bar of chocolate from a box on the shelf behind her and placed it on the counter in front of Mr Simpson. 'You certainly seem to prefer dark chocolate to milk,' she said in a low voice as a way of prolonging the conversation.

'You're right there. We'll make a detective of you yet,' he teased, handing her sixpence.

She blushed and tingled all over. Hastily, she turned and placed the money in the till and gave him his change. As he left the shop, she rested her elbows on the counter and gazed after him, wondering if the day would come when he would notice that she was growing into a woman. She would be seventeen before Christmas.

'Stop daydreaming,' said Mrs Wright, nudging her daughter's elbow. 'He was joking when he said he'd make a detective of you.'

Wendy heaved a sigh. 'I know it was a joke. So who's the bigamist, Mam?'

'Never you mind, girl. You help the lad get those newspapers in the bag and out on the bike.'

Wendy did as she was told, steadying the bicycle as the youth heaved the bag into the holder at the front of the machine. Once he was seated, she gave him a push to get him started and watched him sail off down the road. She stood a little longer, breathing in the polluted air and gazing at a tram rattling by. A worker making his way to the tobacco factory pushed past her and entered the shop. She followed him in just as the sun went behind a cloud.

As Wendy served the man, her mind wandered to thoughts of Tilly Moran. Would she arrive today or was she already regretting saying she would take Uncle Robbie's room? She thought enviously of her uncle and aunt away on the briny, heading towards foreign parts. Now, that would be an adventure! Life could be a little dull at times. She thought of Mr Simpson and wondered what his first name was and whether he already had another case to keep him busy. She tried to imagine what it would feel like to be kissed by him and closed her eyes briefly.

'Wake up, girl,' said the customer. 'Yer haven't given me my change.'

'Sorry,' said Wendy, handing him his tuppence.

The next few hours passed slowly without much of note happening. She would be in sole charge of the shop later when her mother went shopping. Perhaps Tilly Moran would have arrived by then.

Wendy was in the back spreading jam on bread when she became aware of raised voices coming from the shop. She hurried out and was in time to see an angry-faced young woman step away from her mother. Mrs Wright had a hand to her face and was swearing like a trooper. Wendy was shocked because she had never heard her mother swear before.

'What's up? What's going on?' demanded Wendy.

'You run and find the bobby, girl!' panted her mother. 'This cow has just assaulted me.'

'That's because you interfered in my affairs,' cried the woman, banging her fist on the counter. 'Yer should have minded yer own business. Now the police have gone and arrested me husband.'

'He's not your husband, you stupid woman,' yelled Mrs Wright.

'He's as good as! We were happy. I'm having his baby. What's going to happen to me and the baby now? He'll lose his job, might go to prison. How am I going to cope?' she wailed.

'It's not my fault! Lay the blame where it belongs on that two timing man of yours,' said Mrs Wright, her face screwed up with pain.

'It is your fault. Yer shouldn't have interfered.'

'Oh, shut up, you silly girl. Don't yer care that he's got a wife already?'

'Of course, but I love him. She was a mistake and nagged him to tie the knot before he went off to war,' said the woman, wringing her hands. 'What am I going to do?'

Wendy's sympathy was roused. 'Do you really want me to get the police, Mam, or shall I make us all a cup of tea?'

'No, you bloody won't,' said Mrs Wright, lowering her hand to reveal a right shiner.

'Blooming heck, Mam, she's given you a black eye,' said Wendy.

'Yeah! And you want to go and make her a cup of tea. Not bloody likely. She needs a warning from the bobbies if nothing else. You go and find ours on the beat. Then you can go the butcher's and see if he's got a bit of steak for this eye.'

'Yer don't really think I'm going to hang around here waiting for a bobby to come, do yer?' said the woman. 'I'm off!'

As she hurried out of the shop, she bumped into a girl in the doorway.

'Stop her!' called Mrs Wright.

But it was too late, she had gone.

'What's going on?' asked Tilly, coming further into the shop and placing her Gladstone bag on the counter.

Wendy smiled at her. 'So you've come.'

'Yes. The room is still available to me, isn't it?'

'Of course,' said Mrs Wright. 'But you've picked a bad time to arrive, girl. That one you let get away, did this to me.' She lowered her hand.

Tilly gasped. 'That's some black eye! How awful!'

'I'll say it is,' said Wendy, nodding. 'Go and have a look at it, Mam.'

'I'll do that after you go and fetch a bobby and me steak. I know where that woman lives so she won't get away with this.'

'What about Tilly?' asked Wendy. 'Who's going to see to her?'

'She can see to herself,' said Mrs Wright, touching the skin beneath her eyes gingerly. 'You showed her the room so she knows where to stow her stuff.'

Tilly cleared her throat. 'Freddie brought me in the car. I've got a few more things that need bringing in and taking up.' She paused. 'Is there anything I can do for you before the pair of us go up?'

'No. My eye won't stop watering until I have that steak. Take some money out of the till, Wendy, and get going,' said Mrs Wright.

Wendy did so. Then Freddie came in with a couple of boxes in his arms. 'Where do I put these?' he asked.

'Follow me,' said Tilly.

'No, he doesn't,' said Mrs Wright, seizing hold of Tilly's arm. 'You're not going upstairs with him, unchaperoned. You can wait until our Wendy comes back.'

Freddie placed the boxes on the counter and stared at Tilly's landlady. 'I'm a married man and I haven't got time to hang around here, Mrs Wright. I have to get back to work and I still have a few more things to bring in yet.' He brought his head closer to the older woman's. 'That's a bad black eye you've got there.'

'A woman gave it to her,' said Tilly.

Mrs Wright let out a scream. 'You don't have to tell him! I'll trust the pair of you to get out my way and take your stuff upstairs.'

Freddie and Tilly did not need telling twice but before they went, he asked, 'Do you get many women fighting round here, Mrs Wright? I don't know if it's a safe place for our Tilly.'

'Of course not,' said Rita Wright indignantly, drawing herself up to her full height of five feet, two inches. 'This is a respectable household.'

Freddie's lips quivered. 'I'll believe you. Well, I can't hang around here all day. I've a proper job to do.'

Mrs Wright said, 'Yeah, you go. I'm going to have to keep my eye on the shop until our Wendy gets back.'

Tilly was giggling as she carried her Gladstone bag upstairs. 'I know I shouldn't laugh,' she said. 'But Mrs Wright saying she was going to keep an eye on the shop with that black eye of hers tickled me.'

'I wonder why the woman hit her?'

'I'll try and find out and let you know,' said Tilly.

Freddie dumped the boxes on the bed and gazed about him. 'Not bad. I'll be able to tell the family you've a nice room. Mind you, I'm still not certain I should be leaving you here, Tilly.'

'Don't be daft,' said Tilly. 'That woman's not going to hit

me. Besides, Wendy is fetching a bobby. See how safe I am? The police will be keeping an eye on this place. I've struck lucky!'

Freddie shook his head. 'I'll go and get your desk. You can carry up your chair.'

She followed him out. 'Don't say anything about what happened to the others, Freddie. I don't want them worrying about me.'

'OK,' said Freddie. 'But if you do get into trouble, Tilly, just let me know and I'll come and sort it out.'

She thanked him, thinking that while it was reassuring her family were concerned about her, she hoped that they would not be coming over here by the minute to check up on her.

CHAPTER SIX

Tilly was smiling as she stowed away her clothes and books, hung a towel on the rail of the wash stand, put her old rag doll on her bed and her toiletries and Bible on the dressing table. She placed typing paper on her desk next to her typewriter, as well as a couple of sheets of carbon paper. In a drawer she put her spare typewriter ribbon, pencils, rubbers and her fountain pen and ink. Then she went downstairs, curious to know why the woman who had brushed past her earlier had given Mrs Wright a black eye.

'So how are you feeling, Mrs Wright?' asked Tilly, on entering the sitting room.

'It's his fault. I should never have helped him,' said Mrs Wright, holding the steak to her eye. 'But when he came into the shop and showed me that man's photograph, I knew I couldn't keep quiet.'

'What man?' asked Tilly.

Mrs Wright stared at her from her one good eye. 'Never you mind. It's a private matter but I should have known he wouldn't keep quiet about where he got his information from.'

'Mam, I'm sure Mr Simpson didn't snitch on you,' said Wendy, not wanting her hero to prove to have clay feet. 'Maybe she worked it out for herself. I mean, so many people come into this shop and chatter away about their lives that we know a lot about them. We also know when strangers move in.'

'Maybe. Although, I wouldn't have thought she was that bright. She should have spotted that bigamist swine was a bad 'un straight away,' said Mrs Wright.

'What about you and Dad? You were always saying he was hopeless as a father and a husband, so why didn't you spot his faults before you married him?' demanded Wendy, crossly.

Her mother reddened. 'Never you mind! Don't you get personal with me, girl. What a thing to say in front of the lodger! Which reminds me...' She stared at Tilly.

'You want paying,' said Tilly.

'Yeah. Two weeks in advance.' Mrs Wright held out her free hand.

'I'll need to go back upstairs,' said Tilly.

Mrs Wright dropped her hand. 'OK. It can wait. You can give me it later. Right now, if you could put the kettle on and make us a cuppa, it would be a help.'

'OK.' Tilly went into the kitchen but left the door open.

'D'you think they will put him in prison, Mam?' asked Wendy.

'Probably. The law's not going to let men get away with being bigamists,' said Mrs Wright.

'But what about her having his baby? It's a bit of a mess, isn't it?'

'Let it be a warning to you, girl,' she said darkly. 'You can't trust men, even the best of them. Take my brother for instance. I never thought he'd go and marry again at his age. I mean, he made a mistake the first time, didn't he? I thought we'd have him with us until he passed away.'

'Don't you think you should be pleased that Uncle Robbie's found happiness at his time of life?' asked Wendy. 'I think he and Aunt Eudora love each other.'

'Love! Happiness! It doesn't last, girl. You mark my words. You'd best get your head out of the clouds – stop reading those women's magazines!'

There was the sound of a bell jingling and footsteps, then silence. Tilly presumed someone had come into the shop and Wendy had gone to serve them.

A few minutes later Tilly carried in a tray and placed it on an occasional table in front of the sofa where her landlady was sitting. 'How do you like your tea, Mrs Wright?' she asked.

'Strong and sweet,' said the older woman.

Tilly poured the tea. 'Is there anything else I can do for you?'

'Besides pay me?' asked Mrs Wright, placing the steak on her saucer and then sipping her tea. She was silent a moment and then said, 'Know anything about books?'

Tilly was puzzled about what she meant by that question. 'I read a lot and possess a few books of my own, and I want to write a novel of course.'

'I've a pile of books upstairs,' said Mrs Wright. 'The old ladies left them and nobody's claimed them. Our Robbie left books behind, as well. I had the boys dump them in one of the empty rooms. If you get the chance, perhaps you could have a look at them and see if they're worth anything.'

Tilly's interest was roused. 'You mean you want to sell them?'

Mrs Wright put down her cup and dabbed at her watering eye with the steak. 'If you can get a decent price for them, all well and good, but there's quite a lot of them.'

'I'll have a look and see what I can do,' said Tilly. 'If there are as many books as you seem to be saying, have you thought of a lending library?'

Mrs Wright stared at her. 'What d'you mean?'

'Have you ever been in Boots, the chemist? They lend books out for a penny a time. With your having knocked two shops into one, you have the space for some bookshelves.'

'There, I knew you were a clever young woman, you being able to type and all,' said Mrs Wright, smiling lopsidedly as her face had swollen slightly.

'Where are the books? I could look at them now. I won't be going to sign on at the Employment Bureau until tomorrow.'

'You can't miss the room, it's the last along the landing.'

Tilly went upstairs and decided to change into an older frock before looking at the books, thinking they might be dusty. But before making a start, perhaps she should pay Mrs Wright for her bed and board.

Mrs Wright was still sitting where Tilly had left her but she was not alone. She was talking to a policeman and Minnie had arrived home from school and was sitting beside her on the sofa. The girl's eyes were on the young man, who was writing in a notebook. In fact, she was batting her eyelashes at him. Tilly hoped Mrs Wright was unaware of her behaviour and turned to go back upstairs. Only to pause when Mrs Wright spoke her name. 'Hang on, Miss Moran. If you don't mind, take our Minnie with you.'

'Mam!' protested Minnie. 'I want to hear what happened.'

'I'll tell you later. Now go, go!' Mrs Wright made shooing motions.

Minnie clicked her tongue against her teeth, got up and swept out of the room with her nose in the air. Tilly hurried after her. The girl stopped at the foot of the stairs. 'What did you think of him?'

'You mean the policeman?' asked Tilly.

'Who else?' asked Minnie with a predatory gleam in her eye that shocked Tilly. 'Not bad looking, is he?'

Tilly was about to say *Too old for you* when she remembered Don and the age difference between them. 'He's OK. But I would have thought he'd have no difficulty finding himself a girlfriend of his own age.'

Minnie grimaced. 'You're right. Thank goodness there should be plenty of lads around of my age in a few years, so I can have a pick of the bunch, although I do prefer older men. I feel really sorry for our Wendy, she's not going to be able to pick and choose. Mind you, I doubt Mam will let her go even if someone did ask her out. Our Wendy is far too useful to her.' Without waiting for Tilly to comment, Minnie continued up the stairs.

Tilly followed her and then, when the girl stopped outside a bedroom door, she walked past her to a door at the end of the landing. Tilly was about to open the door when she heard footsteps behind her. 'This isn't your bedroom? What are you doing here?'

Tilly told her. Minnie looked vaguely interested. 'Mam would do anything to make some extra money. Do you really think your idea will work?'

'Don't know until it's tried and tested,' replied Tilly. 'I don't know your mother's customers, do you?'

'You mean are they readers?' Minnie ran her tongue along her teeth and did not immediately answer her own question but appeared to be giving it some thought. 'Depends on the books. Most who come in buy a newspaper, some of the women buy the *Red Letter* magazine. Mam reads that. I do, too, when she's not looking. Some good stories in it. So are you going in?' Before Tilly could open the door, Minnie flung it open for her.

The room was dimly lit because the curtains were drawn, so immediately Tilly went over to the window, avoiding the numerous books piled up on the floor, to let in some light. Then she turned and looked at the books, thinking there must be a couple of hundred there.

'Some are thick and heavy and most don't have pictures,' said Minnie, leaning against the wall.

'Most adult books don't have pictures,' said Tilly. 'If you've looked at them, then perhaps you can tell me some of the authors.'

'Sure. There are some popular ones. Mam would have a fit if she knew I'd read a couple of them,' said Minnie, sounding amused.

Tilly thought that Mrs Wright sounded like Alice and for a moment shared an unspoken fellow feeling with Minnie. 'Are there any Ethel M Dell, John Buchan, Elinor Glyn or Edgar Rice Burroughs?' asked Tilly.

'You mean the American who writes the *Tarzan* stories,' said Minnie, referring to the last name.

'He also writes fantasy and science fiction,' said Tilly, kneeling down on the well-worn rug next to the books.

Minnie chuckled and knelt beside her and picked up a book

from a pile. 'Can you imagine two old spinsters reading about an ape man?'

'Why not? He meets Jane, doesn't he? So there's a bit of romance,' said Tilly, running her gaze down the spines of books. The two famous women writers she had mentioned where well represented.

'But would they want to swing through the trees?' asked Minnie. 'Actually,' she continued, 'there are some *Tarzan* books here. Uncle Robbie liked reading them.'

'But I'm sure he didn't read this,' said Tilly, picking up a copy of *The Way of the Eagle* by Ethel M Dell.

Minnie grinned. 'Mam's read that. She said it was rubbish. Daft of her to say that because I immediately wanted to read it.'

'What about Wendy?'

'She wouldn't admit it to me,' said Minnie. 'I like stories about adventurous, arrogant, rich men. I'd like to marry a man like that but fat chance I'll have of doing so. Maybe if I became a stewardess on a liner?' she mused, scrambling to her feet. 'I'll leave you to it. I'll go and change and then see where Mam is up to with the bobby. I'll make the excuse that I've come down to peel the potatoes. See you!' She fluttered her fingers and left the room.

For a moment Tilly did no more than kneel there, thinking about what the younger girl had said. Alice would have called Minnie a precocious little madam but only time would prove to Tilly if that were true. She could be all talk. She got on with looking at the books, setting some aside that she thought should be popular, but decided if a library in the shop was to succeed, then they would need to buy some recent titles. From what Minnie had said about her mother,

Tilly was almost convinced that Mrs Wright would not be prepared to fork out on new books. It would also cost money for bookshelves and a ledger for the names and addresses of the borrowers, a date stamp and an ink pad. Maybe it would be best if she kept quiet about the idea of a library for the moment. At least until Mrs Wright brought the subject up again herself.

But Minnie's mention of the stories in the *Red Letter* magazine had given Tilly an idea. She would buy a copy of the magazine, read it and try to come up with a short story that would suit its pages. Hopefully, she might be able to make a few bob that way.

Tilly went downstairs. She could hear Mrs Wright's and Minnie's voices coming from the kitchen and presumed the policeman had left and they were preparing the evening meal. She wondered when the boys would arrive home from school as she went into the shop. Wendy was serving a customer and Tilly waited until the other girl had finished before asking whether she had a copy of the *Red Letter*.

'No. It's not out until tomorrow and last week's would have been used to light the fire,' said Wendy. 'I didn't realise you read it.'

'I've read Alice's copy sometimes.'

'And now you've got to buy your own,' said Wendy. 'You could always read our copy.'

'I'll do that, if you don't mind.'

'Although, it does mean you'll have to wait until we've all read it,' said Wendy.

Tilly decided that she didn't want to do that if she wanted to refresh her memory as to the kind of stories the magazine published, but she did not say so. Instead, she thanked Wendy and went looking for Mrs Wright to hand over the money for her keep.

There was a tantalising smell of cooking coming from the kitchen and she headed for there, finding to her surprise that it was Minnie who was standing over the gas stove, frying slices of potatoes and onion. Her mother was watching her and was still dabbing at her eye but this time it was with a handkerchief and not the steak.

'I've your money, Mrs Wright,' said Tilly.

'Thanks, girl,' said the older woman, taking the money from her and placing it in the pocket of her pinny. 'You happy with a couple of eggs tossed in with this?'

'Yes,' said Tilly, who was so hungry by now that bread and jam would have done her.

'Good. I'm glad you're not a fussy eater. I can't abide fussy eaters,' said the older woman. 'You can set the table for me – that's if you don't mind. What with this eye.'

'Shall I set places for your boys, as well?' asked Tilly, glancing over at the kitchen table.

'You might as well,' she said. 'Not that our Davy will be in just yet. You can bet he'll be in the park, kicking a ball around believing he's going to make it into the Liverpool team one day. I don't know how many times I've told him to come home first and change his shoes, but will he listen?' She shook her head and a tiny smile played round her mouth.

It was obvious to Tilly that Mrs Wright had a soft spot for her younger son. 'What about Peter?'

'Oh, he'll be in soon. It's Scouts tonight, so he'll be wanting to eat early and get into uniform and be on his way.' She added, 'Cutlery is in the left table drawer and tablecloths are in the right.'

'Thanks,' said Tilly, and she proceeded to take out a tablecloth and spread it over the table.

'So, you came over here to be near your dad,' said Mrs Wright, removing plates from a shelf.

'That's right.'

'You think you'll see much of him?'

'I hope so.'

'Why didn't you set up home with him?'

Tilly looked at her in surprise. 'He works for Mrs Black.' She corrected herself, 'I mean, Mr and Mrs Bennett.'

'But he did work for her first, didn't he? I believe they've known each other for years,' said Mrs Wright, placing the plates on the table.

'Yes. From before I was born,' said Tilly.

'It's a long time and he hasn't always worked for her, has he?'

'No. She gave him a job and a roof over his head when he needed it.'

'She must be fond of him to do that,' said Mrs Wright. 'I mean, he was in the asylum, wasn't he?'

Tilly was beginning to feel extremely uneasy. Where were all these questions leading? Tilly thought of Alice and her feelings for both her father and Eudora Bennett. Surely there couldn't be anything more behind her hatred for them than what Tilly had always believed: that her sister hated her father because of his violent behaviour towards their mother and herself, and disliked the former Mrs Black purely because she was a medium and healer, and their father had sought her help?

'Yes, he was in the asylum but he's much better now,' said Tilly, praying her landlady would ask her no more questions.

It was a relief when the door opened and Peter entered the kitchen. He paused in the doorway, staring first at Tilly, then his mother. 'Our Wendy said a woman attacked you. Golly, that's some black eye, Mam! Did you hit her back?'

'As if I would respond to violence with violence,' said Mrs Wright, giving a sniff that was similar to the one Minnie had given earlier. 'Not at all the way decent people should behave. Isn't that right, Miss Moran?' she said. 'Doesn't the Bible say we should turn the other cheek?'

'Yes,' said Tilly, wondering why it was that sometimes Mrs Wright called her Miss Moran and then at other times *girl*. She could not remember if she had addressed her as Tilly yet. There were definitely several sides to Wendy's mother, she decided. Was it possible that earlier she had been hinting there was more to her father and Eudora Bennett's relationship than that of healer and patient and subsequently employer and employee? But why should the woman be interested in their past?

'Our Minnie would have hit her,' said Peter, going over and peering closely into his mother's face. 'It's gone all purply.'

'She'd have deserved it,' said Minnie, glancing over her shoulder at him. 'Probably Mam never got the chance to retaliate.'

'What a thing to say,' said her mother, glaring at her. 'I believe the law should deal out judgment and that's why I've complained to the police.'

Tilly was beginning to feel really sorry for the woman and was tempted to say so but guessed she would be out on her ear if she did. Instead she asked where she would find the salt and pepper to put on the table and whether she should cut some bread.

'You do that, girl,' said Mrs Wright absently. 'Bread in the crock and knife in the drawer.'

'Is Miss Moran having the first egg?' asked Minnie, glancing at Tilly.

'Yes. Then Peter because he'll be going out and you'll need to get a move on,' said Mrs Wright, 'because I'll be going out later, too, and I want to fry my steak.'

Tilly almost blurted out *You're going to eat that steak after you've handled it? I don't know how many times you've pressed it against your face!* But she remained silent, knowing that she could not behave the way she would have at home. Besides, perhaps Mrs Wright would wash the steak.

As soon as she had eaten Tilly decided she would go upstairs and see if she could come up with some ideas for a story. If not, then she would read one of the books piled up in the spare room and try and forget what Mrs Wright had insinuated about her father and Eudora Bennett.

'Are you OK? Got everything you need?' asked Wendy, popping her head through the half-opened bedroom door.

Tilly looked up from the book she was reading. 'I'm fine. You finished in the shop?'

'Yes. I've closed up. Is it all right if I come in?'

Tilly put down her book on the bedspread. 'Of course.'

Wendy closed the door behind her and came further into the room. 'Bed comfortable?'

Tilly nodded and glanced at her bedside clock. 'You're late closing.'

'It's Mam who sets the hours and she thinks we can catch the late evening passing trade if we stay open. I wonder if it's worth it on any night other than Friday and Saturday.' Wendy yawned and pulled out the chair from the desk and sat down. 'So what do you think so far? That woman hitting Mam hasn't put you off living here, has it? That's never happened before.'

'No,' said Tilly, smiling. 'There was a time in Chester when members of my family were staring down the barrel of a gun.'

Wendy's eyes widened. 'You're joking!'

'No. Swear it on the Bible,' said Tilly, placing her hand on hers at the side of the bed.

'It must have been terrifying,' said Wendy.

'It was for Freddie and Clara and Dad,' said Tilly, settling herself to tell the tale. As she talked she remembered how her father had been the hero of the hour, risking his life to save his granddaughter from being kidnapped. It had been the first time Tilly had met her father and what daughter could not have been impressed by his bravery, especially as he lay bleeding on the ground?

'You seem to have gone off in a trance,' said Wendy, stirring Tilly from her thoughts. 'So what finally happened to Bert?'

'Well, you've heard the saying *He who lives by the sword, shall die by the sword*?' said Tilly.

'Yes,' replied Wendy, her eyes wide. 'Are you saying?

'He was shot with his own gun and died.'

'Blooming heck!' Wendy smiled and said solemnly. 'So should all baddies perish.' She got up from the bed and went over to the window. 'Do you want your curtains closing? It'll help shut out some of the noise of the traffic.'

'Thanks,' said Tilly.

Wendy drew the curtains and then glanced down at the typewriter on the desk. 'Have you done any writing this evening?'

'No. Too many things on my mind.'

'I wish I could type,' said Wendy wistfully, touching the keys.

'It's not that difficult if you put your mind to it and concentrate – and practise, practise, practise. You can always have a go when I'm not here,' said Tilly, 'as long as you don't waste too much paper.'

Wendy's face lit up. 'Do you really mean it?'

'I wouldn't say it if I didn't mean it,' said Tilly, smiling. She got up from the bed. 'I'd better go the lavatory before I settle to sleep.'

'I'll come with you,' said Wendy.

As they went downstairs together, she said, 'Fancy a cup of cocoa?'

'Don't mind if I do but only a small cup,' said Tilly, thinking of the trek from her bedroom to the outside lavatory during the night. There was so much she was going to have to get used to living here. Hopefully, in time, she would settle down and build a new life for herself.

CHAPTER SEVEN

'What would you do with this weather?' asked Tilly of no one in particular. She'd had such a strange dream last night and, what with it being her birthday and having only the one card from Kenny and Hanny, she felt out of sorts.

'You're not going out in it, are you?' asked Wendy, glancing over to where Tilly stood just inside the shop doorway, gazing out at the pouring rain.

'I have to. I need to go into town to register at the Employment Bureau.'

'Why don't you hang on for a bit? It's only early and you don't want to get caught up in the parades.'

Tilly came back into the shop. 'What parades?'

'It's the Twelfth of July. Orangemen's Day. Surely you've heard of it, even in Chester?'

'Of course, I have. I just forgot.'

'They'll be crowds in town. It's a shame about the rain because the procession is worth seeing if you've never seen one before. The men will be wearing all the regalia of the various lodges and the women and kids will be dressed in pretty frocks. A couple will be dressed as William and Mary with long curly wigs and costume of the times. Then there's the bands. They play some really stirring music. "Sons of the Sea and We're all British Boys" is one. Very patriotic.' Wendy sighed. 'The poor kids! All their pretty dresses will get soaked – but at least the rain should dampen the ardour of any troublemakers.'

'You mean if the Orange and Green clash?' said Tilly, having read about such conflicts in the local press in the past.

'Yeah! And what with the troubles in Ireland right now and the violence between Sinn Fein and the Black and Tans, there could be even worse trouble than usual over here.'

'Surely the police will stop any fighting,' said Tilly, frowning.

'It depends if they want to get involved. Some have been badly injured in the past, you know.'

Tilly did not know but she was suddenly feeling a long way from home. Liverpool appeared to belong to a different country altogether compared to Chester. 'I suppose I'd still better take a chance,' she murmured. 'I can't be putting it off. I need to get a job as soon as I can.' If she didn't then she was going to be in financial trouble despite the crisp two pound notes she had found inside Kenny and Hanny's birthday card.

Tilly drew the brim of her hat further down so as to keep the rain out of her eyes and stepped outside, wishing she had not forgotten to pack her umbrella before she left home. She was about to cross the road to the tram stop when she collided into someone and he stood on her foot. 'Ouch!'

He threw her a hasty, 'Sorry, love.'

Then he was gone, leaving her with a brief impression of a fairly good-looking, clean-shaven man in his early twenties with nice teeth. When she turned round he had vanished and she presumed he had gone inside the shop. She dismissed him from her thoughts and crossed the road. Almost immediately, a tram came rattling along and she climbed aboard and found herself a seat. She gave the conductor the money for her ticket and then gazed out of the window at the passing scene. Fortunately there was only the one hold up at the top of Brunswick Road, where they had to wait while a bedraggled procession marched past from the direction of Shaw Street.

Once in town, Tilly had little trouble finding the Women's Employment Bureau and filled in the relevant registration forms. At that moment there were no jobs available but it was suggested that she call in several times a week to see whether any work had come in. She decided not to get despondent so early in her search. After all it was her birthday and she did have money and was free to wander around the shops, even if she planned on keeping her money where it was, safely in her handbag.

She soon discovered that there were several summer sales on. The Bon Marché had Shantung silk at two shillings and eleven pence, ha'penny a yard. She could not help thinking about Alice and what she could do with a few yards of the fabric. With her sister's eye for design and skilful fingers, she could create a lovely dress in no time. She wondered if there might be a card from Alice, Seb and the children when she arrived back at the Wrights' home. She had hoped but not expected one from Don, so would not be too disappointed if one didn't arrive, despite his never having missed her birthday since they met. With her father being so forgetful, she didn't think that he would remember her birthday.

She continued to wander around town despite the rain and, eventually, came to another clothes shop called Phillip's and its window was full of blouses: crepe-de-chine ones, beautifully smocked in shades of champagne, sky blue and pink. She longed to buy one but at twenty-nine shillings and sixpence, they were well out of her price range.

She wandered on and eventually came to WH Smith and Son in Tithebarn Street. She went inside and scanned the shelves of books, observing the titles and names of publishers and reading the opening pages. There was a notice advertising the latest and forthcoming releases. Tilly was always on the lookout for new titles. She could not afford to buy books but made a note of the titles and authors, making a resolution to join the local library and order them. Thinking of this reminded her of the piles of books above the shop and that she was supposed to be doing something to make money with them. Perhaps she should see if there were any second-hand bookshops in Liverpool.

Tilly was on her way out when she saw another notice propped up on a table. It read: *Red Letter* novels, No 1 out on sale today.

Red Letter! thought Tilly, the magazine read by Alice, Wendy, Minnie and Mrs Wright, as well as thousands of women in Britain today. Obviously, the publishers were breaking out into another line. She could not resist buying a copy of the slim novel as it was reasonably priced; after all, it was her birthday.

After making her purchase she left WH Smith's and, as it was still raining and she was feeling a little tired now, she decided to catch the tram and go to visit her father.

* * *

'Hello, Tilly,' said Joy, emptying some scraps on a plate just outside the back door. 'I believe it's your birthday today. Many happy returns. I suppose you've come to see your dad?'

'Yes, thanks. Is he around?'

'He's down under the trees at the bottom of the garden.' Joy straightened up. 'He's been acting stranger than usual today.'

Tilly's heart flipped over. 'Strange in what way?'

'The talking to himself is not unusual but his asking for a prayer book certainly is,' said Joy with a faint smile.

'A prayer book!'

'Exactly. Why should your dad want a prayer book? According to Alice and Kenny he was against the church.'

Suddenly, Tilly thought of a reason why her father might want a prayer book. 'Did you have one handy?'

'Of course. I go to church off and on. I'm thinking of going along to St Margaret's next Sunday. I believe it's high church,' said Joy. 'Smells and bells, I rather enjoy that kind of service. Theatrical.'

'Kenny does, too. I'd sometimes go to the cathedral with him,' said Tilly, smiling. 'Anyway, I'd best go and see Dad.'

'If you find out what he wants the prayer book for, let me know.' called Joy after her.

She raised her hand in acknowledgment and went down the garden. Fortunately it had stopped raining and she was keen to discover if her father had managed to get a tin box for the baby bones and whether he was preparing for a burial service. She soon discovered that was exactly what he was about. She found him, gazing down into a hole with what looked like a large cash box on the ground beside it.

'Hello, Dad! Were you going to go ahead without me?' she asked.

He glanced at her and his weather-beaten face broke into a smile. 'I willed ye to come and here yer are.'

'Yes. I've been to the Employment Bureau and thought I'd pop in and see you before going back to my digs.'

'I'm glad yer did. I was hoping yer could say a few words over the little lad. I've looked in the book but there's too many words and I thought you could pick something short.'

'Why a little lad, Dad?' she asked, curiously.

'We lost a lad, Flora and I,' he murmured.

Tilly was filled with sadness at the thought of this dead little brother she would never know. Taking the prayer book from her father, she noticed that he had placed a marker at the beginning of *The Order for the Burial of the Dead*. Silently, she read the first reading from the New Testament before flicking over the pages and deciding that simply saying the prayer of committal and the Lord's Prayer would be adequate.

'When you've placed the tin in the ground, Dad, I'll begin,' she said, a tremor in her voice.

He stared at her and did as she said and then asked, 'Is there anything else I should do? I was thinking that perhaps I should scatter some soil on the lid.'

She nodded. 'Of course!'

He did so as Tilly intoned, '"Forasmuch as it hath pleased Almighty God of his great mercy to take unto himself the soul of our dear...' she hesitated and then took a deep breath, 'brother here departed, we therefore commit his body to the ground; earth to earth, ashes to ashes, dust to dust; in sure and certain hope of the Resurrection to eternal life through our Lord Jesus Christ; who shall change our vile body, that it may be like unto his glorious body, according to the mighty working, whereby he is able to subdue all things to himself. Amen."'

Mal muttered, 'Amen.'

'Now the Lord's Prayer, Dad, that we can say together,' she said huskily, noticing the uncertainty in his face. 'Surely you know the Our Father?'

He nodded. 'But I can't imagine what it's like having a father that cares. Mine left when I was only little and Mother hated him for it.'

Tilly wondered if this was a reason why her father hated the Church and its God. 'Would you like me to say it?'

'Aye, lass.'

Tilly did so and then closed the prayer book. Mal began to shovel some earth on top of the makeshift coffin. 'I bought a rosebush,' he said. 'It's a bonny one with a red flower and several other buds. I'll plant it now, shall I?'

'I don't see why not.' She watched him at work in silence and when he had finished, he looked up at her as if for approval. 'That's lovely, Dad. You'll always know where the baby is buried now.'

'Aye.' He looked satisfied as he put the spade away just inside the door of the outhouse. Then he turned to her. 'Am I right in believing it's yer birthday today, lass?'

'Did Joy tell you?'

'Aye, lass. I'm sorry I didn't remember by myself. I thought perhaps we could do something together. Is there anywhere that yer'd like to go?'

Tilly thought about his suggestion and said, 'What about if we go to the Palladium and see a film?'

'If that's what would please yer, lass, I'm willing,' said Mal. 'I've never seen a film before.'

'Never! Honestly, Dad?'

He grinned. 'Honestly.'

Tilly smiled. 'Then you're in for a treat.'

'It'll be my treat,' he said. 'I'll pay because it's yer birthday.'

She was not going to argue with that but decided she would buy a bag of sweets from the shop for them to eat inside the cinema. 'We'll go this evening. I'll need to go home and get changed and have something to eat.'

'I'll smarten myself, too,' he said, 'and see yer later, lass.'

'Will we meet outside the Palladium? You do know where it is, Dad?'

'Aye,' he said firmly. 'I've dropped off Mr Bennett there once or twice.'

'We'll meet about five o'clock,' said Tilly, kissing his cheek and thinking that she would return the prayer book to Joy and then be on her way. As she walked up the garden, she experienced that feeling again that she was being watched. She glanced towards the neighbouring wall and spotted a woman's face.

'Hello!' she called, changing direction and heading towards the wall. Instantly, the woman vanished. Tilly tried to find a foothold in the brickwork to hoist herself up but it was a no-go. She decided that the woman must have something to stand on. Had she seen Mal bury the box and heard Tilly say prayers? If Miss Parker had, did it really matter? She decided not and returned to the house.

She found Joy in the kitchen and there was a mouth-watering smell of baking. 'So what did he want the prayer book for?' asked the older woman.

Tilly decided she could trust Joy with the truth. 'Dad found a baby's skeleton in the garden and decided it needed a Christian burial.'

Joy stared at her as if she didn't quite believe her. 'Pull the other one.'

Tilly smiled. 'Honest! I said a couple of prayers and he's planted a rose bush to mark the spot. Here's your prayer book back.' She placed the book on the table.

'I wonder if it was the old woman's,' said Joy. 'Perhaps she got herself into trouble and the father went away and never came back. Maybe he died.'

'Gosh, Joy, you've as much imagination as I have,' said Tilly, startled.

'Perhaps it was stillborn.'

'I thought of that. Poor little mite.'

Joy nodded. 'Best say nothing to anyone else.'

Tilly agreed and then remembered the neighbour. 'By the way, next door was spying on us again. Is the master of the house back yet?'

'I haven't seen him but then I'm not forever looking out of windows or over walls.' Joy went over and cautiously checked the contents of the oven. Then she turned to Tilly and said, 'Are you doing anything special for your birthday?'

'Yes. Dad's taking me to the flickers this evening. I don't think he'd object if you wanted to come, too,' said Tilly.

'No thanks. I see enough of your father but come back here with him and we'll have a drink and a piece of cake.'

Tilly's eyes lit up. 'Is that the cake in the oven now?'

'Yes. I might even put a few candles on it.'

Tilly hugged her. 'You are kind, Joy.'

Joy smiled and pushed her away. 'I don't need any soft

soap. I hope the pair of you have a nice evening together.'

So did Tilly, still surprised that her father had never seen a film in his life. Of course, he might have forgotten doing so but whatever, she felt certain he would enjoy the treat.

Tilly linked her arm through her father's as they headed for the entrance to the cinema. It was a continuous performance and there were two films showing. One called *Eye for an Eye* and the other *Island of Adventure*. Tilly felt a stir of excitement and could not wait to get inside the auditorium. The famous Russian actress, Alla Nazimona, was in the first film that, according to the poster outside, was a tale of vengeance. The other one was said to be set on a South Sea Island. How she wished films could be in colour instead of black and white. Perhaps one day they would be but for now she had to content herself with things as they were.

They had missed the start of *Island of Adventure* but it was obvious something exciting was happening because of the accompanying music. It was really stirring stuff full of crashes and rippling key notes. As they lowered themselves into their seats. Tilly could see that there were natives up on the screen fighting with white men and the faces of the women there expressed terror. She took a bag of sweets from her handbag and offered it to her father. She needed to give him a nudge and hold the bag out in front of him because his eyes were glued to the screen.

Without looking his hand fumbled inside the paper bag and he drew out a toffee twirl and rammed it in his mouth. She took a pear drop and relaxed in her seat. Somewhere nearby a boy was reading aloud the words up on the screen. Probably to a granny or granddad who was either unable to read or due to bad eyesight could not make out the words. Half an hour passed. Suddenly Mal sat bolt upright, muttering to himself as there came another loud crash of music.

Tilly darted him a glance. 'You OK, Dad?' she whispered.

'It's not right,' he said. 'They shouldn't be doing that. It's cruel. It's wrong.'

'It's only a film, Dad. They'll get their comeuppance, you'll see.'

He was silent for a few minutes and then he shot to his feet and shook his fist at the screen. 'Get out of there, lassie!' he shouted. 'Ye're in danger!'

Tilly jumped out of her skin. 'Sit down, Dad,' she hissed, pulling on his jacket.

'Nooo! She needs help,' he cried.

'Will yer shut up and sit down, old man,' said a man behind them. 'Yer spoilin' the film.'

'I canna sit down,' said Mal, turning on him. 'Not when the lassie is in trouble. Where's yer heart, man?'

'In me bloody chest! Where d'yer think, Granddad?'

'I'm no yer granddad,' growled Mal. 'Now shut yer mouth or I'll shut it for yer.'

'Is that a threat?' asked the man, getting to his feet.

'Sit down, Dad,' said Tilly, worried that a fight was about to break out and he might get hurt.

Mal looked down at her. 'Is that you, Flora?'

Tilly's heart performed an odd leap. 'No, Dad. It's Tilly.' She was suddenly scared and stood up. 'Perhaps we'd best go.'

'Tilly!' His tongue seemed to be savouring the name.

'Yes, Tilly. I'm your daughter.' She clutched his sleeve. 'Come on. Let's go.'

'About bloody time,' said the man behind them. 'Let them

past, folks, and then we can get back to the bloody film.'

Mal stiffened and he turned back to the man. 'I don't like yer language. There's women present.'

'What's going on here?' interrupted a new voice.

Tilly looked towards the aisle at the end of the row and saw an usherette standing there with the commissionaire.

'Nothing to worry about,' she said politely. 'My father's just having one of his funny turns. The war, you know.'

'The war! He's too bloody old to have fought in the war,' said the troublemaker behind them. 'He's a loony,' he added with a snigger.

Tilly saw red. 'My dad is not a loony!'

She pushed the man and he fell backwards. His seat had sprung up, so instead of landing in comfort, he caught his back on the hard edge. A yelp of pain escaped him and he slid to the floor.

'Oh my,' said Mal. 'Yer shouldn't have done that, lassie. I think we'd better get out of here.'

Tilly was horrified by what had happened. 'Yes, we'd best. Sorry, sorry,' she said.

'Let them out, let them out,' ordered the commissionaire.

The people in the rest of the row got to their feet. A woman gave Tilly a push in the back. 'Go on, queen, get out before yer land yerself in anymore trouble.'

Once Tilly and Mal were outside in the foyer, the commissionaire wanted their names and address. Without a second thought Tilly gave him false information and then, seizing her father's hand, she ran out of the cinema with him, knowing she would not dare show her face at the Palladium again for a long time.

It came as a surprise to find that the sun was shining outside.

She and her father exchanged glances and he chuckled. 'Yer might not be Flora but ye've got plenty of guts, lass. I don't know what I was thinking of getting myself all worked up the way I did. But those pictures, they seemed so real.'

Tilly agreed but felt concerned that her father had not been able to distinguish make-believe from reality.

'Now where shall we go?'

'You know who I am now, Dad?' she asked.

'Yer my daughter, Tilly. I only forgot for a moment because yer look so like yer mother when she was young.' He offered her his arm and she slipped her hand through it.

'Shall we go to the park?' she asked.

'Aye. It'll be pleasant in the park. Trees and grass and birds. It'll be peaceful, like,' said Mal.

Tilly agreed.

They made their way along West Derby Road, passing Wright's shop on the other side until they turned into Sheil Road and crossed to the other side. Her father took her through some public gardens and along Denman Drive until they eventually came to Newsham Park. They strolled in silence until they reached the boating lake. There, they paused on the bridge to watch the ducks squabbling over the crusts a woman and some children were throwing to the birds.

Tilly took out the bag of sweets and offered it to her father. He took a bon-bon and popped it into his mouth. She thought about the swans and ducks and boats on the River Dee on a summer's evening and puzzled over whether her sister had ever seen this side of their father. She tried to imagine what Alice would have thought if she had been in the cinema with them. No doubt she would have said that their father was a bad influence on her because Tilly had reacted violently to the man behind them. Tilly had never thought herself capable of reacting in such a physical way to aggression. Yet she had felt such a strong need to protect her father because sometimes he seemed childlike to her. Perhaps her mother had understood him much more than Alice could ever know. She felt the need to talk to someone about it. But who could she speak to about such a disturbing episode?

They returned to the house a short while later to find Joy reading a newspaper in the garden now the sky had cleared and it had turned into a fine evening. Nanki Poo was sprawled at her feet and he opened one eye as they approached. Joy glanced up at them. 'You're home earlier than I thought you'd be.'

'We decided we didn't like the film,' said Tilly, 'so we went for a walk in the park.'

'I'll put the kettle on,' said Joy, folding the newspaper.

'No! You stay where you are,' said Tilly, placing a hand on her shoulder. 'I can make tea.'

'Thanks. I was just reading an article in the paper so I'll finish it.'

'What's it about?' asked Tilly.

'A woman who wants a separation from her husband because he tortured her by bringing mice home and setting them free in the kitchen. He even tried to put one down the front of her frock,' said Joy, pulling a face.

'What an odd way to behave,' said Tilly.

'It's the kind of thing our Bert would have done if he'd thought of it. I still find it hard to believe sometimes that we're rid of him forever,' said Joy. 'Most of us like to believe we're safe in our own homes, but it's far from true.' Her expression was sad.

Tilly could think of nothing to say to comfort her, remembering Joy's brother Bert had been responsible for the death of their younger sister. She took the bag of sweets from her handbag and dropped them on top of the folded newspaper. 'Help yourself while I put the kettle on.'

Joy took out a bon-bon and was about to offer the bag to Mal but he was no longer where he had stood a couple of minutes ago. She glanced down the garden and saw him vanish inside the outbuilding. She opened her newspaper and finished reading the article before getting to her feet and going inside the house.

'The judge gave the woman a separation,' she said to Tilly. 'I wouldn't bother making a cup for your dad. He's gone off to his quarters and will no doubt forget about us.'

'Is he often that forgetful?' asked Tilly.

'Sometimes he is and sometimes he isn't. Mother's the same,' said Joy. 'You've got to remember neither of them are spring chickens. Mother seems to remember the past better than the present. She still believes Bert's alive and God's gift to humanity.'

Tilly spooned tealeaves into the pot. 'Dad went a bit peculiar in the cinema. He believed what was happening on the screen was real and briefly thought I was my mother.'

'That must have given you a shock,' said Joy, sounding sympathetic.

'It did! Then a man behind us got really nasty and said Dad was a loony. That's why we left.' Tilly sighed. 'I won't be taking him the cinema again.'

'Sounds sensible,' said Joy, taking milk from the larder and placing it on the table. 'I'm sorry your birthday hasn't been as good as you hoped but at least you can have some cake.' From the larder she produced an iced cake with a candle in the middle. 'Happy birthday, Tilly, and may you have many more of them.'

Tilly flushed with pleasure. 'Thanks!'

Joy produced a box of matches and lit the candle. 'Now blow out the candle and make a wish.'

Tilly was not sure what to wish for because there were several things she wanted but she decided on one thing dear to her heart and crossed her fingers as she blew out the tiny flame.

CHAPTER EIGHT

Liverpool: Autumn 1920.

Tilly limped into the shop and was relieved to see that there were no customers waiting. Wendy was serving cigarettes and a newspaper to a young woman, whilst Mrs Wright had her head together with a middle-aged woman, who appeared vaguely familiar. Tilly placed her handbag on the counter and leant on it. She slipped off her left shoe and looked inside it. Yes! A nail had come right through the sole. She resisted inspecting her foot and eased the nail from her shoe. The young woman brushed past Tilly, almost knocking her off balance.

'What's up?' asked Wendy, peering over the counter at Tilly's foot.

'A nail. It went right through my sole and stocking and into my foot. It feels really sore,' said Tilly.

The woman talking to Mrs Wright paused in mid-speech and turned and looked at Tilly. 'Yer'd best wash that foot right away, girl. Yer don't want it getting septic and ending up with blood poisoning killing yer.'

'You're a right cheerful one,' said Mrs Wright, smiling and giving the woman a poke in the arm with her elbow.

'I'm just advising the girl,' said the woman.

'Yes, yes, she is,' said Tilly, recognising the woman who had been in charge of the shop on the evening of the Bennetts' wedding. 'I don't know where that nail's been so she's right.'

Wendy lifted the counter flap. 'You'd better come in. Did you have any luck?'

'No.' Tilly sighed. She had never thought it would be this difficult to find a job. 'All the ones I've gone after they either want a young man, or I'm too old or too young for the money they want to pay an employee.' If it hadn't been for the belated birthday card from Seb and Alice with a postal order inside, she would be absolutely broke by now. As it was she had not been able to visit them and neither had they been to see her. Perhaps her sister was still vexed with her. Tilly dreaded the thought that if she didn't find a job soon, she would have to swallow her pride and ask for help from her family. She didn't want to do that because she could too easily imagine what Alice would have to say. Besides, she would be distanced from her father if she had to return to Chester. If only the short stories she had sent to the *Red Letter* had not been rejected, she would have got her foot in the door and the publisher would have looked with favour on her next offering. One thing was for certain: she had to spend more time writing and at least the last rejection letter had been encouraging.

'Never mind,' said Wendy, resting her elbows on the counter. 'I mean you have skills. Mam's not going to kick you out and something is bound to turn up sooner or later.'

'Yous still looking for a job, girl?' asked the woman.

'Yes! Mrs Pain, isn't it?' said Tilly.

The woman looked gratified. 'Yer've a good memory.'

Tilly smiled. 'If I have it's not helping me to get a job. You haven't seen an office job advertised on your travels, have you?'

Mrs Pain pursed her lips. 'Now, I can't say yeah to that but there might be one coming up at the insurance office in Prescot Road where I clean. Miss Langton's assistant is leaving to get married. Nineteen, she is, and a plain little thing but she's managed to catch a man. Still, I reckon she's not half as clever as yous are.'

'You flatter me, Mrs Pain,' said Tilly, managing a smile despite the pain in her foot. 'What do you suggest I do? Go there and ask whether there is the likelihood of a position be coming vacant in the near future?'

'If yer mean by all those words what I think yer mean, then why not, girl? The early bird catches the worm. But I'd advise you not to dolly yerself up.'

Tilly was puzzled. 'Why?'

'There's women that don't like a girl that catches the men's eye. They think they're flighty. It's down to jealousy, if yer ask me,' said Mrs Pain.

'Are you talking about the woman you mentioned. Miss Lang—Miss Langton?'

'That's her!' Mrs Pain nodded her head vigorously. 'Miss Langton! Must be in her forties, I reckon, and already grey and as miserable as sin. Don't want to discourage yer, girl, but I thought I'd best warn yer. But if yer desperate and use yer nous, then I reckon yer could get on the right side of her and the job could be yours.'

Tilly did not know what to think. On the one hand, she was

grateful to Mrs Pain for telling her about the job, but on the other, she didn't make it sound very attractive. Still, beggars couldn't be choosers and so she would have a go at getting the post. 'I appreciate your help, Mrs Pain. Where is Prescot Road? Perhaps I could go along there tomorrow morning and enquire.'

'All yer've got to do is catch the tram along Sheil Road and when yer come to the end of it, get off and turn right. Then yer cross the road and walk along for a bit and yer'll come to the Friendly Assurance Society office. It's the only one along there.'

'Thanks,' said Tilly in heartfelt tones, despite her mixed feelings.

Mrs Pain's face creased into a smile. 'Good luck, girl. I'm sure you can do it.'

Tilly smiled. 'I'd best get myself organised.'

'I'll come upstairs with you,' said Wendy. 'I can leave you looking after the shop for ten minutes, can't I, Mam?'

'Yes, but don't be long,' said Mrs Wright.

As the two girls went upstairs, Wendy said, 'You just missed Mr Simpson this morning.'

Tilly was always just missing the detective and, although curious to see what he was like, she was not that bothered about meeting him. 'Did he want anything other than his newspaper and chocolate?'

'He's got a new case.'

'What is it?'

'He said it's not wildly interesting but it'll help pay the bills. He's taken on another part-time job for a salary because work has been slow in coming in since the bigamy case,' said Wendy.

'That's a couple of months ago,' said Tilly, thinking of the poor woman who had been left pregnant and without a husband. Fortunately her family had stepped in to help her, Mrs Wright had not pressed charges and she had got off with a warning.

'I know! He said if it weren't for his savings and his sister, he'd be in the workhouse.'

Tilly gasped. 'I hope he was joking.'

Wendy fiddled with a strand of mousy hair. 'I hope so but these are tough times, as you know, Tilly.' She tucked her hands up her sleeves. 'They reckon in Liverpool alone there are three hundred more men out of work every week and there's ex-soldiers who can't find jobs. Alongside that there's these strikes going on. Even the printers are at it and it says in the *Echo* that there might be no newspapers next week if matters don't improve.'

'Whatever will you read, Wendy?' joked Tilly, knowing the other girl was an avid reader of the local paper.

They had reached Tilly's bedroom and she opened the door and went inside. Wendy followed her. Tilly sat on the bed and eased off her shoes. 'I should have brought up some hot water to soak my foot,' she said.

'I'll go down and get you some,' said Wendy, picking up the jug on the washstand and hurrying out of the bedroom.

Tilly moved to a chair because the bed was a little too high for her feet to touch the floor. She removed her garters and rolled down her stockings. The sole of the left one was bloodied and she dropped it on the floor and, with difficulty, looked at her foot where the nail had pierced it. Mrs Pain had put the wind up her a bit and she hoped the cut would not grow worse.

A few minutes later Wendy re-entered the bedroom,

carrying the steaming jug. She poured the water into the bowl and said, 'I hope it's not too hot for you.'

'If it's too hot for me, then it's going to be too hot for the germs that cause trouble.' Despite her words, Tilly felt the water with her elbow and let it cool down a little before plunging her foot into it. To take her mind off it, she said, 'So Mr Simpson never told you what his latest case was about?'

'Something to do with a missing dog.'

'A missing dog? That sounds really exciting.'

'There's no need for you to make a joke of it,' said Wendy seriously. 'It's a valuable dog! It has a pedigree, just like Uncle Robbie's Pekinese has. They cost a lot more than tuppence ha'penny, pedigree dogs, you know.'

'I should imagine they would,' said Tilly, bending down and rubbing the sole of her foot. 'So what plans does he have to find it?'

'I didn't have a chance to ask,' answered Wendy gloomily. 'He was in a hurry. I might never find out.'

'Cheer up! You just might if he's already told you as much as he has done,' said Tilly.

'Maybe you're right,' said Wendy, her expression brightening. 'Anyway, I'd best go. Mam will be complaining if I don't shift myself. By the way, if I were you, I'd cut a sole out of cardboard and put it inside your left shoe before you wear it again.' She left the room.

Tilly remained where she was with her foot in the bowl, thinking about what Wendy had told her and also about the vacancy that would soon become available. She only hoped that her foot would feel better so that she could have a try at putting herself forward to get the job.

* * *

'You do look smart,' said Mrs Wright, inspecting her lodger the following morning.

'I was hoping I looked dowdy,' said Tilly, dismayed. It was the reason she had decided to wear the charcoal grey costume with the well-worn white blouse.

'I think it would be impossible for you to do that,' said Wendy, resting her elbows on the counter. 'Not with your figure and coloured hair, it-it's just so-so bright.'

'Even with a hat on?' asked Tilly. 'Perhaps I should stuff it all under my hat and pad out my figure so I look dumpy.'

Wendy was about to say *But you haven't got a fat face!* But Tilly had already gone.

She reappeared a short while later. 'What do you think?' she asked, glad that there were no customers in the shop. She tried to do a twirl and almost overbalanced.

'What have you done to yourself?' asked Minnie, making a sudden appearance. 'You look older an-and...'

'And what?' asked Tilly.

'I don't like to say. Perhaps you should put on some lipstick.'

'Certainly not,' said Mrs Wright. 'There'll be no painting of lips in this house.'

Minnie pulled a face. 'You're so old-fashioned, Mam. What's wrong with a girl adding a bit of colour to her lips?'

'It's not right. If God had meant us to have bright red lips then he'd have given us them,' said Mrs Wright. 'It's-it's of the devil and painting your face says something to a man about a girl.'

'What?' asked Minnie with an innocent expression. 'And you never go to church, Mam, so I don't know what you're going on about the devil for. I don't believe he exists.'

Her mother turned almost puce. 'That's enough. Just you believe me when I say men think a girl is giving them the old come-on if she paints her face.'

'Come-on what?' asked Minnie, inspecting her fingernails. 'You'll have to explain, Mam. I need to know as much as I can when I go out into the wide world.'

Her mother seized her arm and dragged her out of the shop into the room at the rear.

'If you ask me,' said Wendy, 'our Minnie already know more than is good for her.'

'I'd agree,' said Tilly, smiling.

'Whatever you do, don't smile,' said Wendy hastily. 'Look as sober as you can. You'll dazzle her and she'll—'

Tilly blushed and pulled a face. 'OK. I get the message. So what d'you think about these?' From her handbag she produced a spectacles case and put on plain lenses glasses.

'Where did you get them from?' asked Wendy.

'I bought them secondhand. I wanted to try out a look for one of my characters.' Her voice trailed off as the door opened and a customer entered.

'Gosh, they change the real you even more,' said Wendy. 'And you're wearing flat shoes, too,' she added.

'Why d'you mention that?' asked Tilly. 'I have to walk there and I can't risk my foot getting worse.'

'You need heels to go with that costume but I understand why you need to look sensible.'

'That's what I want to hear. I want Miss Langton to believe me to be a sober, sensible person,' said Tilly, removing the spectacles, only to bump into the man standing behind her. She glanced up at him from mischievous hazel eyes. 'Excuse me.'

He stepped aside and held the door open for her. 'My pleasure,' he said, his gaze washing over her.

'Thank you,' said Tilly, having a vague feeling she had seen him before. Then she was gone.

'Who was that?' asked Mr Simpson, closing the door behind her.

'Our lodger,' said Wendy, beaming at him. 'Good morning, Mr Simpson. What can we do for you? Your usual paper?'

'Yes, please, Miss Wright,' he answered. 'I didn't know you had a lodger.'

'Since July,' informed Wendy, folding a copy of the *Daily Post* and handing it to him. 'She's going to be a novelist one day but in the meantime she's looking for a proper job. Is there anything else I can do for you, Mr Simpson?' She felt like batting her eyelashes at him but didn't have the knack.

'I noticed she mentioned Miss Langton,' he said.

'Do you know the woman?'

'I've met her. She's what you'd call *a bit of a tartar*. I feel sorry for your lodger if she's going after a job in her office.'

'Tilly's desperate for money. If she doesn't get this job, then she might have to go and live back at home in Chester.' Wendy sighed. 'Is there anything else I can do for you, Mr Simpson?'

He appeared to collect himself and brought his head down so it was on a level with hers. 'You can do me a favour.'

She almost answered *I'd do anything for you* but instead said, 'What is it?'

'I wondered if you'd put this poster in your window?' He took a roll of paper from beneath his arm and opened it up and spread it on the counter.

Wendy gazed down at the photograph of the dog. 'Is this the one that's gone missing?'

'Yes. It answers to the name of Bruce.'

'You don't think it's been run over?'

'No. It would have been found and a report made.'

Wendy felt in a bit of a dilemma. 'I'll have to ask Mam.'

He looked disappointed. 'If you must.'

She felt mean not saying yes straight away but she knew that if her mother saw the poster and she had not mentioned it then she would tear it down immediately. She went to the door and called her mother.

Mrs Wright came into the shop and stared at Mr Simpson. 'What is it?'

'Mr Simpson asked if we could put this poster in the window for him, Mam. It's of a valuable missing dog.'

'I don't like dogs,' said Mrs Wright, stony-faced.

'What's that got to do with it, Mam?' asked Wendy. 'It's not going to leap out of the poster and bite you.' She could not resist a smile in Mr Simpson's direction. He winked at her and she felt a glow warm her whole being.

'Don't be cheeky, girl,' said her mother, before addressing Mr Simpson. 'It'll cost you sixpence for it to go in the window for a week.'

He hesitated and then nodded. 'Let's hope it'll bring us some results.'

'Why didn't the owner put up posters?' asked Wendy.

'Why didn't she go to the police?' asked her mother.

'She did but believes they don't take cases of missing dogs seriously,' replied Mr Simpson, 'and the dog means everything to her.'

'So how did she get to hear about you?' asked Mrs Wright.

'Word spreads,' he said. 'But just to help it along, I also placed another advertisement in the *Echo*.'

'Smart,' said Wendy, clearly impressed.

Her mother sniffed. 'Why bother paying you? She could get another dog easily enough.'

'She likes this one.'

'I hope you find it,' said Wendy, wishing her mother would keep quiet.

'Thanks, love.' He smiled at her and handed over a sixpence. 'My address is on the poster if anyone comes in and says they have information as to Bruce's whereabouts. Hopefully I'll see you tomorrow.'

He tipped his trilby and walked out of the shop.

'You can put up the poster,' said Mrs Wright, staring after Mr Simpson. 'And I wish you'd stop staring at him out of goo-goo eyes. He's not for you, girl. I'm going in to chivvy our Minnie up to go out and look for a job. And while I think on, remind me to ask Tilly about those books upstairs. She still hasn't done anything about them.'

Wendy nodded and picked up the poster and found some sticky tape to put it up. She thought of Tilly and of how she would have a lot to tell her when she returned.

Tilly had not taken the tram to Prescot but in every other way she had obeyed Mrs Pain's instructions to the letter, so she had no difficulty in finding the Friendly Assurance Society office. Even so, she had butterflies in her stomach because she was not feeling a bit like herself but a character in one of her stories. She stood a moment outside the door to put on the spectacles; then taking a deep breath, she entered the building.

A young woman stood in front of a filing cabinet with her back to Tilly. She could hear her humming to herself. There was a desk with a typewriter and a pile of paper, as well as an in tray, out tray, and an ink stand.

Tilly cleared her throat. 'Excuse me.'

The girl appeared not to hear her, so she spoke louder. This time the girl turned and looked at her. 'Can I help you? Is it about a burial policy?' she asked, eyeing Tilly's sombre garb.

Her question gave Tilly an idea; one that might rouse the woman in charge's sympathy. 'As it happens, I have recently lost someone, but that's not why I'm here. I'm desperate for work and I heard that there might be a job going here soon,' she said eagerly.

The girl smiled. 'I don't know who told you but it's my job that's becoming vacant. I'm getting married.'

'So I heard. Congratulations,' said Tilly, clutching her handbag tightly with both hands. 'You're a fortunate young woman in this day and age.'

'That's not what Miss Langton thinks,' said the other girl promptly. 'She's forever going on about marriage no longer being the only career open to a right-minded woman.' She dropped her voice. 'According to her every girl should be concentrating on leading an independent life free of men. Mind you, she missed the boat years ago.'

Tilly thought the girl was being rather unkind to Miss Langton and guessed she would not say such things about her if she were not leaving to be married. But before Tilly could speak there was the sound of footsteps approaching the other side of the door leading to an inner sanctum. The door opened to reveal a woman in her forties. She was tall and thin and wore a calf-length skirt in a dogtooth pattern of green and black, topped by an eau-de-Nil cotton blouse. Her brown hair was twisted up on the top of her head in a tight chignon. 'Who's this?' she asked sharply.

'My name is Matilda Moran and I heard that a job was becoming vacant here so I'd like to apply for it,' replied Tilly in a quiet, well-modulated voice.

The woman raised her eyebrows. 'I would like to know how you heard about this job.'

'From someone who comes to this office. I forget her name right now but she seemed pretty certain of her facts.'

'Hmmm! Well, news does get around,' said the woman, sitting down at the desk. 'I am Miss Langton, secretary to Mr Holmes, the manager. Have you any references with you?'

'Yes,' said Tilly, glad that Seb had given her a glowing reference, not that it had done her much good so far. The other two she had in her possession were written by the headmistress of her former school and her typing course tutor. She opened her handbag and removed a thick envelope and handed it to Miss Langton.

The woman waved her to a seat and opened the envelope. She removed the sheets of paper and read what was written there. Then she stared at Tilly. 'You seem to be well thought of by all and sundry. I will, of course, be checking theses references to see that they are genuine and will need to consult Mr Holmes about your filling the position available before it could be offered to you.'

Tilly could not believe her luck. She knew the references to be genuine so did not care about the woman checking up on her. Of course, this Mr Holmes might be a problem but she did not see why he should not wish to employ her. 'Thank you.'

'I have to tell you that the position here is unlikely to earn you the wage of your previous one. You're quite young to have been employed as a secretary.'

Tilly agreed. 'I was very fortunate to be taken on by a family friend. I do understand that matters are different over here but I am willing to work hard to advance myself.'

Miss Langton stared at her fixedly. 'There is no room for advancement here, Miss Moran, so if that is your plan forget it. If you wish to advance in the insurance business then you will have to eventually move elsewhere. Unless you plan to marry as soon as possible?'

'I have no such plans, Miss Langton,' assured Tilly. 'Rather I would learn from you and so gain valuable experience,' she added, remembering what Mrs Pain and the girl listening to them both had said.

'I am pleased to hear that.' Miss Langton's expression thawed. 'You seem a sensible young woman and it is possible when you are a few years older that a position might open up in one of the other sub offices or even our main building down at the Pierhead.'

'That gives me hope,' said Tilly, venturing a smile.

'There is one other thing I would like to know, Miss Moran.'

Tilly smoothed her face and said, 'Yes, Miss Langton?'

'I see your former position was in Chester. Why have you come to Liverpool?'

'To be with my father,' answered Tilly, without hesitation. 'My mother is dead, you see, and he was all alone.'

'I see. Well, you have my condolences, Miss Moran. If you'll give me your address in Liverpool, I will be in touch.'

Tilly thanked her and left the building, hoping Miss Langton would not look too closely into her background. She had not exactly told a lie but she had not told the exact truth either, she needed this job. She removed the spectacles and replaced them in her handbag, deciding to do a bit of window shopping before heading back to the shop.

'So how did you get on?' asked Wendy, leaving the magazine open on the counter as Tilly entered the shop.

Tilly removed her hat and shook her red-gold curls loose. 'I'm hopeful. Miss Langton is going to write and let me know. She has to check my references and consult the manager. I suppose there's always the possibility that there might be other applicants. I'll probably have to be interviewed by him, as well. But it'll be worth it if it helps me on the way to a profession that will pay me more money eventually.'

'You're talking about your writing?'

'Yes. But I can't afford to give all my time to it just yet. I need to earn and save money to do that. I can't sponge off people and I've no intention of starving in a garret. I've already sent off short stories and have written down some ideas for my novel.' Tilly wondered what Wendy would think if she told her that one of her ideas had come from something she had read to her from the *Echo*. It involved an illegitimate child being left on a doorstep of a rich childless couple.

'What about the books upstairs?'

Tilly frowned. 'I'd forgotten about them.'

'Mam hasn't. She wants you to do something about them,' said Wendy.

'OK. Right now, I'm going to change out of these clothes. I wonder if your mam would still be interested in my idea about a library? It would mean speculating to accumulate. We'd have to have bookshelves made to fit in here and we'd have to have a register for borrowers and buy labels, and a date stamp and pad, and probably some new books that are popular so not easy to get out of the library without a wait.'

'I'll mention it to her,' said Wendy, opening the flap for her to pass through. 'By the way, you saw Mr Simpson this morning.'

'I did?' said Tilly, gazing into Wendy's rosy face.

'He was the one who held the door open for you.'

'Oh! I've bumped into him before.' Tilly smiled. 'I think it was outside the shop the day of my birthday. He had nice teeth.'

'Once seen never forgotten,' said Wendy, and sighed. 'He brought us a poster to put up in our window. Didn't you notice it?'

'I can't say I did but then I wasn't looking,' said Tilly.

'Go out and have a look,' said Wendy. 'There's a reward for any information.'

Tilly went outside and gazed at the poster of the dog. She smiled to herself, thinking that the great detective had been hired to find a missing dog. Bigamists, dogs, what next? She went back inside the shop.

'I bet he wishes he could be more like Sherlock Holmes or even Sexton Blake, tracing jewel thieves or spies.'

'I wouldn't be surprised,' said Wendy. 'Trouble is that I'm sure private detectives get paid more money between the pages of magazines and books than in real life, and there's always a risk they could get shot or even killed.' She shivered. 'He's much safer doing what he's doing than playing at Sexton Blake.'

Tilly agreed and went upstairs, thinking she needed to work more on her book. She had started off with her hero being the baby left on the step and had not got much further. Perhaps when he grew up he could have nice teeth like Mr Simpson. For a moment she wished she had looked her best when he had held the door open for her, instead of so dowdy. She berated herself for caring what another man thought of her when it was Don she eventually wanted to marry. Anyway, she could not afford to be thinking too much about real men if she was to create a fictitious hero for her readers to fall in love with.

CHAPTER NINE

'A couple of letters have come for you,' said Mrs Wright, placing them on the table in front of Tilly.

'Thanks.' Tilly finished her toast and eagerly picked up the envelopes. It was a week since she had gone along to the office of the Friendly Assurance Society and had almost given up hope of hearing from them. One of the envelopes was brown and rather large and when she shook it something inside slid up and down. Curiosity would have had her open that one first but as it did not have a Liverpool postmark she opened the other one first.

'Would you believe it?' said Minnie, interrupting her perusal of the letter.

'Believe what?' asked Peter, glancing at his sister, who was reading last night's *Echo*.

'A crocodile was found in a dustbin in Paris,' she answered.

'Shush,' murmured her mother. 'Tilly's reading her letter. Anything about that job you went after, girl?'

'Yes.' Tilly darted a relieved smile at her landlady. 'I have an interview with the manager the day after next.'

'Well, let's keep our fingers crossed,' said Mrs Wright. 'You owe me money.'

'I'm sorry about that,' said Tilly, her cheeks burning with embarrassment. 'But I have been sorting those books out upstairs and writing stories and sending them off.'

'The man thought he was drunk and seeing things but it turned out that it was definitely a crocodile,' said Minnie, glancing across at Tilly. 'Wouldn't you like to put that in a book?'

'Only if it was a murder mystery and about to gobble someone up and then leave the remains in the yard and disappear.'

'Oo-er! What a thought,' said Peter, grinning. 'But what if, like the crocodile in *Peter Pan*, it had swallowed something precious.'

'You mean like a clock?' asked David. 'Tick-tock.'

'No! Jewellery.'

'Now that's more like it,' said Minnie, glancing at Tilly as she slit open the larger envelope. 'There was something about a man being charged with housebreaking the other day. He'd been released from Dartmoor on license but failed to report to the police.'

'Where was this?' asked her mother.

'The robbery was in Liverpool. He went and pawned a watch and that led to his arrest. Don't you think an authoress could find all kinds of plots for books out of the newspaper, Tilly?'

Tilly lifted her head. 'You talking to me?'

'It doesn't matter,' sighed Minnie. 'What's in the envelope?'

'Don't be nosy, girl,' admonished her mother.

'I'm not being nosy, just interested,' said Minnie.

Tilly said shortly, 'It's a letter from my brother-in-law and a

belated birthday letter from a friend. Now, if you'll excuse
me?' She got up and left the kitchen and hurried up to her
bedroom.

She dropped the letter from Miss Langton on her desk and
then sat on the bed and took out Seb's letter and postal order.
She stared at the latter, not wanting to cash it but knew that
if she didn't, then she was going to have to pawn something.
She found the contents of his letter worrying but had to accept
there was little she could do to help Georgie over the measles,
except pray. She could not even visit because Seb had told her
to stay away. Fortunately the other two children had already
had the disease and recovered without any lasting effects. She
could only hope that Kenny and Hanny's twins would not
catch it from him.

Setting aside Seb's letter and the postal order she picked up
the envelope that Seb had said had come in a letter for him
from Don. Inside it were two photographs. She glanced at
them and then decided to read the letter first. It was brief and
to the point and she felt deeply disappointed because she had
missed his long descriptive letters in his sprawling handwriting.

Dear Tilly,

*I'm sorry to have missed you when I arrived in Liverpool.
I hope that there will be a chance for us to meet in the future.
In the meantime I hope you had a happy 17th birthday.*
Don.

The words were so flat that she wanted to weep but instead
she swallowed the lump in her throat and looked at the
photographs again. Her heart felt as if it was being squeezed
as she gazed at Don's face. He had shaved off his moustache

and looked younger. He was resting against a car and in the background was what appeared to be line after line of crosses.

She turned the photograph over to see if there was a message on the back and read *Lest we forget*. Obviously, he believed that she was capable of working out that the words had a double meaning: to remember the fallen in the war and what had been between them. According to Seb's letter Don had sent a couple of other photographs; one of which was of Clara's father's grave in Flanders. Tilly was deeply touched by his thoughtful action and felt a fierce longing to see him and say how sorry she was to have missed him. She looked at the other photograph and saw that it was of her and Don with Seb and Alice's children in the garden in Chester. Don had taken it with some kind of delayed action attachment. He had hold of her hand and they were both laughing. When she thought of his damaged foot, she wondered how he had managed to move so fast to include himself in the picture. She remembered how he would have overbalanced if she had not grabbed hold of his hand. She turned over the photograph and saw that he had written *Oh, happy day!*

She blinked back tears as she placed the photographs and letters in a drawer. It had not slipped her notice that there was no address on Don's letter. Was that because he would not be staying in one place for the next few months or did he mean he did not expect her to answer his letter. She picked up the postal order and knew that she must cash it and immediately write and thank Seb for his generosity and also ask after Alice and the children, especially Georgie. She found some comfort in the thought that most likely Don would still keep in touch with Seb and hopefully sooner or later she and Don would be in touch again.

After Tilly had written a letter of thanks and brought her family up to date with her search for a job and expressed concern about Georgie, she went downstairs, intending to visit the post office. She found Wendy in the shop talking to the man whom Tilly now recognised as Mr Simpson.

His voice trailed off and he stood waiting as if expecting Wendy to introduce them to each other. Tilly smiled and held out a hand to him.

'I believe you're the famous detective, Mr Simpson,' she said.

His eyes gleamed as he took her hand. 'I think you mock me, Miss Moran.'

'You know my name! No wonder my ears were burning,' said Tilly, freeing her hand. 'I believe you're on the Case of the Missing Dog.'

'Not so missing now, Tilly,' said Wendy, uncertainty in her eyes as she looked at the pair of them.

Tilly cocked her pretty head on one side. 'Is that true, Mr Simpson?'

'Certainly, it's true,' he said. 'I've solved the case but sadly not to my client's satisfaction.'

'Why is that?' enquired Tilly, ever curious about other people's lives.

He hesitated.

'Client confidentiality?' she asked, having read enough detective stories to know of such things.

'Yes,' he said regretfully.

'I hope she still paid you,' said Tilly.

'Fortunately I asked for some expenses up front and she was fair enough to cough up the rest of my fee.'

'It would have been terrible if you'd been left out of pocket after all your hard work,' said Wendy.

'You can say that again,' he murmured, glancing down at her.

'Do you have another case to work on?' asked Tilly.

He switched his attention to Tilly. 'Not yet. But something is bound to turn up. At the moment I have some insurance claim investigation work.'

'You can talk about that?'

'Not specifically,' he said firmly.

'I understand,' said Tilly. 'It was nice talking to you, Mr Simpson.'

'And you, Miss Moran.'

Tilly turned to Wendy. 'I'm off to the post office. I'll see you later.'

'Yes. I'll see you later,' echoed Wendy.

The shop door had no sooner closed behind Tilly than Mr Simpson said, 'I'd best go. I need to visit the bank and then the office to see if there's any post or enquiries.'

'I'll see you tomorrow then, Mr Simpson,' said Wendy in a small voice.

He nodded, and hurried from the shop.

Hearing footsteps behind her, Tilly turned and saw Mr Simpson. 'I believe we're going in the same direction, Miss Moran,' he said.

'You're going to the post office, too, Mr Simpson?' she asked, wondering if she could persuade him to tell her how he solved his last case.

'No, but I need to catch the tram into town and will pass the post office.' Tilly was silent, waiting to hear what he said next. She heard him take a deep breath. 'You look very different from the last time I saw you, Miss Moran, and I wondered whether you'd like to visit the cinema with me one evening.'

Tilly stopped dead and stared up at him. 'Why should I want to do that, Mr Simpson, when we've only just been introduced?'

'But introduced we've been,' he retorted swiftly. 'I thought a visit to the Palladium?'

'No, thank you, Mr Simpson. I scarcely know you.' Tilly could hardly tell him that she avoided the Palladium like the plague, concerned in case the commissionaire should recognise her and embarrass her or even send for a bobby and have her arrested. 'Good day,' she said firmly, and hurried away.

Tilly cashed her one pound postal order and bought stamps and envelopes and then left the post office. There was no sign of Mr Simpson so she presumed he had caught the tram into town. After posting her letter, she decided that perhaps a treat for herself and the Wrights was called for, so she dropped into the bakery on the corner of Lombard Street and bought some currant buns. Then she returned to the shop, wondering if she could work a private detective into her novel.

Wendy looked up as she entered the shop. 'So you went the post office?'

'Yes,' said Tilly, startled by the question. 'That's where I said I was going. Mr Simpson walked part of the way with me and then he went and caught the tram into town. I then went to the bakery and bought some buns for us to have with a cup of tea. My brother-in-law sent me a postal order, not that I've mentioned being hard up.' She produced the bag with a flourish.

'That's nice.' Wendy hesitated. 'What did you talk about?'

'Sorry?'

'You and Mr Simpson.'

'Nothing in particular. I was tempted to ask him about his cases as I thought it might be fun to have a private detective in my book but—'

Wendy interrupted her. 'He wouldn't tell you anything. Client confidentiality.'

'That's right. Anyway, his cases don't sound very exciting.'

'Bigamists and missing dogs,' murmured Wendy.

The girls exchanged looks and laughed.

'I'll go and put the kettle on,' said Tilly, and hurried into the back.

The following day dragged by because Tilly was impatient to get the interview the next day over with and know if she had got the job. She tried to write but could not settle and ripped up several sheets of precious paper. She talked to Mrs Wright about buying more books but she raised her eyebrows in horror and told her to forget the idea for the moment. Tilly decided if the worst came to the worst and she did not get the job, then she would try and get a job in a factory, or even as a housemaid. Both would surely be useful in gaining information and experience of the way other people lived. The downside was that she would have to work damned hard and would not have time for her writing.

The day of the interview arrived and Tilly decided to wear exactly what she had worn the last time she had visited the insurance office. As it was, she did not get to be interviewed by the manager, Mr Holmes, because he had been called away urgently and so Miss Langton asked her further questions and then seemingly distracted and bored by the whole situation, told Tilly she had the job and to report for work the following Monday.

Tilly could scarcely believe she had gainful employment at last and during the next few days was on pins, wondering if she would receive another letter saying that it had been a mistake. When Monday arrived and no such communication had arrived, she rose early and got ready for work.

'Well, I hope everything goes well for you, Tilly,' said Mrs Wright. 'It's always difficult starting something new but at least you seemed to have fitted in here well.'

Tilly agreed that on the whole she had fitted into the Wright household without too much upheaval on either side. Was that because they were prepared to accept her as a paying guest whilst at the same time treating her as one of the family? Having a decent room of her own certainly helped her to cope with them and although there were comforts she missed, she had adjusted to doing without them. Mrs Wright was the person whom Tilly found the most difficult in the family to feel at ease with and maybe that was because Tilly had never had a proper mother. How different would her life have been if her own mother had lived? She decided to think about that another time. Right now she had a job to go to and despite what she had been told about Mrs Langton, she was glad to have it.

If Tilly had neither needed the money nor not been so interested in people, she might have been tempted to pack up the job within days. It held no challenge for her, consisting mainly of opening the mail and placing it on Miss Langton's desk to sort out, filing, making tea, running errands, and, depending on their status, seeing callers in and out. Some of these were insurance collectors and the odd one could be amusing, telling her tales about some of the people he visited. But she told herself that it was a job and her meagre wage would pay the rent and her fares and the couple of shillings that remained she would save for essentials when the need arose.

So the weeks passed during which Tilly heard from Seb and Alice that Georgie was much better but sadly the measles had left him with weak eyes and he would need to wear spectacles. Fortunately the twins had managed to avoid catching the disease, which could only be a relief at their age.

Tilly answered their letter, saying how sorry she was to hear about Georgie's eyesight, but she prayed that with the right treatment his eyesight would improve. She sent him a children's book that she had found amongst the books upstairs for Alice to read to him and also asked Seb to let her know if he heard from Don. She determined to try and visit them but it was not easy due to her job, visiting her father, household chores and lack of money. Everything was so dear and there were even more food shortages, which some put down to the terrible weather during July and August.

At least Tilly was able to spend a few hours writing a week and even sent off a couple more short stories. Tilly took to scanning the newspapers even more than she had in the past for ideas. It amazed her just how much crime there was in Britain and how many murders took place. One in particular caught her eye. Perhaps because the girl was the same age as herself and a typist, as well. Her battered body had been found hidden beneath shingle on a beach and the police had put bloodhounds on the trail to try and catch the murderer. Why would anyone want to batter a seventeen-year-old typist to death? The thought caused a shiver to run down her spine. Had it been a crime of passion? Tilly determined to follow the story in the following days in the hope of finding out what had happened. She also noticed that trouble was brewing in the ship repair industry. As for the murdered girl, which the newspapers took to calling *The Beach Mystery,* it turned out that the girl had got friendly with a Frenchman and when her boyfriend had found out about it he had killed her in a jealous rage. Tilly decided that it was, perhaps, best to avoid falling in love at all costs.

The return of the honeymoon couple and the arrival of Robbie Bennett at the shop was to stir his sister into agreeing with Tilly's plan for a library. It was Wendy who told him about it when he handed her some books that he and Eudora had read whilst on their honeymoon for anyone to read; they were almost brand new and best sellers. He thought it a good idea and said so.

'But I'd have to fork out for shelves and other paraphernalia,' his sister protested.

'Oh, come on, Rita. You'll be doing your customers a service and once it takes off, you'll make money,' said Robbie. 'Winter's coming and you're closer than the public library and people read more during the long dark evenings.'

'He's right, Mam,' said Wendy, feeling a stir of excitement. She was convinced that Mr Simpson was likely to borrow books, which meant more opportunity to talk to him.

'I tell you what,' said Robbie. 'Me and Mal will make the shelves for you and I'll even pay for the wood.'

'OK! If you're willing to do that then I'll give it a go but if it doesn't work out, then Tilly will have to find a dealer to take them away,' said Mrs Wright. 'I should have had her do that in the first place instead of humming and hahing about this library idea.'

'I think it's a bit much expecting her to do something with the books in the first place,' said Robbie. 'She's your lodger, not your lackey '

'Yes, but,' Rita's mouth tightened. 'I'll say no more. If it brings in some money I suppose she'll have proved herself.'

'I suggest a joining fee of sixpence,' said Robbie, rubbing his hands together and smiling. 'That will bring you in some money straight away.'

Rita was pleased with that idea and so, having been given the go ahead, Robbie measured the wall, where it was decided the shelves would go, and left to visit the wood yard.

Tilly was pleased when she arrived home from work on an unexpectedly warm and sunny October day to be told that her library idea was to take fruit.

Mr Simpson was to be Wendy's first customer, paying over his sixpence without complaint, as well as a penny to take out a book. She was surprised to see that he chose *A Princess of Mars* by Edgar Rice Burroughs.

'I didn't know you liked that kind of book,' she said

'There's lots you don't know about me,' said Mr Simpson cheerfully. 'I'm interested in what lies out there in space.'

Wendy wasn't. Her feet were firmly fixed on Earth, although she found the thought of dancing beneath the stars with Mr Simpson infinitely romantic. Whether he could dance or not was one of those things that she did not know about him and did not like to ask.

'I thought you'd have gone for one of our mystery stories,' she said.

'Once upon a time I would have but now I want to escape

work.' He grimaced. 'I'd best be on my way.'

'And how is the detecting business?' she asked hastily, in order to keep him there a bit longer.

'I've another private case but at the moment, I'm busy with an insurance investigation.'

'What's it about?'

'Now, Wendy, you should know better than to ask that.' He shook his head at her.

'Sorry,' she said. 'But is it exciting?'

Mr Simpson shrugged. 'No more so than my last case. A lot of hanging around and following certain gents, using up my shoe leather. With a bit of luck I should have the case sewn up after the weekend.' He tucked his newspaper and book under his arm and added casually, 'How is your lodger, by the way? I haven't seen her for a while.'

'That's because Miss Moran works full time in an office and in her spare time she has lots to do.'

'I suppose she writes then?'

'Yeah. She's working on a novel and I think she might have a detective in it.' Wendy hesitated before adding, 'She doesn't write by hand but has her own typewriter and allows me to practise typing on it. I don't always want to work behind the counter of this shop, you know. I could do office work if I got really good at typing. Do you have a secretary, Mr Simpson?'

'No.' He cleared his throat. 'I could help her with her research if she wanted, not tell her any secrets, just how I go about things. Perhaps you could mention it to her?'

'Mmm! I suppose I could do that,' said Wendy, lowering her eyes and fiddling with a corner of a newspaper as she wondered whether he had heard a word she had said about her own ambition. She decided there was no way she was going to encourage him and Tilly to spend time together.

'Thanks. I'll see you then.' He walked out of the shop with a jaunty air, passing another customer coming in on the way.

The woman stopped in her tracks and stared at the shelves of books.

'That's new,' she said.

Wendy sighed and gave the customer her full attention, explaining about the library. Immediately the woman went and studied the shelves, joined and left with an Ethel M Dell. Wendy was convinced that Tilly's idea was going to be a success and almost envied her when several more people joined the library and said what a good idea it was.

When Tilly arrived home, she was delighted to be told the news and scanned the names and addresses and titles of books in the register. 'I'm really pleased. I'm glad your Mr Simpson has joined. It's interesting that he's an Edgar Rice Burroughs' admirer.'

'I found it strange but that's men for you. I suppose if they can't find adventure here, then they will look for it in outer space in fiction,' said Wendy.

Tilly nodded. 'At least you get the thrills without the danger in books and films. She remembered the last time she had been the cinema and was reminded of her father. 'I must go and see Dad soon but not tonight. I'm tired.'

'You go and put your feet up,' said Wendy, salving her conscience about keeping quiet about Mr Simpson's suggestion that he help Tilly with her research. After all, hadn't somebody said that all was fair in love and war?

CHAPTER TEN

The wind was whipping the branches of the trees in Newsham Park and along the drive. It was really menacing with the wide expanse of the darkened park on one side. Leaves swirled through the air and the pavement was slippy with their dampness. The damp was penetrating the hole in the sole of her shoe and, despite having her hat pulled down over her ears and her coat collar up, Tilly felt chilled to her backbone, having forgotten to pack her winter coat when she had left Chester. She wished that she had gone straight to her digs but had told herself when she had left work that the weather could be worse tomorrow.

She kept her head down against the wind and so did not see the man coming towards her until they collided. She was sent flying by the force of his shoulder catching the side of her head and landed on her bottom. 'Damn!' she groaned through gritted teeth.

'Are you all right? I didn't see you there.' A hand reached down and gripped her upper arm and he dragged her to her feet.

'I'll live,' she gasped, clutching the sleeve of his tweed overcoat with one hand and rubbing her bottom with the other. She felt slightly sick and could do no more than lean against him for the moment.

'Terrible weather,' he said in a posh sounding voice.

Tilly glanced up at him but could make out little of his face. The brim of his trilby cast his upper features in shadow so she could only see his square chin, a sculptured mouth and a thin black moustache. 'Yes, terrible,' she agreed. 'I always pity sailors in weather like this.'

He made no comment, only saying, 'Can you stand alone now? Only I have an appointment and am in a bit of a hurry.'

'Yes, of course. I wouldn't like to delay you,' said Tilly, straightening up immediately, despite still feeling unsteady on her feet. 'If I fall flat on my face I'm sure someone else will come along and pick me up,' she added beneath her breath.

He must have had extremely good hearing because there was the slightest of pauses before he said, 'I beg your pardon?'

She flushed. 'Sorry. I didn't mean you to hear and it was rude of me to say such a thing. It's just that I still feel a bit dizzy.'

Another pause before he said, 'Perhaps I could escort you to wherever you're going. I suppose the person I'm meeting can wait.' He took her arm.

'It doesn't matter. Please, go. I can cope,' said Tilly, infusing a note of cheerfulness in her voice.

'Now you're being awkward, Miss...?'

'Moran. I'm visiting the Bennetts and I think I'm nearly there.'

'They are my new neighbours and it will take us only moments to reach their house.'

Tilly could not disguise her interest and stared at him intently. 'So you're Mr Parker.'

'Yes. Leonard Parker. Are you related to the Bennetts? I have yet to meet them as I've been kept rather busy for the last few months and I believe they've been away.'

'Yes. Aren't you in shipping?' said Tilly, as they walked slowly along the pavement.

'I own a shipyard. You might have heard how bad matters have been in the shipyards and docks these past few months.'

'Go slows, strikes,' said Tilly. 'But I was under the impression that most of the disputes had been resolved now.'

'That remains to be seen. It has been an extremely costly business and I have to ask myself how long will it be before trouble breaks out again.'

'I shouldn't imagine the wives would want their menfolk out on strike at this time of year, not when they've families to consider,' said Tilly.

'No. But I can see us having trouble with coal supplies to stoke the ship's boilers due to the miners' unrest and strikes. Supplies of coal and coke are already low throughout the country and dwindling.' He stopped abruptly. 'What a subject of conversation for a young lady. Much too serious,' he said ruefully.

'I'm interested in what's going on in my country and the wider world.'

He smiled. 'Very commendable, Miss Moran. But we are here now and I must leave you. May I apologise again for knocking you over. Perhaps we will meet again.'

'Apology accepted. Although, the fault was as much mine as yours,' she said, returning his smile.

'I hope the rest of your evening is enjoyable.' He raised his hat.

'Thank you. I hope the same for you.'

His mouth was suddenly grim. 'I doubt it. But then life seldom goes the way we wish it to, does it?' He did not wait for her to answer but hurried away.

Tilly rested a hand on the gatepost, aware of a throbbing at the base of her spine. She watched him stride away purposely along the drive. She wondered where he was going and who he was meeting. Then she shrugged and pushed open the Bennetts' gate and went up the path and along the side of the house to the rear. She knew the way so well now that doing it in the dark did not bother her. The glow of the oil lamp in her father's quarters could clearly be seen and she expected that she would find him there.

She was halfway down the garden when she suddenly noticed a shadowy figure and a moving beam of light where her father had begun to clear an area of brambles and weeds. Her heart missed a beat and she wondered if there was possibly a tramp hiding there. Then she realised that was a stupid thought because he wouldn't be carrying a torch. Suddenly Mal's voice spoke to her out of the darkness.

'Is that you, Tilly?'

'Yes, Dad!' She wondered what he was doing there and how he had known it was her without shining the torch on her. 'How did you know it was me?'

'I heard yer speaking to someone at the front gate.'

So the answer was as simple as that, thought Tilly. 'What are you doing there in the dark?' she asked, approaching across the grass with care.

'Just checking something.'

'What?' She drew close to him.

'You don't want to know,' he said, glancing down at the newly dug earth and placing something in his pocket.

'I do. Otherwise, I wouldn't have asked,' said Tilly.

'Not telling yer. Secret.' He moved the beam of the torch and shone it in her face.

She put up a hand to shield her eyes. 'Don't do that, Dad! You'll blind me.'

He lowered the torch. 'Sorry, lass. What about a cup of tea?'

'Yes. I'd like a cup of tea. I came to ask if you could do something for me.'

'Anything I can do I'll do it for you, daughter.' He sounded pleased and then surprised her by switching off the torch. For a few moments Tilly could not see anything; she could hear her own breathing and that of her father, as well as the wind in the trees and the barking of a dog. 'Come on,' he urged, taking her arm. 'I've some scones and jam that Joy gave me. She said that sugar's come off the ration so we'll be able to have more sweet treats. You'd like a couple of scones with your tea, wouldn't you?'

'Yes, Dad. I'm hungry. I've come straight from work.'

'Enjoying the job, are you?'

She sighed. 'It's a job. I'm thankful that I can earn my keep.'

'That's good. We need to work. It makes us feel useful.'

'I'm not working to feel useful, Dad. I need the money. I have to support myself now I'm no longer living with Alice and Seb.'

'Alice?' He frowned. 'Alice ran away from me. I didn't want to hurt her and I need her to forgive me. Flora always forgave me.'

Here we go again, thought Tilly, convinced as time passed that her father would never be rid of his guilt.

'We visited her grave. Roses on the grave,' he muttered. 'Alice threw them away.'

'Put it out of your mind. It's in the past. Right now I need your help.'

'Good. I like to be of help.' Mal entered the outhouse and led her past a car parked on the ground floor towards a wooden ladder at the rear of the building. Tilly followed him up to a large room that ran the length of the building and was divided into living and sleeping quarters by a partition. Tilly knew from a previous visit that there was no plumbing in the building and that her father used the outside lavatory adjacent to the house and carried water from an outside tap at the top of the garden for his needs.

Mal waved her to a well-worn sofa before putting a match to one of the rings of the camping stove he used for making tea, warming up soup and frying himself a chop or egg and bacon. After putting on the kettle, she watched him take something from his pocket and place it in a tin.

'So what is it yer want me to do for yer, lass?' he asked,

Tilly winced as she eased herself down onto a cushion. 'Have you ever mended your own shoes, Dad?' she asked.

'Aye, lass. Is it that what you want me to do for you? Mend a shoe?'

'I have a hole in one of them from where a nail went through the sole.' She took off her shoe and showed it to him.

'I could fix that, get some leather off-cuts from the cobbler. I have a last downstairs.'

'A last?'

'Aye. I'll go and get it.'

'You don't have to go now, Dad,' she said hastily.

'Aye. I do. I might forget about getting the leather as soon as you go but if the last is there, staring at me with your name attached to it, I'll remember.'

She smiled. 'If that's what you want to do.'

He jerked his head. 'Aye. Ye keep yer eye on the kettle, lass.' Picking up his torch, he left her and went downstairs.

Tilly pushed herself up from the sofa and went over to the table, curious as to what her father had earlier placed in the tin. She took off the lid and looked inside. There were several items there such as a peacock's feather, the kind of pebble one might pick up off a beach, a fir cone and several coins, but right on top was what appeared to be a badge with a bird emblem engraved in it. When she picked it up and turned it over she was proved wrong – it was a button. Where had it come from?

She put it back and took two cups and saucers from a shelf and placed them on the table. She poured milk into the cups and thought about Mr Parker, wondering how old he was and whether, with his posh voice and being in shipping, he would have escorted her to the gate if he had known she was the gardener's daughter. She realised she was in a peculiar position class wise; not that she had any time for class division these days. She found the scones and placed them on a plate in the middle of the table. When the kettle boiled she made tea. Her father had still not returned so she went and stood at the top of the ladder and called down to him.

'I won't be a minute,' he shouted. 'I think I've found it.'

A few minutes later he was back upstairs, brandishing a cast-iron implement that appeared to have two human shaped feet. He stood it on the table on one of them. 'There ye are, lass. Come back in a couple of days and I'll mend that shoe for yer,' he said. 'And I might as well put a new sole on the other while I'm at it. I bet it's wearing thin.'

She agreed. 'I'm doing more walking now, Dad, than I've ever done.'

He stared at her worriedly. 'Yer've lost weight and yer need some fat on yer during the winter. Keeps yer warm.'

She agreed but knew there was nothing she could do about that. So sooner or later she was going to have to visit her family in Chester, not only to see how they were but to collect her winter coat.

She poured out the tea and as they drank and ate the scones, she told him about meeting Mr Parker. Mal did not interrupt her but when she finished, he said, 'He shouts at her.'

'Who?' asked Tilly, surprised.

'Her! The nosy one who looks over the fence and watches what I'm doing. I told her to go away and complained to Eudora about her. She said most people were nosy and we've nothing to hide.' He frowned and muttered. 'She wants to be friends with the neighbours, but why? Yer can't always trust those living close to yer and that woman is funny in the head if ye ask me.'

Tilly had thought that a possibility and suspected that Alice would have said it was like the kettle calling the pot black where her father was concerned. 'Have you ever had a proper conversation with her, Dad?'

'No, lass. And I don't want to either. I'm staying away from strange women. There was another one that called round there and I didn't like the sound of her at all.'

'Why?' asked Tilly, wondering if Mr Parker had a lady

friend, one of these bright young things you could read about in the newspapers.

'She had a voice like a rusty gate and was as common as muck. I heard them talking. They didn't know I was listening.'

Tilly wondered what on the earth the beautifully spoken Mr Parker could have to do with a woman her father referred to as common as muck. 'What were they saying, Dad?'

'She was threatening him but he was as nice as pie to her and said that he would see her right.'

'Perhaps she was a wife or daughter of one of his workers,' said Tilly.

'Yer could be right, lass, but I was glad when she left because she reminded me of Mother,' said Mal dourly.

They fell silent after that and soon after Tilly left. To her dismay, when she went outside she discovered that the wind had suddenly dropped and a freezing fog had descended. Fortunately it was not yet dense enough to prevent her finding her way and she arrived back at the shop safely. She found Mrs Wright just closing up and was informed that Wendy, Minnie and the boys had gone to the Palladium, having been given complimentary tickets by their uncle.

'At least they shouldn't have any trouble finding their way home from there,' said Tilly.

'How was your father?'

'OK.'

'Did you see Mrs Bennett?'

Tilly shook her head. 'Only Dad. I'll go up to my room now, if you don't mind? I'm tired and there are a few things I have to do.'

'You've had something to eat?'

Tilly nodded. 'But I wouldn't mind a hot drink. OK, if I make myself a cocoa?'

Mrs Wright said, 'You do that and you can make me one while you're at it.'

Tilly went and made the cocoa. She took hers up to bed with her. That night she had the strangest dream of a soldier coming towards her through a fog. He was followed by an old woman holding a kite in the shape of a big bird. It swooped down on the soldier and then the three of them vanished into thin air. She woke with a start and, despite her aching back and bottom, she wrote down the dream while she could remember it before going back to sleep again.

When Tilly woke the following morning, it was so cold in the room that she did not want to get out of bed. But she dragged herself out from beneath the covers and padded across the cold linoleum to the window to check on the weather. She could hear no sound of traffic and when she drew back a curtain, she could see only a blanket of fog. She was filled with mixed feelings. It looked like there would be no getting to work that day, which meant she would be short of a day's wages that week but a day off was extremely attractive. She went back to bed and snuggled beneath the blankets and went back to sleep.

Wendy woke her by hammering on her bedroom door. 'You've overslept, Tilly. We all have!'

Tilly yawned and glanced at her alarm clock and saw that the hands stood at ten o'clock. She sat up in bed, winced and remembered colliding into Mr Parker last evening. 'Is it still foggy out?' she called.

'Yes. The newspapers haven't come this morning and only one customer has been in. Mam went outside and she couldn't see her hand in front of her face. Minnie hasn't gone to work and the boys have stayed home from school.'

'I'm not surprised,' said Tilly. 'You could get lost in this weather. I'm staying at home, too.'

'So what are you going to do with your day?'

Tilly did not have to think long about that. 'I'll work on my novel,' she replied.

'Would you like me to bring you some tea and toast up?'

'Thanks,' said Tilly, pleased at the suggestion.

She slipped out of bed and went over to the washstand and hesitated before pouring out some cold water. She splashed her face with it and washed her hands and, shivering, decided that was enough cleanliness for the moment. She found clean clothes and put them on as swiftly as she could: vest, bodice, knickers, thick black stockings, a petticoat and an old, long woollen skirt, jumper and cardigan. Then she dug out a pair of gloves from which she had cut the end of the fingers and put them on. Only to find when she sat down on her chair at her desk that its hardness caused her extreme discomfort.

'Damn that Leonard Parker,' she muttered. Getting up and putting her hand inside her lower garments, she gingerly felt the bone at the base of her spine. Could she have cracked it? Even if she had there was nothing a doctor could do. One couldn't put a splint there, and besides, she could not afford a doctor's fees. She was just going to have to suffer.

'You decent, Tilly?' called Wendy.

'Yes.'

She unlocked the door and Wendy entered, carrying a breakfast tray. Tilly took a pillow from her bed and placed it on her chair and, slowly, lowered herself onto it.

'What's to do with you?' asked Wendy, placing the tray on the desk.

Tilly explained.

'Blooming heck!' Wendy sat in the basket chair and smiled. 'So you've met the mysterious Mr Parker at last. Is he good looking? How old is he?'

'I'd need to see him in the light to gauge his age. I can tell you that he has a black moustache.' Tilly reached for her cup of tea and took a sip.

Wendy raised her eyebrows. 'That's a great help. Most men in Britain have moustaches. Why I wonder?'

'Fashion. Besides, I should imagine men find it difficult shaving under their nose. Easy to cut yourself. Have you seen a cut-throat razor?'

'Yes. Scary,' said Wendy.

'Of course, there could be another reason,' said Tilly. 'Facial hair is a sign of manliness. Think of Samson in the Bible, when he was tied up by Delilah and all his hair and beard cut off, he lost his strength.' She smiled as she reached for a slice of toast.

'Mr Simpson doesn't have a moustache,' said Wendy thoughtfully.

Neither does Don, Seb, Freddie or Kenny, thought Tilly.

'The king does but the Prince of Wales and the Duke of York don't,' said Wendy.

Tilly nodded. 'You're right. So what does that say about men and their opinion of themselves?'

'I don't know,' said Wendy. 'So is your hero going to have a moustache or be clean shaven?'

'I'll have to think about that,' said Tilly, reaching for her notepad and reading what she had written during the night. 'Perhaps he'll be an ex-soldier.'

'Not an ex-policeman?' Wendy could not resist asking.

Tilly raised her eyebrows. 'Why?'

'I'll leave you alone,' said Wendy hastily, not wanting Tilly to think too deeply about what she had just said. She got up and hurried from the room.

Tilly finished her breakfast and after visiting the lavatory, she returned to her room and began to write.

'What do you think of this?' asked Wendy, looking up from a newspaper when Tilly came in after leaving her shoes with her father a couple of days later. She had worn high heels to work and taken in a cushion and travelled on the tram. Neither had gone down well with Miss Langton.

Tilly groaned, thinking of the woman's reaction. When Tilly had explained the reason she needed the cushion, the woman had completely flown off the handle, saying that young women these days mollycoddled themselves too much. Then she had gone on about taking a day off because of the fog and then she had accused Tilly of being responsible for files going missing, as well as other items from the office. Tilly had denied the charge and Mr Holmes had come out of his domain and told Miss Langton to keep her voice down and that it was common sense that had kept himself and Miss Moran at home during the foggy weather. After that Miss Langton had not spoken to Tilly at all but stormed out of the office at lunchtime and not returned for several hours. No doubt she had believed because Mr Holmes had business elsewhere she could get away with absenting herself. Tilly had coped alone, not that she had minded doing so because she had worked in the office long enough to know Miss Langton's job as well as her own. She had managed to deal with the agents and clients' business and maybe that had caused Miss

Langton to be even more bad-tempered when one had praised Tilly's capability to do her job. There had been several nasty moments and Tilly was concerned that the woman would do her best to get rid of her in the not too distant future.

'Do I need to know, Wendy?' she murmured, removing a glove.

'It could give you ideas for your novel,' said Wendy, and read out, 'During the disastrous bad weather the Bishop of Liverpool fell when a tram was brought to a sudden halt in the fog.'

'I knew about that,' said Tilly, trying to be patient. 'It happened outside St Margaret's Church. I heard some women talking about it in the post office, although, why you think I should want to put the Bishop of Liverpool in my novel, I don't know.'

Wendy pulled a face. 'It wasn't so much the bishop as the things that can happen in the fog. There was a death. A woman drowned in the Leeds-Liverpool Canal. It's believed that she mustn't have been able to see where she was going and fell into the water.'

'Poor woman,' said Tilly, interested despite wanting to get upstairs and relax. 'Has she been identified?'

'Has who been identified?' asked Mr Simpson, entering the shop and placing his library book on the counter. 'Good evening, Miss Moran. I haven't seen you for a while,' he said, gazing into her pretty face, flushed by the wind.

'No, Mr Simpson. Somehow we keep missing each other,' she said, smiling. 'I hope you're well.'

'Better for seeing you,' he said. 'Although you appear to have lost weight. I hope you're in good health?'

'I'm fine. It's all the walking I do,' said Tilly.

Wendy cleared her throat. 'There's a couple of things you might be interested in in the newspapers today, Tilly,' she said. 'The fashion page for instance. You might like to hear what Jacqueline says about what colours redheads like you should wear.'

'I know I shouldn't wear red,' said Tilly, deciding to humour her.

'According to *our expert* that's a mistake,' informed Wendy. 'She says that certain shades of red can be worn with conviction.' She wrinkled her nose. 'Whatever that means. Do you know what a *tailleur* is?'

'It sounds French,' said Mr Simpson.

'Wait a minute,' said Tilly. 'I think it's a kind of jacket.'

'You could be right,' said Mr Simpson.

'It says a *tailleur* of red-brown to wear over a vest of ochre organdie,' said Wendy loudly. 'So it sounds like a jacket. It says it can be worn with a toque of waxed ribbon in a red-gold shade to match your hair. You need to wear bronze shoes and silk stockings, as well,' she added.

Tilly laughed. 'Does Jacqueline say how much this is all going to cost?'

Wendy shook her head. 'A few bob I should imagine.'

'Probably pounds and pounds. Now if my sister read that description she could make the whole lot for almost next to nothing,' said Tilly.

'I should imagine you'd look lovely in such an outfit, Miss Moran,' said Mr Simpson.

The colour in Tilly's cheeks deepened. 'You've a silver tongue, Mr Simpson. I couldn't afford it anyway.'

Wendy frowned and quickly turned a page. 'Well, what about this, Tilly? There's an advertisement about a short story competition in the *Red Letter*. The prize is publication and five shillings.'

'Now that is interesting,' said Tilly excitedly. 'I suppose the entry form will be in this week's *Red Letter*?'

Wendy nodded.

'Right! Give me a copy,' said Tilly, opening her handbag and taking out thrupence. At the moment she didn't have a clue what to write but was hoping inspiration would strike once she sat down at her typewriter.

Wendy handed the magazine to Tilly, who asked them to excuse her and she went into the back of shop. She said a quick hello to those present and hurried upstairs. An idea popped into her head and by the time she had changed out of her dark suit into a skirt, jumper and cardigan, her idea had developed further.

She placed a sheet of paper in her typewriter and gazed at it for moment before typing 'The Lady in Red'. Having never been to Paris she was going to have to use her imagination. She had read about it and reckoned a mention of the Eiffel Tower, Notre Dame Cathedral, the Left Bank and the River Seine glistening in the moonlight would give the reader a flavour of the city. But should her story be purely a romantic tale or should her lady in red be a woman of mystery? She thought of the Russian actress, Nazimona. Perhaps it should be about an aristocratic lady escaping the Bolsheviks and meeting a British soldier who was a spy? There was a lot of interest in events in Russia at the moment and the Western allies, horrified by the murder of the Russian Imperial family, had sent armed forces to help the White Russians.

Tilly began to type, her imagination taking flight, and for the next hour or more she was in a different world. Only to have to re-enter the real one when Peter banged on her bedroom door and shouted, 'Supper's ready, Tilly!' She groaned because she needed to polish the story and retype it.

She ate her meal without really noticing what she was eating but remembered to thank her landlady before returning to her room. This time she retyped her story with no typing errors and made a carbon copy. Then she put the top sheets in an envelope with the entry form and a stamped addressed envelope. She had a good feeling about her effort and planned on posting it the following morning on her way to work.

To Tilly's surprise, Miss Langton made no mention of the events of yesterday, and to the girl's ever greater surprise, Mr Simpson entered the office halfway through the morning.

'Mr Simpson! What are you doing here?' she asked.

His face lit up. 'Miss Moran, how nice to see you. I'm here to see the boss.'

'Is he expecting you? Is it urgent?' asked Tilly. 'Miss Langton is in with him right now. Do you want me to let him know you're here or are you prepared to wait until she comes out?'

'I can wait.'

Tilly offered him a seat. He sat down whilst she continued with her filing. She was conscious that he was watching her. 'So what do you think of this woman who fell in the Leeds-Liverpool Canal, Miss Moran?' he asked.

She glanced at him. 'What should I think, Mr Simpson? I don't know the woman.'

'She was insured by this company.'

'I didn't know that but most likely Mr Holmes and Miss Langton will have heard of her.'

'No doubt. She was a pawnbroker.'

'Was she?' said Tilly.

Mr Simpson nodded. 'I still have contacts in the police force and it appears that she was also known to the police.'

Tilly stared at him. 'You say that as if—'

'They suspected her of being a fence in receipt of stolen property.'

'Gosh!' Tilly felt a thrill of excitement. 'I didn't realise you were involved with such goings on.'

He smiled. 'Perhaps that's why you didn't accept my offer to help you with your research, Miss Moran?'

'What offer?'

'My offer to supply you with useful information about criminals and police procedure for your novel,' he said. 'Perhaps Wendy forgot to mention it to you.'

'She did. No doubt she has a lot on her mind,' said Tilly, deciding to seize the opportunity to gain information from him whilst neither Wendy nor Miss Langton was present to interrupt them. 'Do the police suspect foul play? Is it possible that there was a falling out amongst thieves and she was pushed into the canal on purpose?'

Mr Simpson stood up and began to prowl about the office. 'You have plenty of imagination. As it is nothing can be proved but the police are very interested to see who takes over her business. Her solicitor says she has no close family, only a nephew in America.'

'So it's doubtful he could have murdered her.'

Mr Simpson nodded and stared at a notice on the wall. 'It's a puzzle to the police what she was doing wandering along the canal at that time of evening in the fog.'

'How close are we to the Leeds-Liverpool canal?' asked Tilly.

He smiled. 'A good way away. It travels from the docks, cuts through Kirkdale, Bootle and on through Litherland, Maghull and cross country through Lancashire to Leeds in Yorkshire.'

'And her shop is where?'

'Scotland Road, which is near enough to the canal for her to walk there.'

'So will it be this distant relative who will arrange her funeral? A bit difficult if he's living in America.'

'The funeral can go ahead without him because it would take time for him to get here,' said Mr Simpson. 'The solicitor is seeing to the arrangements.'

'I see.'

At that moment the door into Mr Holmes's inner sanctum opened and Miss Langton came out. She started when she saw Mr Simpson there. 'What are you doing here? Have you been waiting long?'

'Only a few minutes,' said Mr Simpson, 'and Miss Moran has looked after me fine.' He gave Tilly a smiling glance and then said, 'I'll go in. See you again, Miss Moran.' He tipped his hat and after giving a knock on Mr Holmes's door, opened it and went inside.

'Well!' exclaimed Miss Langton.

Tilly avoided her eyes and continued with her filing, hoping the woman was not going to find fault with her again or she could see herself looking for another job.

CHAPTER ELEVEN

'Good evening, girls,' said Mr Simpson, placing a book on the counter. 'It's blinking cold out there.'

'Cold enough for snow?' asked Wendy. 'What do you think, Mr Simpson, will it snow for Christmas this year?'

'The weather could change again by then.'

'So what will you be doing for Christmas, Mr Simpson?' asked Tilly, wondering why she had not seen him at the insurance office since his mention of the pawnbroker's death.

He smiled at her. 'We Scots don't celebrate Christmas to the same extent as you do south of the border, Miss Moran. The New Year is more important. We call it Hogmanay.'

'I know that,' said Tilly, resting against the counter and taking a foot out of the shoe her father had repaired and wriggling her cold toes. 'I'm half-Scottish. My dad was born in Scotland.'

'So was I, apparently. My father died in India and then my mother passed away when I was only five years old. Her sister and husband took in me and my sister. They're both gone now and their son was killed in the war.'

'No doubt you'll be spending Hogmanay with your sister?' asked Wendy.

He shook his head. 'She's going up to Scotland to stay with a cousin for a week. She hasn't been well and she's lost her job. I thought the break would do her good. Mostly likely I'll just have a wee dram with some friends.'

'You're always welcome to come here for Christmas or Hogmanay, Mr Simpson,' said Wendy earnestly. 'You could first foot for us.'

He smiled. 'That's very generous of you but hadn't you better ask your mother first?'

'And if I do and she says yes?' she asked.

'Then maybe I'll pop by,' he replied, glancing at Tilly.

She took the opportunity to ask him if he had heard anything else about the pawnbroker who had fallen in the canal and whether the solicitor had heard from the nephew in America.

'Seems he never came back from the war and there are no other relatives as far as we know,' said Mr Simpson, strolling over to the bookshelves and scanning the titles there. He took out a book and brought it over to the counter. 'Have you read this, Miss Moran?' he asked. '*The Thirty-Nine Steps*? It's a good yarn.'

'Yes, I have, it's a great adventure.'

'I often read old favourites,' he said, handing it to Wendy. 'And what will you be doing for Christmas and New Year, Miss Moran?'

'I hope to visit my family in Chester,' said Tilly. 'Although if it snows, I can't see me going anywhere.' She paused. 'So what will happen about the pawnbroker's shop and possessions?'

'A notice will be put in several newspapers asking anyone related to her to get in touch with the solicitor, where they might learn something to their advantage,' he explained.

'I wonder if anyone will come forward,' mused Tilly.

'Only time will tell,' said the detective.

She nodded. 'I'd best go and change. I'll see you again, Mr Simpson.'

'I look forward to that, Miss Moran.'

She nodded, a slight smile on her face as she left the shop.

During the next few days there was a fall of snow but it did not last long and public transport continued to operate despite the freezing cold weather. The newspapers forecast a bleak Christmas what with frozen pipes and a million unemployed, and in the Rhondda Valley the coal miners had suddenly downed tools again, which meant coal shortages and electricity cuts.

For Tilly there was at least some good news in that she won the *Red Letter* short story competition and received her five shilling prize in time for the festive season. Unfortunately, due to work commitments, she did not get the chance to visit her family over the Christmas season but determined to visit them before the New Year.

Robbie Bennett dropped by with presents for the whole family, including a couple for Tilly, one of which was a matching set of scarf, hat and gloves, knitted by Hanny and given to Joy. He and Eudora gave her a book. She was touched by their generosity and thanked him, apologising that she didn't have anything for them.

'We didn't give to receive, Tilly,' he said, patting her shoulder. 'I've also some news for you. Freddie telephoned to say that Clara had given birth to a baby boy two days ago.'

Tilly had almost forgotten that Clara was having a baby because she had been so taken up with her own life. 'Are they both well? What are they going to call him?'

'Nicholas. After St Nicholas. You know, Father Christmas.'

'I know,' said Tilly, smiling and thinking he looked a little like Father Christmas himself with his mop of pure white hair.

'And mother and son are both fine,' he added. 'They asked Joy to let you know and Eudora also told me that I'm to tell you that we're throwing a party on New Year's Eve and you're all invited.' He beamed at them.

Minnie's face lit up. 'They're you are, Mam. We've been invited to a New Year's party, which means none of us will have to cook that evening.'

'But what about Mr Simpson?' asked Wendy, looking dismayed. 'I said he could first foot for us.'

We'll just have to tell Mr Simpson we're going to be out,' said her mother. 'I'm not going to miss out on free food and drink.'

'Who's Mr Simpson?' asked Robbie, glancing around the circle of faces.

'He's a private detective,' said Wendy. 'He comes into the shop most days and has hardly anyone in the way of family.'

'Bring him along then,' said Robbie jovially. 'The more the merrier.'

Wendy exchanged looks with her mother. 'Is that all right with you, Mam?'

'I don't see the harm in it,' said Rita. Having downed a couple of glasses of the sherry her brother had brought her, she was in a fairly good mood. 'After all, it is the season for good will towards all men.'

'Tell him to be prepared to do a turn,' warned Robbie.

'Although, on second thoughts best keep quiet about that as we definitely need more men and don't want to put him off!' He chuckled.

'He could first foot for you,' said Wendy casually. 'After all he is dark and handsome.'

Robbie gave his niece a keen look. 'If you say so, love. We want everything to go well this year.'

Don't we all? Tilly thought. She looked forward to the party next Friday, wanting to have some fun, and she also saw it as an opportunity to see her father. She planned returning to Newsham Drive with Robbie Bennett today, taking the present she had made for Mal. She had bought some wool out of her winnings and knitted him a pair of socks. Sometime during the week she would visit Chester straight from work and stay a couple of hours and then get the last train back to Liverpool. She would need to buy a present for the baby, having already bought some inexpensive little gifts for her nieces and nephews but nothing for the adults. She had sent Christmas cards but had not received one from Alice and Seb and hoped that was only because it had been lost in the post. She did not want to believe that she was out of favour with her sister again. Should she mention to her father that she planned on visiting Alice and the children? Tilly decided to see what kind of mood he was in. What if he decided he'd go with her? What would she say then?

'Do you think Tilly will make the effort to come and see the new baby before he's out of nappies?' said Alice, putting down the *Weekly News* and getting to her feet.

It was the Wednesday evening after Christmas. She had hoped her sister might have visited over the Christmas holiday despite the difficulties of travelling but Tilly had not done so and Alice was feeling more than annoyed. She had been just as hurt when Tilly had not made the effort to see Georgie during his illness.

'That's a bit sarcastic,' murmured Seb, glancing up from the book he was reading. 'She is working and probably hasn't got the money to spare for the fare.'

'I bet she makes the time to see Dad,' said Alice, wrapping her cardigan tightly round her and wandering over to the darkened window.

'That was her purpose in going over there and he does live within walking distance. I'm sure she'll come if she can,' said Seb.

Alice glanced over her shoulder at him. 'You always make excuses for her,' she said crossly. 'I don't see why she couldn't afford to come this time. You did enclose a postal order in her Christmas card, didn't you?'

'Yes, but perhaps she didn't receive it.'

'Why shouldn't she have? You posted it, didn't you?'

'I gave it to Freddie to post.'

Alice glanced at him. 'Freddie! What day was that?'

'Can't remember.'

'Perhaps he forgot to post it, what with the baby coming,' suggested Alice.

'Damn!' Seb frowned. 'It might still be in his pocket.'

'Surely he would have found it by now. He could have posted it but it mightn't have reached her until after Christmas,' said Alice agitatedly. 'She might think I'm right off her. I mean, I didn't answer her last letter because I was annoyed with her for not coming to see Georgie.'

'I told her not to come,' said Seb, getting up and going over to his wife. He put his arms round her and drew her against him. 'If she comes this week I don't want you making her feel guilty.'

'If you say so, but what if she starts going on about Dad?'

'Why should she when she knows how you feel? As long as you don't bring him into the conversation and say something nasty about him, then I'm sure everything will be fine.'

'He's mentally unstable.'

Seb sighed. 'Hanny said that Joy told her that he's a lot better. He might still talk to himself but he's not alone in doing that.'

'She told me that Joy said that he's always digging holes.'

'That's what gardeners do,' said Seb reasonably.

'But he doesn't plant anything, just digs them and then fills them in.' She looked up at her husband. 'You must admit, Seb, that's peculiar.'

'He's not getting any younger. Perhaps he's buried something and forgotten where he put it.'

'I suppose it's possible but if it's a plant what does it matter where it goes?'

'It could be treasure,' teased Seb, kissing the side of her neck.

She rubbed her cheek against his. 'Now you're being silly.'

'No, I'm not,' he protested. 'I'm sure there are people who bury their money because they don't trust banks and think of it as foolproof way of deceiving burglars who might break into their homes. Perhaps it's even possible your old dad found the old lady's money and decided to leave it where it was for the moment and then forgot where it was. Now he's trying to find it again.'

Alice laughed. 'Honestly, Seb, you should be the writer, not our Tilly. Well, if the old spinster did bury some money, I hope he doesn't give it to Mrs Black.'

'Mrs Bennett,' corrected Seb.

Alice groaned. 'I hate the thought of her having the same married name as me. Perhaps you should take your father's name of Waters.'

Seb said firmly, 'No. I've been Bennett all my life and customers know me by that name. I'm not changing it now.'

'Not even for me?'

'Not even for you. Think of the children and their school. Their friends would be asking why they had a different name. No. We're Bennetts and we'll stay Bennetts.' Seb kissed her lightly. 'I often wish that Robbie Bennett had been my father rather than my natural one. He's a much nicer man – he's prepared to employ your father and provide him with a roof over his head. Hopefully, they'll do so until he dies.'

'Unless he goes off the rails,' murmured Alice. 'If that were to happen and he hurt Tilly, I know what I'd want to do to him.'

'Shush! Why should he? I hope you don't even hint that such a thing could happen to Tilly. Promise me you won't mention your father to her?'

Alice hesitated and then promised.

Seb could only hope that his wife would stick by her word.

Tilly was humming a carol as she crossed Queen's Park footbridge in Chester. She had asked Miss Langton if she could leave the office slightly earlier and the woman had said she would ask Mr Holmes. As it was Miss Langton seemed to have forgotten to tell her what he had said, so Tilly had slipped out the office while the other woman was taking dictation in his office.

Tilly paused in the middle of the bridge and gazed down at the surface of the river where stars were reflected. A once familiar damp smell filled her nostrils. She remembered the many times she had crossed this bridge with the children or walked along the riverbank with Alice or Hanny. It was good to be home. She was feeling so much better about everything since she had received Alice and Seb's card, especially as there had been a postal order inside. She hoped they would forgive this being a flying visit. Alice might suggest she should have left it to the weekend, but what with the party on New Year's Eve and work on New Year's Day, she would be tired out by Sunday.

She straightened up and continued on her way. As she walked up the path towards Victoria Crescent she experienced that odd feeling you sometimes get when returning to a place that had once been so familiar that you took it for granted and didn't really see it properly. She decided to visit Clara, Freddie and the baby first and see Kenny and Hanny at the same time. Hopefully the twins would still be awake, but as they were only two years old, chances were they would be in their cots and fast asleep. Still, she could have a peek at them looking angelic in the Land of Nod.

The front door was opened by Hanny, who threw her arms about her. 'I told Clara and Freddie you'd come. I just knew you wouldn't be able to resist the baby and would need to see for yourself that Clara was OK.'

'Of course I had to come,' said Tilly, warmed by Hanny's welcome. 'But I didn't come just for that reason. I wanted to see you all.'

'We've missed you,' said Hanny, drawing her further into the house. 'I wish I could have visited you in Liverpool before now but what with the twins being such a handful and Mother going more peculiar by the day, I just couldn't manage it.'

'I understand,' said Tilly, returning her hug. 'How's Kenny? I'm glad the twins are so well.'

Hanny said, 'He's well. Janet's managing to string words together and I plan to teach her colours, numbers and her alphabet as soon as possible.'

Tilly groaned. 'Say you didn't buy the twins alphabet books for Christmas? Because that's what I've bought.'

'As it happens, no, we didn't. Kenny couldn't resist buying a secondhand train set and a book about animals and birds for Allan. As well as colouring books with crayons for them both. We bought a doll for Janet and a simple jigsaw and pretend sweet shop. She had the clothes off the doll in no time and then had terrible trouble getting them on again.'

'I'm sorry I missed it.'

'You should have seen their faces on Christmas morning. I still think they're a little young to understand what it's about but they did enjoy it all.'

'Perhaps I'll be here next Christmas,' said Tilly.

'Let's hope so,' said Hanny, linking her arm through Tilly's. 'Now, do you want to see the new mother and baby first? I must admit I can't get enough of my new nephew. He has lovely brown eyes and a mop of black curly hair.' As they climbed the stairs, she added, 'I thought you might come this evening.'

'Why?'

'Because Joy phoned the office and told Kenny that the

Bennetts were throwing a party on New Year's Eve and you were invited along with the Wrights, so I guessed you wouldn't wait to see the new baby until the New Year.'

Tilly paused on the stairs. 'You haven't mentioned the party to Alice, have you?'

'No. I know how she feels about Eudora.'

'What about Kenny? He just might—'

'Forget it. He'll want to keep her happy.' Hanny called out, 'Tilly's here!'

A door opened on the first landing and Freddie appeared. He smiled down at her. 'Hello, our kid. I wasn't sure you'd come but Hanny was convinced you would. Did you have a nice Christmas?'

'It was OK. Different to any other I've spent but the Wrights have made me feel like one of the family.'

'Good. Come in and see the baby.' He held out a hand to her and she took it. He pulled her up the last few steps and, still holding her hand, led her into the bedroom that had once been Kenny and Hanny's. Even before she went over to Clara, who was nursing the baby, Tilly was aware of that special baby smell. It took her back to the day Alice had given birth to James and the relief she had felt that her sister had come through the ordeal safely. Tilly could never forget that her mother had died giving birth to her. She wondered if she, herself, would ever marry and have a child, and briefly she thought of Don and blond-haired babies.

'Hello, Tilly! How kind of you to come all this way in the dark to see us,' said Clara, stretching out a hand to her.

Tilly took it and squeezed it gently. 'I'm glad you're all right.' She gazed down at the baby and, not for the first time, thought about the miracle of life. A year ago this child had not even been conceived and now here he was, a fully formed human being, exhibiting his parents' dark hair and Clara's brown eyes. She felt an unexpected yearning inside her.

'Well, d'you like him?' asked Freddie.

'What's there not to like about him? He's so handsome.'

'That's what Alice said,' commented Clara, smiling. 'She thinks he's like Seb.'

'Well, you are cousins,' said Tilly.

'You are going to see them while you're here?' asked Clare seriously. 'They've missed you, you know.'

Tilly perched on the side of the bed. 'Of course I'm going to see them. What kind of a sister do you think I am?'

'Alice could have done with your help when Georgie was ill.'

Freddie darted Clara a warning look.

'I'm sure,' said Tilly, flushing. She moved away from the bed. 'You've got to understand, Clara, I have a job to do and there's Dad. Besides, Seb told me to stay away.'

'Of course. It's really none of my business.'

Tilly said, 'Of course it is. You're family. Alice coped, anyway, because she's an experienced mother.' She paused. 'I don't want to tire you out and I haven't much time. I bought a present for the baby.' From the shopping bag she produced a parcel and placed it on the bed. 'It's only a small thing. He really is a lovely baby.'

'Thanks,' said Clara, reaching out and touching Tilly's hand. 'You didn't have to buy a present, you know. I do understand if you're a bit hard up.'

Tilly said nothing and withdrew her hand. 'Hopefully I won't leave it so long next time.'

'We'll let you know when the christening is to be,' said Freddie.

'Thanks,' said Tilly, turning to Hanny who had kept in the background. 'Where's Kenny?' she added.

'I'll take you to him,' said Hanny.

With a tarrah, Tilly left the bedroom.

As soon as they were out of earshot, Hanny said, 'Clara's fond of you, you know.'

'She's fonder of Alice.'

'Yes. And Alice hasn't been herself since you left; Clara's concerned about her.'

Tilly sighed. 'Georgie will be going to school in no time at all and it could be she's worried about having time on her hands.'

'I don't think it's that,' said Hanny.

'I hope you're not going to say she's still worried about Dad harming me, are you?'

'No, but—'

'Don't, please,' pleaded Tilly. 'He'd never harm me.'

'Perhaps we'd better drop the subject,' said Hanny, leading the way into the twins' bedroom where they found Kenny with a twin on his knee.

He looked up at Tilly and smiled. 'So you've come at last.'

'It looks like it,' she replied, bending down and kissing his cheek and then that of his daughter who had inherited his red-brown hair. She thought how much her father would like to see this granddaughter who was named after his first wife. Tilly handed a present to her niece, who immediately tore off the wrapping and then handed the book to her father and said, 'Dank you,' to Tilly.

She smiled, kissing her again. The other twin was asleep in his cot, so Tilly gave his present to Hanny. Then they talked in low voices for a short while before she made her farewells and set off to see her sister.

The front door was opened to her by her eldest nephew, James. He took one look at her and then turned and bellowed, 'Aunt Tilly's here!'

Then he faced her again and said, 'You should have been here for Christmas. It wasn't the same without you. Mam can't tell a story like you do.'

'So you missed me?' said Tilly, smiling down at him.

'Naw!' said James, grinning. 'Come in. Dad's making cocoa and Mam's made macaroons.' He lowered his voice to a whisper. 'Don't tell her but they're not as good as Granny Waters'.'

'I wouldn't dare,' whispered Tilly, feeling a rush of love for him. She wanted to hug him but decided that at ten he might consider himself to old for hugs. She made do with ruffling his hair. 'So did you get nice presents? And how's Flora and Georgie?'

'They're both in bed but I don't have to go up for another half hour.' He seized her hand and dragged her inside the house. 'I can read to you and then you can tell me a story in bed.'

'I'll certainly listen to you read, love, but I don't know if I'll have time to tell you a story,' said Tilly regretfully.

James's face fell. 'But you've only just come.'

'I know. But I've work in the morning and woe betide me if I don't get there on time. Miss Langton would have my head.'

'You mean she'd chop it off?' he asked, giggling.

Tilly laughed. 'No, but she'd make my life even more difficult than she does now.'

'But you have to stay or Flora and Georgie won't get to see you,' he said in wheedling tones.

'I can't, love,' she said, hating to disappoint him.

'Please, Aunt Tilly,' he asked.

'You heard your aunt,' said Alice, appearing in the drawing room doorway. 'If she can't stay, she can't stay.'

Tilly stared at her sister and wanted to rush over to her and ask how she was and say that she was sorry she'd stayed away so long, but there was something in her sister's tone and stance that made her think Alice would not welcome such a display of affection. Instead, she walked over slowly and said, 'Hello, Alice. It's good to see you.'

'So the prodigal has returned,' said Alice.

'Hardly. I haven't wasted an inheritance in riotous living,' said Tilly lightly. 'Are you OK?'

'Why shouldn't I be OK? Come in and sit down for a few minutes before you have to go back.'

'I don't want Aunt Tilly to go back,' said James. 'At least not just yet.'

His mother turned to him. 'You go and tell Daddy to make an extra cup of cocoa.'

The boy hurried away.

Tilly watched his sturdy figure. 'He's grown,' she said.

'What did you expect?' asked Alice. 'He wasn't going to waste away because you weren't here. Neither was Georgie.'

Tilly was hurt. 'I don't deserve that remark. I love Georgie and besides, Seb told me not to come. How is he?'

'Adaptable. You know Georgie.'

Tilly smiled. 'Yes. He's always been an easygoing little boy.' She paused. 'James looks so well. How's he doing at school?'

'Fine. He has Kenny's gift for drawing and his father's application to work. Come and sit down and get a warm,' said Alice. 'It's cold out.'

'It's bitterly cold,' said Tilly, following her sister into the drawing room. She placed her shopping bag on the floor beside the sofa and drew off her gloves. Her gaze scanned the room to see if there had been any changes and noticed the piano was still in its corner. She longed to sit on the piano stool and run her fingers over the keys. It seemed a long time since she had lost herself in music.

'So, how are things with you?' asked Alice politely, waving her to the sofa. 'Seen anything of Dad?'

Tilly stiffened. 'Yes. He would have liked to have come with me but I told him I was going straight from work. I knew you wouldn't want him here.'

'At least you've got that much sense. I believe he's been digging holes all over the garden.'

Tilly looked at her in surprise. 'He is a gardener but it's the first I've heard that there's holes all over the garden. I haven't seen any for a start.'

'Apparently he fills them in again. Seb thought he might have found treasure and then forgot where it was.'

'He could just be turning over the soil.'

'At this time of year?' said Alice.

Tilly thought of the baby skeleton and debated whether to tell her sister about it but decided to keep quiet. 'Why not?'

Alice smiled but did not pursue the subject. 'So how was your Christmas? By the way, thanks for your card. Did you get ours?'

'It came late but was gratefully received.' Tilly removed her coat and hat and sat down on the sofa.

Alice ran an eye over her appearance. 'You didn't buy anything new for Christmas?'

'No. I had to make do.'

'Seb thought you might be hard up.'

'I'm managing.' Before Tilly could say anything else, Seb entered the room carrying a tray of steaming mugs. 'It's good to see you, Tilly. Enjoying your independence?'

Tilly smiled appreciatively and took one of the mugs. 'Will you be annoyed if I say yes?'

'Of course, not,' said Seb, 'although we miss you.'

'Macaroon, Aunt Tilly?' said James, offering the plate to her.

'Thanks.'

Tilly was aware that Alice was watching her as she bite into the macaroon. 'It tastes good.'

'You don't have to try and get round me,' said Alice. 'I know they're not as good as Gabrielle's.'

'Have you heard anything from Seb's mother?'

'You mean, did we see her at Christmas?' said Alice, breaking off a piece of macaroon and feeding it to the cat. 'No. Apparently she was tied up rehearsing for a pantomime for some charity. Obviously it was more important than spending Christmas with her only grandchildren.'

'She did send them some decent presents,' said Seb.

'She sent me a Noah's Ark with lots of animals,' said James, sipping his cocoa. 'You'll have to come and see it, Aunt Tilly.'

'Don't bother her,' said Alice. 'You heard your Aunt Tilly. She hasn't got time.'

'I don't know why she can't stay the night and catch an early train,' said James plaintively. 'Daddy could run her to the station.'

'Now there's a thought,' said Seb, cocking an eye at Tilly. 'What time do you have to be in the office?'

'Nine o'clock,' said Tilly, her spirits lifting. It would be great not to have to rush off so soon.

'I could get you to Birkenhead by eight o'clock. You shouldn't have any trouble catching a train to Liverpool in time,' said Seb.

Tilly looked at her sister. 'If that's all right with you?'

Alice shrugged her shoulders. 'Why shouldn't it be? Your old room is still there. All you have to do is make up your bed and put a hotty in.'

'Thanks,' said Tilly, looking forward to spending even a little time with her nephews and niece.

Her sister grilled her later, not only about her job but also about the Wrights and whether she saw much of the other Mrs Bennett. Tilly was able to answer honestly that she saw little of her. Fortunately, her sister did not ask her what she was doing on New Year's Eve. She could imagine blue smoke coming from Alice's ears if she told her that she was going to a party at Eudora's house. So the evening passed quite pleasantly and she took the opportunity to have a bath. There were only two things that marred Tilly's enjoyment: the first was knowing that her father would so have enjoyed talking to his grandson. The second was that there was no mention of Don Pierce. Tilly assumed that Seb hadn't any news but she was concerned that this silence might mean that something bad had happened to him on his travels. The thought scared her.

CHAPTER TWELVE

'Damn! The engine won't start,' said Seb, entering the kitchen blowing on his hands. He held them out to the fire. 'I was going to drop Freddie and Kenny at the yard on the way but now we'll all have to walk.'

Tilly was dismayed. 'What d'you mean it won't start? I've got to get to work.'

'It must be the cold. I'm sorry, Tilly,' he said, looking concerned. 'But I'm sure your boss will understand in the circumstances.'

Tilly was not as convinced as he was because it was not Mr Holmes she would have to face but Miss Langton and her unpredictable temper.

'Not to worry. I'll just have to walk to the station and hope the trains will be running on time and I'm not too late.'

She stood up and went to fetch the winter coat she had taken from her wardrobe. At least her feet were more sensibly clad since she had rediscovered the fur lined button boots that Alice and Seb had given her as a present last Christmas. She turned to the children, who were having their breakfast.

'Sorry, loves, but I'm going to have to go.'

'But you'll come again soon, won't you, Aunt Tilly?' asked Flora, getting up from her chair and going to hug Tilly round the waist.

'As soon as I can,' said Tilly, stroking the silky soft hair that was the same colour as her own. 'Or you can come and visit me.'

Flora looked at her mother. 'Can we do that, Mum?'

'We'll see,' said Alice. 'Now say your goodbyes and finish your breakfast.'

Goodbyes said, Tilly felt quite tearful as she waved to the family standing on the front step. Then she asked herself what she was getting upset about. At least she had managed to see them before the old year was out and hopefully she would visit them again in the not too distant future. Now she had to get to work and, fingers crossed, she would get there on time.

'What time do you think this is to be coming in to work?' demanded Miss Langton, her eyes hard and cold. 'I will speak to Mr Holmes and no doubt he'll tell you to collect your things and go.'

'You mean he'll sack me?' said Tilly, unable to conceal her dismay.

'It's what you deserve. Making eyes at the men who come in here and stealing things.'

'Stealing!' Tilly's dismay was replaced by anger. 'That's defamation of character, Miss Langton. I've never stolen a thing in my life. I'm going to complain to Mr Holmes about what you've just said.' She made for the manager's office.

'You'll do no such thing,' said Miss Langton, seizing hold of Tilly's coat. 'Just go!'

'No!' Tilly attempted to shrug off her hand. 'You've gone too far this time.'

Miss Langton clung to her for dear life. 'All right. Perhaps I've made a mistake. We'll forget your tardy timekeeping this once but don't let it happen again.'

'I've always been on time,' said Tilly, wondering what was up with the woman, the way she changed her mind from one minute to the next.

'Let's forget what I said,' Miss Langton smoothed down Tilly's sleeve.

Tilly removed her hand. 'I can't let it pass that you called me a thief. I want an apology.' She darted a challenging glance at the older woman and watched her inner struggle.

'All right,' burst out Miss Langton. 'You really are most impudent but perhaps I was a little hasty and it would be difficult to replace you right now.'

Tilly realised that was the closest she was going to get to an apology. If she had not needed the job so much she would have walked out, but instead she accepted Miss Langton's apology and hung up her coat. Then she went over to her desk and stowed her handbag and the carrier bag containing her other coat and shoes under the desk. Fortunately, the rest of the day passed off without any further unpleasantness.

The sight of the sleet coming down caused Tilly to button her winter coat up to her chin and pull down her new woolly hat over her ears before braving the elements. She decided it was not an evening for walking home and caught a tram. As she entered the shop she removed her hat and shook the sleet from it.

'D'you mind?' asked Wendy, giving a delicate shiver as several frozen drops landed on her face. 'So why didn't you come home last night? Decided to stay at your sister's, did you?'

Tilly nodded. 'James wanted me to stay, so I let myself be persuaded, only for the car not to start this morning. I ended up being late for work. Then Miss Langton completely lost her trolley and said I made eyes at all the men that came into the office and that I was a thief into the bargain.'

Wendy gasped. 'That's terrible. What's wrong with the woman, calling you a thief?'

'I was furious and I almost got an apology from her. Anyway, I've still got my job, thank goodness,' said Tilly. 'Although, I don't know how long I'll be able to stick it out.'

'You should write more short stories,' said Wendy, opening the flap for her. 'A nice romantic one set in spring.'

Spring, thought Tilly, wishing it was here now. As she went into the back, she wracked her brains trying to come up with an idea for another story.

Mrs Wright was in the kitchen, ironing. Tilly greeted her and apologised for not coming home last night. She explained what had happened as she shrugged off her coat and sank into a chair by the fire and eased off her sodden gloves.

'I gathered that's what happened,' said the older woman. 'So have you decided what you're wearing tonight?'

'Tonight? What's tonight?' asked Tilly.

'You can't have forgotten it's New Year's Eve and we're going to the Bennetts', girl?'

She smacked her forehead. 'Yes, I had!' Her face brightened. 'I'd better go up now and pick something out to wear.'

'That's a new coat you're wearing,' said Mrs Wright. 'Hang it on a chair in front of the fire to dry out.'

'It's not new and neither are the boots,' said Tilly. 'They're at least a year old, but thanks, I will need to dry it out if I want to wear it this evening.'

'Let's hope the weather changes before then,' said Mrs Wright. 'Well, pick out a dress, girl, and if it needs ironing I'll do it for you. But before then you can make a cuppa for me, you and Wendy and you could make yourself a slice of toast if you're hungry. I decided it was a waste of time to cook for us all when there's bound to be loads of food at the party. Let's hope this weather changes before eight o'clock; we don't want to get soaked before we get there.'

'Did Wendy ask Mr Simpson about going?' asked Tilly, putting on the kettle. There was no sign of the rest of the family and she wondered where they all were.

Mrs Wright hung a dress on a hanger and hooked it over the picture rail. 'I believe so. I just hope she's not getting too fond of that man.'

Tilly glanced at her landlady as she placed the flat iron on the fire. 'Why should you think that? I know she talks to him and is always glad to see him but is it any more than that?'

'You tell me, girl. I don't want her getting any fancy ideas in her head about him. I want her here, helping me. It's her duty as the eldest girl.'

Oh dear, thought Tilly. If it was true that Wendy fancied Mr Simpson, then she felt sorry for the girl. Of course, she would make any man a good wife. She could clean and cook and looked after the shop, so must have some kind of business head on her shoulders. But how did Mr Simpson feel about her? As far as Tilly could make out, he didn't appear to see Wendy in a romantic light at all. In fact, Tilly was convinced it was her he fancied. How did she feel about him? She liked him and was interested in the work he did, but she didn't really know him, so could say no more than that. She considered marriage and thought that a good wife or husband was worth their weight in gold. She thought of Don and prayed he was safe. She wanted him alive and enjoying the work he was passionate about.

It suddenly struck her that 'Worth her Weight in Gold' was a good title for a romantic short story. Now, what profession could she give her hero? How about his being a mining engineer in South Africa, returning to England, having made his fortune. A confirmed bachelor he had never considered taking a wife until he met the almost Cinderella figure of the lovely but hungry and orphaned Eve. Tilly's thoughts whirled with possibilities.

'Tilly, you've gone into a trance,' said Mrs Wright in a loud voice. 'The kettle's boiling.'

'Sorry,' said Tilly, warming the pot and then making the tea. 'I was thinking.'

'Now there was me thinking you had turned into a statue,' said Mrs Wright sarcastically. 'So what dress is it to be for the party?'

Tilly did not answer but stared into space before dashing out of the kitchen. She had to write her thoughts down before they escaped.

'That Tilly,' said Mrs Wright, when her daughter came in from the shop for a warm, having served a rush of customers. 'She dashed off upstairs as if she had a pack of hounds after her.'

'Did she say why?' asked Wendy, taking a sip of tea.

'No! Although maybe she decided she'd better get a move on if she wants me to iron her dress for the party. And while

I think about it, girl, I don't want you making eyes at Mr Simpson,' said her mother.

Wendy's face turned beetroot. 'I don't know what you mean, Mam!'

'Oh, yes, you do. I'm not having you getting yourself into trouble just so he'll marry you.'

Wendy gasped. 'Bloody hell, Mam! What a thing to say to your own daughter. You should know me better than that.'

Her mother stared at her hard. 'I'll have none of that swearing. I'm not blind and I don't want you forgetting I need you here. Besides, he's too old for you.'

'No, he's not,' denied Wendy. 'And he'd notice me more if Tilly weren't here,' she muttered.

'I must admit she's a looker and she could catch him if she wanted,' said Mrs Wright. 'She did ask if he was coming to the party, so maybe she is interested in him.'

The little confidence Wendy had was seriously dented by her mother's words. She almost wished that she was not going to the party if it meant watching Tilly and Mr Simpson flirting with each other. But it was too late to get out of it now. Besides, was she ready to give up on him without a struggle?

By the time Mr Simpson arrived at the shop, Wendy was fraught with nerves. There was a glow about Tilly when she came downstairs, wearing a dress that had such style that Wendy felt a frump in comparison to her. When Mr Simpson commented on Tilly's appearance, Wendy could have wept.

'That's a really nice frock you're wearing, Miss Moran,' he said.

'Thank you, kind sir,' said Tilly, smiling up at him. 'It used to be my sister's but she passed it on to me.' The gown was of green velveteen and fitted snugly about her waist and hips.

The neckline was scooped and trimmed with lace and revealed the slightest hint of cleavage. There was a stole of the same green velveteen to match but she would be wearing her warm coat and hat, gloves and scarf to go out in. Tilly had only worn the gown once before but she had decided that tonight was a fitting occasion to put it on. She was feeling elated. She had rattled off her story on her typewriter in no time and although it needed touching up here and there, she was convinced that she would sell it.

'Call me Grant,' said Mr Simpson.

Tilly's smiled deepened. 'If that's what you wish, Mr Simpson. I mean Grant and you can call me Tilly.'

'May I call you Grant, too, Mr Simpson?' asked Wendy.

He glanced down at her and smiled. 'Of course, Wendy. Why not? We're all friends here, aren't we?'

'Of course, we are,' said Tilly, smiling at them both.

'Well, if you've settled that,' said Mrs Wright dryly, 'we might as well be on our way. At least the sleet's stopped and we haven't far to go.'

Grant offered both girls his arm and with one either side of him, they hurried outside and made their way to Newsham Drive, followed by the rest of the Wright family.

'You do look nice, Tilly,' said Joy, helping her off with her coat.

'Thanks. It was one of Alice's,' said Tilly. 'The family sent their love, by the way.'

'You managed to get to Chester then?'

'I stayed overnight and was late for work.' She pulled a face. 'I was threatened with dismissal.'

'But they didn't sack you?'

Tilly shook her head. 'How's Dad?'

'His usual self,' said Joy, hanging Tilly's coat in the cloakroom and accepting Mrs Wright's from her. 'You know he's been digging holes.'

'I didn't until Alice told me.' Some of Tilly's high spirits evaporated. 'She thinks he's mad.'

'Alice would. She won't give an inch where your father's concerned. I've decided that perhaps his digging these holes and filling them in again is to do with some kind of plan he has for spring planting,' said Joy with a twinkle. 'By the way, Mr and Mrs Bennett will expect you to do a turn on the piano. She remembers how good you were as a girl when you had music lessons at her house in Chester.'

Tilly said, 'I haven't played for ages. I had hoped to have a go on Alice and Seb's piano but I didn't get a chance.'

'You don't forget things like that,' said Joy, encouragingly. 'It's like riding a bike. Why don't you go and have a practise now while the drawing room is empty?'

Tilly hesitated, aware that the Wrights and Grant Simpson were watching her. 'Go on,' urged Minnie. 'We're all waiting to hear if you're as good as Miss Kirk says.'

'All right,' agreed Tilly. 'But don't blame me if my playing causes you to put your hands over your ears.' She turned to Joy. 'Should I ask Mr Bennett's permission first?'

'If it makes you feel better then do. Last time I saw him he was in the kitchen talking to your father.'

Tilly thanked her, adding, 'Do you think Dad will stay for the party this time?'

'I shouldn't think so. You know what he's like,' said Joy. 'But at least you'll be able to have a word with him here instead of traipsing down the garden.'

'Can I come with you?' asked Grant, surprising Tilly.

'Why?' she asked bluntly.

'A couple of reasons,' he said easily. 'First I'd like to thank Mr Bennett for inviting me to the party and secondly I heard from that police sergeant I know that your father is a brave man. Apparently he had the guts to face a kidnapper with a gun. It takes nerves for an unarmed man to do that and I admire him.'

His words touched Tilly. 'Thank you,' she said huskily.

'Can I come, as well?' asked Wendy, slipping her hand through Tilly's arm. 'I'd like a word with Uncle Robbie.'

'Perhaps we should all go,' said Mrs Wright, her eyes on her eldest daughter.

Tilly said, 'Could the rest of you follow us on in a few minutes. Dad doesn't like being surrounded by too many people all at once.' Without further ado, she hurried from the hall, accompanied by Grant and Wendy.

To Tilly's surprise she found several people in the kitchen but her father was not one of them. 'Hello, Mr Bennett,' she said, 'I was hoping to find Dad here.'

Robbie turned and faced her. 'Sorry, Tilly. You've just missed him. He's taken Nanki Poo for a walk.'

Tilly could not conceal her amazement. 'In the dark! What if he was to fall over something?'

'You're thinking he's gone over to the park. Well, he says he won't go into it,' said Robbie, 'so stop worrying, Tilly. And let me introduce you and Wendy and...' He raised an eyebrow in Grant's direction.

'This is Mr Grant Simpson, Uncle Robbie.' Wendy stepped forward. 'He's the friend I spoke to you about. He's a private investigator.'

'Thank you for that, Wendy,' said Grant in a vexed undertone.

She flushed and fell silent, moving away from him.

Robbie and Grant shook hands. 'May I introduce our next door neighbour, Mr Leonard Parker,' said Robbie.

The two men shook hands and then Leonard turned to Tilly. 'I think we've already met,' he said, holding out his hand.

'That's true,' said Tilly, placing her small one in his strong grasp. She gazed into his handsome face and felt her cheeks warm with the admiration in his vivid blue eyes. 'Miss Moran, isn't it?'

'You have a good memory, Mr Parker.'

'So where did you meet?' asked Grant.

'We met outside,' said Leonard, continuing to stare at Tilly. 'It was blowing a gale.'

'Later the fog came down and you could scarcely see your hand in front of your face,' said Tilly.

'I literally picked you up off the ground.'

'You were in a hurry and I wanted to get out of the wind,' she said in a breathy voice.

Grant Simpson cleared his throat. 'Mr Bennett, Tilly came to ask your permission to practise on your piano.'

'You certainly have it, Tilly,' said Robbie. 'Now, Mr Parker, perhaps I can introduce to my niece, Wendy?'

Tilly withdrew her hand from Leonard's and stepped aside to allow Wendy to stand in her place. 'If you'll all excuse me. I'll go and practise my piano playing.'

She hurried away, wondering why she was feeling the way she did when she hardly knew Mr Parker. How old was he? As old as Grant and Don? Did it matter? Suddenly she wanted to lose herself in her music because her insides were churning. Hopefully her fingers had not lost their skill and she would calm down. She did not want to make a hash of her playing and prove an embarrassment to the Bennetts and their guests.

It was a relief to discover that after a few hesitant starts and discordant notes, the music flowed beneath her touch: Sonatas, dance music, popular music hall songs and even a hymn or two composed by Charles Wesley. She even rediscovered that peculiar crashing piece that she had toyed with when Seb was missing during the war.

'You're good,' said Wendy, appearing suddenly. She rested an elbow on the top of the piano. 'It's not fair. You can write, you can play music and you're witty and pretty. What chance have I got?'

Tilly stopped playing and glanced up at her. She did not pretend to not understand what Wendy meant by that question. How could she after what Wendy's mother had said to her. 'You underestimate yourself.'

'He's annoyed with me because I let slip that he's a private investigator,' said Wendy gloomily.

'I don't suppose it really matters and he'll probably forget about it in a few days,' murmured Tilly, playing a few notes.

'I hope so.'

'What do you make of Mr Parker?' asked Tilly.

'Struck.'

Tilly lifted her eyes and stared at her. 'What do you mean by that?'

'You knocked him for six.'

Tilly did not speak but she felt her cheeks grow hot. 'I don't want to get involved with either of them. I want to write. You keep your eye on your Mr Simpson, the great detective, and

I'll make sure I don't see too much of him.'

'It's no use,' muttered Wendy, toying with a sheet of music. 'Mam will put her spoke in even if he did start fancying me.'

'It's your life. Don't be so defeatist.' Tilly closed the piano lid and stood up. 'I'm hungry. Do you know when the food's going to be served?'

'You can help yourself now,' said a voice behind them.

Tilly had regained her composure and could now look Leonard in the eye without it affecting her breathing. 'Thank you, Mr Parker. I'm starving.'

'I hardly think so.' His blue eyes ran over her figure. 'You look ravishingly beautiful.'

Tilly forced herself to laugh. 'Oh, please, Mr Parker, you'll be turning my head. I'm only an office girl and I have to keep my feet firmly on the ground.'

'That's not quite true,' said Wendy. 'Don't you believe her, Mr Parker! She's far more talented than that: Tilly's a writer.'

'A writer?' He gazed at Tilly. 'You look a bit young to be published.'

'But I am. Only articles and short stories,' said Tilly, 'but—' Wendy interrupted her. 'She's writing a novel.'

'A novel?' Leonard gave Tilly a teasing smile. 'I suppose it's a romance?'

'I'm not yet sure what genre it'll fit in,' she said. 'Now if you'll excuse me, Mr Parker, I really am very hungry.' She made to brush past him but he stopped her by taking her arm. 'So what do you think of crime novels? Have you read this new author, Miss Christie? She has a silly little foreigner for a detective.'

'Hercule Poirot,' said Tilly, feeling as if his fingers were burning through the sleeve of her dress. 'Yes, I've read her first book and I disagree with you. I thought he was clever to work out the identity of the murderer.'

'He's something of an oddity, you must admit. In real life he wouldn't have a chance to get near the body or ferret out the murderer. It was quite a clever murder so I do admire Miss Christie. Poison is a woman's weapon.'

'You think so?' asked Tilly.

Grant was suddenly on the other side of Tilly. 'I believe Miss Christie worked in a pharmacy during the war,' he said, 'so she knows her poisons.'

'Fiction reflecting real life, you think?' said Leonard.

Wendy decided to join in the discussion 'There was a case a few months ago of a Yorkshire farmer who was accused of the attempted murder of nine people,' she said.

'Really?' asked Grant, looking interested.

Wendy nodded. 'He poisoned a box of chocolates and then offered it round. He had forged a will and they had dared to contest it, so he was really annoyed with them, I guess.'

'What poison did he use?' asked Tilly, fascinated by the snippets of information Wendy found in the newspapers.

'Strychnine. It's what they use to kill rats,' said Wendy. 'It makes you think, doesn't it?'

'Makes you think what, Miss Wright?' asked Leonard.

'That the means of getting rid of someone you want out of the way is surprisingly ready to hand,' she said slowly. 'Not that I want to get rid of anyone,' she added hastily, looking at Tilly.

Tilly raised her eyebrows. 'You've given me an idea. But food first.'

Mr Parker laughed. 'So the mention of strychnine in the chocolates hasn't put you off your supper, Miss Moran?'

'No, Mr Parker. It certainly hasn't.' Tilly removed his hand from her sleeve and left the room without a backward glance.

The others followed. 'I've never met a girl like her before,' said Leonard.

'You mean you've never met a writer?' said Wendy, thinking of what Tilly had said to her earlier. 'Well, now you have, Mr Parker, perhaps you'd best make the most of it. It's possible that one day she might put you in a book and you'd both be famous.'

'Now there's a thought,' murmured Leonard. 'Although, to be honest, Miss Wright, I'm a man who much prefers to remain in the background. If you'll excuse me.'

He left her and Grant, staring after him.

'What do you make of him?' asked Grant.

'He seems nice enough,' said Wendy, glancing up at him.

A frowning Grant said, 'You're such an innocent, Wendy. I'm going to get something to eat.' He walked away.

Wendy felt like stamping her foot. Instead, she followed him to the buffet table where she found Tilly helping herself to food. She was just about to speak to her when Eudora came up to them and said, 'Tilly, how lovely you look this evening.'

'Lovely food, Mrs Bennett,' said Tilly, biting into a sandwich. 'You'll have to excuse me. I'm really hungry.'

Eudora brushed back a strand of pure silver hair amongst the black and smiled. 'You eat up, dear. I like to see people with a healthy appetite.'

'Wendy was telling us about a man who tried to kill nine people by poisoning a box of chocolates. What do you think of that?' Tilly took another bite of her sandwich, which contained tinned salmon and was delicious.

'I'm never surprised by the strange behaviour of the human

race,' said Eudora. 'It's what makes life so interesting.'

'I'd agree,' said Tilly.

'For instance, your father and those holes he kept digging and filling in a short while ago.'

'I know. It's odd,' said Tilly. 'Perhaps it was moles. Have you asked him about them?'

'No. I'm sure he had his reasons and, besides, he's stopped now the frost has made the ground too hard to get his spade into it.'

'What if he starts up all over again in the spring?' said Tilly.

'Then, dear, I really would have to speak to him.' She patted Tilly's shoulder. 'Now, you eat your fill and have a glass of champagne. I'm looking forward to hearing you entertain us later.'

The rest of the evening passed off smoothly. Tilly played the piano and was clapped and cheered. She looked for Leonard Parker amongst those listening but he seemed to have vanished and she was aware of disappointment. She saw her father briefly but made no mention of holes. What was the point if he was no longer digging them? By the time midnight chimed she had forgotten all about them, cheering in the New Year as church bells and the ship hooters on the Mersey sounded a welcome. She had managed to survive the past six months, almost independently of her family. She could only hope that she could continue to do so during 1921 and prayed that it would be a healthy, happy year for all those she loved and cared about.

PART TWO

February–September 1921

CHAPTER THIRTEEN

'Listen to this,' said Wendy, glancing up from the newspaper as Tilly entered the shop.

'Go on,' she said, resting her elbows on the counter and fixing her with a stare. 'I could do with some entertainment right now. Something that will make me laugh. That woman will be the death of me.'

'I presume you mean Miss Langton? Well, this should tickle you.' Wendy read out aloud, '*Weird Merseyside spook, remarkable manifestation and its effects in vicarage. It was felt but seldom visible. Panic-stricken maids leave due to nerves whilst dog barks at the vicar's favourite chair.* Apparently, the vicar died ten years ago,' she added.

'You should read that to your Aunt Eudora,' said Tilly. 'She might be able to help them get rid of the ghost.'

'No, I daren't do that because Uncle Robbie wants her to have nothing to do with getting in touch with the spirits,' said Wendy. 'Do you believe in ghosts?'

Tilly shrugged. 'I've an open mind. Anything funnier than that?'

Wendy turned over a page. 'There's a piece about the latest in the Sex War.'

Tilly straightened up. 'Go on?'

'It happened in America. Apparently girls at various churches have refused to keep company with men who smoke – while the men will have nothing to do with girls who wear knee-length skirts, silk-stockings, paint their virgin cheeks or have hairstyles that hide their ears.'

Tilly crinkled her nose. 'What's wrong with hiding their ears?'

'Perhaps it's a new hairstyle.'

'Anything else?'

'Yes. It's in America again.'

Tilly thought fleetingly of Don and could not imagine him being against the modern girl. 'So what's it say?'

'A judge in Springfield, Ohio, has ordered a waist-high curtain to be hung before the jury-box so that the lower extremities of women won't distract the police as they give evidence.'

Tilly smiled. 'He and Miss Langton would make a pair. She's forever going on about the length of my skirts, saying they're too short when they're at least an inch below my knees. She told me that she's had complaints.'

'Do you believe her?'

'No. Because I'd be able to tell if anyone who came in disapproved of my legs.' She chuckled. 'I've had a couple of wolf whistles.'

'That's what's probably got up her nose,' said Wendy. 'Seen anything of Mr Parker?'

Tilly said casually, 'No. And I'm not planning to. I told you I've no time for men. What about Grant? Have you seen him?'

'Not for a week or so,' said Wendy, folding the newspaper. 'And when I did see him he seemed to be in another world. I don't think he heard half of what I said.'

'Perhaps he has a case that's exercising his mind,' suggested Tilly.

Wendy sighed. 'Well, if he has, he's keeping it to himself like the good private investigator he is.'

Tilly said no more but went into the back, said hello to the family, and went upstairs to change. She felt slightly guilty because she had made no mention to Wendy about having seen Grant, herself. He had visited the insurance office several times since the beginning of the New Year. Apparently, he had known Mr Holmes when he was a policeman attached to Tuebrook police station. She decided that next time she saw him then she would try and persuade him to spill the beans about his latest case.

'Good morning, Miss Moran,' said Grant, breezing into the office a few weeks later. 'Miss Langton!' He inclined his head in her direction and received a sour look for his effort.

'Good morning, Mr Simpson,' said Tilly, smiling at him. 'What can we do for you?'

'It's not your place to ask such a question,' snapped Miss Langton from over by the filing cabinet. 'I'm in charge here. What is it you want, Mr Simpson?'

'To see Mr Holmes. There's been an interesting development,' he said, striding over to the manager's office and knocking on the door.

Miss Langton immediately scurried after him. 'You must let me enquire whether he's available first,' she said.

A voice called, 'Come in.'

'There, he can see me,' said Grant, winking at Tilly. He went inside and closed the door in the secretary's face.

Miss Langton spun round. Swiftly, Tilly lowered her head to the figures she was entering in a ledger.

'Did you say something?' asked Miss Langton.

'No,' said Tilly, keeping her eyes on her work.

'You sniggered then.'

'No, I didn't. Why should I?'

'Because you thought it was funny.'

'Thought what was funny?' asked Tilly. 'Did you tell a joke?'

The woman marched over to where Tilly was sitting and slapped the desk. 'I do not make jokes.'

'No,' sighed Tilly, and lowered her head to her work again.

'He winked at you. You're a flirt. When you first came here, I thought you were different from those other girls. Now you're nothing but trouble.'

'I'm not a flirt,' said Tilly fiercely, throwing her pen on the desk. 'And I'm not a troublemaker either. All you do is pick, pick, pick on me. You can't stand it that I'm young. You want to be young again and have men find you attractive. Perhaps you regret never having married.'

The colour drained from Miss Langton's face and the skin around her nose and mouth looked pinched. 'How dare you! You will leave now!'

Tilly hung onto her temper, realising she should not have let her tongue run away with her. 'I'm sorry, Miss Langton, I shouldn't have said that. Your private life is none of my business.'

'I don't want your apology,' said the older woman breathing heavily. 'I want you out.'

Tilly's control over her temper slipped. 'It's not your place to fire me,' she said. 'As soon as Mr Simpson comes out the office I'm going to speak to Mr Holmes and tell him you've been victimising me.'

Miss Langton turned puce. 'You will *what*?' She leant across the desk and slapped Tilly across the face.

Tilly's head jerked back with the force of the blow and she let out a cry.

Mr Holmes's door opened and he said, 'What's going on here?'

'She-she w was impudent,' gasped Miss Langton. 'I will not put-put up with such behaviour in my office.'

Grant had followed the manager out and stared at Tilly, who had a hand to her cheek. 'What did she do, Tilly?' She did not answer, only lowering her hand. 'She hit you?'

'She asked for it,' said Miss Langton, collapsing into a chair and burying her face in her hands.

Mr Holmes sighed. 'Miss Moran, are you badly hurt?'

'I'll survive,' said Tilly, reaching for her pen with trembling fingers.

'Then perhaps you could go to the bakery and bring us some buns back and we could have a cup of tea?'

'OK,' said Tilly, getting to her feet. 'How many buns and do I take the money out of the petty cash?'

'Four, Miss Moran. We'll have one each,' he replied, 'and yes, use the petty cash. Thank you.'

'But surely you're not going to allow Miss Langton get away with hitting Miss Moran?' burst out Grant.

Tilly darted him a glance as she fetched her coat and hat and shook her head.

'I'll deal with this in my own way, Grant,' said Mr Holmes

firmly. 'Now if you'll wait for me in my office.'

Grant looked at Tilly and hesitated. She managed a small smile and shrugged on her coat before turning away. She stopped in front of Miss Langton because it was the older woman who was in charge of the petty cash but her shoulders were shaking. Tilly decided to get the key herself and take the money. This she did and then left the office.

It was a relief to be out in the fresh spring air and she took her time walking to Blackledge's bakery, knowing there would be changes ahead.

'Who did that to yer?' asked the woman in the bakery.

'Did what?' asked Tilly, handing the money over and taking the bag of buns from her.

'Yer've finger marks on yer face, luv.'

'Have I?' Tilly touched her cheek and felt the bruising made by Miss Langton's fingers. Tilly had never been hit before and the experience had shocked her. Suddenly she wanted to weep and hurried out of the shop, pulling her hair over her cheek.

Miss Langton was still sitting where she had left her, so Tilly put on the kettle and made the tea. She poured out two cups and put them on a tray with a plate with two buns on it. She knocked on the door of Mr Holmes' office.

'Come in!'

She entered, carrying the tray.

Immediately Grant rose from his chair and took it from her. 'Are you OK, Tilly?'

She nodded, and quickly left.

Miss Langton had still not moved when Tilly poured out their tea and carried a cup over to her. 'Tea, Miss Langton,' she said.

The woman shook her head.

Tilly sighed and placed the cup and bun on the desk and sat down and drank the sweet tea and ate the bun, wondering what would happen next.

Half an hour later Grant and Mr Holmes came out of the inner office. 'If you'll let me have your report as soon as possible, Grant, I'd appreciate it,' said Mr Holmes.

'Sure,' said Grant, and shook his hand.

Tilly had looked up when they appeared but now she lowered her eyes to her work again. She knew when Grant stopped in front of her desk. 'Are you OK, Tilly?' he asked again.

She nodded. 'Don't worry about me. I'll be fine.'

'I'll see you at the shop.'

'OK.'

Tilly did not watch him leave, aware that Mr Holmes was speaking in a low voice to Miss Langton. The woman got up and went into his office with him. Tilly stayed where she was for a couple of minutes before getting up and creeping over to the door. She placed her ear against it but could not make out what was being said, so returned to her desk. Shortly afterwards one of the insurance collectors came in and she had to deal with him.

It was to be three-quarters of an hour before Miss Langton emerged from Mr Holmes's office. He stood in the doorway and beckoned Tilly. She stood up and went into his office with him. He waved her to a chair and she sat down.

'I'm extremely sorry about what happened, Miss Moran,' he said. 'It was bad behaviour on Miss Langton's part but I'm afraid I am going to ask you to leave.'

'What?' Tilly had not known what to expect but she knew this was wrong. She pushed herself to her feet. 'It's not fair!'

'No, it's not,' he said. 'Please sit down again, Miss Moran. I want to explain a few matters to you.'

'All that matters to me is that I'm going to be without a job. Do you know what that means, Mr Holmes?'

His frown deepened. 'Of course I do. I'm well aware of the employment situation in this country, but you will not go empty-handed and I will write an excellent reference.'

'I don't understand,' said Tilly. 'If you consider me such a good worker, why are you sacking me?'

He fiddled with the pen on his desk. 'You are young and you are pretty, as well as intelligent, Miss Moran. Miss Langton has none of these attributes but she is loyal and hard-working.' Tilly made to speak but he silenced her with a raised hand. 'I doubt she has told you that she has an invalid widowed mother and that she has to support the old woman as well as herself. She has to pay someone to look in on her during the day and cook her a meal. Miss Langton's life is not easy. I was a friend of her father's and I feel some responsibility for them.'

'I see,' murmured Tilly, able to pity the woman but she still did not like her.

'I will see you are paid three months' wages, Miss Moran, and hopefully that will give you some breathing space and time to find another job,' said Mr Holmes.

Tilly's spirits lifted. She was out of a situation that she had found difficult but would still be able to pay for her bed and board until summer.

'Thank you, Mr Holmes. I do appreciate that you accept that what happened was not my fault.'

He nodded. 'I will get in touch with head office and see that this matter is dealt with swiftly and everything will be in the post before the end of the month.' He stood up and so did Tilly.

'Perhaps it's best I leave now,' she said.

'Yes.' He held out a hand to her. She took it and shook it and then, picking up the tray of crockery, she carried it out of the office.

Tilly did not speak again to Miss Langton but washed the crockery before putting on her coat and hat and leaving the office for the last time. Once outside, she was filled with such a sense of freedom that she wanted to sing and dance. Instead, she decided to cross the road and head for Newsham Park, hoping to find her father in the Bennetts' garden.

'Good morning, Tilly,' Eudora greeted her. 'What are you doing here at this time of day? Why aren't you in work?'

Tilly turned and looked at Eudora, who had Nanki Poo on a lead. 'It's a long story,' said Tilly, opening the gate.

'Then why don't you come in and tell me about it? If you were wanting to see your father, he's gone on an errand for me and won't be back for some hours,' said Eudora. 'Have you had lunch?'

'No,' said Tilly.

'Then come in and have a sandwich with me. It's Joy's day off and she's gone to see the Queen.'

'The Queen?'

'Yes.' Eudora's dark eyes twinkled down at her. 'Surely you can't be unaware that the King is at Aintree for the racing and the Queen and Princess Mary are in town presenting some awards or opening some building or other while they're here.'

Tilly gave her a blank look. 'I had no idea, which is surprising because Wendy generally keeps me up to date with everything that's going on in Liverpool.'

'I see. Well, it's Grand National week. If you've got any money to spare, Tilly, even a sixpence, Mr Bennett and I will put it on a horse for you when we go to the races on Friday.'

Tilly said, 'What about thrupence?'

Eudora chuckled, and followed her round to the back of the house.

Once Nanki Poo had been fed and the sandwiches and tea made, Tilly and Eudora sat down at the kitchen table. 'Now, tell me what's happened,' she said.

Tilly proceeded to tell her everything and Eudora listened without interruption. But when Tilly had finished her tale, the older woman clapped her hands and beamed at her. 'But this is excellent, Tilly. I need a part-time assistant and here you are!'

Tilly stared at her warily. 'What kind of assistant? You're not taking to the stage again are you and doing readings?'

Eudora pulled a wry face. 'No, my dear. That side of my life is completely over. My new work certainly involves meeting people's needs but at a different level. It's charitable work.'

Tilly swallowed the remains of her sandwich and hesitated before saying, 'I can't work for nothing, Mrs Bennett. I need a job that pays as the money I'll be getting will run out. It's not that I wouldn't like to help you for free but you must realise how it is. If I want to be independent I need to support myself.'

'An admirable aim,' said Eudora, offering Tilly another sandwich.

'Thanks,' she said, taking one.

'The charity I am involved in will willingly pay for your help. I wasn't suggesting that you would be an unpaid volunteer such as myself.'

'Oh!' exclaimed Tilly, relieved.

'Of course, we cannot pay you a large wage but if you find you love the work, then you'll end up with more hours than you could possibly want.'

'So what is this job?' asked Tilly.

'I'm a member of the Friends of the Seamen's Widows and Children's Charity connected with the Liverpool's Seamen's Orphanage,' said Eudora. 'Although my work does not involve raising money for children who have lost both parents, but for the wives and children of seamen lost at sea or killed in accidents at the docks. Some mothers naturally want to look after their children in their own homes but, to do so, some need help. One of my tasks is to visit some of these families and see the conditions they live in. By doing this I discover how best to provide for their needs. You'd be shocked, my dear, by how poverty stricken some families are.'

'But what would I do?' asked Tilly.

'It would be useful if you came along with me and made notes while I talk to the families. I'm not as young as I was and sometimes I can't always hear properly what they say. You could type up the notes and you'll be paid for that, too. When you're more experienced then you'll be able to visit without me and eventually take a trainee with you.'

Tilly's eyes gleamed. 'It sounds a very worthwhile job.'

'My dear, it is,' said Eudora, patting her arm. 'And it will open your eyes to a different side of life altogether, which will help you in your writing.'

'When do I start?' asked Tilly, bursting with enthusiasm.

Eudora said, 'There are a few matters I need to sort out first. I'll fill you in on them tomorrow. We'll have lunch and you can see your father then.'

Tilly agreed and shortly afterwards she left and made her way to the shop.

'What are you doing home?' asked Wendy.

Tilly explained.

'Gosh,' said Wendy, looking slightly envious. 'You have fallen on your feet.'

'Haven't I just,' said Tilly with a smile before going upstairs. She changed into something more comfortable and settled herself at her desk, then placed a sheet of paper into her typewriter and began to type.

The following day Tilly arrived at the Bennetts' house just before noon and was welcomed by Eudora. 'Joy's not back from the shops yet and Robbie's already left for a rehearsal at the Palladium,' she informed her. 'I thought a light lunch, my dear, in light of what's going on in the world today. People are starving in Europe and Asia, you know. I saw photographs in a magazine the other day that wrenched my heart. I have a friend in America who sends magazines over to me after she's read them. Perhaps you'd like to take one home with you? They're not all misery but have some very interesting articles.'

'Thanks, I would,' said Tilly, dipping her spoon into the homemade lentil soup.

'Have you seen any more of our neighbour?' asked Eudora, taking bread from a plate in the middle of the table.

The question surprised Tilly. 'You mean Mr Parker or the relative who lives with him?'

'Mr Parker.' Eudora's pale brow puckered. 'A good-looking man and charming on the outside but I suspect he's a deep one.'

'What do you mean – a deep one?'

'Only that I sense he's hiding something'

Tilly felt a strange tingling on the back of her neck, remembering that, according to Joy and Hanny, Eudora Bennett could *see* things that others could not. Yet she found herself defending Leonard Parker. 'He seemed honest and open to me.'

'Naturally. Clever people who have something to hide often present such a front. Remember Bert Kirk?'

'How could I forget him? He shot Dad and tried to destroy the family.'

'Indeed, he did.'

Tilly frowned. 'You're not saying Mr Parker would behave in such a way?'

'I don't know him well enough to say that, Tilly, but I sense that he's a man with secrets.'

Again, Tilly felt that tingling at the nape of her neck. 'Have you read *Jane Eyre*, Mrs Bennett? If you have you won't have forgotten the hero.'

Eudora's eyes twinkled. 'Mr Rochester, who kept his deranged wife locked up in the attic and would have married Jane bigamously.'

'You read my mind!'

'Not really. We were talking about Mr Parker and secrets. I just put two and two together. I think the woman next door is exactly who we believe her to be and that is a poor relation, who is slightly backward but quite capable of doing housework and cooking for him.' Eudora stood up and cleared away her utensils and made a pot of tea. 'I can admire him for taking her in but then it probably means he doesn't have to pay her a wage.'

Suddenly, Tilly felt resentful towards Eudora for sniping at Leonard Parker in that nasty way. Then the moment passed and she knew that the attraction she had felt at their second meeting was stronger than she realised. She finished her soup and got up to wash their bowls and cutlery.

'You don't have to do that, Tilly,' said Eudora, placing two slices of Dundee cake on a plate. 'Joy would have seen to them.'

'I like to be useful,' said Tilly.

Eudora smiled. 'Then perhaps it's time we talked about the reason why you're here. You can also pour out the tea.' Tilly did what she said and then sat down at the table. 'You played extremely well at my New Year's party, by the way,' added Eudora, 'which has given me another idea but I doubt it will come to fruition for some time.'

'What's that?' asked Tilly.

'A concert in aid of the seamen's orphans and widows. One that we could also put on as entertainment for them, as well. We'd need good amateurs, such as yourself.'

'You mean you'd want me to perform on stage in front of people?' croaked Tilly, almost overcome by excitement.

'Yes. And you could accompany some of the singers. I believe Seb's mother is back on the stage, performing for charity. Now, if we could persuade the Liverpool Nightingale to sing for us next Autumn, I think that would be a feather in our cap, don't you?'

'You think she would do it?' asked Tilly doubtfully. 'I mean she and you don't exactly—'

'Hit it off? Oh, I think I could persuade her. I know things about her that if even a whisper got out.' She smiled.

Tilly felt that tingle again and thought there was rather a wicked gleam in the older woman's dark eyes. 'You mean you'd blackmail her?'

Eudora raised her eyebrows. 'Blackmail is not a nice word

to use, Tilly. But I'm only human, my dear, and she once accused me of murder.'

'Gosh,' said Tilly, looking shocked. 'That's not nice.'

'No, it isn't. As if I'd do away with the man we both loved.' She took a deep breath. 'Anyway, concert apart, you want to know about Monday and where I'll be taking you.'

'Yes,' said Tilly, wondering about the secrets that were locked up in Eudora's heart.

'Have you ever been to Scotland Road? Well, Scotty Road, as the locals call it, has something of a reputation. There is a pub on every corner and even the police are wary of visiting the area after dark on their own.'

'But we won't be going at night-time, will we?' Tilly reached for a slice of Dundee cake and bit into it.

Eudora smiled. 'Certainly not. But it would be sensible even during the day to not stand out. We will dress simply and carry little money on our persons. These are tough times, as we both know, and it would be foolish to put temptation in the way of desperate people.'

'Will my own clothes do?' she asked.

Eudora looked her over. 'You look very pretty in green and white but it would be best if you have something dark and plain. There are so many women dressed soberly since the war and we want to blend in. You'd be surprised by how many working class people hate do-gooders.'

'But surely some must welcome those who would help them?' asked Tilly, taken aback.

'Of course! But they don't want their neighbours knowing they're accepting charity.'

'What about help from the church?'

'The church does what it can but large numbers have

drifted away since the war. They question the reality of a caring God when so many brave men were killed and taken from them,' said Eudora.

'What about the Government?'

Eudora shrugged. 'Some politicians have made a start in trying to change the lives of the poor but increases in taxes aren't welcomed by the rich.'

'Surely life has to improve for the poor, otherwise there could be a revolution, the same as in Russia?'

'I doubt it, my dear. Life will certainly get worse before it gets better but one day the lot of the working classes will improve.' She added in a voice that quivered, 'Not in my earthly lifetime but certainly in your children's. In the meantime, I have to do what I can to help the needy. I want you here on Monday at ten o'clock,' she said firmly.

For a brief moment Tilly thought of those words – *your children's* – and whether Eudora really could *see* the future. She felt that tingle again, thinking of Don and guiltily of Leonard Parker, too.

Eudora said, 'Any questions, Tilly?'

Tilly forced herself to concentrate on the matter in hand. 'Will Dad be driving us?'

Eudora's eyebrows shot up. 'Certainly not! Haven't I just explained matters? We go incognito, Tilly.'

Tilly flushed. 'You make me feel like a spy.'

'Well, it will certainly give you something to put into one of your stories, dear, won't it?' she said with a laugh. 'Now, finish your tea and cake and go and see your father. I have a little job I want him to do for me later.'

Tilly did as Eudora said and found Mal cleaning the car. 'Hello, Dad.'

He did not immediately respond and she wondered if he was getting deaf in his old age. She went and stood the other side of the car so he could not avoid seeing her. 'Hello, Dad,' she repeated.

'There yer are, lass!' Mal dropped his polishing cloth on the front passenger seat and held out his arms to her. 'I'm really glad to see ye. I've been worried.'

'What is it, Dad? What's wrong?' she asked, giving him a hug.

He glanced about and then whispered, 'I found a body and I've forgotten where it is.'

She could only think that he meant the baby's skeleton. 'You buried it under the trees, Dad, at the bottom of the garden. You planted a rose bush on top of it.'

He looked doubtful. 'No.'

'Yes. Come on, Dad. I'll show you where it is.' She slipped her hand into his and led him to the bottom of the garden and pointed at the rose bush that already had leaves unfurling.

Mal shook his head. 'That's not it, lass.'

'Of course it is,' she said patiently. 'You've just forgotten, as you said.'

His weather-beaten face puckered in thought and he shook his head. 'No.'

Tilly sighed. 'Perhaps you should dig it up and then you'll see I'm right.'

'No,' he said. 'I'll find it and yer'll see I'm right, lass.'

She decided it was a waste of time arguing with him. Instead she told him about working for Eudora's charity, helping the orphans and widows of seamen. He seemed interested and when she told him that most likely she would be performing in a concert next autumn, his face lit up. 'I'll have to go. I have to see my daughter play before all those people.'

'You won't mind being amongst so many people, Dad?' she asked.

He hesitated. 'I have to do it.'

Tilly stayed a little longer talking to him and then she took her leave. As she reached the Bennetts' front gate she heard her name being called and saw Leonard Parker standing on the pavement outside his house.

'Miss Moran, how nice to see you again,' he said.

'Mr Parker.' Tilly felt the colour rise in her cheeks. He was looking very smart in a silver grey suit and on his handsome head he wore a homburg. He had an overcoat over his arm and in his hand he carried a briefcase. 'Are you off to your office after lunch?'

'I'm off to see my solicitor.' He looked at her expectantly. 'And what are you doing here?'

'I have a new job working with Mrs Bennett.'

He looked surprised. 'What kind of work?'

'For a charity, helping the orphans and widows of seamen.'

'Ahhh! Good works! Although, there are some men in the shipping business who make me very angry.'

'You mean because you've lost money due to the strikes?'

'Yes.' The muscles of his face tightened. 'If this was the old days and I was a pirate I'd have made them walk the plank.'

'You're not serious,' said Tilly, startled.

A small smile played round his mouth. 'Of course not. But perhaps you could have a pirate in one of your stories? You could make him a lord who had fallen on hard times due to the devilish actions of other pirates.'

Tilly returned his smile. 'What a good idea! He could rescue the heroine from another pirate ship and they could end up living on a tropical island.'

'Perhaps she could be the daughter of the villain,' said Mr Parker promptly. 'A Cinderella figure who had no idea that her father was a blackguard.' He raised his hat. 'Good afternoon, Miss Moran. A pleasure talking to you.'

'Good afternoon, Mr Parker.' An amused Tilly watched him stride off along the Drive towards West Derby Road, forgetting Eudora's warning and her vow to have nothing to do with men.

CHAPTER FOURTEEN

'I see you've dressed as I advised and that you're nice and early, dear,' said Eudora, opening the door to Tilly the following Monday. 'Come in. Joy will make us a drink before we go.'

Tilly followed her into the kitchen where Joy was slicing vegetables. 'Hello, Tilly,' she said, glancing up at her. 'You raring to go?'

'It'll be interesting, I'm sure,' said Tilly.

'Make us some mocha coffee, Joy? There's a dear,' said Eudora.

'Seb's mother used to make mocha coffee,' said Tilly. 'I often had it at Alice and Seb's house.'

Eudora waved her to a chair. 'I used to wish that Alice would come and see me after your mother passed over. I always felt I could have helped her, if only she had not hated me so. Perhaps before I become spirit, she might have a change of heart and seek me out before it's too late.'

Tilly was startled by her mention of becoming spirit and was reminded of what Eudora had said last week about *not in her earthly life.* Was it possible the medium could foresee her own death? Tilly felt that cold shiver again but kept quiet about what she was thinking. When she finished her mocha coffee, Eudora said that they would need to be on their way. Tilly followed her outside.

'Good morning, ladies!'

Tilly felt her pulses race and looked to where Leonard Parker stood on his own path, drawing on a leather glove. 'Good morning, Mr Parker,' she said.

'Good morning,' said Eudora, nodding in his direction. 'You off to your shipyard?'

'Indeed. The devil finds work for idle hands, Mrs Bennett, so I like to keep busy.' He raised his hat, smiled at Tilly, and then walked away.

She could feel the warmth in her cheeks and was aware of Eudora's speculative gaze. 'A very attractive man,' murmured the older woman. 'But do remember what I said, dear. Now come along.'

Tilly fell into step beside her, hoping she would not give her another warning about the dangers of attractive men. She need not have worried because the rest of the day was to provide them both with more important matters to consider than Tilly's attraction to Eudora's handsome neighbour. Tilly was suitably shocked by some of the homes they visited and she realised just how fortunate she was, herself.

The poorest of all the families they visited were the Doyles. Mrs Doyle had four girls and three boys. She was dressed in what appeared to be several layers of clothes that had seen better days. Her breath smelt and she was missing a number of teeth. Tilly could only guess at her age and thought it likely that she was younger than she looked. No fire burnt in the kitchen grate and only one torn curtain was nailed over the window, where a sheet of cardboard had replaced a broken pane of glass. Tilly could feel the draught coming through it and could imagine how cold the room would be in winter if the pane was not replaced. She made a note of it.

The eldest child was Patricia, who was ten years old and as skinny as a rake with lank brown hair and fierce, rebellious grey eyes. Tilly knew that she should have been at school with the other three children of school age – Micky, Jimmy and Kathleen – but according to her mother she couldn't manage without her and that was why she was at home, helping to take care of the three children under school age. The girl had the baby, Anthony, wrapped inside the thin shawl she wore and it whimpered in its sleep.

Tilly was desperate to help this family, so it came as quite a surprise when they left without handing over even a few pennies and offered no promise of help. 'Why didn't you give them just a few coppers?' she burst out. 'You could see the family were in dire straits.'

'Yes, Tilly, I could,' replied Eudora calmly. 'But you mustn't allow yourself to become emotionally involved or you'll be no use to me at all. Your job is to write down their names and ages and most urgent needs. To give that mother even a few coppers would have been a mistake. She drinks, dear. Couldn't you smell the gin on her breath? Obviously she's getting money from somewhere. Perhaps she gets the children to steal or maybe she sells her body for it.'

Tilly gasped. 'Her body! You mean she—?'

'Yes!'

'I can't believe any man would want her,' said Tilly frankly.

'To be crude, my dear, even now when women outnumber

men, there are still men who have to pay to go with a woman and any port looks the same in the dark.'

Tilly was shocked into silence.

'I fear for the children, especially the eldest and the youngest.'

Tilly found her voice. 'I can understand your fear that the baby might die but why Patricia?' Eudora did not answer and Tilly continued, 'Do you think the children would be better in the orphanage?'

'There are only so many places in the orphanage, Tilly,' said Eudora. 'With help they can survive and Patricia is the one with whom we will liase. You must befriend her. She might only be a child, herself, but I'm sure she has a sense of responsibility towards the other children. No doubt she is still grieving for her father and is angry with life but she will also be scared of losing what remains of her family.'

'So what do we do?'

'If you're willing you can return here later today. You can take warm clothing for the baby and other children, as well as milk and food. They'll also need wood and coal for the fire. I'll see that the latter is delivered.'

'Where will I get the rest from?'

'We have a second hand clothing and dried and tinned goods depot. Milk and bread you'll have to buy fresh. I'll give you money for them.'

'How will I carry all this?'

Eudora smiled. 'A second-hand perambulator should do the job. We have one of those, too. You'll not stand out pushing that through the streets in this area. And let's hope that the mother doesn't pawn the clothing and blankets for gin.'

'You really think she would do that?'

'When the craving is on them, some women would sell their

own children,' said Eudora, with a hint of sadness in her face. 'I don't think Mrs Doyle is that far gone yet. Often it's living without hope that turns them to drink, so we need to encourage her to believe there's something for her to look forward to.'

Tilly thought how it was hope that had kept Alice sane when the news had come that Seb was missing during the war and she wanted to give this family hope.

Tilly's heart was beating heavily as she waited for someone to answer the door. It had taken her much longer than she had imagined to gather everything together, place it in the pram and wheel it there.

'Who is it?' shrilled a voice.

'It's Tilly Moran from the Seamen's Friends. I was here earlier with Mrs Bennett.'

Bolts were drawn back and the door opened to reveal Patricia standing there with the baby balanced on her narrow hip. 'What is it yer want?'

'I've clothes, blankets, food and stuff for your family,' said Tilly in a low voice.

The girl's face went blank with surprise and then she gazed down at the pram and smiled. 'In there?' she asked, a lilt in her voice.

Tilly smiled. 'Yes.'

'Yer'd best bring it in but yer can't stay,' whispered Patricia.

'I don't want to stay,' said Tilly frankly. 'I'm late and I've other things to do, so if you could get out the way?'

The girl moved aside, hushing the baby when it whimpered.

'What's goin' on?' asked a child's voice out of the gloom.

'Mind yer business, Kathleen,' Patricia hissed, 'and stay where you are.'

Tilly heaved the pram into the front room, feeling the pull in the muscles of her back and neck. She was breathing heavily by the time she had wheeled it further into the dimly lit room. 'Hasn't the wood and coal arrived yet?' she asked.

'No! Nuthin's come and Mam's got a-a visitor, erm...' Her voice trailed off.

'Mrs Bennett said she would see to it, so you can be sure it'll come soon. Do you want me to hold the baby while you unpack everything?'

She sensed the girl hesitate. 'No. The kids'll help me. Yous can go.'

'Fine.' Tilly made for the front door but then hesitated. 'Have you no lighting in here?'

'We ain't got gas. I've a stub of candle in the kitchen.'

Tilly made a decision, and despite Eudora having told her they would be visiting some other families known to her tomorrow, she said, 'I'll bring you some tomorrow.'

'No! If the coal and wood comes we'll have light.' Patricia touched her arm. 'Please, go.'

'What about matches and newspaper?' Tilly dipped a hand in her pocket and produced a thrupenny bit. 'Here, use this to buy them.'

Patricia seized the money. 'Thanks! Tarrah.'

Tilly closed the door behind her, wondering about Mrs Doyle's visitor. Was it a man? If so, then possibly Eudora Bennett was right. Poor kids! What influence was their mother's behaviour having on them? Tilly shook the thought away. Right now, she could not wait to get back to the Wrights' and have something to eat, wash herself all over and fall into bed.

* * *

Tilly had been home for about half an hour when Grant entered the shop. Wendy was serving a customer, so he had to wait until she had finished before approaching her. Wendy's heart began to race.

'Hello, Grant, this isn't your usual time to call. What can I do for you?'

'Hello, Wendy. I wondered if Tilly was around.'

Wendy was about to say that she was upstairs but changed her mind. 'What do you want her for?'

'To offer her a part-time job,' he replied. 'I only found out this morning that she's lost her last job, so I've decided that I need a secretary. Someone to be in the office when I'm out on a case, to tidy up my files, type my letters and invoices and answer the telephone.'

Wendy could have spat nails but all she said was, 'You have a telephone?'

'A new acquisition.' He smiled. 'I came to the conclusion that it's essential for my work.'

Wendy did not want Tilly to work for him. 'Oh, what a shame! Tilly has already found another job. She's working for my Aunt Eudora.'

Grant's face fell. 'Oh! That's a bit of a blow.'

'I'm sure it is but I'm afraid that's life,' said Wendy sympathetically. 'Are you on a case now?'

'I just turned one down.'

'Why?' Wendy thought he must have money if he could turn jobs down.

'It's a missing doggy case and I have my suspicions about what's happened to the poor beast because of what happened to the last one that went missing. You remember Bruce?'

'You mean the one that we put up a poster about in the window?'

He nodded. 'There's quite a bit of meat on even a small dog and what with so many hungry people about—' He stopped abruptly.

Wendy stared at him and gulped. 'You mean someone ki-killed poor Bruce and served him up for dinner?'

'Damn! I didn't mean to tell you that and I've upset you now. Sorry.' He reached out and squeezed her hand.

'But how-how can you be so sure?' Wendy wanted him to go on holding her hand and her fingers curled about his but he did not appear to notice.

'When I was in the police force during the war there was a period when dogs and cats went missing, so we raided this particular restaurant and it was as we suspected – they'd been serving them up to their customers.'

Wendy gasped. 'I know meat was scarce during the war but to take someone's pet.' She shook her head sadly. 'How did you find out?'

'Dog collars and tags in the bins. You think people would be more careful about disposing of the evidence, wouldn't you? Anyway, I'm sure that time will prove that's what's happened to this little doggy and I don't want to have to tell the owner.'

'I can understand your feelings,' said Wendy in heartfelt tones. 'Do you have any other cases?'

'A couple have come in and I've insurance investigation work to keep me busy, as well.' He brought his head closer to hers and whispered. 'You'd be surprised at how dishonest some people can be, Wendy. They think nothing of telling a string of lies to cheat the insurance companies.'

'People,' she said on a note of disgust. 'So what are you

going to do about a secretary? I wish I could help you. I can type a little and I do have some spare time. I'm sure I could get used to answering the telephone when you're out of the office and when you're in I could make you tea.'

His face softened and he touched her cheek with a finger. 'I appreciate the offer, Wendy, but I've a feeling your mother wouldn't like the idea.'

'I know you're right but,' Wendy stopped and the corners of her mouth drooped. 'It would have been something different to do.' Her cheek seemed to tingle where he had touched it.

'Don't you like working here?' He sounded surprised.

'It's all right. I know I should count my blessings.'

'That's the ticket,' he said, smiling. 'Give Tilly my regards and tell her I hope to see her soon.'

'Of course, I will,' said Wendy, having no intention of doing anything of the sort. 'See you tomorrow?'

'All being well,' he said, leaving the shop without buying anything.

Wendy salved her conscience by telling herself that despite Tilly's job with Eudora being only part time, she needed time to do her writing. It was likely that if Tilly knew Grant needed a part-time secretary, she would accept the position. Thrown together in each other's company they might fall in love and where would that leave Wendy's hopes and dreams? She had done the sensible thing and what Tilly did not know would not harm her.

'Good morning, Miss Moran!' Leonard Parker tipped his hat. 'You here again?'

'Yes,' said Tilly, thankful that she no longer blushed when he spoke to her. It was over a month since she had started working for Eudora and it had been an extremely busy time. 'You off to your office?'

'Not today. I've other business to see to and it can't wait. How are the widows and orphans? Better for your having visited them, I'm sure.'

'I hope so. Some are really, really poor. I had no idea of the suffering some families go through and I'm glad to be of help to them.'

His eyes sharpened. 'Don't get yourself too involved, Miss Moran. You might end up suffering for it yourself. Some of these women would diddle you out of your last penny.'

'Diddle?' asked Tilly.

'Trick you.'

Tilly looked surprised. 'I don't know how you'd know that. Surely you wouldn't come across such women in the circles you move in?'

'Certainly not in my social life or the shipyard but I do have my fingers in other pies.' He smiled. 'I hope you have a nice day, Miss Moran.'

'I hope the same for you,' she said, wondering what other businesses he had.

As Tilly walked up the path to the Bennetts' house she had no idea what her day would hold and that was what made the job interesting. Fortunately the money Mr Holmes had promised her had arrived in the post and so her need to earn more was not overwhelming. But sooner or later she would have to find another job. She worked three days a week and she had visited the Doyles several times. Patricia kept her standing outside on the step but she was obviously grateful for the help the family received. Tilly was convinced that Patricia still stayed away from school and had told Eudora about her suspicions.

'It is worrying but unless we report Mrs Doyle to the school board, there is little we can do,' she had said.

'Shouldn't we do that?'

'You'd lose the girl's trust and it's important that we keep that if we're to help the family,' said Eudora. 'It would be best if the mother could find a job.'

Tilly wondered what kind of job Mrs Doyle could do. She had recently read about a training scheme for war widows, organised by the Government, and had mentioned that to Eudora, as well.

'A good idea, Tilly, but I doubt Mrs Doyle is the kind of widow that the training scheme would help,' she had said. 'The woman just hasn't got the right kind of brain.'

Tilly felt certain that Patricia had a good brain but without education how could she use it to her advantage? She was frustrated, wishing she could do more to help her. Eudora reminded her several times that the Doyles were not the only family in need. They had visited various other families and Tilly had typed up reports. She had also visited the charity's office and several times she had called in at the depot where donated clothing, bedding and food were stored. On one occasion she was given the task of helping sort out newly donated garments into women's and children's and taken them to the laundry.

Tilly entered the kitchen to find not only Joy there but Eudora, Robbie and her father. Mal was looking the worse for wear and he had a sleeve rolled up, exposing a swollen elbow painted with iodine.

'What's happened?' she asked, placing a hand on her father's shoulder.

'We've had a burglary,' said Eudora.

'When did it happen?'

'Just before dawn. If it hadn't been for Nanki Poo and your father we might have been killed in our beds. As it is poor Nanki Poo is dead.' Her voice trembled. 'Your father tackled the man but he managed to get away.'

'That's terrible!' Tilly sank onto the chair next to her father. 'Are you all right, Dad?'

'I wish I could have held onto him but he was a wiry bugger and managed to slip out of my grasp,' he muttered. 'Damn fella kicked my legs from under me and I fell.'

'You did your best, Mal,' said Robbie gruffly, his shoulders slumped and his face a picture of misery. 'I just hope the police have some information on the swine.'

'You've sent for the police?' said Tilly.

Robbie nodded. 'They shouldn't be too long coming.'

'Don't want to talk to the police,' mumbled Mal. 'They might think I lied and suspect me.'

'How can they, Dad, when you've been injured?' said Tilly, covering one of his work-worn hands with hers. 'You're worrying unnecessarily. Besides, we all know you'd never hurt Nanki Poo.'

'Of course, he wouldn't,' said Eudora. 'And he'd never steal from us either.'

'Did the burglar get away with much?' asked Tilly.

'As far as we can see he's taken a couple of ornaments I brought back from my journey to the Orient. They're irreplaceable,' said Eudora sadly.

'Just the same as Nanki Poo,' said Robbie, a suspicious dampness in his eyes.

'Is there anything I can do?' asked Tilly, feeling deeply sorry for them.

'No, dear,' said Eudora, toying with the bracelet on her wrist. 'Best you go home. We won't be doing any visiting today.'

Tilly nodded. 'What about tomorrow?'

'Maybe. Call round, anyway, and I'll make up my mind then.'

'I'll leave you to it then if there's nothing I can do. I don't want to be in the way.' Tilly kissed her father's cheek. 'I'll pop in and see you tomorrow, Dad.'

'Thanks, girl!' He patted her hand.

Tilly said her goodbyes to the others and left the house. On her way back to the shop, she could not help wondering whether Eudora would give her another day's work to make up for not working today. If not then she was going to be a day short in her wages. She sighed but told herself there were plenty worse off than herself and she was not going to waste her day mooning around and worrying about things. She would try and finish that pirate story she had begun.

As she entered the shop, a familiar voice said, 'Tilly!'

'Hello, Grant,' she said, smiling.

'I didn't expect to see you here at this time of day,' he said, grinning at her. 'Wendy said you were working for Mrs Bennett.'

Tilly glanced at Wendy and wondered if it was her imagination that she did not look pleased to see her. 'I only work part time and I should have been working today, but there's been a break-in at the Bennetts' house and I was told to go home. It was a bit of a blow all round. The burglar killed poor Nanki Poo and Dad was injured trying to prevent him from escaping.'

'Did he get away with anything?' asked Wendy.

'Some irreplaceable valuables that Mrs Bennett brought back from the Orient,' replied Tilly. 'They've sent for the police. Dad's not looking forward to being questioned by them.'

'No one likes being questioned by the police but I'm sure he'll be fine,' assured Grant. 'But tell me, did I really hear you say that you only work part time?'

'Yes, that's right.'

Grant smiled. 'Would you like another part-time job, putting in a few hours at my office a few days a week?'

Tilly's face lit up. 'Do you really mean that?'

'Of course I do! Otherwise, I wouldn't have said it.' He glanced at Wendy. 'I thought you might have mentioned the job to Tilly.'

'No. I forgot and she's been so busy.'

'Not too busy to put in a few hours for the great detective,' said Tilly, darting Grant a teasing look. 'I could do two and half days for you if that would suit?' she added.

'It suits me fine,' he said, delighted. 'Perhaps you'd like to accompany me to the office now?'

'Of course I will.' Tilly glanced at Wendy. 'Will you tell your mam about the break-in? She might want to go and visit them.'

'Yes, OK,' answered Wendy. 'Poor Nanki Poo. I liked that dog.'

'Me too,' said Tilly. 'Your Uncle Robbie is really upset. I'll see you later.'

She left the shop with Grant. 'Where is your office?' she asked him as they stood on the pavement waiting to cross the road to the tram stop.

'Fenwick Street, near the Corn Exchange,' he answered. 'Do you know the area at all?'

'Can't say I do,' she answered.

'It's within walking distance of the Pierhead.' He took her elbow as a tram going in the opposite direction rattled by. They crossed the road, avoiding a cyclist and horse and cart. 'Now it's spring and will soon be summer it'll be pleasant walking down to the Mersey and watching the ships coming and going while you eat your lunchtime sandwiches.'

'That does sound nice,' said Tilly. 'But what's it like in winter?'

He grimaced. 'You can stay in the office because there's a hell of a wind that blows up from the river. It'd chill your blood.'

Tilly smiled. 'It can be really cold living by the Dee in winter.'

'That's where your sister's house is?'

'Yes. A mist rises off the water and it can be really scary when it's just getting dark,' she said softly. 'Then when the sun starts to rise and shafts of sunlight shine through the mist, it looks really beautiful.'

'You sound quite poetical,' said Grant. 'Do you miss it?'

'Sometimes,' she said. 'But I bet the Mersey can look just as good when the sun's dancing on the water.'

Grant laughed. 'The colour of the Mersey doesn't lend itself to poetry. It's khaki or mud coloured and it's almost the same with the Leeds-Liverpool canal where it passes through the city.'

His mention of the Leeds-Liverpool canal reminded her of the woman who had drowned there in the fog last autumn. 'Any more news of your pawnbroker?'

Grant hesitated.

'You don't have to tell me.'

'If you're going to be working for me then perhaps I can,' he decided. 'The police are putting it down as an accident because they have no proof of it being otherwise. But interestingly, someone has been in touch with her solicitor with the information that when the poor woman was young, she gave birth to an illegitimate son.'

'Gosh!' Tilly stared at him. 'What happened to him?'

The woman doesn't know but thought that she should come forward with the information. I think she was hoping that there would be a reward.'

'And was there?'

'I think she was given something for her efforts.'

'So will they be able to trace him?' asked Tilly. 'And what about the father?'

Grant shrugged. 'Who knows? The baby was registered but under the pawnbroker's maiden name and the father's name was left blank.' He paused. 'Here comes the tram.'

CHAPTER FIFTEEN

Tilly led the way to a front seat upstairs and sat down, wondering if he would continue with that conversation, but he didn't, saying, 'I enjoy sitting here,' as he sat next to her and gazed down at the road ahead. 'I pretend I'm the driver.'

Tilly smiled. 'I like watching people. I find them interesting.'

'That's one of the reasons I enjoy being a detective.'

'Are you on a case now?'

He nodded. 'The result of which I hope means the couple stay together. The husband suspects his wife of seeing another man while he's at work, so he's hired me to keep an eye on her.'

'It can't be an easy task.'

'I don't enjoy following women around but it's part of the job.'

'I suppose it's the only way you'll get to know if she's innocent,' said Tilly.

'I don't think he wants to divorce her but one of the neighbours has filled his head with doubts and the uncertainty is torturing him.'

'Why doesn't he just ask his wife point blank if she's seeing another man?' asked Tilly.

'Life is never that simple in the so called grown-up world, Tilly.' He grinned. 'My client has told me that his wife would be terribly hurt if she knew he didn't trust her.'

Tilly smiled. 'Is his wife a bit of a femme fatale?'

'No. That's what I find surprising,' said Grant. 'She's nothing to write home about.'

'Then she must have hidden depths if he cares so much for her,' said Tilly. 'Will you want me to type up your notes on the case?'

'Of course! And tidy up my files. They're in a bit of a mess.'

'I presume you do have a typewriter?'

He nodded. 'It's not the latest model but I'm sure you'll have no trouble with it. I've been using four fingers but it takes me ages just to type out the simplest letter.'

Tilly thought it was a change having a man confess to not being the best at something.

They left the tram near the Victoria monument, and walked past the bank on the corner into Fenwick Street. The sun had come out and Tilly was wondering how her father was getting on with the police and if they had any idea of who the burglar might be. Hopefully she would find out more when she called at the house tomorrow.

Grant stopped outside a door next to a philatelist shop. On the wall next to it was a wooden plaque with the words *Grant Simpson, Private Detective* painted on it in black. An arrow pointed upstairs and he unlocked the door and led the way up a narrow flight of stairs.

Tilly was pleased when she saw the size of the office but thought it would need a decent heater in the winter. The sunshine coming through the window showed up the dust and also that the glass needed cleaning. Grant switched on a small paraffin heater near a large desk, on which stood a telephone, an ink blotter and an ink stand with pen. There was also a smaller desk on which stood the typewriter he had mentioned, as well as a filing cabinet and a couple of spare chairs. She presumed these were for the clients.

'There's a tiny kitchen where you can make tea,' he said, leading the way to a door that led off the office.

She followed him and discovered that the kitchen really was tiny but there was a sink, as well as gas ring with a kettle on it and a ledge containing cups and saucers below a cupboard on the wall.

'Would you like me to make tea?' she asked.

'If you would. There should still be some milk from yesterday, hopefully, it won't have gone off.' He reached up and opened the cupboard and produced milk, tea and sugar, as well as a packet of biscuits and a box of matches.

She put the kettle on.

'There's also a lavatory,' said Grant. 'I'll show you while the kettle is heating up.' He took her along a corridor.

Tilly was glad about the lavatory being so handy but she suspected he did not have a cleaner. She put the question to him when making the tea.

He shook his head. 'I can't afford one.' He paused. 'You couldn't?'

'What?' asked Tilly.

'Give the office a bit of a clean? I'm sure it won't take you long.'

Tilly almost asked him what job exactly was he was hiring her for? A secretary or a cleaner? But she was so grateful to have this second job that she did not voice the question.

'I'll pay you for your time,' he said hastily, as if reading her mind.

'Do you have polish, dusters, a brush, a mop and disinfectant?'

He opened a drawer in his desk and produced a dirty rag. 'I've been making do with this.'

'Mr Simpson, you ought to be ashamed of yourself!' With a disdainful look, she took the rag from him with the tips of her fingers and dropped it in the wastepaper bin. 'If you want to increase your clientele then we're going to have to improve the look of this place. I presume you have a petty cash box?'

A smile lurked about the corners of his mouth as he opened another drawer and took out a tin. He flicked open the lid and emptied out a pile of copper. 'That's it,' he said.

She took all of the coins. 'I'll visit a chandler's on the way home and the next time I come in here, this place won't know what's hit it.'

'That's the ticket.' His smile widened. 'I'll show you the files now.'

He opened a drawer in the filing cabinet and removed a couple of pieces of cardboard. A piece of string held them together. She removed it and out fell sheets of handwritten notes. Tilly raised her eyebrows and bent to pick them up at the same time as he did. They banged heads. 'Sorry,' she said.

'You OK?' he asked, taking hold of her arm and bringing her to her feet. Their bodies brushed against each other and she stepped back swiftly, avoiding his gaze. He picked up the notes and placed them on the smaller desk. 'You'd best sit down.'

Tilly sat at the desk and rifled through the sheets of paper, pausing when she came across the name of the insurance company that had employed her.

'How is Miss Langton?' she asked, glancing up at him.

'She's been arrested for buying opium.'

'Opium!' Tilly's voice rose to a squeak. 'Where did she get opium from?'

'She's not saying but she bought it for her mother, who apparently is in terrible pain with arthritis,' he murmured. 'Of course, she might have bought it from a Chinaman in Pitt Street. When I was in the police force we raided an opium den in Chinatown,' said Grant, going over to the window and looking out. 'I can tell you there was more going on there than opium smoking. It was a real den of iniquity.'

'But what will happen to her and her mother?' asked Tilly, shocked and concerned.

'Mr Holmes is dealing with it. He's got a solicitor to represent Miss Langton.'

'Will she get the sack? If she does, then he's going to need someone to fill her position.'

'He's had to dismiss her and has already got someone from head office,' said Grant, coming back over to her desk. 'Why? You weren't thinking of applying for her job?'

'No! I do feel sorry for her, though. Miss Langton and all the other women who desperately need help to cope with their lives.' Tilly thought about Mrs Doyle and her gin drinking, which led to neglect of her children. Women who had no man to support them. Miss Langton was fortunate in that she had Mr Holmes as a family friend, and a forgiving one at that!

'People can't break the law and get away with it, Tilly. They have to be taught a lesson,' he said gently.

'So she might have to serve a prison sentence,' murmured Tilly.

'Not necessarily. The court can show leniency. She could just get a fine.'

'But can she afford to pay the fine? Or will Mr Holmes—?'

Grant shrugged. 'It's not your problem, Tilly.'

'I'd like to know what happens to her. You're sure to find out. Will you let me know?'

He nodded and she thanked him before inspecting the typewriter more closely. She was about to ask him another question when the telephone rang. He picked it up and turned his back on her. She placed a sheet of paper in the typewriter and typed *The quick brown fox jumped over the lazy dog.* The keys were a little stiff but that was probably due more to a lack of proper use than the machine needing a drop of oil. She had noticed that dust clung to the base of the keys. She reached into the wastepaper bin for the dirty rag that Grant had taken out and carefully wiped away the dust. She was aware of the murmur of his voice as he spoke on the telephone but could not hear what he was saying properly because he spoke quietly. She picked up the first handwritten sheet of paper and placed it at the side of the typewriter and then placed a clean sheet in the machine and began to copy the handwritten one.

She had typed several pages of notes before Grant replaced the mouthpiece and turned to her. 'I have to go out, Tilly.'

'Yes, Mr Simpson.'

He smiled. 'Perhaps we shouldn't be on first name terms during office hours.'

Tilly nodded. 'That's what I thought. Until what time d'you expect me to stay here?' she asked.

'I hope to be back by five but if I'm not, just lock this door.' He held out a Yale key to her. 'And take the bottom door off the latch and close it behind you. I'll pick up the key at the shop tomorrow.'

'I probably won't be able to work for you in the morning,' said Tilly, taking the key from him. 'I have to call in at the Bennetts' and see if I'm needed.'

He looked disappointed but only said, 'Fair enough. But I'll want you on Thursday.'

She cleared her throat. 'How much will you pay me?'

'I'll match at least what Mrs Bennett pays you and if I find other work for you then I'll pay you extra, as well as expenses.'

She wondered what other work he was referring to, but did not ask because he was already on his way to the door. 'See you later, I hope, Tilly.'

'I hope you have a successful afternoon.'

He gave a twisted smile and closed the door behind him.

Tilly waited a few moments before rising from her chair and going over to the window. She could hear the sound of traffic in Lord Street and the voices of businessmen wafted up to her from below. She saw Grant appear and wondered where he was going. One thing was for sure: she would get to know sooner or later because she would be typing up his report. Right now she would get on with what was on her desk and then she would slip out the office and buy some cleaning materials and give the place a good going over before she left that evening.

Grant did not reappear that day and so Tilly locked up the office and left. Its windows now had a sparkle to them and all the surfaces were dust free, the toilet was shining clean and smelt intoxicatingly of pine disinfectant. She felt that she had done a good day's work and hoped she would be paid accordingly.

When Tilly arrived back at the shop Mrs Wright was holding the fort. She told Tilly that the police had been to the Bennetts' house and the upshot was that they had hopes of catching the burglar.

'Did they say how?' asked Tilly, picking up that night's *Echo* and placing a penny on the counter.

'No idea,' said Mrs Wright, putting the penny in the till.

'How was Dad?'

'I didn't see him. He was burying the dog.'

'In the garden?'

'Where else? Eudora was overseeing the burial. My brother said that he'd rather not watch. He was very fond of that dog.'

Tilly thought, so were the others. By the sound of it the ground was now soft enough to dig holes. She was reminded of what her father had said about a body and wondered if he would start digging holes again. Perhaps she should talk to him about that tomorrow.

She went upstairs and found her bedroom door open. The tap-tap of her typewriter could be heard. Suddenly the noise stopped and she heard a muffled 'Bloody hell!' and then the sound of a drawer being opened.

Tilly walked into the room. 'What are you doing?'

Wendy jumped and dropped the photographs.

Tilly bent and picked them up. 'I'd rather you didn't go nosing in my drawers,' she said stiffly.

'I'm sorry. I was looking for a rubber.' Wendy's expression was defiant. She nodded at the photographs. 'Who is he?'

Tilly looked down at the picture of Don. 'He's none of your

business. But if you must know he's the American who saved my brother-in-law's life.'

'So why is it you have his photograph?'

'You really are nosy,' said Tilly, a glint in her eye.

'He looks older than Grant Simpson.'

'He's twenty-seven and I'll be eighteen in July.'

'Do you like him?'

'Of course I like Don! He's on the side of the angels. He cares about people,' said Tilly, glancing down at his image. He seemed to be gazing straight into her eyes and it gave her a strange feeling. Tears welled up and she brushed them away with the back of her hand. She so missed his letters and he felt so distant from her. 'Could you go now, Wendy, I want to get changed.'

Wendy nodded and moved away from the desk, only to pause in the doorway. 'So how did it go at Grant's office?'

'Fine. Why didn't you tell me about his offer of a job?'

Wendy hesitated before saying, 'I didn't see the point with you working for Aunt Eudora's charity.'

Tilly wondered if that was the real reason but decided not to press the point. 'OK. See you later.' She waited until the other girl had left before glancing at the paper Wendy had practised on. Not bad,' thought Tilly, before scrunching it up and placing it in the bin. But would typing skills help Wendy to get what she wanted?

As Tilly changed into a clean skirt and blouse, she thought of Don and wondered why she had placed his photograph away in a drawer, feeling the way she did about him. Surely it had nothing to do with the guilty attraction she felt for Leonard Parker? As she had said to Wendy, Don was on the side of the angels. She felt somehow that was not true about

Leonard, with his talk of pirates and making the strikers walk the plank. Yet he was so good-looking he caused her pulse to race – a dangerous sensation in the light of Eudora's warning. She would be far better holding Don close in her thoughts. She opened the drawer and removed the photograph of that happy day at her sister's home and gazed at Don's smiling face and her own. Lest we forget, she thought, before wondering what tomorrow would bring.

By the time Tilly was ready to call in on Eudora, Grant had still not arrived at the shop, so she left the key with Wendy to give to him. 'Tell him I'll be at the office at nine o'clock tomorrow morning.'

'OK! You can trust me,' said Wendy.

Tilly hoped so. As she walked to Newsham Drive on what was a lovely spring morning, she decided that if the weather remained fair she would visit her family in Chester the coming weekend. She had still not heard anything about Freddie and Clara's son's christening and hoped they had not forgotten about her. If Joy did not get a chance to telephone Kenny at the yard, then she, herself, would do so.

She hoped the Bennetts were feeling better this morning after the shock of yesterday. They were not getting any younger and this sort of shock wasn't good for people of their age.

But Tilly need not have worried. When she arrived at the house it was to discover that both Bennetts were already out and about. 'But I thought I'd be working today,' she said, dismayed. 'Did Mrs Bennett say when next she'd need me? I can't come tomorrow as I've another part-time job now, working for Mr Simpson.'

'Ahhh! The great detective,' said Joy, smiling. 'She didn't

actually say. Probably because she has a lot on her mind. I know today she and Mr Bennett are seeing their solicitor.'

'Perhaps I'll come back this evening and see if she wants me on Friday. There's something I need to ask her about Mrs Doyle.'

'You do that. I'm sure she won't mind,' said Joy, taking the vacuum cleaner from a walk-in cupboard. 'So what are you going to do now? Visit your dad?'

'Yes. I want to see how he is.'

'He's a bit edgy, if you want my opinion,' said Joy.

That isn't surprising, thought Tilly, leaving the kitchen. She had not gone far down the garden when her father suddenly appeared from behind a bush; his boot narrowly avoided a clump of daffodils. He was clutching a shovel and she thought he looked nervous and excited.

'What are you doing there, Dad? Surely you're not digging holes again?'

'I've found it,' he said in a husky voice. 'I've found the body.'

Tilly's stomach flipped over. This definitely wasn't the spot where they had buried the baby skeleton. 'What body?'

Mal grabbed her sleeve and urged her to come with him. Reluctantly, she allowed him to lead her to a place that he had cleared last autumn. It was close to the dividing wall between this garden and that of Leonard Parker's. There was a mound of soil and what appeared to be a trench. Suddenly she did not want to go closer as there was a smell emanating from it that caused her to gag. Oh, dear God, she thought. Had her father really found another body? She swallowed bile.

'What kind of body is it, Dad?' she croaked.

'A man's! I want yer to look so yer know I'm not lying.

Then we'll bury it again like we did the baby,' he said.

Tilly did not want to do this. Why couldn't he have told Joy about it or the Bennetts?

'Come on, lass,' he said, urging her forward. 'Just a quick peep and then we'll bury it again and yer can say a prayer.'

Reluctantly, she looked down into the trench. There was a body there all right. It was naked and in an advanced state of decomposition. She backed away and threw up behind a bush.

'Are ye all right, lass?' Mal sounded anxious as he patted her shoulder.

'No, I'm not all right,' she said hoarsely.

'I'll bury it again.'

'No!' cried Tilly, wiping her mouth with the back of her hand. 'This isn't the same as the baby's skeleton, Dad. What's a grown man's body doing here? He must have been murdered.' She took several deep breaths before making for the house. She glanced behind her to see what her father was doing and caught sight of a face peering over the wall. The woman bobbed down as soon as she realised she had been seen.

'Come on, Dad!' called Tilly. 'We're going to have to report this to the police. It's a pity you couldn't have told them about it yesterday.'

Mal hurried towards her. 'They might think I killed him,' he whispered. 'I hit a policeman once and they locked me away.'

Tilly tried to remember if Alice or Kenny had ever told her about this but her brain did not seem to be functioning properly. 'You have to tell them, Dad. Anyway, that would have been in Chester when you were ill.'

She linked her arm through his and hurried him towards the house. As soon as they entered the kitchen they could hear the sound of the vacuum cleaner. 'You stay here, Dad. I'll go and find Joy.'

Looking extremely unhappy, he shook his head. 'I'll come with yer, lass.'

'OK!'

They found Joy vacuuming the dining room carpet. She had her back to them so Tilly did not waste time calling to her but went over and touched her shoulder. Joy turned. 'Switch it off,' mouthed Tilly.

Joy did so. 'What is it?' she asked, then frowned as she stared at Mal. 'What's he doing in here in his muddy boots? And you, Tilly, your shoes—'

'Dad's found a body.'

Joy looked startled. 'What!'

'Someone has buried a man's body in the garden,' said Tilly.

Joy swallowed. 'You're not joking.'

'Would I joke about such a thing?' cried Tilly, and sat down suddenly on the nearest chair.

'They might think I did it and I didn't,' said Mal in a trembling voice. 'I'm going to bury it again.'

'Don't be daft, Dad!' Tilly's voice was fierce. 'I should imagine that body's been there for a while.'

'I'm going to have a look,' said Joy firmly.

'Take a hanky with you,' advised Tilly.

Joy looked at her and nodded. 'Do something, love. Put the kettle on and perhaps we could all do with a drop of Mr Bennett's brandy.' She hurried out.

'Wait!' called Tilly, getting up and following her. 'You don't know where the body is.' She turned to Mal. 'Dad, show her!'

Joy paused and popped her head through the doorway and stared at Mal. 'Come on, then,' she said. 'I haven't got all day.'

He followed her while Tilly put the kettle on. Then she decided to see how Joy was coping and went outside. She saw her father shambling down the garden to his living quarters. She called to him but he ignored her. Joy appeared from out of the bushes with a handkerchief pressed to her mouth. Without speaking she hurried up the garden towards Tilly, shooing her inside. They both sat down at the kitchen table and neither spoke for several minutes. Then Tilly realised the kettle was boiling so she got up and made tea.

It was not until they had both had a drink that Joy said, 'Did you notice the cheekbones were smashed.'

'No! Are you going to telephone the police?'

'I should really get in touch with the Bennetts first but as I haven't a phone number and it could be hours before they get back, I suppose I better had.' She got up and left the room.

Tilly was about to follow her to listen in on what she said when she remembered her father. She made another cup of tea and put three spoonfuls of sugar in it and took it down the garden. He must have seen her coming because he came out and stood waiting for her.

He gulped down the tea before asking, 'What's Joy doing?'

'Telephoning the police. It has to be done, Dad. There's nothing for you to worry about. Why don't you come back to the house? I don't like you being here on your own.'

'Yer think the murderer will come back?'

'I haven't even thought of that but why should he? He doesn't know you found the body,' said Tilly.

'It might have been a woman who murdered him,' said Mal. 'Women can be strong. Mother was and used to frighten the life out of me when she got into one of her tantrums.'

'Perhaps it was the woman who lived in the house before the Bennetts,' suggested Tilly. 'The one who buried the baby. He could be the father and years later returned, thinking to take up with her again. She was angry and they quarrelled and she hit him with a shovel. Maybe she didn't mean to kill him but was scared to own up to the crime.'

Mal stared at her, goggle-eyed. 'Ye haven't half got some imagination, lass. Shall we go and see whether Joy's finished telephoning the police and see what they said?'

Tilly sighed. 'OK!'

They went inside the house and found Joy in the kitchen, opening a bottle of brandy. 'I thought we could all do with a tot,' she said.

'Won't Mr Bennett mind?' asked Tilly.

Joy shook her head. 'He's a very understanding and generous man. If he was here he'd be pouring it out for us.'

Tilly made no mention of being under age and not used to spirits but accepted the small glass. 'Dad and I were trying to think who could possibly be the murderer. He thought it might be a woman and so I thought, in that case, it could have been the old spinster who lived here.'

'Don't you start trying to solve this mystery,' said Joy sternly. 'Just because you're working for that private detective you mustn't get carried away. Leave this to the police.'

'I can't help thinking about it,' said Tilly, sipping the brandy cautiously. 'You must be curious about who could have done such a thing?'

'I don't want to think about it,' said Joy firmly. 'I just want the police to come with an ambulance and for them to take the body away and that's the end of it. Let them do their policing somewhere else.'

'They're bound to want to inspect the grounds and ask us questions,' said Tilly.

'Not for long,' said Joy, sitting down by the fire. 'They'll soon go away when they realise it's been there since before we moved here. That part of the garden was real wilderness, if you remember. If it hadn't been for your dad clearing the area and digging it over today.'

'He didn't find it today,' said Tilly. 'He mentioned it to me ages ago and I thought he was talking about the baby's skeleton.'

'I remember you mentioning that to me,' said Joy, 'but it had slipped my mind. I don't know what Mr and Mrs Bennett are going to say.'

They were to find out much later but not before the police arrived in the form of Sergeant Jones. Tilly immediately recognised him as the policeman involved in the case of the wig thief, who had been none other than Bert Kirk. Due to her family's involvement and a shared interest in singing, the sergeant had become friendly with Seb's mother, Gabrielle.

'Sergeant Jones! I forgot you lived not far from here,' said Tilly.

'Miss Moran!' He smiled at her. 'I did hear that you'd come to live this side of the Mersey but I never expected to find you involved in the discovery of a body,' he said, shaking her hand.

'It's Dad who found the body,' said Tilly.

'And it must have been there for some time,' interposed Joy.

Sergeant Jones stared at Mal and said gravely, 'Then perhaps you'd better show me where it is, Mr Moran.'

Mal nodded and, getting to his feet, led the way out of the kitchen. Tilly glanced at Joy. 'I think I'd better go with them in case he gets Dad in a tizzy.'

'You do. See that he doesn't mention having come across the body earlier, too, if I was you.' said Joy. 'It will only lead to more questions and could complicate matters.'

Tilly agreed and hurried out.

Fortunately Sergeant Jones was in no mind to linger near the body and didn't even ask Mal why he'd been digging in that part of garden. Tilly could only presume that Joy had told the police over the telephone that the gardener had found the body, so most likely they'd thought he'd been digging over the ground ready for planting. 'I certainly agree that the body looks like it's been there for a while. But I'm no expert; the detective inspector will have to be brought in on this.'

'I wonder how old he was and what his name was,' said Tilly.

'Hopefully they'll be able to find out,' said Sergeant Jones. 'But it's not going to be easy with him having been stripped of all clothing. Of course, the murderer intended to make it difficult for us if the body was found.'

'No doubt the detective inspector will search the ground looking for clues,' said Tilly. 'It's just like a crime novel.'

'You're right,' said Sergeant Jones, a faint smile playing round his mouth. He clapped his hands and rubbed them together. 'Let's get back to the house. I'd like to telephone headquarters. No doubt they'll want me to stay here and keep an eye on things until they arrive.'

It was as he said and while he waited, Joy made another pot of tea and some toast and they all sat at the kitchen table. The sergeant asked Mal a few more questions and made notes and Tilly was relieved that without her saying a word, her father made no mention of when he had first found the body.

Once the sergeant finishing his questioning, Tilly asked him about Seb's mother. 'I did hear that she's been performing on stage.'

'That's right,' said Sergeant Jones, his ruddy face breaking into a smile.

'Another cup of tea, Sergeant?' asked Joy.

He thanked her. 'Gabrielle still has a lovely voice for her age.'

Tilly said, 'Do you think she'd like to sing in a concert that's being put on in aid of the Seamen's Widows and Children in the autumn? I'm going to be playing the piano.'

'I'll ask her,' said the sergeant. 'Gabrielle has a soft spot for orphans and has performed in a concert for the Waifs and Strays, as well as other charities.'

Tilly wondered what her sister would make of that news. 'Her grandchildren would love to see her, they especially miss her making those macaroons,' she said.

He smiled. 'I'll mention it to her.'

Tilly thanked him, thinking Seb and the children would be pleased if Gabrielle made the effort to visit them. With that settled, they talked about other things. Not long afterwards, the detective inspector arrived with a constable and an ambulance. The inspector spoke to the sergeant and was shown the body. The surrounding area was inspected and after he had a few words with Mal, Joy and Tilly, the body was removed and the police left.

'Just like that,' said Joy, making yet another pot of tea.

'I suppose if it had been a recent murder then they'd have left a constable on guard,' said Tilly.

'They'll be back,' growled Mal. 'That inspector told me not to fill in the hole but if yer ask me he's wasting his time if he thinks he'll find some clues. The rain will have washed anything away by now. Still, he'll be wanting to speak to Eudora and her man.'

Joy groaned. 'I'm just hoping she won't be annoyed with me. She might be sorry not to have seen the body. She might have got some vibes from it.'

'What d'you mean?' asked Tilly.

'With her being a medium! She might have been able to sense something while the body was still there,' said Joy. 'I didn't think about it at the time.'

'Too late now,' said Tilly, thinking that she would have liked Grant to have seen the body, too, with him being an ex-policeman and a private investigator.

'The body might have left an impression in the ground,' said Mal. 'His spirit could—'

'What do you know about such things, Dad?' asked Tilly, surprised.

'I've listened to her talking about the spirit world often enough over the years. If it can happen in a house then maybe it can in the ground,' he said.

Joy got to her feet. 'I think I'll get on with my vacuuming.'

'Is there anything I can do?' asked Tilly.

'If you're hanging around waiting for Mrs Bennett to come back, then you might as well help me. Do some polishing and then perhaps you can play us some music. Get in some practise for this concert.'

'It's ages off yet,' said Tilly. 'But I don't mind if I do,' she added, thinking some music might soothe them all.

She was still playing the piano when the Bennetts returned. By then it was nightfall and they had been shopping. Joy got to them first and was pouring out all that had happened.

'We've got a torch, haven't we, Robbie?' asked Eudora. 'I want to see this grave.'

Tilly had not thought about the trench being a grave but now she did and it made her feel all peculiar. She watched as Robbie opened a drawer in the dresser and took out a flashlight. 'Come on, Mal, you can show us the way,' he said.

They all followed him out into the garden.

'Well, I certainly never expected this when I moved here,' said Eudora, gazing into the trench by the light of the torch.

'It has to be murder, doesn't it?' said Tilly.

'Not necessarily,' said Robbie. 'It could have been an accident and the person responsible panicked and felt they had to get rid of the body.'

'Surely the dead person would have been reported missing,' said Tilly.

'And why bury him here?' asked Joy. 'And his cheekbones were smashed. It must be someone local.'

'I suppose they'll have to go through the missing persons lists from a few years ago,' said Robbie.

'That will only work if he was actually reported missing and maybe he wasn't,' said Eudora.

'Can they find out with any accuracy when he died?' asked Tilly.

Robbie shrugged. 'I don't really know.' He smiled at her. 'I'll drive you home, Tilly. The streets aren't always safe these days and I want to have a word with my sister.'

She was glad of his offer but first she needed to know something before she left. 'When will you next need me, Mrs Bennett? I have another part-time job and I'll be working tomorrow for Mr Simpson.'

'Mr Simpson, the detective,' said Eudora.

Tilly nodded and told her how the job had come about.

'I can see I'll have to be more organised with the times you work for me, dear. Shall we say you'll work for the charity all day Saturday?'

Tilly agreed. It meant she could work for Grant on Thursday and Friday if he wanted her. In the meantime, she could not wait to get back to the shop and tell the Wrights about the body in the garden.

Mrs Wright was surprised to see her brother. 'What are you doing here?'

'Tilly's father found a body in the garden,' he answered. 'So as it's been a bit of a shock all round I thought I'd not only drive Tilly home but take the opportunity to check with you and ask Pete if he'll perform in the concert for the orphans in the autumn.'

'Never mind that right now! What's this about a body?' asked Mrs Wright.

'Tilly can explain. She knows more than I do about it,' said Robbie. 'And the concert is important, Rita. You will let Pete perform? The more experience he gets at playing in public the better.'

She frowned. 'I don't know. He could be better off serving an apprenticeship in the building industry.'

Robbie scowled. 'He has a talent. Besides, have you read the newspapers that you sell recently? There's a million unemployed and although that includes the entertainment business, in my opinion that will boom again. I'm going now. What with the break-in and now this body, I can't be staying here discussing it with you. Eudora needs me.'

He left.

Tilly and her landlady exchanged looks.

'Well?' asked the older woman. 'What about this body?'

Tilly began to tell her what had happened. As she did so, she began to think of a way she might use it in her novel. This story was not going to be the romantic adventure she had originally planned but much more realistic and gritty.

CHAPTER SIXTEEN

The following morning Tilly was waiting outside the office with a bottle of milk when Grant turned up. 'Good morning, Miss Moran. You're nicely on time and you've bought milk, that's good.'

'Good morning, Mr Simpson. Did you have a successful day yesterday?'

He grimaced and took out his keys and slipped one in the lock. 'In one way I had something of a frustrating day but I've thought of a way you can help me.' He pushed open the door, picked up a couple of envelopes from the floor and led the way upstairs.

Tilly put the door on the latch and followed him up. It was not until they were inside the office and she had put the kettle on that she told him about yesterday. 'I presume you didn't call in at Wright's shop first thing this morning, Mr Simpson?'

'No. I'd overslept, so was in a bit of a rush and I didn't want to keep you waiting outside.'

'Dad found a body buried in the Bennetts' garden.'

His eyebrows shot up. 'You're joking!'

'No! Honestly. It had been there for some time.'

'I presume Mr Bennett sent for the police.'

'Joy did. The Bennetts were out and didn't come in until the sergeant and the detective inspector had been and gone and the man's body was taken away.'

Grant let out a low whistle. 'Well, I never. How did he die?'

'His cheekbones were smashed, so someone must have hit him in the face but I didn't look too closely at him. It was Joy who noticed that.'

'Any means of identification on him?'

She poured milk into cups and, keeping her eyes down, said, 'He was in his birthday suit, Mr Simpson.'

'Bloody hell!' exclaimed Grant. Then he apologised for swearing, adding, 'Someone really didn't want him identified.'

'We wondered if he was reported missing and how the police will go about tracing him. What if it was a relative or a lover who wanted him out of the way and they've kept quiet?' asked Tilly.

'I don't envy the police the task of identifying him. You'd be amazed at how many people just walk out of their jobs or homes without saying where they're going.'

'So you reckon it's easy to disappear?'

Grant did not answer because he was opening the post and had extracted a sheet of paper from an envelope. Tilly wondered if he had heard her question but realised that he had a moment later.

'Yes. But if someone really wants them found it can be done, but it takes a lot of time and patience. People need money to support themselves and that generally means finding a job, and that'll be on record. Also, there's a limit to how much a person can alter their appearance. Height isn't so easy, neither is the colour of one's eyes. This letter,' he tapped the sheet of paper with a finger, 'it's from a client and you won't find the case in the files. It's from a so-called gentleman and he wants to know how I'm getting on tracing a woman he wants found. He hasn't even signed this letter with his proper name because he doesn't want a scandal.'

'Can you tell me why he wants her found?' Tilly's hazel eyes gleamed with interest.

'Two months ago a woman knocked on his door and thrust a baby into his arms and said, 'This is yours!'

Tilly gasped. 'And was it?'

'He's admitted to having had an affair.'

'Is he married?'

Grant smiled. 'Good question. As it happens he isn't but he is engaged to be married. He is still living at home with his mother. It was bad luck on him that before he could chase after the woman with the baby, his mother came out of the house. Now she wants to keep the little girl. She's a rich widow and, according to him, used to getting her own way. He's her only son and she's forever threatening to change her will if he crosses her. He's worried that his mother might leave everything to the child. He's absolutely furious and wants the mother found and the baby returned to her.'

'Am I to understand, if he's asked you to trace her, that she's moved from where she was when he was having his affair with her?'

Grant nodded. 'She's an actress with a touring repertory company.'

'So all you have to do is to find the company and hope they'll know where she is,' said Tilly, utterly absorbed in the story.

'Yes. But it's not that easy. He's forgotten the name of the company.'

'What about the name of the play she was in?'

Grant gave a nod of approval. 'You have got a brain in your head. My client! He doesn't even remember the name of the play. What he does remember is the theatre and the name of the role she played.'

'That's something,' said Tilly. 'I'm surprised that in the circumstances he isn't concerned that she might blackmail him.' No sooner had she spoken than Tilly realised the kettle was boiling merrily away and she had not noticed. She switched off the gas and poured water into the teapot.

Grant looked at her thoughtfully. 'You know, Miss Moran, he told me that one of the reasons he wants her found is to give her money to help look after the baby. He said he believes a child should be with its mother.'

'And did you believe him?'

'I admit that I thought it might be a way of him buying her off.'

'But what if she doesn't want to be bought off? What if she wants to continue with her career as an actress and doesn't want the child?'

'You know, you're good at this,' said Grant admiringly. 'I doubt that's occurred to him. He thinks she's left the baby with him because she wants to punish him.'

'Then I'm amazed he hasn't thought of the blackmail angle,' said Tilly, handing Grant's tea to him. 'Can you tell me what you've done so far to trace her?'

'I've visited the Playhouse and spoken to the manager. He was able to tell me the name of the play once I gave him the name of the character.'

'So from that did you get the name of the company?'

Grant nodded. 'Trouble is he had no idea where the company is playing right now and he didn't have time to give me any more help.'

'Surely he must have the name of the manager of the company.'

'He said he has it somewhere. I need to go back and ask him for it.'

'He might have the manager's home address, too.'

Grant smiled. 'Maybe.'

'So you'll tell your client all that when you write back to him?' asked Tilly.

'I'll dictate and you can type it out and see it goes off today.' He added cheerfully, 'I suppose I'd better do a bit more on this case. I've earned the retainer he gave me but now I need more money from him if he wants me to continue. Travelling expenses for a start. It's likely I'll need to travel elsewhere in the country. At least I have her stage name and a photograph.' He opened a drawer and produced a photograph. 'What do you think?'

Tilly gazed down at the black and white print and agreed with him that the girl really was a dark-haired beauty. She appeared to be only a couple of years older than herself. 'No wonder she didn't want to give up her career. Although she should have thought of that before having an affair with our client, Mr X.'

Grant returned the photograph to the drawer. 'Once I get an answer from him, I might need you to take over from me on the other case I'm working on.'

Tilly felt a thrill of excitement. 'You mean you want me to watch the client's wife. The one who's worried she might be having an affair?'

He nodded. 'Unless I get it all tied up before I go off on my travels, but the way things are going so far I can't see that happening. So give it a few more days then you can probably take over from me,' said Grant. 'And thinking about that I need to know what days you'll be working for me and which you'll be working for Mrs Bennett.'

'She doesn't need me until Saturday so I can be here in the office tomorrow as well as today,' said Tilly.

'Perhaps if you ask her about doing Saturdays, Mondays and Tuesdays for her and Wednesdays, Thursdays and Fridays for me. Unless something important comes up, which means that we have to change those days,' said Grant.

Tilly agreed to suggest it to Mrs Bennett. 'Although it's Good Friday this Friday, so I won't be in, and I must remind her that it's Easter Monday on Monday, so I won't be working that day either.'

'Right,' said Grant, blowing out a breath. 'I'm glad you remembered it was the Easter weekend.'

She sat at the typewriter, placed paper and carbon in the machine and waited for him to dictate his answer to Mr X's letter.

Tilly was thinking about Mr X and whether Grant had received an answer to his letter as she walked along the pavement past Leonard Parker's house on Saturday morning. The sudden growling and then barking of a dog startled her and she stepped back as the head of an Alsatian appeared above the fence. The dog's front paws rested on the top of the wood and for a moment she thought it was going to attack her. She screamed.

'Steady, Fang,' said a male voice.

Fang! Tilly could see why the dog had been given that name and shuddered. A hand appeared and gripped the dog's collar. She watched as Leonard Parker clipped on a lead and, by sheer brute strength, dragged the Alsatian away from the fence. 'I'm sorry if he frightened you, Miss Moran. But what with all the goings-on lately my aunt pleaded with me to get a guard dog '

'It's all right. I shouldn't have screamed,' said Tilly, trembling. 'You'll think me a coward.'

'Your reaction was understandable. If he has the same effect on any burglars or murderers I'll delighted.' The dog began to bark again and he thwacked it with the thick end of the lead. 'Shut up, Fang.'

'He'd tear out their throats,' muttered Tilly.

'Rather that than I was murdered in my bed,' said Leonard, smiling.

Tilly said, 'I'd rather not think about either of those things. I wish people would respect the law. Poor Nanki Poo.'

'It was a shame he was killed,' said Leonard regretfully. 'He was unusual and I shouldn't wonder if he was worth a few bob.'

'Of course. He was a pedigree dog,' said Tilly. 'I suppose it was your aunt who told you about the body?'

'Yes! But if she hadn't I'd have found out the next day because the police came knocking on my door asking questions.'

'What kind of questions?' Tilly could not resist asking.

'Damn foolish ones!' he said, sounding exasperated. 'Can I think back a few years and remember any commotion out of the ordinary going on in next door's garden? Did the old lady have any visitors? I ask you! I reminded them that there was a war on – and although I tried to keep my eye on the old girl because I felt sorry for her – I had lots of more important things on my mind. If my father had still been alive then he might have been able to tell them something. They then asked if I remembered anyone going missing in the drive or if I had seen any strangers. I reminded them that there's a park opposite and people are always coming and going.'

'That's true,' said Tilly. 'It makes me wonder why the murderer didn't bury the body in the park.'

'I wondered that, too,' said Leonard, smiling. 'I suppose there was always the fear of him being seen and there is another entry into the Bennetts' back garden, besides going up the side of the house.'

Tilly looked surprised. 'I didn't know that.'

'Yes. There've all got doors in the rear wall that back onto a lane and a grassy area, overlooking the main road. The Bennetts' door is concealed by the outhouse.'

Their conversation was interrupted by the Alsatian growling and then it began to bark. 'Will you quieten your dog, Mr Parker?' said Eudora.

'I'd best go,' Tilly whispered.

'I hope you have a pleasant day and don't allow what's happened to disturb your sleep,' said Leonard.

'I won't,' she said. 'Bye.' Tilly walked up the path to where she could see Eudora standing in the doorway. 'I'm sorry I'm late.'

Eudora's eyes rested on Tilly's flushed face. 'I hope you haven't forgotten my warning, Tilly. Mr Parker is a charmer but he's not for you.'

Tilly bit back a sharp retort. 'We were only talking because of his dog.'

'It's going to prove a nuisance, that dog. I can understand his reason for getting one but I can't do with it barking and throwing itself at the wall or the fence every time we come outside,' said Eudora. 'It needs chaining up during the day or it could get out and savage someone.'

'*The Hound of the Baskervilles*,' murmured Tilly. 'Sherlock Holmes had to shoot the beast.'

Eudora's expression altered and she looked wistful. 'Did you know that Sir Arthur Conan Doyle has developed an interest in spiritualism? Not only did he lose his first wife early this century but he also lost his son and five members of his immediate family during the war.'

'Poor man,' said Tilly softly. 'I know Rudyard Kipling lost his only son. So much sadness. I hope there'll never be another war.'

Eudora sighed. 'It is a tragedy for those left behind and I sometimes regret that I can no longer give them some comfort – but I made a promise. Now come in and have a cup of tea and I'll tell you what I want you to do. I won't be able to go with you to the Doyles after all. I'm having trouble with a builder doing some alterations to one of my properties and I need to speak to him face to face. Mal will be taking me once he and Robbie come back from the police station in Tuebrook.'

'What do the police want with Dad?' asked Tilly, immediately anxious.

'Just to look at some photographs of villains to see if he can recognise our burglar.'

'I hope he won't work himself into a state.'

Eudora smiled. 'Of course he won't. He has Robbie with him and, besides, I gave him a double dose of his tonic.'

Over tea and biscuits Eudora spoke about Seb's mother. 'Joy was telling me that the police sergeant promised to ask Gabrielle to sing at our concert.'

'I thought it might be best my mentioning it,' said Tilly casually.

Eudora fixed her with a stare. 'How tactful you are, Tilly, and you're right, of course.'

'I wonder who's her accompanist.'

'I'm sure she'll let us know if she wanted to bring her own or is happy for you to play for her,' said Eudora.

Tilly wondered what Alice would think of that; her sister had never got on with her mother-in-law at the best of times. Would she be prepared to support the concert if Gabrielle was going to take part?

'You can let me know how you get on with the Doyle family on Monday morning, Tilly. We'll be going to the office as there is a fair amount of typing for you to do and I need to speak to people,' said Eudora.

Tilly remembered what Grant had said about her working days and she mentioned his suggestion to Eudora.

'It sounds a sensible arrangement,' said the older woman. 'It does mean you'll be able to support yourself without needing to ask your family for help. But it does give you less time for working on your novel and I think it important that you continue with your writing.'

Tilly agreed. 'I'll just have to make sure I fit in at least a couple of hours every evening,' she said.

Eudora gave Tilly money for travelling expenses and she set out to catch a tram into town and another that took her along Vauxhall Road. She got off near Burlington Gardens and walked up the street where the Doyles lived. It was the start of the Easter school holidays and she found Patricia watching the younger girls and seven-year-old Jimmy playing out in the street. Tilly presumed Micky, who was nine, had gone to the park to play football with some lads from the street.

'Is your mother in, Patricia?' she asked.

Patricia hesitated. 'Yes, but me uncle's with her and he chased us out.'

'I didn't know you had an uncle. Why did he chase you out?'

'Yer real nosy, aren't yer?' said Patricia with a spurt of irritation. 'But if yer must know he wanted a private word with me mam.'

'I want a private word with her, too,' said Tilly firmly.

'Yer best not having it today,' said Patricia. 'He wouldn't like it that we have the likes of you visitin' us. He's a real hard nut.'

'Is he going to help you as a family?'

A sharp laugh escaped the girl. 'Now that would be the day, wouldn't it? He never came when Dad was home, only when he wanted something from Mam and he could get her on her own. She's his big sister, yer see, and she has a misplaced sense of loyalty where he's concerned.'

'So what does he want this time?' Tilly asked, wondering how Mrs Doyle could help her brother when she couldn't even help herself and her children.

'How the hell should I know?' said Patricia scathingly. 'He wants to keep it a secret, that's why we've been chased out.'

Tilly considered the situation for the moment. 'Well, he's not going to be there all morning, is he? So I might as well hang around until he's gone.'

Patricia sighed heavily. 'I wish yer wouldn't. It'll do no good.'

'Let me be the judge of that. How's Anthony?'

She hesitated. 'He's OK. Although—'

Tilly pounced on the word. 'Although what?'

'He's got a bit of a sniffle and a cough.'

Tilly's eyes narrowed. 'Your mam hasn't pawned those clothes I brought or the blankets, has she?'

'Why d'yer say that?' asked Patricia indignantly. 'I told yer I'm looking out for all of us, especially the baby.'

'I'm glad to hear it,' said Tilly, her voice softening. 'It's just that I know how difficult it must be for you.'

'Yer think yer do but yer don't really,' said Patricia roughly. 'To do that yer'd have to be me and yer can't be me.'

'You're very perceptive,' said Tilly, smiling.

'That's a big word. What's it mean?'

'You've got a clear understanding of who you are and who I am.'

Patricia laughed. 'That's easy, Miss. I'm a nobody and yer a somebody.'

'That's not true!'

'Yes it is!' cried Patricia.

Suddenly there was the sound of a door opening and the girl glanced in the direction of her home. 'What is it?' whispered Tilly.

'It's him,' said Patricia. 'Get away from me. He'll take one look at yer and know what yer are. He doesn't trust anyone according to Mam.' She seized her younger twin sisters, Mary and Maureen, and hurried them away.

Tilly glanced at the man standing outside the Doyles' house, talking to Mrs Doyle, and thought he did indeed look a tough nut. She decided to go for a walk round the neighbourhood and come back in half an hour. Hopefully, by then, she would have a chance to speak to Mrs Doyle.

It was as Tilly was strolling along Scotland Road, gazing in the shop windows that she saw Leonard Parker coming out of a pawnshop. What on earth was he doing there? She was debating whether to go up and speak to him when the man she recognised as Mrs Doyle's brother walked up to him. Whatever they had to say to each other was said in fierce whispers. She wondered how they knew each other and whether Patricia's uncle could possibly work in Leonard's shipyard. Maybe he was arguing about the cut in piecework in the shipyards. But even if she was right about that, it did not explain why Mr Parker was coming out of a pawnshop. It was not the kind of place she would have envisaged him frequenting. Suddenly the two men parted and went in opposite directions.

On impulse Tilly decided to follow Leonard but knew she would have to hurry or she could lose sight of him amongst the Saturday morning shoppers. Fortunately he was wearing a distinctive jacket with a dogtooth pattern, so she had little difficulty in keeping track of him. Even so, she was glad when he left the crowds behind and turned into a street that led towards the docks. Suddenly he came to a halt in front of two large gates and in one of them was a Judas gate, which he opened with a key. He stepped inside and locked the door behind him. Unable to follow him in there, she turned away and headed for the Doyles' house.

There was no sign of the girls in the street, so she knocked at the door. Patricia answered it. 'I thought it might be you,' she said. 'Well, yer've missed Mam because she's gone out on a message. But yer can come in if yer like and have a look at the baby.'

Tilly accepted the girl's invitation. As she entered the kitchen it struck her afresh how little of this world's goods this family had but at least spring had arrived and it would not be long before summer was here and there would be no need for a fire at all.

Patricia took Tilly over to the perambulator where the baby lay. He was well wrapped up but his little nose was running and his cheeks were flushed. She knew something about childish complaints having helped care for her nephews and niece. This little one might just have caught a common cold but if it worsened it could go on his chest and turn into something more serious. Mrs Doyle could not afford to get a doctor out to him and she wondered what was the best thing to do.

'What d'yer think?' asked Patricia.

'You're doing the best you can by keeping him warm but if he should get feverish then let us know.' Tilly took out a scrap of paper and wrote Eudora Bennett's address on it and her telephone number. 'Mrs Bennett will help you in an emergency.'

Patricia looked relieved and took the paper and pocketed it along with the pennies Tilly gave her. 'Thanks. Yer'd best go now, just in case the brother comes back.'

'What does your uncle do for a living?' asked Tilly.

'He works down at the docks. Why d'yer ask?'

'Does he work in a shipyard?'

'Maybe.'

Tilly produced a bag of sweets and handed them to Patricia. 'Share these with your sisters and brothers. I'll see you again soon.'

A smile lit up Patricia's thin face as she took the treat. 'No, yer've done enough. I'll get in touch with Mrs Bennett if we're desperate. I'll miss yer coming but yer best staying away while the brother's on the prowl.'

'If you'd rather I did that then I will,' said Tilly, although she had every intention of keeping an eye on the family without calling at the house. She would need to mention the uncle to Eudora but would leave seeing her until next week. She decided to keep quiet about seeing him talking to Leonard Parker. After all, there might be a completely innocent explanation. Besides, she wanted to get off home and do some writing.

'Have you said something to Grant Simpson about me?' asked Wendy, resting a shoulder against the doorjamb of Tilly's bedroom.

'No. Why should you think that?' Tilly lifted her eyes from her typewriter. She thought the other girl looked pale and strained. 'I'd rather you didn't disturb me when I'm writing but if you want to talk, then come in and shut the door behind you. You're letting in the noise of Pete practising and that's distracting me, too.'

Wendy did as Tilly suggested and closed the door and sat on the bed. 'How's it going?' she asked.

Tilly pulled a face. 'I've had to rewrite what I'd already done because my heroine decided she wasn't going to do what I originally planned for her. My hero isn't behaving himself either. He's going to get himself into real trouble if he's not careful.'

'What are you going on about?' said Wendy, staring at her as if she were mad.

'Don't ask,' groaned Tilly, removing a sheet of paper and

turning it over so she could type on the back. 'So what's this about Mr Simpson?'

'He hasn't been in the shop for days.'

Tilly thought about her last conversation with her employer. 'It's possible he's away on a case, making the most of the Easter weekend,' she said cautiously. 'I can't swear to that but it's a possibility.'

'What case?' asked Wendy, perking up.

'It's confidential so I can't talk about it,' said Tilly, taking a bag of sweets from a drawer and popping a chocolate lime into her mouth. She offered the bag to Wendy, who shook her head.

'No thanks. I eat too many sweets. If Mam knew the times I helped myself she'd have a fit. Fortunately, she's more out of the shop than she's in. Visiting her cronies from the old street. Mrs Pain for one. D'you remember her?'

'Yes,' said Tilly. 'She's the cleaner who told me about the job in the insurance office, isn't she? I haven't seen her around for a while.'

Wendy nodded. 'That's because she's developed terrible rheumatism in her knees.'

'Poor old thing. Surely she must be entitled to the old age pension.'

'Hell, Tilly, you have to be seventy to get that and five bob doesn't go far these days.' Wendy wandered round the bedroom and picked up a magazine lying on the floor in a corner. 'You didn't buy this in our shop,' she said.

'I don't know what you're talking about.'

Wendy plonked the magazine on the desk. 'It's American, it's got the dollar sign on.'

Tilly glanced at it. 'Your Aunt Eudora gave it to me. I haven't had a chance to look at it yet.'

Wendy sat on the bed and began to flick over pages. 'It's got lots of pictures. Oh, look! It's got a photo, the same as the one you have in the drawer.'

Tilly sighed. 'You're going to have to go. I can't concentrate.'

'Look!' Wendy came over to her and placed the open magazine on top of a pile of paper. 'It's sad, isn't it? I wonder where me dad's buried. I'd like to visit his grave one day and put some flowers on it.'

Tilly looked at the picture of the war graves and realised that Wendy was right. It was the same as one of those that Don had sent to her; that meant he must be working for this magazine. She felt a stir of excitement as she read the prose beneath the photograph and then began to read the article from the beginning and looked at the other photographs. There was a picture of Don with a smiling blonde, who had her hand on his shoulder. It gave her quite a shock seeing him with a woman.

'He must be clever,' said Wendy. 'Just like Grant Simpson.' A sigh escaped her. 'Bet he has money, too.'

Tilly did not answer but found herself wondering whether Don and the blonde were close friends. How old was the magazine? She turned to the front and saw it had been issued several months ago. He could be anywhere with this blonde for company. She felt an ache inside her. What if he had decided to marry a woman of his own age, believing because Tilly had failed to meet him in Liverpool that she did not care enough about him?

Tilly dropped the magazine on the floor and turned to Wendy. 'Now you've shown it to me, will you go, please?' she said fiercely. 'I've work to do.'

'OK! I'm going but what about Grant Simpson?' asked Wendy.

'He told me to go into the office on Wednesday. I'll find out then whether he's been away or not.'

Wendy nodded and left the room.

Tilly picked up the magazine, turned to the photograph of Don and the blonde. She gazed down at it for a moment, with tears in her eyes, before throwing the periodical into a corner.

CHAPTER SEVENTEEN

'Hey, Tilly!' called Grant, waving to her from across Fenwick Street the following Wednesday.

'Mr Simpson,' she said, clutching the bottle of milk and smiling as he arrived on the pavement in front of her. 'Did you go away? Wendy said you haven't been in the shop.'

'Ahhh, young Wendy. She makes me smile, that girl,' said Grant.

'Why is that?' asked Tilly, watching him unlock the door.

'Because she's always so welcoming and keeps me informed of what's going on in the wider world. In a way it was she who gave me an idea about the actress case.'

'What idea was that, Mr Simpson?' asked Tilly, following him inside.

'Newspapers. They inform us about who's performing and what's on in the various cities and towns. There's also a newspaper specifically for those in the entertainment business. Since reading one I've discovered that life is tough for some in the business. Quite a number are out of work. There's been a drop in stage work.'

'Do you think it's because people can't afford to go to the theatre or due to the growth of cinemas?'

'Both play their part, I should imagine. It's also true that some of the top singers are now recording their voices, so those who can afford to buy a gramophone don't have to go out to find entertainment – they can play records of the great singers in the comfort of their own home.' He paused to open the door upstairs and crossed the room to his desk. 'Put the kettle on, Tilly, I'm parched and desperate for a cuppa.'

She did so before asking, 'So did you find your actress?'

'Not yet. But I did visit the manager at the Playhouse and he gave me the home address of the company manager. So I decided to visit the house in Bolton and was able to talk to his wife. She gave me the name of the theatre and city where the company were performing and so I went there.'

'But you said you didn't find her?'

'That's because she's left the company. She was spotted by one of these film makers and apparently she's now making a film at a studio down in the south of England.'

'So you're going to go there?' asked Tilly, hoping this meant she would do some detecting.

'I thought it wiser than writing to her in case she took fright and decided not to see me,' said Grant, sitting down at his desk. 'Besides, I'd like to meet her because I'd like her version of things. I plan to catch a train south in exactly,' he glanced at the clock on the wall, 'an hour and a quarter.'

'So what about your client who suspects his wife of having an affair?' asked Tilly.

'Mr Nuttall. You can take over there, Tilly.' He pursed his lips and tapped his fingers together. 'Her first name is Phyllis.

While I was watching her I was thinking how useful a camera would be.'

'A camera?'

'Yes, but even the watch-pocket "Klimax" would set me back three to eight quid, depending on the model.'

'But why do you need a camera?'

'I suspect the husband could be one of those men who is going to be difficult to convince that his wife isn't up to something naughty. I know that sounds peculiar but the man has no confidence in himself when it comes to women.'

Tilly glanced at him as she spooned tealeaves into the pot. 'What makes you say that?'

'She's a good few years younger than him. He's a weedy looking man who's going bald. He does have a good job with a bank; one of those in this street. He's worried she married him for his money and is now tired of him. He saw my plaque and that's when he got the idea of having her followed.'

'So what have you found out about her?'

'She's out every afternoon. Some days she goes to Stanley Park and sits watching the mums with their kiddiewinks feeding the ducks. Other times she goes to Walton Road and looks in shop windows and talks to babies in prams. She also tap dances.'

'Tap dances!'

Grant nodded. 'It's growing in popularity in America and now has crossed the Atlantic. I suppose it has its roots in clog dancing.'

'Do you think it's possible she could be having an affair with the teacher?'

'I did spot her leaving the building with a man. I followed them but there wasn't anything lover-like in their behaviour. Of course, that could be deliberate if they thought they might be seen. I suppose the thing to do is join the class and watch them together but tap-dancing isn't me.'

Tilly smiled.

He chuckled. 'Don't look like that! Of course, I could surprise myself and be good at it but I don't think so. Now is that cup of tea ready? I'm going to have to go soon.'

Tilly poured out the tea and put a couple of biscuits on a plate. 'Do you have a photograph of Mrs Nuttall.'

He nodded and produced one and gave it to her.

Tilly saw a pleasant looking woman with fair hair and smiling eyes. 'She looks nice, not the sort of woman you'd think would be having an affair.'

'But who knows what thoughts lurk behind those eyes. You only need to read the newspapers as Wendy does to know that you can't tell a murderer from just looking at one.' Grant bit into a biscuit and munched.

Tilly thought of the good looking Bert Kirk and knew that to be true. 'Have they any children?' she asked.

'No.'

'And how long have they been married?'

'Six years. She's in her mid-thirties and he's pushing fifty.'

Tilly nodded, thinking she should have no trouble keeping an eye on the woman and maybe she would get some more material for her novel, too. 'There's just one more thing,' she said. 'I don't know Liverpool that well and I could get lost.'

'Not with this you won't,' said Grant, producing a map of Liverpool.

'You think of everything,' said Tilly, taking it from him.

'I do my best,' he said. 'Good luck.'

'Good luck to you, too,' she replied.

* * *

Tilly stood across the road, seemingly reading a newspaper, and saw the front door of the house open and Phyllis Nuttall come out. The woman had a good figure, which was shown to advantage in the close-fitting royal blue costume she was wearing. Tilly decided it was unlikely that she was going tap dancing because all she carried was a small handbag. Tilly watched her head in the direction of the main road. She folded the newspaper and went after her. She had a quick, determined walk and Tilly had trouble keeping up with her. Fortunately, it turned out Mrs Nuttall was only going as far as the local church hall.

A notice outside informed Tilly that there was to be a lantern slide show by a visiting missionary that afternoon. Such a visit seemed out of keeping with the kind of woman who would have an affair. Even so, Tilly decided to go inside because it was just possible that perhaps she was meeting someone in there.

Tilly sat at the back of the hall and fixed her gaze on Mrs Nuttall's hat. It was a distinctive piece of blue headgear that sat at an angle on her fair hair and had a small poke crown and narrow brim decorated by a bunch of artificial forget-me-nots. After a brief introductory talk the slide show commenced. The film had been shot in Africa and there were pictures of the countryside and wild animals. Tilly sat up straight when she saw a gorilla. What a creature! It was huge and had such a human expression in its eyes that she felt sorry for its capture. The scene changed and there were shots of a mission school with happy, smiling native children singing.

The scraping of a chair being pushed back dragged her attention away from the screen and she realised it was Mrs Nuttall who had got up and hurried out. Tilly rushed outside and found her leaning against the railings.

'Are you all right?' asked Tilly, with concern.

The woman did not answer but hastily dabbed her eyes and hurried away. Tilly let several minutes lapse before following her to Stanley Park. Mrs Nuttall appeared to be walking aimlessly along the paths, past shrubs and beds filled with spring flowers. Then they came to the lake and she sat down on a bench where some mothers and toddlers were feeding the ducks.

Tilly stepped back into cover provided by a huddle of rhododendrons and watched with a heavily beating heart as a man came striding towards the bench. Was she about to witness an assignation? No. He walked past Mrs Nuttall without a glance.

Several minutes passed without anything happening. Tilly began to feel foolish, asking herself why the woman should go to the hall if she planned on a lovers' tryst here? Why had she rushed outside? Something had upset her but what?

Suddenly Tilly felt the patter of raindrops on her hat and shoulders and watched as Mrs Nuttall rose from the bench and hurried away. Tilly followed her home and watched the door close behind her. What should she do? Stay or go? Perhaps she would come out again but with an umbrella this time. Would Grant expect her to carry on keeping an eye on the house? Tilly decided that perhaps she should stay. An hour passed and Tilly was getting wetter and colder because the rain was coming down in sheets. At last common sense prevailed and she gave up and left for home. She was shivering with cold by the time she arrived at the shop and her feet were sloshing about in her wet shoes.

'Goodness me, Tilly, you look like a drowned rat,' said Mrs

Wright, glancing up from serving a customer. 'Get inside, girl, and get out of those wet clothes.'

Tilly did not waste any time doing what her landlady said but lifted the flap with numb hands and hurried into the back where she could hear voices. All talk stopped as she entered the room and there were several indrawn breaths.

'Bloody hell, Tilly!' exclaimed Wendy. 'You look like a—'

'I know – a drowned rat,' she said in a shaky voice, trying to tug off her sodden gloves. 'So would you if you'd been standing in the rain as long as I have.'

'We got wet coming home from school,' said Davy, 'but not as wet as you.'

'Come over to the fire,' said Minnie. 'Davy, you get out the way. We don't want her catching pneumonia.'

'I need to take my shoes off,' said Tilly. 'I'll get the rug wet.'

'Never mind that,' said Wendy.

Both sisters dragged her towards the fire and peeled off her outdoor clothes as well as her cardigan, which was damp, too. 'I reckon you're soaked through to your knickers,' said Minnie, looking at her skirt.

'Shut up, Min,' hissed Wendy. 'Not in front of the lads. Get upstairs and find Tilly some dry clothes.' She turned to her brothers. 'Boys, out!' she ordered.

They did not argue but went into the other room. Wendy helped Tilly off with her jumper and skirt before going over to a cupboard in one of the alcoves. Tilly stood in front of the fire with her eyes closed while her underwear steamed and the heat penetrated her chilled body. She held out cold hands to the fire as Wendy draped a towel about her shoulders.

'You're going to have to strip everything off,' said Wendy. 'I can't believe you got this wet waiting at the tram stop.'

'I didn't. I tell you, Wendy, detecting isn't what I thought.'

'What is it then?' asked Wendy, taking a smaller towel out of the cupboard and placing it over Tilly's head and beginning to rub her hair vigorously.

'Damn, that hurts,' croaked Tilly. 'I watched her but it was just a waste of time. I got wetter and colder. I still feel cold.'

'Stop nattering and get your underwear off and start rubbing your body to get the circulation going.'

Tilly tried to comply with what the other girl said but it wasn't easy because her hands had started to tingle and itch. Wendy helped her. It was a relief when she was naked and wrapped in a warm towel.

'You'd be best in bed,' said Wendy.

'I need a hot drink,' whispered Tilly.

Minnie entered the room with an armful of clothes. 'I brought these,' she said.

'Never mind them,' said Wendy, waving her away. 'I think Tilly should be in bed. You make her a hot drink and a hottie and I'll go up with her.'

Minnie opened her mouth to say something but one look at Tilly and she dropped the clothes on a chair and put the kettle on.

Within half an hour Tilly was tucked up in bed with a hot water bottle after having a cup of tea. She fell asleep but woke some time in the middle of the night, feeling shivery and with a terrible headache and a sore throat, and wanting the lavatory. She managed to stumble to the lavatory but had to cling to the wall on the way back to her bedroom because she felt so dizzy. She wondered how she was going to get up in the morning and go to work. Yet she must because she had to keep her eye on Mrs Nuttall.

Tilly tossed and turned for the rest of the night, feeling hot one minute and cold the next. It was a relief when morning came and Wendy brought her a cup of tea in bed. 'Thanks,' mumbled Tilly.

Wendy stared down at her. 'You not feeling too good?'

'I'll be all right,' said Tilly, her voice husky. 'I have to keep my eye on Mrs-Mrs Nut-tall this afternoon.'

'Who's Mrs Nuttall?' Wendy placed a hand on Tilly's forehead, which was burning. She frowned and helped Tilly to sit up, and then gave the cup to her before perching on the side of the bed.

Tilly sipped the tea.

'So who's Mrs Nuttall?' repeated Wendy.

Tilly hesitated and then told her. 'So you see why I have to go?'

'Don't be daft! You've caught a chill and if you don't look after yourself you'll end up with pneumonia. You're not going anywhere.'

'I need the money,' croaked Tilly. 'And, besides, it's the first bit of detecting I've done for Mr Simpson and I don't want to let him down. He's gone away on a case and left me in charge.'

'It'll be the last time you'll be doing anything for him if you don't listen to what I say,' chided Wendy.

Tilly laughed weakly. 'It could well be so because he won't trust me with another case if I fail him.'

'I'm getting Mam. She'll tell you what's what,' said Wendy.

She hurried downstairs and into the shop, where her mother was sorting out the newspapers. 'Tilly's got a fever. She's insisting she's got to go into work and keep an eye on some woman, but I think if she's not sensible, Mam, she could end up with pneumonia. I was wondering whether to nip over to Uncle Robbie's and speak to Aunt Eudora. I mean, she used to be some kind of healer and she could give her something to bring down the fever. After all, that charity she works for does employ Tilly.'

'I suppose so,' said her mother, frowning.

'It would save on doctor's fees,' said Wendy.

Her mother nodded. 'You carry on here. I'll go and have a look at Tilly.'

Rita hurried upstairs and into Tilly's bedroom. She found her on the floor, slumped against the bed. 'What are you doing, girl?' she asked, getting her hands beneath her armpits and heaving her onto the bed.

'Have to watch Mrs Nuttall,' she muttered.

Placing a hand against Tilly's burning forehead, Rita tutted. 'You're not going anywhere. Now get back into bed.'

Tilly was too weak to argue and clambered beneath the bedcovers. She lay down and closed her eyes. Her head was banging away and when she tried to swallow her throat really hurt. She moaned, feeling more miserable than she had ever felt in her life before. Perhaps she would die. If she did then she was going to let a lot of people down.

'So will I go and speak to Aunt Eudora?' asked Wendy, as soon as her mother entered the shop.

'Yes! We don't want her family saying we didn't do all we could for her,' said Rita.

'Shall I fill a hot water bottle for Tilly before I go to work?' asked Minnie, coming into the shop. 'She's moaning up there.'

'You do that,' said her mother. 'You'll have to get the cold one from her bed.'

Wendy said, 'I'll nip up and get it and tell her I'm going for Aunt Eudora.'

Before her mother could stop her, Wendy rushed upstairs. Tilly had thrown off the bedcovers and lay curled up, shivering. Wendy saw the cold hot water bottle and grabbed it before drawing up the bedclothes so they covered Tilly's shoulders. 'Tilly!' she called. 'I'm going to get Aunt Eudora. She'll make you better.'

'Mrs Nuttall,' muttered Tilly.

Wendy said, 'You mustn't worry about her.'

Suddenly Tilly shot out a hand and grabbed her wrist. 'Help me. You follow her.'

'Me!' cried Wendy.

Tilly's hand slid from Wendy's wrist and dropped onto the bed and her eyelids closed. Wendy felt her pulse, which was rapid, and tucked her arm beneath the bedclothes. Then she hurried downstairs, placed the cold hot water bottle on the kitchen table, put on her hat and coat and left the house.

Wendy almost jumped out of her skin when the Alsatian let out a flurry of barks and its head appeared above the fence. 'Go away, dog,' she yelled, and ran up the Bennetts' path and round the back. She let herself into the kitchen and found herself the object of several pairs of eyes.

'Wendy! What are you doing here so early?' asked Robbie.

'Tilly's ill. She got soaked yesterday and she's burning up,' panted Wendy, staring at Eudora. 'We've kept her in bed. I thought you might be able to give her something, you having been a healer.'

Eudora glanced at Joy. 'Oh dear,' said the latter, looking worried. 'Do you think I should get in touch with Kenny and have him tell Alice?'

'No,' said Eudora firmly. 'I'm sure Tilly wouldn't want us to do that unless matters become desperate.' She drained her teacup and stood up. 'I'll just get a few things and then I'll be with you, Wendy.'

'Should I let her dad know?' asked Wendy.

'Not just yet,' said Eudora. 'We don't want him getting upset anymore than he is already at the moment.' She hurried from the kitchen.

'I hope Tilly's going to be all right,' said Robbie, looking concerned.

Wendy sat down suddenly because she had gone weak at the knees. 'So do I.' She realised just how much she wanted Tilly to get better despite her having the job with Grant Simpson that she would have liked herself.

'Hello, Tilly, dear,' said Eudora, helping her to sit up against the pillows. 'I just want you to swallow this for me.'

'What is it?' muttered Tilly, forcing her eyelids open and trying to focus on Eudora's face.

'Medicine, dear. It'll make you feel better. Now, open your mouth.'

Wendy watched as Eudora persuaded Tilly to drink the draught she had made from various herbs and dried berries that she had crushed into a powder. Wendy prayed it would do the trick. She watched Tilly's throat move and heard her utter a tiny cry of pain as the medicine went down. Then Eudora kept Tilly's mouth closed with a gentle hand as she lowered her against the pillows.

'How often will she need to have one of them?' asked Wendy.

'Every four hours,' replied Eudora. 'But try to get her to

drink weak milkless tea sweetened with honey or rosehip syrup if she complains of being thirsty. A watch will have to be kept on her, especially during the night.'

'Perhaps we should send for her sister,' said Wendy.

'No!' Eudora turned quickly and stared at her. 'Alice has young children and a husband to take care of and it's the same with Hanny.'

Wendy hesitated a moment before saying, 'Tilly's worrying about watching some woman for Mr Simpson. He's gone away and left her in charge. It's the first bit of detecting she's done and she's worrying about letting him down. She asked me if I could take over for her and I would, except—'

'I'll let you have Joy,' said Eudora. 'She can stay with Tilly while you're watching this woman.'

Wendy's face lit up. 'Thanks. Will you speak to Mam about it?'

'I'll get your Uncle Robbie to speak to her. She'll take more notice of him than me.'

Wendy agreed. Once Eudora had left the bedroom, she sat for a few moments gazing down at Tilly and then she looked for her handbag and opened it. Inside she found what she was looking for: a photograph, an address and a map book of Liverpool.

Wendy was glad that the storms of the other day had passed and, although it was blowy, the sun was shining. The front door of the house opened and a woman stood in the doorway. Wendy recognised her from the photograph in her pocket. Smart dresser, she thought, as Mrs Nuttall shoved a bag under her arm and a purse in the pocket of her jacket. She glanced in Wendy's direction but the girl's head was buried in a newspaper. Suddenly a giggle burst in Wendy's throat as she peered through the holes she had cut in the newspaper and stared after Mrs Nuttall as she walked along the street. When she turned a corner, Wendy folded the newspaper and hurried after her.

Two hours later she was still following Mrs Nuttall, whose behaviour she found puzzling. If there was any truth in her husband's suspicion that she was having an affair during the afternoons, she was going a strange way about it. She had wandered up and down Walton Road, looking in shop windows, bending and talking to babies in prams but always walking away as soon as their mothers appeared. So far there had been no hint of an assignation with a man and Wendy was getting hungry and thirsty.

Wendy was just considering buying a meat pie in a nearby bakery when she saw Mrs Nuttall seize hold of the handle of a pram and ease off the brake. The next moment she was hurrying along the road with it. What was the woman doing? Wendy was tempted to shout *Stop, thief!* but did not want to draw attention to herself or to warn Mrs Nuttall that her actions had been seen. She soon realised that the woman was heading for home. She must be mad, thought Wendy. You can't take a baby home without your husband and the neighbours being aware of it. Babies needed feeding and changing and could cry a lot.

She watched Mrs Nuttall wheel the pram up her path and round to the back of her house. Wendy hesitated before following her. She was in time to see Mrs Nuttall lifting the baby out of the pram.

'What d'you think you're doing with that baby?' asked Wendy quietly, not wanting to startle Mrs Nuttall into dropping the child. As it was, the baby began to wriggle and suddenly slide from beneath her arms. Wendy sprang forward and put a hand to its bottom and held it there.

'You've got no right to follow me here!' cried Mrs Nuttall, clutching the baby tightly now. 'I don't know who you are but see what you've done? You've hurt my baby.'

The child began to cry.

'It's not your baby,' said Wendy.

'Yes, it is.'

'No, it isn't. I saw you wheel the pram away from the shop that the mother had just gone inside.'

Mrs Nuttall's lips quivered. 'You're fibbing.'

'And you're a thief,' said Wendy.

The woman's face crumpled and tears filled her eyes. 'You-you don't understand. That mother stays in that shop for ages, gossiping and laughing. She doesn't want a baby. I want a baby and can't have one.'

Wendy felt sorry for her but thieving was thieving and you just couldn't let people get away with it. 'You have to give it back.'

'No!'

'Of course you do!' cried Wendy. 'If you hurry up before the mother sends for the police, you can always say you made a mistake. That you were taking care of a baby for your sister, friend or cousin and that you wheeled the wrong pram away because it was the same make and colour.'

Mrs Nuttall stared at her, rocking the crying baby awkwardly. 'Who are you?'

Wendy had no intention of revealing her identity. 'You're wasting time. Let's get this baby back to its mother.' Mrs Nuttall made no move to do what she said but it was obvious she was filled with indecision. 'Come on!' cried Wendy. 'Or it's going to be too late. The police will be involved and you'll end up in prison and what will your husband say to that?'

'All right!' she said, her lips quivering. 'I'll do what you say but you have to come with me.'

Wendy was not so sure of that. She did not know this woman and she just might be crafty enough to try and put the blame on her if the police were to get involved.

'No. You have to do this yourself but I'll be keeping my eye on you to see that you give the baby back,' said Wendy. 'You can be sure of that.'

Mrs Nuttall stared at her a little longer and then suddenly placed the baby in the pram, tucked in the covers, fastened the apron and released the brake. Then she stormed off.

Wendy had to run to keep her in sight because she travelled so fast and, to her amazement, when Mrs Nuttall arrived in Walton Road, it appeared that the alarm had not been raised. Was it be possible that Mrs Nuttall had been right when she said that the mother stayed in the shop for ages without checking on her child? Wendy decided that for whatever reason the mother had not yet missed her child: Mrs Nuttall had been very fortunate. She deposited the pram outside the shop and walked away. A few moments later a young woman came out and dumped a bag of shopping on the pram's apron, smiled at her baby and chucked it under the chin.

Mrs Nuttall came striding towards Wendy but she did not stop when she came alongside her but walked right past. That suited Wendy, who headed for the tram stop and home, hoping Tilly was much better and she could tell her what had taken place.

As it happened, Tilly was still not well but her temperature had come down. She was still being kept in bed but she was up to carrying on a conversation. 'You're never going to believe this,' said Wendy, pulling up a chair and sitting at the side of the bed.

'What am I never going to believe?' croaked Tilly. Her eyes still felt heavy and she ached all over.

'Your Mrs Nuttall doesn't have a lover. What she wants is a baby.'

'What? How d'you know that?'

Wendy told her what had happened that afternoon and Tilly found the whole episode hard to believe at first. 'It's the gospel truth. Honest,' said Wendy.

Tilly's head flopped against the pillows and she stared at her for several minutes without speaking while she considered what she knew about Mrs Nuttall. 'It would explain why she goes to the park and watches the mothers and toddlers feeding the ducks. And why she ran out of the talk given by the missionary – I remember he was showing slides of children at the time. Then there was the walking up and down Walton Road, talking to the babies.' She sighed. 'She might have been crazy to do what she did but it shows how desperate she must have felt.'

'It was still wrong of her,' said Wendy.

'I agree,' said Tilly. 'And what a foolish thing to do. She must be out of her mind.'

'If she's in such a state she might do the same thing again,' said Wendy. 'Grant will have to tell the husband so he can deal with it. At least he should be pleased his wife isn't having an affair. But going out every afternoon on the off-chance of stealing a baby – she probably needs to see a head doctor.'

'No!' squeaked Tilly, then burst into a flurry of coughing.

'I'll get you a drink,' said Wendy, and she vanished downstairs.

When she returned, Tilly drained the glass and then sank against the pillows, exhausted. 'The husband doesn't want her to know that he suspected her of adultery and hired a private detective. Unless she confesses what she's done to him, he can't talk about it to her.'

'So what happens?' said Wendy. 'What do we do? Keep on watching her in case she tries again?'

Tilly sighed. 'Until Grant comes back, I suppose you'll have to. It's his case. He'll have to tell the husband what you saw and let's hope he'll know what to do to prevent her stealing any more babies.'

CHAPTER EIGHTEEN

'Good morning, Wendy! Has Tilly left for the office yet?'

'Mr Simpson, you're back,' said Wendy, beaming at him. 'Did you have a successful journey?'

'Fairly successful,' said Grant cautiously, picking up his newspaper. 'Tilly mentioned that to you, did she?'

'She mentioned you were away but didn't tell me what your journey was in aid of.'

'That's good,' murmured Grant, reading the front page headlines. 'So will she be long getting ready? I thought we could go into town together.'

'Tilly hasn't been well. She won't be going into the office today.' Wendy dropped her voice. 'She got soaked while keeping watch on Mrs Nuttall.'

Grant stared at her. 'Is she going to be all right?'

'She's on the mend but Aunt Eudora insists that she's not to get up until there's no sign of fever at all and she can't go out until the cough's gone.'

'Hell!' said Grant, looking worried. 'Can I see her?'

'Can you heck!' said Wendy firmly. 'I'm surprised at you

for suggesting such a thing.'

A slight flush darkened Grant's cheeks. 'I only wanted to talk to her.'

'I should think so but you might tire her out. Besides, I can tell you all you need to know about Mrs Nuttall.' Wendy crooked a finger and beckoned him closer. He lowered his head so that it was on a level with hers. 'I've been watching her and I can tell you she's not after a fancy man but a baby.'

'A baby? How d'you know this?'

A customer came in and so Grant was kept waiting for an answer. He drummed his fingers on the counter and watched Wendy joking and laughing with a young man with a limp. He was accustomed to having Wendy's undivided attention and found himself irritated at her flirting with the young man.

Wendy waved to the customer as he went out and then with a smile on her face, turned back to Grant. 'He's a lovely bloke,' she said.

'I've never seen you flirting before,' said Grant.

She looked puzzled. 'Me, flirt? I was just being nice to him. He's had some bad luck and when that happens you don't want miserable faces round you, do you?'

Grant agreed. 'So, Mrs Nuttall?' he asked.

Wendy explained what she had seen and he stared at her with increasing amazement. 'I didn't know you had it in you to be so firm in such circumstances,' he said. 'I owe you my thanks but I suspect my client is going to have very mixed feelings when I tell him what has happened. He might ask for my advice and I don't know what to say.'

'Perhaps a holiday,' said Wendy. 'She needs to get away and try to forget what happened. A second honeymoon. Who knows what might happen?'

He grinned. 'That's a brilliant idea. Thanks, Wendy. You give Tilly my regards and tell her not to worry about her job. It'll be there waiting for her when she's fit for work again.'

'I will.' She added casually, 'If there's any other help I can give you, then you only have to ask.'

'I'll bear that in mind,' he said. 'I probably owe you some money for your time.'

'Forget it,' she said generously. 'I was glad to help you and Tilly out.'

'You're one in a million,' he said, leaning forward and kissing her cheek. Then he hurried out, forgetting to pay for his newspaper.

Wendy touched her cheek, thinking that was a really sweet gesture. Could it be that Grant was beginning to notice that she was growing into a woman at last?

It was halfway through the morning before Wendy had a chance to go upstairs and speak to Tilly. She took her a cup of tea and knocked on her bedroom door before entering. 'Mr Simpson has been in, Tilly, and he sends you his regards.'

The hump beneath the bedcovers shifted and Tilly's head appeared. 'Did you tell him about Mrs Nuttall?'

Wendy nodded. 'He was amazed.'

'I should think he would be,' said Tilly, sitting up in bed. 'Is that tea for me?'

'Who else?' Wendy smiled and passed it to her. 'He said you're not to worry about work but your job will still be there for you once you're fit.'

'That's a relief,' said Tilly. 'Although I suppose I shouldn't have expected him to behave differently. I wonder what Mr Nuttall will do about his wife.'

'I suggested that he takes his wife on holiday. A second honeymoon,' said Wendy.

'That's a good idea,' said Tilly, staring at her as if she had never seen her before. 'You've really come up trumps, Wend.'

Wendy flushed. 'Glad you think so and if there's anything more I can do for you?'

'A book! You can bring me up a book,' said Tilly.

'You must be feeling better,' said Wendy. 'How about a nice boiled egg and some toasted soldiers?'

'I think I could manage that,' answered Tilly, smiling.

It was to be almost May before Tilly was fit enough to start work and she could not wait to be out and about again. It seemed ages since she had seen Grant or her family in Chester. Joy had phoned them to let them know she had been ill but was on the mend and that she would visit them soon. Unfortunately, she missed baby Nicholas's christening. Mal had called in and seen her but he had not stayed long. He had told her, though, that he had been unable to identify the burglar from the pictures the police had shown him. So on a sunny Wednesday morning, she set off for the office in Fenwick Street. She was impatient to find out from the great detective what had happened on his journey south to see the actress.

'Good morning, Miss Moran.' Grant grinned at her and made to hug her but she backed away. 'Sorry,' he said. 'Just pleased to see you.'

'It's good to be out and about,' said Tilly, smiling at him. 'I'm raring to go.'

'And you've remembered the milk,' he said, indicating the bottle she clutched in her hand.

'Yes.'

'Then let's get inside and you can put the kettle on. There's quite a lot to catch up on with your having been absent for so long,' he said, opening the door. 'But I'm sure you'll manage it.'

'You've had several more cases?'

He nodded. 'More to do with the insurance investigation work I do but there's another divorce snoop pending and two missing persons, as well as a jewellery and cat theft,' he replied. 'A Mrs Goldberg out Sefton Park way is the lady who has asked me to get involved in the latter.' He looked pleased. 'It's good to have some money coming in again.'

'How did you get on with the actress? Did you find her?'

'Yes. Her film name is Sylvia Adams. She offered me money to tell my client that I couldn't find her,' said Grant. 'She's had another big break and had been given a part in a series of films being made in America. She's a very attractive young woman and it's not just that she's lovely to look at. The producer has taken a shine to her and she knows that if he was to discover she'd had a baby then she might lose her chance.'

'Why didn't she just go for help to an unmarried mother's institution and give the child up for adoption when it was born if she had no intention of keeping it?'

'Because her grandmother offered to help her. She had once been on the stage herself and promised to look after the baby while Sylvia carried on working. The problem occurred when the old woman died unexpectedly, leaving Sylvia in a fix.'

'That's the trouble with life,' said Tilly. 'You can make all kinds of plans and then something happens and spoils everything.'

Grant nodded. 'She did say that she had considered putting

her daughter into an orphanage but she kept thinking of Oliver Twist.'

Tilly stared at him. 'I don't know if I believe her.'

He shrugged and sat at his desk and fiddled with the blotter. 'She was thrilled to bits when I told her the mother wanted to adopt her daughter. I suspect it's already occurred to her that when the child's paternal grandmother dies that she might be included in her will. She was talking about when she, herself, is in the money, she might just want to see her daughter again.'

Tilly was astounded. 'How will the child feel about that?'

'Sylvia thinks she should welcome her with open arms. You know these actresses, they live in a make-believe world.' He grinned. 'Anyway, I rather liked her despite everything. I was happy to take her money.'

'What about your client?'

'Don't like him. Besides, she asked me to promise to keep my eye on her daughter and to keep her informed about her progress. So that means she's my client now because she's going to pay me for doing that.'

Tilly said, 'I wouldn't have believed people would behave in such a way.'

'Truth is often stranger than fiction. That's why in real life people get away with all sorts of things. Murder, even. If you put some things that happen in a book and dress it up as fiction, your readers just might believe you.'

Suddenly Tilly wanted to be back in her bedroom, sitting at her typewriter. She had done little writing since catching a chill but had been fortunate enough to have several stories that she had sent away earlier accepted.

'What about the Nuttall's case?'

'Thanks for reminding me. I meant to tell you that Mr Nuttall was shocked and upset by the information I gave him but the next day he got in touch and said he would take his wife away for a long holiday and hopes that will do the trick.'

'She needs more than a holiday,' said Tilly. 'If she still doesn't have a baby she needs something to fill the hours. You said she tap danced. I wonder if she's good enough to take part in the concert for the orphans?'

Grant's expression was thoughtful. 'That's not a bad idea. I'll mention it to him at some time.'

Tilly smiled. 'Perhaps she might even want to adopt an orphan.'

'Don't let's get ahead of ourselves, Tilly. One step at a time. Now let's get to work.'

Tilly was in a hurry when she left work at the end of the day. She had promised to go the cinema with Wendy, as Robbie had given them complimentary tickets for the Palladium. She ran to the tram stop but groaned when she saw the length of the queue.

'Hello, Miss Moran. How are you this evening? I haven't seen anything of you recently.'

At the sound of Leonard Parker's voice Tilly felt that strange tingling inside her and she turned to look at him. 'Good evening, Mr Parker. I've been ill and that's why you haven't seen me.'

He looked concerned. 'Nothing serious, I hope.'

'A severe chill.'

'I'm sorry.' He gazed at her intently. 'Yes. I can see you've lost some of the bloom from your cheeks.'

'I know! I look terrible! But I'm definitely on the mend now and summer's on its way. I'm planning on a trip on the ferry to visit my family in Chester soon.'

At that moment a tram came rattling along and there was a concerted surge towards it. Tilly was knocked off her feet and only saved from being trampled on by Leonard grabbing hold of her and dragging her out of the crowd. She clung to him, getting her breath back.

'What do you say, Miss Moran, to us popping into a Kardomah for a coffee?' he suggested. 'I reckon in half an hour the queue will have vanished and you won't have any trouble catching a tram. There's something I'd like to ask you.'

'Oh, I'm not sure if I have the time,' she said, thinking of the proposed visit to the cinema.

'It'll only take half an hour. Surely you can spare me that time?' He smiled.

Tilly felt suddenly weak at the knees and decided that perhaps half an hour was not very long. Besides, she was curious to know what he had to say to her. 'OK. Just for half an hour.'

He looked pleased and, taking her arm, escorted her to Dale Street and the Kardomah café situated between a plumber's merchant's shop and Liverpool China and India Tea Company. They were shown to a table and Leonard drew out her chair and waited until she was comfortably seated before sitting down himself. He asked her if she would like a cake with her coffee.

'Yes, please,' said Tilly, despite having a feeling this little excursion from the normal was going to take more than half an hour – and wondering whether Don would care if he knew that she was sitting here with another man drinking coffee.

She felt an ache inside her, wondering about the blonde in the photograph and whether she and Don were lovers.

He gave their order and then sat back and gazed across at her. There was an expression in his eyes that brought a blush to her cheeks. Lowering her gaze, she drew off her gloves. 'This is an unexpected treat for me,' she murmured. 'I only started back at work today.'

'I didn't see you at the Bennetts' this morning.'

'Oh, I have another part-time job. I work for Mr Simpson's detective agency.'

He stilled. 'I thought your other occupation was writing.'

'It is! But I have to support myself doing other work as my writing income isn't enough for me to live on.'

'Don't you have family that would help support you while you write your novel?'

'Oh yes, but I want to be independent.'

He reached across the table and placed his hand over hers. 'Now, why doesn't that surprise me, Miss Moran? I suspected you of being a free spirit. If you had been older I should imagine you'd have been a suffragette, smashing windows and insulting members of parliament before the war.'

'I don't know if I'd have gone that far,' said Tilly, wondering if she should attempt to free her hand from that strong grasp. 'But-but my sister went to London and attended a rally in Hyde Park. She heard Mrs Pankhurst speak.'

'Ahhh! The great woman rallying her troops.'

Tilly nodded. 'Although I can't say I admired her behaviour during the war or since. She doesn't seem to care very much for her poorer sisters and their rights.'

'But at least she got the vote for women.'

'Only some women,' said Tilly. 'I'll have to wait years

before I can vote. Unless the law changes before I'm thirty.' She withdrew her hand. 'So, Mr Parker, what is it you wish to speak to me about?'

'I wondered if you'd heard anything more about the identity of the body and whether the burglar had been captured yet.'

Tilly was surprised he should ask her. 'Surely you could have asked the Bennetts about that?'

'True. But I'd rather not. They haven't taken Fang to their hearts and that creates an awkwardness between us. I regret it but I feel I do have to protect my property.'

Tilly decided it was wiser to not state an opinion about Fang. 'I can only say that I can't answer your questions because I don't know the answers. Although I suppose if either had happened, I would have been told.'

He nodded. 'It must be frustrating for the Bennetts that the police have not made any progress.'

Tilly said, 'Naturally they would like to hear of the capture of the burglar and recover their property but I suppose the police have a lot on their plate. One is always reading in the newspapers about some crime or other taking place.'

'Perhaps what they need is to hire your boss,' said Leonard. 'Didn't I meet him at the Bennetts' New Year's party?'

'Yes.' Tilly's brow knit. 'But Mr Simpson has enough on *his* plate at the moment.'

'And in what capacity do you work for him?'

'I do secretarial work and also help in his investigations sometimes.'

'You mean you spy on people.'

Tilly reddened. 'I wouldn't call it spying.'

'Please, don't take offence but isn't that what detectives do?'

'No! They investigate.' She was almost wishing that she had not agreed to come with him now. 'They use their brains to think matters through.'

'And no doubt they go through a lot of shoe leather trying to find out what people are about?'

There was a look in his eyes that caused Tilly to wonder if he could have caught sight of her that day she had followed him. What had he been doing in the pawnshop and talking to Patricia's uncle? She cleared her throat. 'Yes. But I've only worked on one case so far and that was to do with a client who suspected his wife having an affair. Fortunately, she wasn't. So you see, Mr Parker, we clear the innocent. Thanks for mentioning the shoe leather. I'll have a word with Mr Simpson about claiming expenses for it,' she said rather stiffly.

'I'm glad I've been of some help to you.' He paused. 'Perhaps now I can get to the real reason I asked to talk to you.' He leant towards her. 'How would you like to attend a soirée with me?'

'A soirée!'

He smiled. 'I know, it reminds one of another century. It's at the home of a business acquaintance of mine. There'll be music, conversation and supper.'

Tilly was so surprised by the invitation that she did not know how to answer him. Why had he asked her? How would her family feel if she answered yes? She thought again about Don, too. Not that she had to tell anyone about seeing a man but even so... 'When-when is it?' she asked.

'Not for six weeks but I thought I might as well get in early.'

'That would be July.'

'Yes. The second week in July. I'm sure you'll find it interesting.' His eyes gleamed as he leant across the table towards her. 'Look upon it as material for your novel. The women's gowns alone will take some describing. Your readers will imagine themselves dressed in such clothes and picture themselves waltzing with some handsome stranger.'

'You should try your hand at writing yourself, Mr Parker. You've certainly got a way with words,' said Tilly dryly. 'I'll need to think about it.'

She was already wondering what on earth she had in her wardrobe that could match anything these women he mentioned would be wearing.

'You can let me know sometime next week,' said Leonard. 'If we don't bump into each other before then, you could put a note through my letterbox when you call next door.'

'Yes, of course, I could do that,' she agreed, thinking it would save any embarrassment if she turned down his offer. She noticed the waitress coming towards them. 'Here's our coffee and cakes.'

They did not talk whilst they ate and drank. Tilly's head was still in a whirl over the very idea of his wanting to take her out. It seemed strange to her when they hardly knew each other.

'More coffee, Miss Moran?' asked Leonard, smiling. 'Or may I call you Tilly and you can call me Leonard?'

She supposed their being on first name terms was a step forward. And he really was extremely handsome and charming. The kind of man not only Eudora Bennett had warned her against but Hanny, too. 'If that's what you wish,' she answered. 'But I'm afraid I have to leave. I'm going to the cinema this evening.' She reached for her gloves.

'The cinema! I hope you enjoy yourself. I prefer the theatre myself.'

'I like the theatre, as well,' said Tilly instantly. 'But the films have something different to offer.'

'Far away places with strange-sounding names?'

Tilly smiled. 'You could say that, Mr. Leonard.' She rose to her feet. 'I'd best be going. Thanks so much for giving me this treat and for your invitation. I'll be in touch.'

He stood up. 'I hope it will be yes. Take care of yourself, Tilly. We don't want you falling foul of something nasty again, do we?' he said smoothly.

'No.' She hurried from the café, still undecided whether to accept his invitation or not. It would certainly be an experience. If Don had been in touch then she would not have even considered accepting the invitation. But as things stood between them at the moment, then... She sighed and decided not to mention it to anyone for the moment.

'You're late,' said Wendy in an accusing voice, as soon as Tilly arrived home.

'Sorry. The queues at the tram stops were terrible. I won't keep you long. I just need to have a quick wash and change. I'll eat my supper later.' Tilly disappeared upstairs before Wendy could say anything else.

Shortly afterwards when they crossed the road to the Palladium, Wendy asked Tilly how she had got on at the office. 'Fine,' answered Tilly. 'Lots of work for me to catch up on and Mr Simpson told me that Mr Nuttall is taking his wife on holiday. Isn't that nice?'

'It would be lovely with the right man,' said Wendy. 'Are you going to be doing anymore detecting for him?'

'Possibly. I'll let you know.'

They arrived outside the cinema and Tilly was glad that the commissionaire did not even spare her a glance. Yet once inside the magnificent auditorium, she found it difficult to concentrate on the screen. Her thoughts alternated between thinking of those moments in the café with Leonard Parker and what Grant Simpson had told her that morning about Sylvia Adams. How could she use these experiences in her novel? Her tummy rumbled, reminding her that she had not had supper and despite the bag of sweets Wendy produced, Tilly was glad when it was time to go home.

As soon as she had eaten her dried-up supper, she went upstairs and sat at her typewriter and began to write. That night, Tilly dreamt she was dancing with Leonard Parker in a sumptuous gown with Don sitting on the sidelines watching her with such an expression on his face that she felt terribly guilty. Then she remembered the blonde in the magazine article and was hurt and angry. She told herself that what was sauce for the goose was sauce for the gander. She woke up with the conviction that she would miss out on a great opportunity if she turned down his offer. But what could she wear? She had nothing suitable in her wardrobe and even her best dress might look out of place. Was she going to have to buy a new outfit?

Her question was to be answered within the next few days when Wendy read out to her a description of the latest Parisienne design for a walking outfit from 'Jacqueline's Mirror of Fashion'.

'The couturiers have devised a tunic of very fine lace, falling over the front of the dress, but having no back; the sides of this tunic are taken in the stitches of the sleeves, producing a wing-like effect when the arms move. This wing-like effect is also seen on tea gowns and evening dresses, in which case the ends of the tunic are frequently caught up at each wrist in a

bracelet or bangle.' Wendy glanced across at Tilly over the newspaper. 'How d'you fancy one of them?'

'I do,' she replied truthfully, taking the copy of the *Echo* from the other girl. 'I'll post off the design to my sister.'

Wendy's eyes widened. 'You're serious!'

'Of course I'm serious. I'm sure she'll enjoy the challenge of copying it.'

'But where will you go to wear a dress like that?'

'A soirée,' said Tilly, her eyes sparkling as she lifted the counter flap.

'Where?'

'Look it up in a dictionary,' called Tilly.

She did not pause to talk to the rest of the Wrights, only greeting them as she passed through the room. She needed to cut out the description of the gown and send it to Alice. Perhaps it might be worth suggesting the dress could be her eighteenth birthday present and explain why she needed such a gown. Fingers and toes crossed, Alice would agree to do as she asked. So Tilly dashed off a letter and posted it the next morning.

She was alone in the office a couple of days later when she received a telephone call, not from Alice but from Seb, wanting to know the name of this man Tilly had mentioned in her letter.

'How did you get this number?' she asked.

'I got in touch with the operator,' said Seb. 'So who is this bloke who wants to take you out?'

She told him and was glad that Grant was out of the office as she sensed he wouldn't be pleased at the thought of her going out with Leonard.

'What does this Mr Parker do?' asked Seb.

'He's in shipping,' replied Tilly, adding, 'He's perfectly respectable and it's not as if I'm going to be alone in his company.'

'How did you meet him?'

'At a New Year's Eve party at the other Bennetts' house. We've met several times since and he took me for coffee and cake the other day. But this is the first time he's asked me out,' said Tilly.

There was a silence at the other end of the line. 'I'd better not mention that to Alice or you won't be getting your dress,' said Seb. 'Leave it until next week before you come. Alice has your measurements and she knows the kind of material and colour that would suit you. She'll probably tack it together before you arrive, so you can try it on. Take care.' He rang off.

Tilly let out a relieved sigh. She would write a note to Leonard Parker that evening and drop it through his letterbox next time she was at the Bennetts'.

CHAPTER NINETEEN

'Good morning, Tilly!' said Robbie, looking up from the newspaper.

'Good morning, Mr Bennett!' She smiled at him, clasping her handbag in both hands in front of her. She felt slightly jumpy, having just popped her note through Leonard's letterbox and been barked at by Fang. She hoped her note would not be torn to shreds.

She glanced around the drawing room, wondering where Eudora was and murmured, 'Mrs Bennett hasn't forgotten I was coming today, has she?'

'No. But an unexpected telephone call meant she's had to go and visit someone in a hurry.'

Tilly was curious about the emergency. 'It isn't to do with the Doyles, is it?'

'She didn't mention any names.'

'Did she leave a message about what she wanted me to do today?'

'I'm to take you to the hall where they're going to have the concert.'

Tilly was surprised. 'She made no mention of it to me.'

'That's because they've only recently settled on a building and booked it for rehearsals and two nights in September,' said Robbie. 'There might be a couple of other people there sounding out the acoustics. A few have enquired about an accompanist, so you could have your work cut out.'

Tilly felt a little nervous but excited, as well. 'What about Pete?'

'He doesn't have to see the place yet,' said Robbie. 'Besides, I think he's doing something with the scouts this weekend.'

'Oh, I didn't know that,' said Tilly. 'So when will we be going?'

'After our cup of tea.'

A moment later the door opened and Joy entered carrying a tray. 'Did you hear that dog, Mr Bennett? One of these days he's going to have someone's throat.'

'He certainly makes me jump,' said Tilly.

'Perhaps I should get another dog,' said Robbie, getting up and taking the tray from Joy and placing it on the table. She poured out the tea and handed a cup first to him and then to Tilly.

'Have you heard anything more about your burglary?' asked Tilly.

'They've questioned your father again and searched his quarters,' said Robbie.

Tilly almost spilt the tea Joy handed her. 'Surely they can't suspect him?'

'I told the inspector they were making a mistake,' said Robbie. 'He said they had to make sure because they reckon the spate of burglaries this year is due to someone giving the burglars inside information. Myself, I think they're stumped and feel they have to be seen to be doing something.'

'Is Dad OK?' asked Tilly.

'I don't think he's going to put his head in the gas oven,' said Joy. 'Unlike this poor girl found reading a novel while she killed herself. Apparently she had been doing things she oughtn't with men in the park.'

'That's terrible,' said Tilly, thinking there had been a lot of suicides reported in the newspapers since the war.

'I wonder what novel she was reading,' said Robbie.

Joy and Tilly glanced at each other and raised their eyebrows. 'It didn't say,' murmured Joy.

'Perhaps I should pop down and see Dad,' said Tilly.

'He's gone with Eudora,' said Robbie. 'I dropped the pair of them off in St Anne's Street.' He drained his cup. 'Shall we go, Tilly? I've the use of the car, so it won't take us long to get there. I'll introduce you to the woman in charge and then I'll have to leave. You'll have to make your own way home.'

'That's OK,' said Tilly.

He glanced at Joy. 'I was hoping this charity work with the orphans would take Eudora's mind off the other business, but—'

'I thinking you're worrying unnecessarily, sir,' said Joy. 'I can't see her taking Mr Moran with her; she would have taken me. Besides, she gave you her promise.'

'You sound very sure, Joy,' he said.

'That's because I am. You stop worrying, sir, and go and buy that instrument you want.'

He drained his cup, got up and patted Joy's shoulder in passing.

Neither Tilly nor Robbie spoke until they were halfway along Sheil Road. 'Are you nervous at the thought of performing in front of an audience in the autumn, Tilly?' he asked.

'I am a bit. Although I don't suppose people will notice me as an accompanist. Their eyes will be on the singer.'

'You won't be performing solely as an accompanist but as a performer,' he said. 'You're a very attractive young woman and will be noticed. It could be the means of your earning some extra money.'

That thought had not occurred to her and she could not help wondering how she could possibly fit in any extra hours in her day to practise and perform in the evening if she was to support herself and continue with her writing. 'What about you, Mr Bennett? Will you be performing?'

'I'm not sure yet. I'm not getting any younger, Tilly,' he said. 'Indeed, I'm thinking of cutting down my hours at the Palladium. If the management don't like that idea then I'll leave. I can't see orchestras continuing much longer in cinemas now most are showing two films instead of one. It costs more to pay an orchestra and a pianist could do the job much cheaper. I've thought of teaching at home,' he added.

'You mean giving piano and clarinet lessons?'

'Yes. I'm sure I'd enjoy it. I've mentioned it to Eudora and she seems pleased with the idea.'

Tilly thought it an excellent idea. After that they both fell silent, trying to see into their futures. When they reached Kensington, Robbie parked outside the hall and then led the way inside. He introduced Tilly to the woman in charge and was about to leave when a familiar voice said, 'Hello, Robbie. I didn't expect to see you here.'

Both he and Tilly turned and stared at the woman wearing a pencil slim navy blue calf length skirt and floral blouse with a royal blue cardigan. Her jet black hair was held back with a couple of tortoiseshell combs and an odd expression lurked in the brown eyes that glinted at the pair of them.

'Well, I'm not surprised to see you, Gertie,' said Robbie. 'The sergeant gave me the impression you'd sing for the orphans.'

'Gabrielle, if you please, Robbie,' said Seb's mother. 'I'm happy to use my gift to help the poor kiddiewinks and their widowed mothers.' She placed a hand on her breast. 'I, too, am a widow and know how it feels to be a woman left without a man.'

'But you're not poor,' he said.

'That's no thanks to you,' said Gabrielle, 'but then, if you hadn't deserted me, I probably wouldn't be where I am now.'

Robbie stiffened. 'We've been through all this before. I didn't desert you.'

Tilly detected tension in the air and decided to cut in. 'Will I be accompanying you, Mrs Waters?' she asked.

Gabrielle glanced at Tilly. 'I'd like that. I know you're a talented amateur.'

Robbie scowled. 'Tilly's an excellent pianist. She could turn professional if she put her mind to it.'

'But that's unlikely, isn't it? She's working for your wife and some detective agency, I believe,' said Gabrielle.

'I suppose your sergeant told you that,' said Robbie.

She nodded. 'Where is Edie, by the way? I thought she would have been here'

'She calls herself Eudora now, as you well know,' said Robbie. 'She has other business in town.' He glanced at the clock. 'I'll have to be going. See you again, Gertie. Sometime.' He touched Tilly's shoulder. 'Don't let her bully you. See you Monday.'

Tilly smiled. 'Yes, Mr Bennett.'

'Good. I hope you enjoy yourself.' He raised his hat to them both and left.

Gabrielle gazed after him with a frown on her face before turning to Tilly. 'I know this concert seems some time off yet but you'll be surprised at how quickly the time goes. Before you know it, the damn thing is only a fortnight off and we'll be doing rehearsals with the rest of the performers. Then it's only a week off and you start panicking. Practise makes perfect, so I'd like us to meet once a fortnight through June and July and then weekly during August. If we can't practise here, then you can come to my house, Tilly – it's not that far from here.' She clapped her hands together. 'Well, let's get on with it! There's another singer here looking for an accompanist but you can play for me first.'

'I'm quite happy to do that,' said Tilly, glancing up at the piano on the stage. 'Do you know if it's been tuned lately and do you have your music with you?'

'I wouldn't come empty-handed,' said Gabrielle dryly.

Tilly flushed. 'Of course not.'

As they made their way to the stage, Gabrielle said, 'I believe it was your father who found the body in the Bennetts' garden.'

'Sergeant Jones told you,' said Tilly, glancing at Gabrielle's hair and wondering if its colour was due to it having been dyed. She was at least the same age as Eudora, yet not a grey hair showed.

'Who else? I believe you saw it. Not a pleasant experience for a girl of your age.'

'Not pleasant for anyone of any age,' said Tilly, going over to the piano. She lifted the lid and ran her fingers over the keys before sitting down on the piano stool and playing 'A Bicycle Made for Two'. She stopped abruptly and looked up at Gabrielle. 'Can you tell me what else Sergeant Jones said about my father? Apparently the police searched his quarters in connection with the burglary at the Bennetts' house.'

'He doesn't believe your father is in cahoots with the burglar, if that's what's worrying you.'

Tilly said simply, 'Thanks. It helps me knowing that. I trust Sergeant Jones.'

'He's a good, worthy and honest man,' said Gabrielle, a shadow crossing her face.

Tilly stared at her, wondering why that thought should bother the older woman. She knew that Gabrielle had once been arrested and that there was a side to her that wasn't nice. Gabrielle handed Tilly her music and they discussed the songs before having a go at them together. By the end of the session each was feeling quite pleased with the other.

'I never realised what a good voice you had,' said Tilly. 'You're marvellous for your age.'

'There's no need for you to mention my age,' said Gabrielle, looking vexed. 'If you can perform as well as me when you're as old as me, then you can be proud of yourself. I might add that you're not half-bad for *your* age. How old are you now?'

'I'll be eighteen in July,' said Tilly, amused.

Gabrielle sighed. 'So young. I was on my way to America at that age and madly in love with Robbie.' She picked up her music. 'Have you heard anything from my son? How are the children and Alice?'

'I'll be seeing them next weekend. Alice is making me a dress.'

'For the concert?'

'No. I've been invited to a soirée.'

Gabrielle looked suitably impressed. 'By a man or a woman?'

'A man.'

'Well, I hope you make sure he keeps his hands to himself, Tilly,' she said. 'You're a nice-looking young woman and some men will try and take advantage. I presume Seb and Alice know about this man.'

'They don't know him but they know of him.'

'I'm surprised Alice hasn't wanted to look him over,' murmured Gabrielle, pulling on a glove. 'I'll see you here in a fortnight, Tilly, if you'll square that with Edie. Give my love to Seb and my grandchildren.'

Tilly was about to add, *And what about Alice?* but Gabrielle was already on her way and a middle-aged man was approaching the stage. He had sandy greying hair, twinkling blue-grey eyes and a self-deprecating manner. He told her that he had played the dame in pantomimes performed by the local amateur dramatics society and always threw in a couple of comedy songs. He proved to have a fair to middling voice and after they had done a run-through of some songs, he was still yet undecided about which to choose. Both were fairly happy with the other's performance, and they arranged to meet again in a fortnight. After that, he would not be able to come for a month as he was going away.

Tilly had enjoyed herself and felt even better when she came out of the hall into brilliant sunshine. She wondered if she should return to the Bennetts' house and see if Eudora had returned home. She could ask her about the Doyles and check that her father really was all right. But when she called at the house there was no one there, so she returned home and wrote some more of her novel.

It was a slow process because her mind kept wandering, thinking of her father and what Mr Bennett had said about her musical talent, and about Gabrielle and her family in Chester. She thought especially of Alice and the dress for the soirée. Fortunately she had complete faith in her sister and knew she would not let her down. What she might say if she was to hear that the police had searched their father's premises, Tilly dreaded to think. There was also the matter of Gabrielle and telling Alice that Tilly was going to be her accompanist in a concert for the orphans; also that Gabrielle had sent her love to the family.

Tilly's thoughts and feelings were still very mixed when she set out for Chester the following Sunday, after watching the May Day horse parade in Liverpool with Eudora, her father and Joy. She had seen no sign of Leonard, so had no idea if he had received her note or not.

Tilly was greeted with smiles and hugs by her nephews and niece but Alice dragged her away from them, but only after she had promised the older two that she would play a game of croquet with them in the garden and Georgie that she would read him a story.

Alice took Tilly upstairs to her former bedroom and waved a hand to the gown lying on the bed. 'You can try it on and see what you think. You've lost weight since I last made you anything.'

'That's because I'm working harder and I was ill,' murmured Tilly, beginning to undress.

Alice set on the bed and stared at her. 'Joy didn't give us the impression you were that ill.'

'I didn't want you worrying. I caught a chill but I'm fine

now.' She stood in her underwear and reached for the dress, handling it carefully because it was only tacked together.

Alice frowned. 'So who looked after you?'

'Wendy and her mother, and Joy came several times to sit with me.'

'It sounds as if it was serious to me. You shouldn't have kept it from us, Tilly,' said Alice. 'What if you'd died? Did Dad visit you?'

Tilly did not hesitate. 'No. He's as much of a worrier about me as you are.'

Alice looked relieved. 'You believe then that I do still care for you?'

Tilly was astounded by her sister's comment. 'Of course! Why did you think I didn't want you worrying?' She had now managed to get the gown on and turned to look at herself in the mirror.

'What do you think?' asked Alice, getting to her feet.

Tilly gazed at her reflection and slowly smiled. 'You are clever. I love the way you've used bronze satin to make the gown and then made a jacket of beige lace to form the wings.'

'It's not quite as described in the article you sent me but I think it's turned out pretty well,' murmured Alice, 'if I say so myself.'

'You're wasted being just a housewife and mother,' said Tilly, turning to her sister and hugging her.

Immediately Alice said, 'Don't talk like that! Are you happy with the length?'

Tilly nodded. 'If it was for anything else I'd want it shorter but this lower-calf-length is perfect for evening wear.'

'Let me help you off with it. I think it needs to be taken in slightly at the waist.' Alice placed the dress on the bed. 'So tell me more about this man you're going to all this trouble for? How old is he? Younger than Don Pierce?'

Tilly nodded, wishing her sister had not mentioned Don because it made her feel all mixed up. She certainly wished she knew where she stood with him. 'I think so but not much. He inherited his father's shipyard business.'

Alice smiled. 'He sounds promising and lucky he survived the war. Any injuries?'

'Not that I know of and I don't know what he did in the war. Probably something to do with shipping.'

'I'd like to get a look at him. You're not yet eighteen but to get a man like that interested when there's so many other fish in the sea should tell you, Tilly, something about how attractive you are. Even so, we want you to be sure he's the right man for you.'

Tilly groaned as she put on her frock. 'For goodness' sake, Alice, it's the first time he's invited me out - it's not as if he asked me to marry him.'

'I know it's early days,' said Alice earnestly, 'but he might ask you in a few months and you'll have passed your eighteenth birthday by then. Old enough to get engaged and in six months or so you could be married.'

Tilly puffed out her cheeks and then let out a sigh. 'I'm not ready for marriage. I'd need at least a year's engagement or more so I have time to finish my novel.'

Alice said, 'You and your novel! That's just pretend and no one might want to read it. You're only young. What experience have you had of life to put in a book?'

Tilly felt like saying *Plenty after living in this household for years, and what about Dad finding the body in the garden and my getting to see it. Then I've my work with Grant Simpson and the widows and children's charity and concert in a few months.* 'My life hasn't exactly been dull,' she murmured.

'I didn't say it had but getting a man to marry you is much more important,' said Alice, turning the dress inside out.

'My writing's important to me,' said Tilly. 'It's more than just pretend.'

'But this man—'

Tilly hesitated, wishing Don wouldn't keep coming into her head. If he had found someone else then she must stop thinking about him – but her sister was waiting for an answer. 'He could be the one,' said Tilly cautiously, 'but I need to get to know him better and that's why I accepted his invitation.'

Alice smiled. 'Now that is sensible but if you continue seeing him, Tilly, you must bring him to meet us.'

'Yes, Alice,' said Tilly in a long-suffering voice. 'I'd best tell you now I met Gabrielle the other day. We're going to perform in a charity concert together.'

Alice stiffened. 'That woman! Did she mention Seb? Did she ask about the children?'

'Of course she did.'

'But she made no mention of coming to see us, I bet!'

'No. But she sent her love.'

'Her love?' Alice made a derogatory sound.

'You could come to the concert and bring the children,' said Tilly hastily. 'It's for a good cause.'

'I'll think about it,' said Alice shortly. 'Will Dad be there?'

Tilly shrugged. 'Who's to say? It depends if he feels he can cope with the crowd.'

Alice opened her mouth as if to say something sharp about their father but changed her mind. 'You'd best go and play with the children now. I'll get on with this on the machine and then you can try it on again and take it home with you. I'll want to know how the party went afterwards so make sure you come and tell me.'

'Will do,' promised Tilly. 'Although it's not until July.'

Alice looked surprised. 'That's a few weeks away.'

'I know but I wanted to make sure I had a decent dress to wear in time.' Tilly smiled. 'Which I'll have due to my clever big sister.'

'You don't have to butter me up,' said Alice, but she was smiling.

Later, when Tilly was on her way back to Liverpool, it occurred to her that if she didn't hear from Leonard during the next few weeks she would not know, unless she knocked on his door and asked, whether he had received her letter. Something inside her baulked at chasing him up but if he had read her acceptance, then she needed to know where he would pick her up to take her to this soirée.

As it was, Tilly was on pins for the next couple of weeks because she neither heard from Leonard nor saw him. Then towards the end of June when she was calling in on Eudora, she saw him coming from the direction of the park with Fang on the lead. The dog barked as soon as he saw her and strained towards her.

'I think I'd better introduce you to him as a friend, Tilly,' said Leonard, coming up to her. His gaze wandered over her in a lazy perusal.

She did not really want to be friends with Fang, but supposed Leonard had a point. 'Will he stop barking at me if he knows I'm a friend?'

'I can't guarantee that but he shouldn't bite,' said Leonard, smiling. 'He needs to recognise your scent so come closer,

Tilly, and let him have a sniff at you.' She moved closer and Leonard slipped an arm about her waist, causing a delicious thrill to go through her. He introduced her as a friend to Fang. Tilly suffered the dog sniffing her hand and her ankles before Leonard dragged Fang away. 'All done,' he said, kissing the side of her face. 'You were very brave, Tilly, and you're looking your usual lovely self. I was hoping I would see you. I'm so pleased you've accepted my invitation.'

She flushed. 'I was hoping to see you to arrange where you'll pick me up.'

'I've been away on business. Where do you live?'

She told him where the shop was and he raised his eyebrows but only said, 'That's fine. I'll pick you up at seven thirty.'

Tilly thanked him and said that she would see him then. She was wondering what the rest of the day would have in store for her as she walked up the Bennetts' path. She was surprised to find Eudora already dressed in her outdoor clothes. It seemed there was to be no morning cuppa before they left the house that day, nor time to see her father.

'I thought we'd go and give the Doyles a surprise visit,' said Eudora briskly. 'I haven't slept all night. I have a feeling – I worry about those children,' she finished abruptly.

'Me too,' said Tilly. 'But life should have improved for them now it's summer and they're getting regular help.'

'Well, we'll soon find out,' said Eudora.

They caught the tram and Eudora paid their fares and proceeded to tell Tilly about some of the acts they now had for the concert. 'We've a magician and a ventriloquist. I thought there'd be those in the audience who would enjoy a bit of magic; also a comedian.'

'What about a tap dancer?' asked Tilly, remembering Mrs Nuttall.

'You have someone in mind?'

'Yes. But she hasn't been approached yet,' said Tilly. 'I'll try and arrange for you to meet her. She hadn't been well and her husband was taking her on a long holiday.'

'I hope she's better. Let me know when she returns.' Eudora paused. 'So tell me, how are you getting on with Seb's mother?'

'Fine,' said Tilly brightly. 'She does have a good voice.'

'She could certainly belt out a song when we young. Let's hope her voice holds up on the night,' said Eudora.

Tilly changed the subject and asked whether there had been any more news about the body or the burglar.

Eudora shook her head. 'It's so annoying. I had hoped the police would have found out something more by now. I'm beginning to think I'll never see my lovely Chinese vases again and that grieves me.' She sighed. 'But then I tell myself that people are more important than possessions.'

Tilly agreed, thinking that her most precious possession was her typewriter and she would hate it if that was stolen. 'Perhaps they'll be found yet,' she said. 'Have you thought of consulting a private detective?'

Eudora smiled. 'Pushing for business for your other employer, Tilly?'

Tilly protested. 'No. But he has a client who had jewellery stolen, as well as her pedigree cat, and he's doing his best for her.'

'Any progress?'

'He says he has a few leads but doesn't want to say too much.'

They both fell silent and not long afterwards they left the tram and made their way to the street where the Doyles lived. As they approached the house, the front door burst open and Patricia came flying out. She looked like she had been crying and her clothes were torn and her hair a tangled mess. She went past them as if she did not see them.

'Something has happened. I knew I was right! You go after her, Tilly,' instructed Eudora.

Tilly ran after Patricia whilst Eudora made for the house. A man staggered to the door before she could even knock. 'Is Mrs Doyle in?' she asked.

He ignored her question and growled, 'Where's that little slut?'

Eudora could smell onions and stale beer on his breath and stepped back a couple of paces. She decided to revert to the accent of her childhood. 'If yer meant Patty, the girl's ran off. What is it yer wanted her for?'

'None of yer bloody business,' he answered, gazing down at Eudora with an ugly expression on his face. 'Who are yous, anyway?' His eyes were suddenly suspicious as he took in her appearance. 'Haven't I seen yous before?'

'I'm a friend of the family, so mebbe yer have and mebbe yer haven't,' said Eudora.

He stared at her a moment longer and then shoved her aside. She made a grab for his arm but he seized her hand and crushed her fingers, then pushed her away and staggered down the street.

Eudora was aware of palpitations in her chest and knew she had to try to keep calm. She had made herself some medicine to deal with such an event but she did not have it with her. Should she go after him and the girls or go inside and find out what had happened? She decided there would be enough people about to prevent that horrible man from hurting them. She stepped inside the house and found the silence eerie. Then she caught the sound of a snuffle and saw the pram in the corner begin to rock.

She walked slowly over to it and gazed at the baby, who was rubbing his eyes. At least he was all right but where were the other two pre-school children and their mother? It looked like she was going to have to climb the stairs. She stood a moment at the foot of the stairs and took several careful deep breaths before attempting the climb. It was a relief when she managed to reach the top and walked into the front bedroom.

At first Eudora thought Mrs Doyle was sleeping but as she drew closer to the bed, she realised the woman was not breathing. Eudora's heart began to hammer and she had trouble catching her breath. There was no sign of violence, only a carelessly tossed pillow on the floor. Where were the other two children? She forced herself to leave the first bedroom and go into the next. The bed was empty; the bedclothes flung back. She stood listening and it was as if the room was holding its breath. Then she went over and lowered herself carefully onto her knees and peered under the bed. Two frightened pair of eyes stared back at her and she almost collapsed with relief on seeing the twins.

'Come on, Mary and Maureen. Out of there,' she said breathlessly. 'He's gone. I'll look after you.'

They crawled out from under the bed and clutched at her skirts. 'Where's Patsy?' asked one of them.

'She's all right. Miss Moran will look after her. Shall we go and put the kettle on and have a warm drink?' gasped Eudora.

Both nodded. Eudora noticed that they were wearing only

their vests. She told them to put on their clothes and she sat on the bed while they did so, thinking that they needed a bobby and a doctor. Eudora knew she was in no state to go and fetch either and considered the twins too young for such an errand. Hopefully Tilly and Patricia would be back soon and then she could send them for help.

CHAPTER TWENTY

Tilly caught up with Patricia just round the corner of the street past the pub. 'Will you slow down?' she gasped. 'Tell me what's wrong.'

'Can't stop!' gasped Patricia. 'If he catches me, he'll kill me.'

'Who?' asked Tilly, running alongside her.

'Me uncle, of course. He's done for Mam.'

Tilly was horrified. 'You mean—?'

'Dead as a doornail. I saw him doing it. I couldn't believe me eyes.' Her voice broke on a sob.

'You'll have to go to the police,' said Tilly.

'Where the hell d'yer think I'm going?' shrieked Patricia. 'I wouldn't just run out on the twins and the baby! I'm going for help.'

Tilly said no more but ran with her, hoping that Eudora would manage to prevent the uncle from following them and make sure the other children were safe.

The two girls reached the Bridewell on Athol Street and dragged themselves up the steps and inside. Staggering over to the counter they rested against it, breathing heavily.

The desk sergeant looked down at them. 'So what is it you two want?' he asked.

'There's been a murder,' gasped Tilly.

His dark eyebrows twitched together. 'Where? When? Who are you?'

Tilly gave her name and status briefly and the Doyles' address.

He looked at Patricia. 'I knew yer dad,' he said. 'Yer'd best both come through.'

Patricia shook her head. 'Yer've got to get someone there now! 'Cos if yer don't he'll get away and go into hiding and then come back and get me,' she babbled.

'Now calm down, love,' said the sergeant. 'Who's the "he" yer talking about – and who's dead?'

'Me mam!' Patricia's voice cracked. 'And the he's me uncle, her brother. She stole something from him and sold it. He's a bloody thief himself and he was storing stuff in our house before getting rid of it. But now he-he—'

'Shush now,' said the sergeant in a soothing voice. 'Just tell me one thing more – did this fatality happen at your house?'

Patricia nodded.

'Then we'll send someone there right away.'

While he saw to that, he had a policewoman take them to an interview room, where she brought them cups of sweet tea and toast. As they sat beside each other drinking the tea, Tilly was aware that Patricia was trembling. She reached out and took hold of the other girl's hand and squeezed it. 'It'll be all right,' she whispered.

'It's OK for yous to say that but-but what's going to happen to us kids now Mam's dead?' Her voice broke and she began to weep into her tea.

'You'll all be taken care of,' said Tilly, feeling helpless in the face of such misery.

'Yer don't understand,' sobbed Patricia. 'That's what I'm scared of.'

Before either of the girls could say anymore, a policeman came into the room, accompanied by the policewoman who had brought them the tea and toast. She carried a notepad and pencil with her. They both sat across the table from them. 'Now, Miss Doyle, perhaps you can tell me what this is all about – from the beginning?'

Eudora started when she heard the banging on the door and, carrying the baby in her arms, went over to it and asked who was there. When she heard it was the police, she unlocked the door and invited them inside. She told them what had happened since she had arrived and where the body was, and then she sat down and waited.

It was a couple of hours before Patricia and Tilly returned to the house. By then Mrs Doyle's body had been removed and it had been decided between Eudora and the police that the children should go with her and stay at her house until other arrangements could be made. At the moment there was no room for them at the Seamen's Orphanage. As for the uncle, he seemed to have vanished without a trace.

'How long will we be able to stay at your house, Mrs Bennett?' asked Patricia, her face pale. 'I don't want to go to the orphanage. We'll be separated and I've always looked after the others.'

'Hush, dear,' bid Eudora. 'Nobody's going to separate you

and you'll be safe from your uncle with me. You can help Joy in the house and Miss Moran's father will be there to keep his eye out for any intruders.'

'Is he your dad?' asked Patricia, turning to Tilly.

'Yes. Dad's quite strong. He'll look after you,' she promised, hoping Eudora was right and that the police would find the uncle. Until they did so, she suspected that Patricia was in danger.

'So what's all this about a gang of kids staying at Uncle Robbie and Aunt Eudora's house?' asked Wendy, as Tilly came into the shop.

'Weigh us out half a pound of mixed sweets?' asked Tilly, producing a handful of change. 'And tell me how you've found that out so quickly.'

'Our Pete was having a practice there and came running to tell us,' said Wendy, moving to the shelf on which there stood shining bottles of sweets. She removed one and took out the glass top and emptied some sweets into the weighing pan.

'I did hear a clarinet but didn't realise it was him,' said Tilly.

'So give and let's know what's going on,' begged Wendy.

'I'll tell you later. I'm going back to the house with these sweets for them.'

It did not take Tilly long to perform her task and she left Patricia and the children crunching on the sweets in the attic rooms that Eudora had allotted them. She wondered if she would bump into Leonard on her way but she didn't and hurried back to the shop.

By then, it was not only Wendy who was wanting to know what had happened but her mother and Minnie, too. Over supper Tilly told them that Mrs Doyle's brother had smothered her with a pillow and her daughter had been a witness to the murder.

'The poor kid,' said Wendy. 'But why has Aunt Eudora taken them all in?'

'She did what she thought was best for them at the time,' said Tilly. 'I admire her.'

'Our Robbie's not going to like it,' said Mrs Wright. 'He's never had any kids and the noise of them will drive him mad.'

'He was good with us,' defended Peter.

'I like him,' said Davy. 'He takes me to the football matches.'

'Yes, but there's a baby. Robbie was never around when you were a baby,' said his mother. 'Mark my words. He won't put up with those kids for more than a week.'

Rita Wright was to be proved wrong because the Doyle children were still living at the Bennetts' house when Tilly was getting ready for the soiree.

'Wow! You really look somebody in that dress,' said Wendy, gazing enviously at Tilly. 'Who is taking you to this soirée?'

'None of your business,' said Tilly, holding out her winged arms and performing a pirouette.

'It's not Mr Simpson, is it?'

'No!' Tilly stopped and went over to the mirror and checked her hair, rouge and lipstick. 'You don't think I look like a painted doll, do you?'

'No. Although if I was you, I wouldn't let Mam see you.'

'And how am I to prevent that? She's bound to be in the shop or one of the rooms downstairs if you're here.'

'You could wear a mask,' teased Wendy. 'Wouldn't you

rather be going to a masked ball instead of a soirée?'

'If I could dance half-decent that would be fun.' Tilly smiled at her reflection. 'As it is, I'm looking forward to this evening. I could do with a treat.'

Wendy's expression changed. 'I can't believe you were caught up in a murder. It was bad enough when your dad found the body in the garden.'

A shadow crossed Tilly's face. 'I can't believe it myself sometimes. Those poor Doyle kids. I just hope all the grown-ups at the house are keeping a close eye on them.

'What about school?'

'Joy and your Aunt Eudora are doing lessons with them at the moment. It'll be the summer holidays soon and hopefully by September the charity will have worked out what's going to happen to them.'

'The murder got a mention in the *Echo*, you know,' said Wendy.

Tilly turned away from the mirror and picked up her handbag and gloves. 'It didn't say where the children were staying, did it?'

'No.'

'Good. I'd best be going. I'll see you later.'

'You'd best not be late. Have you mentioned to Mam that you're going out tonight?'

'Yes, and I told her that my sister and brother-in-law approve.'

'What about your dad?'

'Your mam didn't mention him,' replied Tilly. 'Which is a good job because I haven't told him.'

Wendy smiled. 'That's OK then. Have a good time. Use the side door then Mam won't see you go.'

The side door was seldom used but for once Tilly made use of it. She was five minutes early but Leonard was waiting for her in a black shiny car. Her eyes lit up. 'Is this yours?' she asked.

'Yes. I bought her a few days ago,' he replied, springing out of the car and going round to the other side to open the door for her. 'What do you think?'

Tilly stroked the side of the automobile. 'She's beautiful. I know something about cars because my family has a car business.' She hitched up her skirt at one side and climbed into the passenger seat. She was aware that he was staring at her ankles and felt her cheeks warm.

He closed the car door. 'That'll be in Chester?'

'Yes.'

'Pity they don't have a place in Liverpool, I could have put some business their way.' He lowered his head. 'You're looking lovely, by the way. That's an attractive gown you're wearing.'

The compliment made her cheeks grow even hotter. 'Thank you.' She watched him get into the driving seat and start the car and did not speak until he initiated the conversation.

'So how's your week been? Interesting?' he asked.

'Yes. A bit shocking actually. I was caught up in a murder.'

'A murder!' He glanced at her before fixing his eyes on the road again. 'How did this happen?'

'You might have read about it in the *Echo*,' she said.

'I've had little time this week for reading the newspapers,' he said dryly. 'Labour troubles: the joiners are on strike. You tell me about it, Tilly.'

So she told him and he listened without interruption until her voice trailed off because suddenly it occurred to her that

Leonard knew the murderer. His knowledge of him might only be slight but she had seen him with Patricia's uncle. Should she warn Leonard about him? But that could mean telling him that she had seen him outside the pawnbroker's in Scotland Road. She remembered the maxim *when in doubt say nought*, and decided to stick to it.

'What a terrible thing to happen to those poor children,' said Leonard, looking concerned. 'Where are they?'

Tilly hesitated. Was it possible that he was unaware that there were children living at the Bennetts' house? 'The charity has taken responsibility for them,' she said, inexplicably feeling the need to cross her fingers.

'That must be a relief to you and Mrs Bennett,' said Leonard.

'It is,' said Tilly.

'So, on a lighter note,' said Leonard, 'did you get a chance to see the prince?'

Tilly had forgotten the Prince of Wales had visited Liverpool to unveil the statue of his grandfather, Edward VII, at the Pierhead. 'No, but I've seen the statue of him sitting on a horse.'

'I managed to get a glimpse of him,' murmured Leonard. 'We're almost the same age but one day he'll be a much more powerful man than I will.'

'He'll need a queen when he's king,' said Tilly. 'I wonder if he has anyone in mind.'

Leonard smiled. 'The newspapers will love it when he decides to take the plunge. There'll be photographs of them, here, there and everywhere – the races, balls, on yachts. There'll be no end to the fascination with the gowns and jewels she wears.'

Tilly agreed that it was a fascinating subject and they discussed the royal heads of Europe and the daughters who might make a suitable wife for the Prince of Wales. He knew much more about who was who than she did and the conversation lasted until they arrived at the house in West Derby where the soirée was to take place.

The door was opened to them by a servant and they were ushered into a drawing room at the back of the house. The room was already half full of people and some had drifted out into the garden with their drinks. They were welcomed by their hostess, who smiled at Tilly and said in a condescending manner, 'What a delightful gown that is you're wearing, my dear, and you so young and pretty. Where did you find her, Leonard?'

'We bumped into each other one stormy evening,' he answered, smiling down at Tilly. 'That was quite a night.'

'So you've known each other some months,' said their hostess.

'Yes,' said Leonard, taking two glasses of champagne from the tray carried by a circulating manservant and giving one to Tilly.

She thanked him and as their hostess continued to talk to him, Tilly moved slightly away and gazed about her. She was conscious of several glances thrown her way and guessed that some women were admiring her gown and wondering about the designer, whilst others ignored her completely. She was aware that some of the men were casting an eye over her in a way that made her feel uncomfortable and she wished Leonard would stop talking to their hostess and take notice of her.

Eventually, he did so and introduced her to several other

people in the room. A couple of the women were friendly and included her in their conversation concerning holidays. One woman was going to the South of France in August, whilst another was taking her children to Devon to a little cottage that her cousin had near Ilfracombe. Leonard stayed close to her most of the time, telling her a little about the different people to whom he introduced her, after they had moved on, in a manner that shocked her a little because it was slightly malicious, if amusing.

It was not until after the mezzo soprano was introduced and was singing her second song that Tilly noticed Leonard was missing. She gazed about her surreptitiously but could not see him anywhere. Then, unexpectedly, she spotted Grant Simpson across the room. He was sitting with a fashionably dressed, extremely attractive woman. Tilly wondered if she was the rich client that she had yet to meet. She hoped he would not notice her because then she would have to tell him that Leonard had brought her here and she sensed the two men had no time for each other.

Leonard appeared just before the mezzo soprano finished her performance. Tilly would have liked to have asked where he had disappeared to but did not like to appear as if she was keeping an eye on him.

A buffet was served in another room and now it seemed that Grant had disappeared but she could see the woman he had been with talking away to another woman. After the food they returned to the drawing room, which had been cleared for dancing. A male pianist was sitting at the piano and he launched into a Viennese waltz.

'Would you like to dance, Tilly?' asked Leonard.

'I haven't danced much although my sister taught me a few

steps so I'm willing to give it a try.' She found herself thinking of Don's injured foot and how she'd accepted that it was unlikely he would ever be able to whirl her around a dance floor. She wondered if the blonde ever thought about such frivolities.

'I should think so, too,' he said with a gleam in his eye. 'Show off that pretty gown you're wearing.'

Tilly was swept onto the parquet floor and, forgetting all about Don and Grant, she gave herself up to the music and the heady intoxication of being held by Leonard. She could feel his breath on her cheek and his hand against her back, pressing her close to him. She thought his lips brushed her ear but told herself that she imagined that fleeting touch.

She was to dance with him several times before the evening came to an end. Tilly had really enjoyed herself and thanked her host and hostess sincerely. 'Leonard must bring you again,' he said.

Leonard only smiled and swept Tilly out of the door and down the drive to where his car was parked. It was not until they were halfway home that he asked her whether she had enjoyed herself.

'Yes, thank you,' she said, giving a delicate yawn and stretching like a cat.

'Then you'll come out with me again?'

She smiled at him. 'I should like that.'

'They liked you. I wouldn't be surprised if I was asked to bring you along to more occasions like this,' he said, with a satisfied smile. 'People are so interesting after they've had a few drinks and let their guard down.'

Tilly did not argue with him. She had made certain that she did not drink too much. Fortunately, she did not care for the taste of champagne. When the car drew up outside the shop and Leonard did not make any immediate move to get out and open her door, she thought that it was odds-on favourite that he was going to kiss her. Especially when he reached out and put an arm round her shoulders and brought her close to him.

Then a voice said, 'Now, none of that, young man.'

Immediately, Tilly realised it was Mrs Wright and swallowed a groan. She must have been watching out for her from the bedroom upstairs. 'I'd better go,' she whispered. 'Thank you for a lovely evening.'

'My pleasure,' he said stiffly, withdrawing his arm.

She sensed his annoyance and found herself whispering an apology for Mrs Wright's interference. She fumbled for the door and managed to open it without much difficulty. 'Goodnight.'

'Goodnight, Tilly,' said Leonard, and he drove off without mentioning when next he would see her.

'I've seen him before,' said Mrs Wright, gazing after the car, 'but I can't remember where. Someone obviously with a bob or two.'

Tilly kept quiet and walked towards the side door, which was open. She had no intention of revealing Leonard's identity because Mrs Wright was bound to tell her brother. He would tell Eudora and she'd tick Tilly off for going out with him and remind her that he was not for her.

Tilly hurried upstairs to her bedroom before she could be asked any questions. She wasted no time washing her face and cleaning her teeth and almost fell into bed, but once there she found she could not sleep. Would Leonard ask her out again? If he did, she would definitely not have him picking her up outside the shop. She tried to imagine what it would have felt like being kissed by him and her body tingled as it had done when she had danced with him. Eventually she fell asleep to have a weird dream with Grant chasing after Leonard with a shovel and Rita Wright standing on the sidelines waving a pair of handcuffs. She woke suddenly and wrote down the dream in a notebook she kept by her bed, just as she had sometimes done in the past.

When Tilly woke on Saturday morning and read what she had written down, she wondered what it could mean; if it meant anything at all. She managed to avoid seeing Mrs Wright, who was in the shop when Tilly came downstairs. She rushed her breakfast and left the house by the side door and headed for the Bennetts' house. She had also been lucky enough to escape too much questioning from Wendy and played down her enjoyment of the party.

Although it was still early, the morning sun was hot and the grass in the park was turning yellow. There had been no rain for a while and the newspapers talked of a drought. As she walked along Newsham Drive, Tilly hoped she might see Leonard but there was no sign of him.

As Tilly went round the back of the Bennetts' house she looked about her for her father and the Doyle children, only to be greeted with the news that Joy had taken all the children to the park and that Mal had run Eudora to the Seamen's orphanage in the car. 'Presumably to discuss with her cronies what to do with these children. That baby kept me awake half the night,' added Robbie, yawning.

Tilly remembered what his sister had said about her brother not being used to small children. 'So you wouldn't have liked a large family, Mr Bennett?' she said.

Robbie cocked an eye at her. 'I realise, Tilly, I've had a lucky escape leading the life I have. I'm just hoping this doesn't go on for long and Eudora can work something out for them quickly. It's not that I don't feel sorry for the poor kids. I do.' He paused. 'So are you off to the hall for a rehearsal this morning?'

She nodded. 'I'll come back here when I've finished and see if there's anything Mrs Bennett wants me to do.'

He yawned again. 'I'm sure we'll have a house full by then and she'll find you something.'

When Tilly arrived at the hall she was disappointed to find that Gabrielle had not turned up but had left a message saying that she was sorry but she could not make it that day. So Tilly returned to the Bennetts' house to find three of the children in the kitchen with Joy. She was showing them how to make gingerbread men. Tilly sat down and watched them enjoying themselves. 'You're good at this, Joy,' she said. 'But aren't you tired after taking them the park earlier?'

Joy nodded. 'I'm enjoying the change and, to be honest, it's Patricia that does most of the running around after them. I just wheel the pram and keep my eye on them. I find it hard to believe from their behaviour that they've lost their mother.'

'I think as long as they have Patricia there, they'll be OK,' said Tilly.

Joy lowered her voice and said, 'Mrs Bennett told me that Mrs Doyle wasn't the best of mothers. Still, she was their mother and they've no parent now, and the uncle sounds a real bad 'un and could end up with a noose round his neck.'

Tilly nodded. 'I wonder what the committee will decide to do with them. It would be sad and wrong if they were to be separated.'

'They wouldn't be the only brothers and sisters for that to

happen to when they're orphaned, Tilly,' said Joy. 'You should know that by now. Even when they're taken care of by aunts and uncles, most can't take all the children when the family is as large as this one.'

Tilly sighed. 'I know.'

It was not long after that that Eudora came home. Tilly thought she looked tired. She was relieved to learn that Eudora had told the committee that she was willing to have the Doyle children living with her for the foreseeable future. Tilly could not help asking, 'What will Mr Bennett say?'

'He'll do whatever I have decided,' said Eudora after the barest hesitation. 'I'm sure it won't be for long. You, Tilly, can help here with the children instead of going out visiting other families.'

That suited Tilly. 'What about their schooling? And I'll need to have time off to practise for the concert,' she said.

Eudora nodded. 'I've had a word with one of the committee members whose husband is on the PCC of St Margaret's church. She thinks he might be able to arrange for them to attend the school there. It's high church and they have lay sisters teaching the children. The Doyle children are Catholics so they should feel reasonably at home there. Mrs Doyle's funeral is on Wednesday. I presume you'll want to attend, Tilly?'

She nodded. 'I'll get a message to Grant Simpson and tell him I won't be able to come in that day.'

So it was settled that Mondays and Tuesdays Tilly would help care for the youngest Doyle children and also Saturdays when she was not rehearsing. She asked Patricia how she felt about the decision.

'Better than being separated,' muttered Patricia, glancing

up from the primer she was struggling to read. 'But it won't last.'

'Nothing lasts for ever,' said Tilly. 'Hopefully when change comes it'll be for the good.'

Patricia did not answer but lowered her eyes to the book again.

The next day, Sunday, was Tilly's eighteenth birthday, so she visited her family. Alice had made a cake and Tilly managed to blow out all the candles in one go but what she remembered most of that day was her conversation with her sister that mainly revolved around her evening out with Leonard Parker and whether he had complimented her on the dress and asked her out again.

Tilly said, 'He said my dress was lovely and that I was pretty but as for asking me out again, Mrs Wright sent him away before we could arrange another outing,' she said.

'He will be back,' said Alice confidently.

Tilly hoped so but she was not counting her chickens yet. Perhaps she would see Leonard tomorrow morning when she was at the Bennetts' house again.

To Tilly's disappointment there was no sign of him or his shiny black car. She tried to put him out of her mind and went to have a few words with her father, who was cutting roses for the house. He had forgotten her birthday but she did not mention it.

'Hello, Dad! How are you today?'

He rolled his eyes. 'I'll be fine as long as those bairns keep out of my garden.'

'It's natural for them to want to play outside,' said Tilly.

'There's the park across the road,' he said.

Tilly smiled, thinking she couldn't argue with that.

Suddenly she sensed movement and glanced to the neighbouring wall. She caught a glimpse of the woman before the head bobbed down.

'Here, lass, take these flowers in for Eudora,' he said.

She hesitated. 'The police haven't bothered you again, have they, Dad?'

'More pictures, more questions,' he muttered. 'I told them that I'd know the man if I saw him again. Mr Bennett said I'm not to heed them. But apparently there's been another burglary in a house in West Derby. That's not far from here.'

Tilly stared at him. 'West Derby? Did they say exactly where?'

'Aye, but I've forgotten. I told them I've never been there – don't know it!' He looked harassed.

Tilly said no more but kissed him on the cheek and went inside.

CHAPTER TWENTY-ONE

'Good morning, Tilly,' greeted Grant, breezing past her to open the door. It was now Thursday, the day after Mrs Doyle's funeral. Eudora had decided that only Patricia should attend the service. It was a sad little ceremony and Tilly was glad when it was over.

'Good morning, Mr Simpson.'

'How are you today?'

'I'm well, Mr Simpson,' she replied. 'How are you?'

'Fine, fine.' He took the stairs two at a time but she followed more sedately. It was not until they were inside the office and the kettle was on that he said, 'So what were you doing at the party last Friday? Did you know there was a robbery there on the Saturday evening?'

'So it was there!' exclaimed Tilly. 'That woman you were with, is she the client with the missing jewellery and pedigree cat?'

'The very one.' Grant's eyes gazed directly into Tilly's. 'I told her I wanted to do some undercover work to catch this thief, so she agreed to take me along to parties with her.

Though she refuses to believe that any of her friends could be in cahoots with the robbers and passing on information.'

'So you believe there's more than one man involved?' asked Tilly slowly.

He nodded. 'She's told me that it's nearly always the same people at these affairs.' He filled his fountain pen from the inkwell. 'One of them is Leonard Parker, but you know that. You were there with him, weren't you?' He glanced up at her.

'Yes! And I had a lovely time,' she said with a hint of defiance.

He stared at her thoughtfully. 'Are you going out with him again?'

'Perhaps.'

Grant forced a smile. 'Good. Then you can keep your eye on him if he takes you along to any more parties.'

'You mean, you want me to spy on him?' asked Tilly, aghast.

'I know,' he murmured, seemingly concentrating on filling his pen. 'It could be dangerous. I suppose I shouldn't have mentioned it to you. You'll be happier here typing and filing.'

Tilly hesitated. 'I want the burglars caught for my dad's sake but Leonard might not ask me out again. I haven't seen or heard from him since the party, and although I've been to the Bennetts', house I haven't seen his big black car either.'

'Perhaps he's away.'

'That's what I thought.' She felt hurt that if Leonard had gone away he had not bothered to let her know. There had to be some way of finding out. She was tempted to speak to his older relative next time she popped her head above the wall and ask where he had gone.

Tilly decided to change the subject for now. 'So how is the

divorce case going and have you seen anything of Mr Nuttall?' she asked.

'I know he's back from holiday because we passed the time of day in the street,' said Grant. 'His wife still isn't A1.'

'Then what about the next time you see him mentioning the concert for the orphans? You could say that you wondered if his wife might be interested in doing a turn?'

'OK,' said Grant. 'As for the divorce case, that's sorted and you can type up my notes and an invoice for my fee.'

Tilly nodded and set to work.

On Saturday she went to the Bennetts' and asked Joy if Mr Parker's car had been seen at all.

'No,' said Joy. 'Apparently, he's gone to America.'

'America! But surely he wouldn't take his car,' said Tilly.

Joy shrugged and Tilly said no more.

July turned into August and the good news was that the wheat harvest had been bountiful and cheaper bread was forecasted. Wendy also pointed out to Tilly the changes in the laws to do with banns of marriage.

'Apparently some people were claiming residency in a parish simply by leaving a suitcase in a room. For some reason it's believed that bigamy was often the result of such marriages,' said Wendy.

Mrs Wright spoke from the other side of the shop. 'You know what's needed, girls? A change in the divorce laws. Too many couples married in haste during the war, only to discover when they had to live together that it had been a mistake.'

Tilly mentioned this to Grant the next day due to his involvement in divorce cases. 'What do you think?'

'I agree with Mrs Wright. The rules for divorce should be

changed but until they are there's still work for me. Even though these adultery cases are fixed sometimes.'

'You mean some of those involved aren't always committing adultery?' asked Tilly, frowning.

Grant smiled. 'Some are, some aren't but are prepared to do what's necessary to be rid of their partners.'

Tilly said no more but she was really having her eyes opened when it came to the whole concept of love and marriage and happy endings.

The Doyle children continued to stay at the Bennetts' house, rehearsals went on for the concert – and still there was no sign of Leonard. Grant told Tilly that there were also no party invitations going out during August and early September because most people were on holiday.

Tilly asked Grant if he had spoken to Mr Nuttall about the concert.

'Damn! I forgot, Tilly. I'll do it next time I see him.'

Tilly wondered if she was wasting her time pushing the idea. After all, it was only a few weeks to the concert now. But he must have seen Mr Nuttall because the following Saturday morning Mrs Nuttall arrived at the Bennetts' house just as Tilly was getting there. She also noticed that Leonard's large black car was parked outside his house again. The sight of it filled her with mixed feelings. Perhaps if it had not been for Mrs Nuttall then she might have hung around outside the house for five minutes or so, but the woman was looking at her as if she knew her.

'Hello,' said Tilly. 'Have you come to see Mrs Bennett?'

'Yes,' answered Mrs Nuttall. 'Should I know you? Your face looks familiar.'

Tilly smiled. 'We have met briefly – outside a church hall

where there was a missionary showing slides of Africa.'

Mrs Nuttall looked relieved. 'So that's where I saw you. Do you know Mrs Bennett well?'

'Yes. I work for the seamen's widows and orphans charity she's involved with and I'll be playing the piano in the concert,' replied Tilly. 'It's for a good cause and it should be fun.'

'Fun?' Mrs Nuttall crinkled her nose. 'You aren't nervous?'

'Of course I am! But I'm sure it'll all come right on the night,' said Tilly. 'Shall we go in?' The front door was slightly ajar, so Tilly pushed the door wide and led the way in.

The door to the sitting room opened and Eudora appeared. She looked careworn but smiled when she saw Tilly and the woman with her. 'You must be Mrs Nuttall.' It was then that Tilly realised that Grant had taken the step of giving Mr Nuttall Eudora's phone number.

'Yes. Mrs Phyllis Nuttall.' The two woman shook hands. 'I believe it was a friend of my husband who mentioned me to you.'

'Yes. But, of course, if you're too busy or feel you don't want to perform then you don't have to,' assured Eudora.

'No. I'm not too busy,' said Phyllis hastily. 'Whether I'm good enough to entertain people is a different story.'

'Shall we go to the hall and you can see how you get on,' said Eudora, smiling. 'I won't be able to stay, I'm afraid, but Tilly will look after you.'

They left the room and were making their way to the front door when a voice piped up, 'Who's that lady?'

Tilly, Eudora and Phyllis looked up in the direction of the voice and saw one of the auburn-haired twins peering through the banister rails. Then a hand grabbed her from behind and

Patricia said, 'Hush, you, it's none of yer business? Sorry, Mrs Bennett,' she called down.

'It's all right, Patricia. Ask Mr Bennett about tickets for the children's matinee. It'll fill a few hours for you. Then Tilly will help look after them this afternoon.'

'What about the baby?' asked Patricia.

Eudora sighed. 'I'm sure if you wheeled his pram into the kitchen then Joy will keep an eye on him.'

Tilly thought it was not surprising Eudora looked so tired. She and Robbie were too old to have to cope with seven children in the house, even with help. Perhaps after the concert changes would have to be made. Tilly felt butterflies in her stomach thinking about performing on stage.

Her father drove them to the hall but Eudora was unusually silent on the journey and left it to Tilly to explain to Mrs Nuttall what working for the charity entailed. It was not until Tilly and Mrs Nuttall were dropped off at the hall and said that they would make their own way home that Mrs Nuttall asked about the children living in the Bennetts' house. Tilly told her briefly of the disasters that had fallen on the Doyle family and the woman expressed suitable dismay at what the poor children had been through.

Then Tilly introduced her to the stage manager and left the pair of them to arrange matters to their satisfaction. Gabrielle had missed a couple of practices but today she had turned up and the rehearsals passed off without any problems arising. After finishing her normal rehearsals, Mrs Nuttall asked Tilly if she would accompany her, too, and Tilly could not see how she could refuse after going to such lengths to involve the woman. After a few false starts it was a relief to discover that Mrs Nuttall had a natural rhythm and Tilly enjoyed being an essential part of the routine.

They parted outside the hall because Mrs Nuttall had decided to go into town and do some shopping. Tilly caught the tram that took her along Sheil Road and then walked to the Bennetts' house. She was about to go inside when a voice hailed her and she turned round to see a smiling Leonard.

'Hello, Tilly. How are you today?'

She felt a spurt of anger, thinking about how she had not heard a word from him for over six weeks. 'I've just been practising for the concert for the orphans,' she said stiffly.

'Ahhh! The orphans! I believe there are children staying in the Bennetts' house.'

'Yes.'

He frowned. 'Where did they come from? Are they relatives of the Bennetts?'

'Perhaps you should ask Mr Bennett,' said Tilly. 'I'd best go in. Mrs Bennett is expecting me.'

'I think you're vexed with me,' he said. 'Perhaps you thought I should have let you know I was going away.'

'It would have been polite,' said Tilly icily, walking away without another word or a backward glance.

CHAPTER TWENTY-TWO

Tilly hurried to the tram stop, hoping there would not be a repeat of the scenes on Wednesday, when the unemployed had gathered outside the town hall in Dale Street, demanding to see the Lord Mayor. It was Friday and that evening was to be the first performance of the concert especially for the children and staff from the Seamen's Orphanage, as well as the families helped by the charity. Earlier, on this September day, there had been scattered showers, but now the sky had cleared, promising a fine evening.

She had decided to wear the dress that Alice had made her for the soirée; this despite the conviction that most eyes would still be on the singers and not her. This was mainly because Gabrielle had said audiences liked a bit of glamour and to dolly herself up. All those in the Bennetts' household except for Joy and the Doyle baby were to be at the performance: Wendy, Minnie and Davy were also going this evening but Mrs Wright would be minding the shop and would attend the show on Saturday with Mrs Pain. Tilly had let Alice know that their father would be attending the Friday performance and so those in Chester would also be coming tomorrow. Grant had bought a ticket and planned to be at the second performance with Mr Nuttall.

Tilly was ready by five o'clock and came into the shop, carrying her music, to remind Wendy that the concert started at seven and to chivvy Minnie and Davy so they wouldn't be late and could get a decent seat. Peter had already gone on ahead to the Bennetts' as he was having an extra rehearsal with Robbie overseeing it.

'D'you know what it said in this old *Echo* that was wrapped round the chips I bought last night?' said Wendy.

Tilly groaned. 'Not now! My head's full of stuff I have to think about.'

'I'm going to tell you anyway,' said Wendy firmly. 'Because it's a woman writer who's said it and it's really got my dander up.'

Tilly's shoulders drooped. 'OK, tell us. But don't be ages. I need to be at the Bennetts' within a quarter of an hour.'

'This writer said a woman's brain is like a musical box compared to a man's, which is like an organ. I thought you being musical and a writer and a woman would have something to say about that.'

'It's an insult to our sex,' said Tilly indignantly, drawing on a beige glove. 'Have you ever heard a musical box? It tinkles merrily along while an organ—'

'I know, I know,' interrupted Wendy. 'It has all these pipes that makes different sounds and it's that powerful it can fill a huge building with noise.'

'Too much noise at times. It can drown out other voices.' She paused. 'There's some truth in that because there are men who love the sound of their own voices and won't allow others to have a say. Anyway, I'm going. See you later.' She hurried out.

When Tilly reached the Bennetts', she noticed that Leonard's car was missing. Part of her regretted being short with him the last time she had seen him but she had been terribly hurt by his lack of consideration. She had to admit that she still found him attractive, but it still niggled her that she had seen him talking to the Doyle children's uncle. She knew why she had kept quiet about that; she did not want to believe that Leonard could be in any way connected with that terrible man. She gnawed on her lip and then told herself there was little point in worrying about it now. What if, due to her mind being elsewhere, she struck a false note? She could imagine what Gabrielle would have to say about that. But she was not going to worry about making mistakes; otherwise the thought might be party to the act. She took a deep breath before heading up the Bennetts' path, thinking she would be glad when it was all over.

As it was, Tilly need not have worried; that evening's performance went off with very few mishaps all round. A juggler who had perfected his act the other day, dropped a ball and the stand up comedian forgot one of his punch lines; Mrs Nuttall missed a step and, surprisingly, Gabrielle's voice suddenly faltered. But on the whole the performances weren't at all bad and she and Peter were note perfect. At the end, they all received thunderous applause and the stage manager assured them that it would all be perfect tomorrow night. 'It's just first performance nerves and you heard the audience's applause,' he said. 'They loved it.'

Mal came to congratulate her afterwards. 'Well done, lass. Yer mother would have been proud of yer. It was a great performance.'

She hugged him. 'Thanks, Dad. I'm glad you enjoyed yourself.'

'Aye. I did. But I'm going to take Eudora and Mr Bennett home now. She's no' so good and needs to rest. You and Patty will be all right with the bairns on the tram?'

'Of course we will. I'll see you later.'

She watched him go, so delighted that he had coped with the evening and enjoyed himself.

'Well done, Tilly,' said Gabrielle, coming up behind her and patting her on the back. 'You're a real trooper. Hopefully tomorrow I won't allow my mind to stray just because Edie was in the audience. Seeing her there took me back to the time when we were young and our names were on the same poster outside theatres.' She sighed. 'We were friends then.'

'If you want a word with her you'd best have it now. Dad's taking her and Mr Bennett home in a minute,' said Tilly.

Gabrielle shook her head. 'Too much water under the bridge and we'd only end up being bitchy to each other.'

'She might thank you for volunteering to be part of the show.'

Gabrielle's face hardened. 'I don't want her thanks. I didn't do it for her but for the widows and their children. I remember what it was like growing up without a father. Mine was a seaman, too, you know. But I don't remember our family ever being offered any help and we could have done with it.' She surprised Tilly by kissing her cheek. 'I'll see you tomorrow, love.'

Tilly wondered whether she should tell her that the whole

family from Chester would be there on Saturday. In the end she decided to keep quiet, just in case the weather should change or a train break down so they couldn't make it after all.

'It went well,' said Wendy, sitting on the crowded tram next to Tilly. The noise of the chattering Doyle children and the younger Wrights was almost deafening. 'Pity Grant Simpson couldn't be there tonight. Will he be there tomorrow?'

'Yes. He's coming with Mrs Nuttall's husband.'

'Mam insisted on my going tonight because there would be that many kids there. I'd have liked to have gone tomorrow. Still, it's over now and I enjoyed it. Our Pete did well and Mrs Nuttall was good – you can see why tap-dancing is catching on over here,' said Wendy. 'There's something cheerful about the sound of those tapping feet. You played well, too,' she added as an afterthought.

'Thanks,' said Tilly dryly. 'Don't forget to tell your Pete how good he was, it'll boost his confidence.'

'OK!' said Wendy. 'But I can imagine Mam saying *We don't want him to get bigheaded, do we?*' She mimicked her mother perfectly.

They both fell silent and then Wendy leant forward and tapped Minnie on the shoulder. She was reading a magazine and obviously trying to ignore the surrounding noise. Even so, she stopped reading and chattered to her sister.

They all got off the tram together but split up. Tilly said, 'I'll see the kids back to the house. I won't be late.'

The Doyles waved to the Wrights and followed Tilly. The twins slipped their hands in hers whilst Patricia brought up the rear with Micky, Jimmy and Kathleen. Tilly was just ushering them through the Bennetts' gate when a shiny black car drew up at the kerb. She paused and then told the children to hurry inside but Kathleen lingered in the gateway. Tilly nudged her and told her to get inside.

Leonard got out of the car and stared at Tilly. 'Did my eyes deceive me, Tilly, or did you have a group of children following you down the drive a few moments ago? I was reminded of the Pied Piper of Hamelin.'

'We had the charity concert tonight in aid of the orphans,' she said.

'So that's why you're wearing your pretty gown.'

'Yes.'

'Did it go well?'

She nodded. 'There's another performance tomorrow, so I'll be playing again. Tomorrow is for the general public and my family are coming from Chester.'

He looked interested. 'Can you get me a ticket?'

'I should think so.'

'Drop it through my letterbox and I'll give you the money when next I see you.'

'OK!' She was pleased by what he said.

'Good.' He smiled. 'I'll look forward to seeing you perform and perhaps you can introduce me to your family.' He raised his hat and headed for his own front door.

Tilly did not move for a moment but her head was in a whirl, imagining what Alice would have to say when she met him. She hoped that she would not gush all over him and say things that would embarrass her. At least she could depend on the others not to do so. Although, it was possible that Seb might mention Don. Somehow she didn't think her brother-in-law would take to Leonard. If only Don had been in touch and she had not seen the photograph of him with that blonde. She sighed and went inside the Bennetts' to discover there was no sign of the children or Eudora.

'Where's Mrs Bennett?' she asked Joy.

'Gone up to bed to have a lie-down. I'm going to take her some tea up. Why?'

'I need another concert ticket for tomorrow.'

'I think they're all gone,' said Joy, 'but you can have mine. Mr Bennett's going to be at the Palladium and I don't feel right leaving her alone with the children and just your dad down the garden.'

'What's wrong with her?' asked Tilly, sitting down on a chair. 'I've noticed she hasn't been herself for a while. She gets breathless and tires easily.'

Joy placed a teaspoon in the sink. 'She's no spring chicken, you know.'

'But she had such life in her this time last year,' said Tilly.

'She's been doing too much since she moved over here, and then to take on the Doyle children, that was pure daft,' said Joy in a low voice. 'I think Mr Bennett will put his foot down and they'll be going sooner, rather than later.'

Suddenly Tilly felt sad, thinking about Patricia and what she had said about change and the family being split up. 'I wish there was something I could do to help.'

'There's only so much that any one person can do. You've done all you can,' said Joy, picking up a tray with a steaming cup of cocoa and a couple of dry biscuits on it. 'The ticket's in the Wedgwood comfit dish on the shelf.'

'I'll make sure you get a refund,' said Tilly, taking the ticket out of its hiding place.

'Never mind. It's all for a good cause,' said Joy. 'You get on home. You've got another big night ahead of you tomorrow.'

Tilly thanked her and left. She popped the ticket through next door's letterbox and walked away, looking forward to having a rest and some time to herself before performing again tomorrow.

Tilly stood on the stage, peering through a gap in the curtains at the rapidly filling hall. Would all the family make it? Or would someone have to stay behind if they couldn't get someone to stay with the younger children and Hanny's mother? Had Leonard got her ticket safely? And what would Grant think if he noticed him here? Her stomach was churning and she wished she could relax.

'Will you come away from there, Miss Moran?' hissed the stage manager. 'The curtain will be going up soon on the first act. Get in the wings and wait your turn.'

'I was just looking to see if my family had arrived,' whispered Tilly. 'I posted their tickets to them.'

'And have they?'

'I can't see them.'

'Well, looking won't get them here any faster. Besides, it's easy to miss people when so much is going on. Now away with you.'

Tilly did as she was told and went in search of Gabrielle, wondering all over again whether she should let her know the family were supposed to be coming. As it was, Gabrielle turned up only minutes before they were due to go on. She was not alone but accompanied by Sergeant Jones.

'He's going to watch from the wings,' she said to Tilly. 'You ready, girl?'

Tilly nodded, thinking the older woman looked magnificent

in a black silk gown with a red floral print that revealed a couple of inches of cleavage. She wore red ostrich feathers in her hair and a red boa about her shoulders. Tilly could imagine what Alice would think when she saw her. They walked onto the stage to a thunderous applause. Gabrielle smiled and bowed and signalled to Tilly with a wave of a graceful hand to take her place at the piano. Tilly felt a calmness come over her as she sat at the piano and began to play the introduction, as she had done so many times in rehearsals, with skill and precision. Suddenly she knew that the pair of them were going to excel for no other reason than that they found pleasure in what they were doing.

'You were marvellous,' said Leonard, pushing his way through the crowd gathered about Tilly and Gabrielle. 'You're much more than an amateur, Tilly,' he added, lowering his head and kissing her cheek.

'Who's this?' asked Gabrielle, eyeing him up and down.

'I think I have one over on you there, mother-in-law,' said Alice, smiling at Leonard. 'If I'm not mistaken, this is Mr Parker.'

He turned to Alice and held out a hand. 'You have to be Tilly's sister. The pair of you look so alike.'

'Yes. But I was only fifteen when she was born,' said Alice promptly. 'Has she told you that I brought her up after our mother died in childbirth?'

'No! I mean, you could almost be taken for twins,' he said.

Alice's smile deepened. 'You flatter me, Mr Parker.'

'He certainly does,' murmured Gabrielle. 'I wonder what he's after?'

Leonard stared at her. 'You sang very well for a woman of your age, Mrs—'

'Waters,' replied Gabrielle.

Tilly swallowed a gasp, wondering how Leonard could be so rude.

Gabrielle added with a sweet smile. 'If you can perform half as well as I can at my age, Mr Parker, then you'll be doing well. Handsome is as handsome does, I always say. Now, if you'll excuse me I have my admirers to consider.' She turned to her grandchildren and said, 'Ready, kiddiewinks? How about if I take you all for some macaroons?'

Seb had been listening with a sense of growing unease to the conversation between the man who might possibly be Tilly's future husband and his wife and mother, and did not like him one little bit. Perhaps he should try and instigate some letter writing. There was always the chance that Don might be back in America again so he would write and tell him how matters were with Tilly and hope his friend would do something. If he didn't then he could lose her.

'Where are you taking them for macaroons, mother-in-law?' asked Alice.

'To my house, it's not that far from here,' answered Gabrielle, glancing at her son's scarred face with a hint of pain in her eyes. 'You don't mind, do you, Seb? The night is young. You've met my friend, Sergeant Jones, haven't you? He'll drive us.'

'Yes, Ma. The sergeant and I have met,' answered Seb patiently. 'But we have to get back to Chester and it's getting late.'

'I'd like to go to Grandma's house,' said Flora, tugging on her father's sleeve.

'Yes, let's stay with Grandma,' said James.

Alice frowned. 'I don't know if that's a good idea.'

Seb said, 'I don't see why not. It is Sunday tomorrow so I don't have to go into work and the children don't have school.'

'Perhaps I should leave you all to sort this out,' said Leonard.

'Yes, that might be for the best, Mr Parker,' said Seb, a glint in his eye.

Leonard turned to Tilly. 'Perhaps I could take you home.'

'Kind of you, Mr Parker,' said her half-brother. 'But my wife and I are staying overnight in Liverpool and we'd like to see a little more of Tilly.'

Leonard's smile vanished. 'Of course. Family! I understand,' he said stiffly, and walked away.

Tilly stared after him, angry at her family's interference in her affairs. 'Now see what you've done,' she said. 'He might not ask me out again.'

'Good thing, in my opinion,' said Kenny. 'He's too handsome for my taste.'

'What has your taste got to do with it?' snapped Tilly. 'It's me that wanted to go out with him.'

'Tilly's right,' said Alice, linking her arm through her sister's. 'You shouldn't have interfered.'

'I think we should drop this subject,' said Seb, frowning at Alice. 'I'm going with Ma and the children to her house. Are you coming with us or staying with Tilly?'

'I won't be staying here,' said Tilly. 'I'm going back to the Bennetts' to tell them and Joy how well everything went this evening.'

'We'll come with you,' said Hanny, linking her arm through Tilly's other arm. 'I want to see Joy and tell Eudora that this idea of hers was marvellous; a pleasure to watch.'

'Well, if you're going to her house,' said Alice, removing her arm from Tilly's, 'I'm not coming.'

'I have my car,' said Gabrielle. 'Seb and Alice, children, why don't you crowd in the back and Sergeant Jones will drive us to my house. I'll make macaroons and your favourite mocha coffee, Alice.'

'You're on,' said Alice, 'although I wouldn't mind a glass of sherry, instead.'

Gabrielle smiled. 'Sherry I can provide.' She beamed at her son and grandchildren. 'Come on, my cherubs, let's go.'

They all left the hall and Tilly, Hanny and Kenny watched them crowd into Gabrielle's car and waved as they drove off. 'So where do we get the tram?' asked Kenny.

'Follow me,' said Tilly, her anger having abated once she saw Alice and Gabrielle being friendly with each other.

The tram was crowded and far too noisy to have a proper conversation, so neither of them made the effort to talk. Tilly was feeling slightly deflated and she thought that was as much a reaction to the fact that the excitement of the evening was all over as it was to her family's interference and Leonard's obvious annoyance. She needed to talk to him but was unsure about exactly what to say.

It was dark by the time they reached the Bennett's house and made their way round the back. Tilly knocked on the kitchen door and pushed it open. 'Got visitors for you, Joy,' she called.

There was no one there but Tilly could hear someone crying. 'It must be one of the children,' she said.

She left the kitchen and went through into the hall, followed by Hanny and Kenny. Suddenly she stopped and they collided into her. 'What is it?' asked Hanny.

Tilly did not answer but could only stare down at the man lying on the carpet in a pool of blood with a spade beside him. She reached a hand behind her and fumbled for one of Hanny's. 'There's a man here. It looks like he could be...' Her voice trailed off and she took several deep breaths, aware of her half-brother coming forward and standing next to her.

'My God! Who is it?' he asked.

Tilly moistened her dry mouth and said, 'It's not Dad. This man is-isn't tall enough.'

'Turn him over,' said Hanny.

'No, wait!' Tilly shouted, 'Joy! Mrs Bennett! Patricia!'

The drawing room door opened and Joy stood there. 'Thank God, you've come!'

Hanny let go of Tilly's hand and hurried over to her sister. 'You're as white as a sheet. Who is this man? What happened?'

Joy clutched her sister's arm. 'He's the children's uncle. He came in here like he owned the place and frightened the life out of us all.'

'What happened with the spade?' asked Tilly.

'Never mind that for the moment,' said Joy, her face quivering. 'Mrs Bennett's dead! She stood up to him and he hit her. Then she collapsed on the floor – her heart must have given out.'

Tilly's eyes filled with tears. 'Where's Dad?'

'He was here. He was doing something in the garden and heard the shouting and the screaming. He came in with the spade in his hand and-and, when he saw Mrs Bennett crumpled up on the floor, he went berserk.'

'Where he is?' croaked Tilly.

Joy blinked back tears. 'He picked her up in his arms and carried her into the drawing room and put her on the sofa. He was weeping.' She swallowed. 'Then he went out and looked at the man and said that he was the burglar,' added Joy. 'After that he muttered something about the police not believing him and left. He took the car.'

Tilly's legs suddenly gave way and she would have sunk to the ground if Kenny had not caught her. He wrapped his arms round her and held her tightly, not uttering a word, only stroking her hair.

'Mr Bennett, where is he?' asked Hanny. 'And have you sent for the police?'

'He's still at the Palladium,' replied Joy, wiping her damp face. 'He was going to quit after Christmas.'

'So he doesn't know,' said Kenny.

She shook her head. 'I don't know how I'm going to break the news to him.'

Tilly lifted her head. 'The police?'

'I telephoned them about ten minutes ago. Patty was against it. She thought we should just bury her uncle in the garden and keep them out of it.'

'Oh, my God!' whispered Tilly. 'It's just like—' She couldn't go on, thinking about her father and worried sick about what he might do.

'I suppose the uncle was another Bert,' said Hanny.

'Could be. But I'm so going to miss her. I loved Mrs Bennett,' said Joy, her voice cracking. 'She was so good to me when Chris went missing during the war, and then Dad died and Mam lost her mind an-and – I don't know what we'll do without her. Mr Bennett's going to be lost.' She put a hand to her mouth and tears trickled down her cheeks.

'Then he's going to need you to be strong,' said Hanny, her own eyes filling with tears.

'What about his sister?' asked Kenny. 'She'll need to know what's happened.'

Tilly struggled to pull herself together. 'We've got to find Dad.'

'And where do you suggest we look?' asked Kenny.

'I don't know.' Tilly's bottom lip trembled.

'What about the children?' asked Hanny.

Joy took a deep breath. 'Patty took them upstairs. She's staying with them. The poor kid. She's only eleven and she's like a mother to them. It shouldn't be so.'

'I'd like to know how the uncle knew they were here,' said Kenny.

Tilly felt even sicker, wondering if Leonard could have told him. She opened her mouth to tell them that she had seen him with the uncle but was prevented from speaking by Joy saying, 'He could have read about the concert in the *Echo* and recognised her picture amongst the faces of the committee.'

'He could have checked a Kelly's Directory or the telephone book for her address,' said Kenny.

'He would have already known it,' said Joy. 'I told you that your dad recognised him.' She stared down at the body. 'That man killed Nanki Poo and he killed the children's mother and Mrs Bennett. I'm glad he's dead.'

'What are we going to do?' asked Tilly, relieved that Leonard seemed to have had no part in their deaths.

'There's nothing we can do but wait for the police,' said Kenny.

The police, thought Tilly, filled with dread. Her father had killed a man even though he was a murderer. They would arrest him and put him in a cell. How would he cope with that?

CHAPTER TWENTY-THREE

'I still can't believe it,' said Robbie, running a hand through his hair. 'I knew she hadn't been feeling too good but I never expected her to die like this.'

'Here, drink this,' said Hanny, who had taken over Joy's role of carer for the moment. Her sister was with the police in the dining room. Just before the police had arrived, Tilly and Kenny had gone to the shop so Tilly could change out of her best dress and inform Mrs Wright and the family of the dreadful news. Hanny expected them back soon. Even as she thought about it there was a sound outside and Kenny, Tilly and Rita Wright entered through the french windows.

Rita immediately went over to her brother and patted his shoulder. 'I'm sorry, Robbie. What a thing to happen, but at least you've your family close by.'

His eyes filled with tears and he took a gulp of brandy. She remained there, patting his shoulder as if he were a child. Tilly exchanged looks with Hanny and Kenny and the three of them left the room and went into the garden. 'Any news about Dad?' asked Tilly.

'None,' said Hanny. 'But I'm sure the police will be searching for him.'

'I'm worried he'll do something crazy,' said Tilly.

'Such as what?' asked Hanny.

Tilly did not say but was remembering Joy and Robbie talking about people committing suicide.

'I'm sure he could get off with manslaughter or self-defence,' said Kenny. 'It depends on what story Joy tells them.'

'They'll still put him in jail,' said Tilly on a sob. 'I don't think he could handle that.'

Silence.

Unexpectedly, Kenny said, 'We were supposed to be at the hotel by now.'

'I telephoned them just after the pair of you left saying that we wouldn't be coming,' said Hanny. 'I didn't think it was right for us to leave Tilly and Joy to cope with this.'

'What's going on?' asked a voice suddenly from the other side of the fence.

The three of them jumped.

Tilly stared at the woman's face that shone pale in the moonlight and wondered whether Leonard now knew what had happened. 'Is Leonard at home?' she asked.

'No. He's still out.'

'Perhaps you can tell him that Mrs Bennett is dead and that the burglar who robbed the house has been caught.'

'I am sorry about Mrs Bennett but glad they've caught that burglar.' She bobbed down again.

'We'd best go in,' said Kenny.

There was a constable on guard outside the kitchen door. 'I've been watching you three,' he said.

Tilly recognised him. 'We've met before,' she said.

He peered into her face. 'Aye. You're the gardener's daughter. I've to keep a watch in case he comes back and sneaks past the man at the front.'

Tilly felt a stab of pain in her heart, wanting her father to come home but terribly anxious about what might happen to him when he did.

That night was to be one of the longest in Tilly's life, comparable to that terrible time when Alice had received the news that Seb was missing. She remained at the house, as did Kenny and Hanny. Rita went back home to her children. Joy sat with Robbie beside Eudora's body, which had been carried upstairs to their bedroom.

The following morning there was still no news of Mal. Kenny and Hanny said they would have to go home. 'We can't expect Clara to look after the twins and Mother, as well as little Nicky,' said Hanny.

'You'll let us know as soon as you hear anything about Dad?' said Kenny.

'Of course!' said Tilly.

She saw them out and, soon afterwards, the children made an appearance, creeping into the kitchen like mice, led by Patricia. Joy told them to sit at the table. Robbie vanished into the drawing room with a cup of tea and a slice of toast. Tilly helped Joy to serve them breakfast whilst Patricia gave the baby his bottle.

An hour later there was a rat-a-tat-tat at the front door, which caused Tilly, Joy and Robbie to make a concerted rush to answer it. On the step stood Sergeant Jones and his expression was grave and filled Tilly with dread.

'You've found Dad,' she rasped.

'Yes. He's been taken to a hospital in Glasgow.'

'Glasgow!' Tilly could scarcely believe it. 'What's Dad doing up there? What happened to him?'

'Perhaps it would be best if I came inside and you sat down,' he said gently.

'Tell me now,' she said in a trembling voice. 'He's dead, isn't he?'

'No, love. He's still alive but it's bad. He crashed into a fallen tree on a country road and has serious head injuries. They found identification on him. Name and address on a card pinned inside an inner pocket.'

'I must see him,' said Tilly. She stared blindly at Robbie. 'I'm sorry about your car, Mr Bennett.'

'The car doesn't matter,' he said in a dull voice.

His shoulders drooped as he turned away and went back inside the house. Tilly signalled to the sergeant to come inside. 'I've put a call through to Chester and they're going to let your brother know what's happened,' he said. 'No doubt, he'll want to go with you.'

Tilly thought he most likely would, but what about Alice?

'Sergeant Jones, do you know if my sister and her husband have left his mother's house yet?'

'I don't know, love. But I could ask Mr Bennett if I could put a call through to the station in Tuebrook. Gabrielle's house is only five minutes away.'

Tilly drew herself up. 'I'd appreciate that.'

It seemed ages before she heard back that Seb and Alice and the children were just getting ready to leave his mother's. She had offered them the use of her car and they were coming here straight away. Tilly could not help wondering what her sister felt about it all.

She was soon to know.

Tilly answered the door to Seb. 'Hello, love,' he said, stretching out a hand to her.

She clasped it. 'Where's Alice?'

'Sitting in the car with my mother and the children. She didn't feel it right to intrude on Robbie's grief.'

'I'll speak to her.' Tilly hurried down the path to the car parked at the kerb.

The children chorused a welcome and she hugged and kissed the three of them before facing her sister. 'So will you come?' asked Tilly.

Alice looked at her as if she was mad. 'You mean, go to Scotland with you? No! Why should I? You know my feelings towards Dad.'

'But he's hurt and could be dying!' cried Tilly.

'I don't care,' said Alice, her face set. 'He can rot in hell for all I care.'

Tilly drew back as if she had been slapped in the face. Gabrielle spoke up. 'That's a wicked thing to say, Alice. With that attitude you'll end up hurting no one but yourself. You have to learn to forgive.'

'You're a right one to talk,' said Alice, clenching her fists. 'You wouldn't forgive your own mother.'

'Yes! And I've regretted it since. Show a bit of compassion. If for no one else's sake but Tilly's. She needs you to do this and so do your children,' said Gabrielle. 'What are you teaching them about the Christian faith if you can't do this?'

Alice reddened, and hearing footsteps, looked up at her husband. Had he heard what his mother had said to her? If he had he was keeping mum but she could guess what his thoughts would be. 'All right! I'll go.'

Tilly's arms went about her neck and almost choked her. 'Thanks!'

'All right, all right,' said Alice, freeing herself. 'But I'd like to know how we're going to get there.'

Gabrielle looked at her son. 'You can take my car – and I suppose my grandchildren can stay with me a bit longer.'

The children cheered. Alice opened her mouth to protest then, at a warning look from Seb, she closed it again.

'If you're not back by Monday evening, I'll take them to your house in Chester and see that they go to school on Tuesday,' said Gabrielle. She ignored the children's groan, saying, 'We'll go on the ferry. It's ages since I've crossed the Mersey on a boat.'

'What about Kenny?' asked Tilly. 'He'll know about Dad by now but if he's coming with us, he needs to get here quickly.'

'He's probably already thought of that and is on his way back to Liverpool right now,' said Seb.

So it proved because Kenny arrived only an hour later in a taxi. Seb had taken the opportunity to top up the tank with petrol and had also filled a spare can. They wasted no time but set off for Scotland. Without even a change of knickers, thought Alice, depressed and anxious at having to leave her children with their grandmother. It had occurred to her that her father might be dead by the time they got to the hospital and found herself remembering the past.

'The last time I went to Glasgow was with Dad,' she said, 'We were in a train crash and he was badly injured. I thought he would die then.'

'You've never told me this before,' said Tilly, hugging her sister's arm.

'That's because I left him to die. I needed to escape from him.' Alice's voice shook.

'But he didn't die,' said Tilly.

'No. He's like a cat with nine lives.'

'Well, let's hope he doesn't run out of lives before we get there,' said Seb.

If Tilly had not been so desperate to reach Glasgow as quickly as possible, she might have enjoyed the journey north, passing through some of the most beautiful countryside in Britain. As it was, she gazed at it unseeingly and could remember little of it later when she looked back on that journey.

It was a nightmare getting through the centre of Glasgow and Seb had to ask a policeman to direct them to the Royal Infirmary. It turned out to be on the edge of the city centre in Castle Street, next to the cathedral. The hospital was a huge building and Tilly's heart sank, wondering how they were going to find her father in such a place. She need not have worried. While Seb found somewhere to park the car, Kenny took charge and before long they were being led along what felt like corridor after corridor to the ward where Mal had been taken. His head was bandaged so that all that showed of his face were his eyes, which were closed.

Tilly reached for one of his bandaged hands and held it firmly. 'Dad!' she cried.

There was no response. She was aware that Alice and Kenny exchanged looks and guessed that they were of the opinion that she was wasting her time and that their father would not survive.

'Do talk to him,' said the ward sister in a soft Scottish brogue. 'It's possible that he might be able to hear ye. At the least, he could sense that yer here.'

'You're from the west coast, aren't you?' said Kenny.

'Aye,' she said, smiling at him.

'I have family there. I haven't seen them for ages but my father grew up in Greenock.'

'He's come home then,' said the ward sister gently. 'I'll leave yer to spend some time alone with him.'

Tilly looked at Kenny and no words were needed for what they were both thinking. Alice said, 'I never imagined this scene in all my life.' Her voice was just a thread of sound.

'Tell him you forgive him,' said Tilly.

Alice did not move a muscle but just stared at that still figure in the bed. She tried to remember what their father had looked like when she was a child. He had always been a handsome man and even in old age he had kept some of his looks. She thought of her mother and how she had died giving birth to Tilly. She glanced at Kenny and saw that he was gazing down at their father. What was he remembering? The violence, the fear of the crazy man their father had been then? Yet when Kenny was just a tot, their father had run from his cruel bigot of a mother, taking his son with him to England. In Chester he had met Alice's mother and she had fallen in love with the handsome Scotsman and married him. Surely she must have seen the need in him, as well as some goodness.

Alice's eyes filled with tears and she reached out a trembling hand and placed it gently on Mal's head. 'I forgive you, Dad. May God forgive you, too.' Her voice was barely above a whisper and she could only hope that he could hear her.

The three of them stayed there until their father slipped away an hour later. 'It was as if he hung on just waiting for us to come,' said Tilly, wiping away her tears.

Alice was the first to leave the bedside and went in search

of Seb. She found him in the entrance hall downstairs and did not need to tell him what had happened. He said that he could tell from her face that she had done what was right.

Afterwards, when the four of them left the hospital, they went in search of a hotel and a meal. When they had reached the coffee stage, Kenny said, 'There's decisions we have to make.'

'Where he's to be buried,' said Tilly. 'Where else but here in Scotland with your mother. It's what he wanted.'

'And it's convenient,' added Alice. 'It's almost as if he arranged it.'

'Maybe he did,' said Tilly sadly.

'I have the deeds to Mother's grave,' said Kenny. 'My grandmother gave them to me. I brought them with me in case I needed them.'

'How long will it take to arrange his funeral,' asked Alice. 'Only I don't want to leave the children too long.'

Kenny hesitated before saying, 'Why don't you and Seb go home and leave the rest to me and Tilly?'

Alice looked at Seb, he nodded, and then at her sister. 'I agree with Kenny,' said Tilly. 'You've done what was needed and you've the children to think about. You don't want Seb's mother reaching the stage where she starts tearing her hair out.'

Alice grinned and, leaning across the table, kissed Tilly on the cheek. 'You do realise this means you can come home to Chester.'

'Don't rush the girl,' chided Seb. 'Let her decide for herself what she wants to do after the funeral.'

Tilly said, 'Thanks. I need time to think through a few things.'

'I wonder if Dad had burial insurance,' said Kenny.

'Eudora Bennett would have known,' said Seb. 'You're going to have to go through his things when you get back, Tilly. Right now there's probably enough money in the business account to pay for the funeral.'

'And if he did have insurance then it can be paid out of the funds when the policy is handed in,' said Alice.

With that agreed no more was said on the matter.

The following day Tilly and Kenny waved Seb and Alice off before going to pick up the death certificate from the hospital. Then they visited an undertaker, who arranged for a minister to visit them at the hotel. He was sympathetic but businesslike and a short private service was arranged in three days' time. In the interim, Kenny visited his cousins on his mother's side, and Tilly went shopping in Sauchiehall Street, where she bought a small holdall, some blacks, underwear and toiletries with money that Kenny gave her. She also visited the cathedral, the library, the museum, art gallery and the cinema, not wanting to think too much about the future just yet.

On the day of the funeral the weather was fair and, although Tilly still felt sad and the service and burial had a dreamlike feeling to it, she managed to keep her chin up and control her tears. Even so, she was glad when it was all over and she could return to Liverpool.

PART THREE

October 1921–March 1922

CHAPTER TWENTY-FOUR

'Are you there, Joy?' Tilly knocked on the kitchen door and opened it.

Joy placed the last batch of scones in the oven and straightened up, dusting flour from her hands. 'Tilly! I heard you were back. How are you, love?'

'I'm OK. I was sorry to miss Mrs Bennett's funeral. How is Mr Bennett?'

'He's as well as can be expected in the circumstances,' said Joy, gazing at Tilly's slim black-clad figure. 'He wants to talk to you.'

'About the car Dad smashed up?'

'No! Of course not. It's something completely different,' said Joy.

Tilly thought there was a slight air of suppressed excitement about her. 'How are the Doyles?'

'They've gone to the orphanage.' Joy sighed. 'It wasn't an easy thing for him to do but Mr Bennett couldn't cope with them here anymore.'

Tilly sat down. 'I suppose I should have expected that. It

won't be what Patricia wanted. She was worried about them being separated.'

'It's better than living on the streets,' said Joy firmly. 'I was talking to one of the policemen the other week and he was saying that the number of barefooted child beggars around is a disgrace, and you missed the riots at the Walker Art Gallery. Thousands of unemployed stormed the place because there was a meeting being held inside and they felt they weren't properly represented.'

'I don't know what I'm going to do,' said Tilly. 'Somehow I feel that the Friends won't want my services now Mrs Bennett's dead. It was she I really worked for and now the concert is over, I feel that part of my life is finished with.'

'You still have your job with Mr Simpson,' said Joy, 'although what about your writing? You should be getting back to that.'

'I wish I could,' said Tilly. 'As it is, I'll have to ask Grant Simpson if he can take me on full time.' She sighed. 'Where is Mr Bennett? I want his permission to go and sort Dad's things out.'

'He's in the drawing room. He's decided to give up the orchestra and give music lessons here in the house.'

Tilly smiled. 'He said he wanted to do that – although I have to confess I thought he might sell up and move away.'

'You mean because of all of the things that have happened here?' asked Joy.

Tilly nodded. 'I thought he might think it an unlucky house.'

Joy shook her head. 'He's not superstitious and he likes the house – loves it being near the park and his sister's close by, and he can easily jump on a tram and go into town if he wants.'

'I'll go and see him then,' said Tilly.

The words were hardly out of her mouth when the door opened and Robbie appeared. 'It is you, Tilly. I thought I heard your voice. I'm sorry about your dad, love.'

'Thanks. And I'm sorry I missed Mrs Bennett's funeral.'

'Not a happy time for either of us,' he said, rubbing his neck. 'But life goes on.'

'I wanted to ask you if I could sort out Dad's things?'

He smiled. 'Of course you can. They belong to you, anyway. The solicitor will be getting in touch with you but I can say now that Mal was one of the beneficiaries in my wife's will. She also had him make a will and I was one of the witnesses. I can tell you that he left you everything, Tilly, which means you inherit the sum that my wife left him.'

Tilly was stunned. 'Are you saying that he didn't leave anything to Kenny or Alice?'

'Yes. But remember that at the time he had no idea that Eudora would leave him money. It's fortunate for you that he died after her. I know she never gave him a proper wage during the time he worked for her. But that was because he was perfectly content having a roof over his head and with her providing him with pocket money and seeing to it that he was kept as healthy as possible. At the time she made her will, she said that she wanted to see him right. She left him a thousand pounds, which will now be yours, Tilly.'

Tilly felt suddenly faint and sank onto a chair.

'I'll make you a cup of tea,' said Joy.

'I'll leave you two to it, then,' said Robbie. 'I'm just going to go into town to Crane's to buy some sheet music and look at a couple of instruments.' He closed the door on them.

'I can't believe it,' said Tilly, shaking her head. 'I feel like nothing is real anymore.'

'She left me money, too,' said Joy, smiling. 'Mr Bennett wants me to stay on as his housekeeper and I will. But I've told him I need a holiday, so when I get my hands on the money, I'm going to take Mother away to give our Hanny and Kenny a break.'

'They'll enjoy that,' said Tilly, her eyes brightening. 'They've had so little time on their own since they married, what with helping to bring me up, as well.' She paused. 'Listen, don't bother with the tea. I'll make myself one down at Dad's place. I need to find the burial insurance policy, if he had one.'

'Oh, he did,' said Joy. 'It's with his will, which is with the solicitor but you might still want to go down there and sort things out.'

'I do. And will you come with me to see the solicitor once I've made an appointment?'

Joy nodded. 'Of course I will. I'm sure Mr Bennett will allow me the time off.'

Tilly thanked her and, leaving the house, went down the garden to the outhouse. The door wasn't locked and she let herself in and immediately it was as if her father was there beside her. She could even hear him talking in her head but it wasn't spooky at all. She went upstairs and into his living quarters but decided not to bother making a cup of tea. Besides, she had no milk.

She wandered around the room, touching this and that and inspecting the few clothes he possessed. She picked up the tin that she remembered peeking inside when he had left her alone once. She opened it and emptied out its contents onto the table: pebbles, peacock feather, coins, fir cones and the bird button. She remembered him picking it up off the ground and putting it in his pocket. She noticed that there were a few threads of khaki cotton attached to it and her brows puckered. It suddenly occurred to her that the button might have some connection with the body that her father had found. Perhaps she should give it to the police. The button might be important.

Tilly put everything back in the tin, including the button, and took it outside with her. She was going to need some bags for her father's clothes and would need to wash them before giving them to the church jumble.

As she went up the garden, a voice said, 'So you're back.'

Tilly did not bother turning her head towards the fence. 'It looks like it. Is Leonard home?'

'No. He's tied up for a few days. Business.'

Tilly thought he seemed to be away more than he was home. She thanked the woman and carried on towards the house. As she entered the kitchen, Joy said, 'I forgot to tell you, Tilly, that there was another beneficiary in Mrs Bennett's will.' She chuckled.

'What's so funny?' asked Tilly.

'You know Mrs Bennett had shares in Kenny and Seb's business?'

'Yes.'

'Well, she's left them to Alice.'

'You have to be kidding!'

'No. Mrs Bennett's sense of humour could be a bit malicious at times. Mr Bennett said the solicitor has written to Alice informing her of her good fortune.'

'I'd like to be there when she receives that letter,' murmured Tilly. 'I think I'll go and visit the family today. Tell them about my good fortune. I'll be back tomorrow.' She placed the tin in her large capacious handbag and left the house.

Seb picked up the afternoon post and glanced through it as he made his way to the dining room. He was surprised to see an official-looking envelope addressed to Alice. He squinted at the postmark and saw that the letter was from Liverpool. Naturally, he was curious about the sender. Surely it couldn't be from Tilly because she must have only just arrived back in Liverpool.

'Letter for you, love,' he said, dropping the envelope on the breakfast table.

'For me?' exclaimed Alice in surprise.

The children glanced at her.

'You don't have to sound as if nobody ever writes to you,' said Seb, good humouredly. He watched his wife rip open the envelope and unfold a single sheet of paper. 'Who's it from?' he asked.

'It's from a solicitor.' She glanced at Seb. 'Why should a Liverpool solicitor be writing to me?'

'Don't ask me. Why don't you read it?'

Alice did so with mounting incredulity and then anger. 'Well?' asked Seb.

She lifted her gaze from the letter. 'You viper!' she exclaimed and flung the sheet of paper at him.

Startled, he said, 'What d'you mean by that?'

The legs of her chair screeched on the floor as she pushed it back. 'You and Kenny both! How could you do business with *that woman* and keep it from me? You know how I felt about her!' Alice's eyes flashed green fire.

Seb knew there was only one person his wife ever referred to as *that woman* and snatched up the letter and read it swiftly. 'Bloody hell!'

The children gasped. 'That's a naughty word, Daddy,' said Flora.

He ignored his daughter. 'Why did she do this? I don't understand.'

'To cause trouble, of course. See, I knew her better than you. What I want to know from you is why you kept her involvement in the company a secret from me these past few years.'

'I think you can guess why,' said Seb, running his hand through his dark curls. 'You'd have told me to refuse her help and the company would have gone bust without it.'

'You could have mortgaged the house.'

His mouth tightened. 'I thought about it but decided her involvement in the company was a better option.' He held up a hand as Alice went to speak. 'Kenny and I knew you'd rant and rave if we'd told you and then gone ahead anyway.'

'I should think I would.' Alice paced the floor. 'I don't know how you could have trusted her. She's deceitful, she's a poisoner, an adulteress...'

Flora and James gasped.

Seb scowled. 'You shouldn't make such accusations in front of the children.' He turned to them. 'You three can leave the table.'

'But we haven't finished,' protested Flora.

He looked at the half-eaten slice of toast on her plate. 'You can eat that in the kitchen while you get ready for school.'

She groaned and flounced out, followed by James and Georgie.

Seb turned to his wife. 'What proof have you that she was any of those things?'

'I don't need proof. I know the kind of woman Mrs Black was,' she said angrily. 'She had my father wrapped round her little finger. He spent money on her that he should have spent on his family.'

'Here we go again.'

'Don't you dare take that attitude! I have cause to feel the way I do about them both.'

'So you've said time and time again. You're just so prejudiced against her that you could never see her good points,' said Seb. 'But I must admit I think it's crazy of her to have left the shares to you.'

'I suppose you think she should have left them to you and Kenny instead of me?' she said tartly.

'I thought she would have left them to Robbie.'

'I told you – she wanted to cause mischief between you, me and Kenny. I know the way that woman's mind worked,' said Alice darkly.

'I doubt that was uppermost in her thoughts but I can believe she did it deliberately to annoy you and put you in a quandary. Hating her the way you do, I expect she thought you might refuse to take anything from her,' said Seb thoughtfully. 'On the other hand, perhaps she considered you might believe she owed you for taking your father away from you. There's also the possibility that she believed if you owned shares in the company you might take more of an interest in it.'

Alice glared at him. 'I suppose Tilly knew about her having shares in the company?'

Seb shrugged.

Alice's eyes filled with tears and, getting up, she hurried from the room.

'Damn!' said Seb savagely, flinging down his napkin and walking out of the room.

Tilly arrived at the house a few hours later. When no one answered her knock, she went round to the back and found Alice digging in one of the flower borders.

'I didn't expect to find you doing this,' said Tilly, gazing down at her sister.

Alice straightened up and put a hand to the small of the back. 'I find it helps when I'm feeling angry and frustrated.'

'Perhaps that's why Dad enjoyed gardening so much,' murmured Tilly. 'You know what the poet says, *You are nearer to God in a garden than anywhere else on earth.*'

'Is that so?' said Alice, ramming the spade into the soil.

'I presume you've received the solicitor's letter,' said Tilly, taking a few steps backward.

Alice glared at her. 'I always believed before Dad came between us that we didn't have secrets from each other.'

'It wasn't my secret to tell,' said Tilly frankly. 'She left Dad a thousand pounds, by the way, and he left me everything in his will.'

Alice stared at her. 'Dad made a will?'

'Yes.'

'I don't know whether to congratulate you or throw a tantrum,' muttered Alice.

'I'll share it with you and Kenny,' said Tilly. 'It's only right.'

'Rubbish!' said Alice. 'You gave him your time so you deserve it. I'm glad you have a nice little nest egg but don't go squandering it on something stupid.'

Tilly felt like stamping her foot. 'Honestly, Alice, when are you going to accept that I'm grown-up now and have plenty of common sense.'

'What about marriage to Mr Parker?'

'I doubt that's a possibility. I haven't seen him since the concert.'

Alice put down the shovel. 'Shall we have a glass of sherry to celebrate our inheritances?'

'That would be nice.' Inwardly, Tilly sighed with relief.

She linked her arm through that of her sister and walked up to the house with her. Once they were settled in the drawing room with a glass of sherry and a plate of homemade biscuits, Tilly asked, 'So what are you going to do with your shares?'

'I haven't given it much thought because I've been too angry.'

'Then think about it now,' persisted Tilly. 'I presume you're not just going to hand them over to Seb?'

'No, I'm not,' said Alice firmly. 'I think I'll sell them back to him and Kenny.'

Tilly grinned. 'And what will you do with the money?'

Her sister did not answer immediately but stared into space. 'You know what I'd really like to do,' said Alice earnestly. 'I'd like to have my own little hat shop.'

Her words made Tilly sit up. 'You've a real talent when it comes to hats but would Seb allow it?'

Alice's mouth set in a stubborn line. 'I don't see why not. Georgie will soon be at school and I could get someone to help in the house.' She paused. 'Or you could come back home! Free board and lodgings and you could do a couple of hours a day in the shop. I'd pay you. You could open the shop early so I could see them off to school and you could pick them up afterwards. Having a business is not the same as having a wife who has to work to help with finances.'

Tilly frowned. 'I'm not coming to live here and be your lackey. Anyway, male pride being what it is, Seb won't want people thinking that he can't support you in the manner to which you're accustomed.'

Alice scowled. 'You are mean. Why can't you come back here and help me out? Now Dad's gone there's no need for you to stay in Liverpool. Unless you still think that Mr Parker is interested?'

Tilly gave her look. 'No, he's not the reason.'

'So you say. I'll get help in. I'll persuade Seb, don't you worry. Why should either of us care what the neighbours think when buying the lease on a little shop will keep me happy and make up for his keeping secrets from me.'

'I don't know why you've never had another baby.'

Alice refilled their sherry glasses. 'Because, although I love my children, I don't want to go through all that again: pregnancy, nappies – babies are hard work. Seb agrees.'

Tilly could not imagine them abstaining from sex. She wondered whether her sister had read Marie Stopes' books *Married Life* and *Wise Parenthood*, which had been published in 1918. The author had shocked the church by advocating birth control and her books had been called obscene by some but they had sold in the thousands. 'I'll say no more,' said Tilly, sipping her sherry.

There was a sound from outside and the next moment Seb entered through the french windows. He smiled at Tilly. 'I'm glad to see you back. You OK?' He bent and kissed her cheek.

'She's come into money,' said Alice, holding up her face for his kiss. 'That woman left Dad a thousand pounds and he left everything to Tilly in his will.'

Seb whistled. 'You lucky duck, Tilly.'

'I did offer Alice a third of it but she refused,' said Tilly. 'But perhaps I should buy her shares and that way she'll have money of her own to do with what she wants and it'll save the company forking out. I'll give the shares to Kenny and that will ease my conscience.'

'So Alice told you about the shares,' said Seb, grinning. 'Did she tear a strip off you, as well?'

Tilly nodded. 'But I knew already because Joy told me. Eudora Bennett left her money, as well. She told me that she's going to have a holiday and take her mother with her.'

'That will be nice for Hanny and Kenny,' said Seb, pouring himself a small whisky. 'Your idea is a very generous one, Tilly. I appreciate it for one because business is still tough. Did your dad leave anything else?'

'The solicitor has the insurance policy,' said Tilly. 'But there is this, too.' She opened her bag and removed the tin.

'What on earth is in that?' asked Alice.

Tilly smiled. 'I thought the kids might like it.' She took off the lid and emptied the contents on to the occasional table. 'You know how we all pick up things that we like and put them in a box or tin. These are Dad's.'

Alice stared at the collection. 'I'd never have believed it of him.' She picked up the peacock feather and brushed her cheek with it. 'Flora will love this.'

'There's several foreign coins here that James will like,' said Seb, rooting through them. 'And what's this? It looks like a medal but—'

'It's a button,' said Tilly glancing at him. 'Dad picked it up in the garden. I did wonder...'

'Wonder what?' asked Alice.

'It's American,' interrupted Seb. 'It's off a soldier's uniform.'

Tilly experienced a thrill of excitement. 'Do you know anything more about it?'

'No.' Seb stared at it thoughtfully. 'But I know someone who might.' He glanced at Tilly. 'What if I do a tracing of it and send it to my friend in America?'

'Your friend in America?' asked Tilly. 'You don't mean Don Pierce? I thought he no longer kept in touch.'

'I think he'll find this interesting.'

Tilly was assaulted by all sorts of emotions. 'Is he still a bachelor? It's just that I saw a photograph of him with this woman—'

Seb shot her a keen look. 'I know nothing about any woman, but, do you still want me to go ahead?'

Tilly did not hesitate. 'Yes! Why not? It's not only that I'd like to solve the mystery of how an American soldier's uniform button got in the garden – but I'd like to know the truth about the blonde who was with him in the magazine photograph that I saw.'

Seb nodded.

'You could ask the neighbours if there'd been any handsome American soldiers calling at the house during the war,' suggested Alice.

Seb shook his head. 'That's the last thing she should do.'

'Why not?' asked Alice.

'I know why not,' said Tilly, a quiver in her voice. 'It might have been pulled off a uniform worn by the body Dad found. We know the corpse met with a violent death.' She felt odd thinking about it. 'Should I show it to the police?'

'What for?' asked Alice, staring at her. 'I think you're allowing your imagination to run away with you. So Dad found a button in the Bennetts' garden. Anyone could have dropped it there. Perhaps a young woman visiting the house had an American sweetheart who had given her one of his buttons as a keepsake after the war.'

'Now whose imagination is running away with them?' asked Tilly sweetly. 'And it was your suggestion to ask the neighbours about handsome American soldiers. Besides, we have no idea if he was good-looking or not.'

Seb said, 'I'd keep quiet about your dad's find at the moment, Tilly. I wouldn't mention it to anyone.'

There was a note in his voice that sent a shiver down Tilly's spine. 'If that's what you think, then I'll do what you say.'

'Good,' he said, smiling. 'So what are your plans, Tilly? Will you still carry on working for the charity and the private detective agency?'

Tilly shook her head. 'No! Once I get my hands on my inheritance I'm going to give up work and write my novel. I'll look for new digs where I can have peace and quiet and—'

Her sister looked alarmed but before his wife could speak, Seb said, 'Don't say it, Alice. It's what Tilly wants and as your father has given her the means to do it, allow her to have a go.'

'All right,' said Alice, thinking that he had opened the way to bring up her plans when the time was right. 'But she could have digs in Chester,' she suggested.

'No, I'm staying in Liverpool,' said Tilly firmly. 'I'll be able to visit you more often and I'll stay here tonight. How's that?'

Seb smiled. 'That's fine.'

After that the conversation became more general and when the children came home, Tilly found it really heart-warming to see the way they searched through their grandfather's collection, laying claim to this or that and carrying their treasures upstairs to their bedrooms. She enjoyed her time with her family, slipping along to Hanny and Kenny's and telling them her plans, as well as playing with the twins. She popped in and saw Clara and Freddie and the baby. Clara said something that took Tilly by surprise.

'Do you think Eudora will try and get in touch with Mr Bennett?'

Tilly stared at her. 'You mean, from the Other Side?'

'Yes,' said Clara.

Freddie, who was nursing his son, raised his dark eyebrows. 'I'd love to be there if she did.'

Tilly said, 'Mr Bennett would run a mile from any psychic phenomenon. He didn't like what she did as a medium.' She paused. 'But I'll make you a promise – if anything weird does happen, I'll let you know.'

CHAPTER TWENTY-FIVE

'Hello, Tilly,' said Wendy, pausing in the act of filling a box with slabs of toffee as Tilly entered the shop. 'You OK?'

She nodded and placed several empty brown paper carrier bags on the counter. 'Sorry about not being here last night but I decided I needed to see my sister.' It was another hot day and she wiped her perspiring brow.

'Understandable,' said Wendy, her grey eyes resting on Tilly's face. 'So what are the carrier bags for?'

'I have to get rid of Dad's stuff, so I might as well get it done now,' said Tilly. 'Have you seen Grant this morning?'

'Yes, and I told him you were back.'

'Good.'

Wendy hesitated. 'I didn't tell you yesterday but while you were in Scotland he asked me to help him out – and I know what you're going to say – I'm not to make a habit of it.'

Tilly smiled. 'I wasn't going to say anything of the sort. What kind of help did you give him?'

'I did a little bit of typing and then I went to a party with him.'

Tilly stilled. 'A party?'

Wendy flushed. 'Yes. He told me it was to do with an insurance claim. I had to circulate and keep my ears and eyes open while he checked out a few things in the house.'

'There hasn't been another jewellery robbery, has there?'

'Not jewels. More what he calls *objects d'art.*'

'I see. Stuff like your Aunt Eudora's Chinese vases.'

Wendy said, 'I suppose so. I wonder where they ended up. Grant's convinced there's a gang working for a Mister Big. He has an idea who it might be but he's keeping mum at the moment.' She paused. 'I suppose you'll be wanting your job back now?'

'No, I won't,' said Tilly, smoothing out the carrier bags. 'I've come into money. Dad made a will and left me everything. It mightn't have been much if your Aunt Eudora hadn't left him a thousand pounds in her will.'

Wendy let out a whistle. 'Lucky you! I suppose you'll be moving out of here and going back to Chester?'

'Out of here, yes – but I haven't made up my mind yet where I'm going. I need some quiet place where I can get on with my novel.'

Wendy's grey eyes gleamed. 'Good idea! But we'll miss you and you could have trouble finding a place. I don't know what Grant will say when I tell him you'll no longer be working for him.'

'He might ask you to continue working for him on a part-time basis,' suggested Tilly.

Hope flared in Wendy's eyes and then died. 'I'd like that but I can't see Mam agreeing. It was OK when it was just temporary but she wants me here. I can just see him finding a blonde bombshell for an assistant and he'll fall in love with her and they'll get married and that'll be that.' She sighed.

Tilly gave her a severe look. 'You shouldn't be so pessimistic. Your mam could always get Mrs Pain to fill in here and give her a break.'

'She'll say she can't afford to pay her,' said Wendy gloomily.

'Why is that? She must give you a wage.'

'No, she doesn't. Mam gives me a couple of bob for spends and buys my clothes, and when I say to her I'm getting older and how about my having a proper wage, she just says that she provides me with everything I need so that's equal to a wage.'

Tilly frowned. 'That's not right in this day and age. The suffragettes fought for votes for women and now women are trying to get equal rights on wages and that with men, so they can support themselves. It's not right. Your Minnie has a job and gets a wage. Surely she has something for herself and gives money to your mam for her keep?'

'Yes, but the problem is that after Dad was killed I saw it as my duty to do what I could to help Mam and I was stupid enough to say I didn't expect any pay then. She's never forgotten it.'

'But that was then and this is now. You must argue your case for leading your own life a bit more,' said Tilly. 'Why don't you suggest to Grant that you take my place and if your mam gets on her high horse and tells you to get out then I'll help you out of my inheritance.'

'I can't take money from you,' said Wendy firmly, 'but I will do what you say and speak to Grant about working for him part time.'

Tilly's face broke into a smile. 'Good for you. Right now I'm going to change into something plain and start clearing Dad's place out.'

'You, look plain?' Wendy laughed. 'Never.'

Tilly said, 'You're so nice. Now open the flap and let me through.'

Later, when Tilly was packing her father's clothing and linen ready to be washed or cleaned, it suddenly struck her that with a few feminine touches her father's quarters could make a suitable place for her to live in while she wrote her novel. It was certainly quiet here at the bottom of the garden. Yet it was near enough to the house if she needed to speak to someone. Of course, Robbie Bennett might not be in favour of the idea; on the other hand, he might agree to rent it to her.

Tilly decided to waste no time asking him and hurried up to the house. She entered the kitchen like a whirlwind, only to stop abruptly when she saw Robbie sitting at the table, nursing a clarinet in his hand.

He glanced up at her and smiled. 'What do you think, Tilly? It's Pete's birthday soon and I thought he deserved a new clarinet after playing so well at the concert.' He held it out to her.

'It's a lovely instrument,' she said, taking it from him and admiring its shiny newness. 'I'm sure he'll love it.'

'I thought he could come here and practise. I'm going to do my darndest to help him get a career in music,' said Robbie.

'Mrs Wright's not going to like that,' said Joy.

Robbie shrugged and took out a cigarette case. He lit a cigarette and blew out a couple of smoke rings. 'I think I can sweeten her up and get her to see things from my point of view. I'm a rich man now and could make her life a whole lot easier.'

Tilly said, 'I was talking to Wendy before and she was saying how much she'd enjoyed working for Grant Simpson while I was away. I've decided to give up my job with him and suggested she carries on working for him in my place. She seems to believe that her mother will be completely against it but has decided she'd like to continue working for him, part time, if he agrees. I suggested Mrs Pain might be willing to take her place but Wendy said her mother wouldn't want to pay out on wages.'

Robbie's eyes narrowed as he stared at Tilly through a spiral of cigarette smoke. 'The trouble with my dear sister is that she had such hard times before I returned to England that she's terrified of being without again. Thanks for mentioning it to me, Tilly, I'll deal with it.'

Tilly smiled. 'Thanks. I'm very fond of Wendy.'

'So am I. She's a good girl.' He paused. 'Have you finished down at your dad's place?'

'Not quite,' said Tilly. 'I want to ask you something. May I sit down?'

He waved her to a chair. 'What can I do to help you?'

She folded her arms on the table and leant towards him. 'I want to rent Dad's place. It would be ideal for me to do my writing there. It's quiet and I'd be undisturbed by people passing to and fro. What do you think?'

Robbie did not answer her immediately and for a moment Tilly thought he would turn her down. Instead, he said, 'I've got an idea. What do you say to your putting in a few hours a week keeping the garden tidy in lieu of rent. I know you used to help Mal occasionally and Joy told me that you looked after the garden for your sister when you lived in Chester.'

Tilly got up from her chair and went to give him a hug. 'That's really generous of you. Thanks. I'll need a break from writing occasionally and looking after the garden will suit me down to the ground.'

'And if it gets really cold in winter, you can move into the house,' said Robbie. 'Your dad was a tough nut, but you could have one of the spare bedrooms.'

'That's really good of you,' said Tilly, touched by his thoughtfulness.

'It's my pleasure. I'm sure Eudora would approve,' said Robbie. His expression suddenly altered. 'The pair of you might think I'm mad but sometimes I feel as if she's at my elbow, advising me what to do when I'm unsure which way to go.'

'And why shouldn't she be?' asked Joy. 'Her spirit will be really strong.'

Robbie looked at her. 'I wouldn't argue that Eudora had a strong personality but if you dare to suggest, Joy, that we should try and get in touch with her via the spirits, forget it!' He took a deep lungful of cigarette smoke. 'I'm content just imagining she's there and remembering just how much she had to say was down to pure common sense.'

Joy said, 'OK. You're the boss. Right now I'm thinking that Tilly will need some help moving her things from the shop so she's going to need a man and a handcart.'

Robbie nodded. 'I'll arrange it. I'll even come back to the shop with you, Tilly. No time like the present if you'd like to move in today. I'll use the opportunity to talk over a few things with our Rita.'

'That would be really helpful,' said Tilly, pleased that everything had been settled so quickly.

Robbie stubbed out his cigarette in an ashtray and stood up. 'I'll go and phone now about hiring a handcart. We'll only need it for a couple of hours at the most.'

Whilst he telephoned, Tilly explained to Joy about her father's clothes and bedding. 'You don't have to take them to the laundry. I can fill the boiler now and, as long as the weather stays dry, I'll have them on the clothes line in no time,' said Joy.

Tilly thanked her and now that that task was dealt with, she only had to wait for Robbie to finish his telephone call and they could go to the shop together.

'So you're leaving us as quickly as I thought you would once I heard you'd come into money,' said Rita, pouring boiling water into the teapot. 'Although, I must admit I thought you'd be going back to Chester, not staying in your father's old place.'

'It's perfect for my needs,' said Tilly.

'Humph!' The older woman pursed her lips. 'D'you really think people will want to buy your book once you've written it?'

'Why shouldn't they?' said Tilly stoutly, despite a sudden sinking feeling. Perhaps she was deluding herself, believing she had some talent.

'These are hard times. People haven't the money to spend on non-essentials,' said Rita.

Robbie shook his head at her. 'Don't put the girl off. I've found that when times are tough people need taking out of themselves. Let her have a go and if it doesn't work – although I don't see why it shouldn't as she's proved she can write by having short stories published – then she can do something else.'

'Thanks, Mr Bennett, you make me feel a whole lot better,'

said Tilly, her spirits lifting again. 'Mrs Wright isn't the first person to think I'm wasting my time but I'm determined to prove that I can do it. Right, now I'll go up and start packing my things, if you don't mind.'

'You do that, Tilly,' he said. 'I need a few private words with my sister.'

'Well, if you're going up. Take your cup of tea with you,' said Rita, pouring it out and thrusting the steaming cup at her. 'And you'll still have to pay me to the end of the month.'

'I will,' said Tilly, steadying the cup on the saucer. 'As soon as I get my inheritance.'

'And when will that be?' asked Rita.

But Tilly had gone, leaving Robbie to talk to his sister about his plans for Pete and giving her a good reason as to why Wendy should be allowed to spread her wings a bit and work regularly for Grant Simpson.

As Tilly packed her clothes and books, she wondered what her father would think if he knew that she was moving into his place and doing his job. As she packed the sheaf of notes she had made for the plot of her novel and the first few chapters she had written, she prayed that no more dead bodies would turn up. Of course, that was extremely unlikely, seeing as how the police had done a fair amount of digging in their search for clues. She picked up the magazine that Eudora had given to her and opened it at the article with Don and the blonde's picture. She gazed at them for a moment and then placed it with her notes; the letters and the photographs he had sent her, though, she placed in her handbag, planning on rereading Don's old letters.

She stripped the bed and folded the bedding and then carried it downstairs. She had to make several trips and made sure not to forget the potted geranium that her father had given her and her rag doll. A lump filled her throat and she wiped away a tear as she took a final look around the bedroom that had been hers for the last fifteen months; then she went downstairs.

She found Robbie talking to Wendy in a low voice in the kitchen. From the expression on her face, Tilly presumed that she was pleased by what he was saying. She left them and went outside the shop to see if there was any sign of the man with the handcart. There wasn't but she decided to wait outside and watch out for him, thinking that she was going to have to write letters of resignation to both Grant and the Friends of the Seamen's Widows and Children's charity that evening.

The man was ten minutes late but as he helped pile Tilly's possessions into the cart, Wendy, Mrs Wright and Robbie came out of the shop.

'I suppose we'll still be seeing something of you,' said Rita Wright.

'I suppose you will,' said Tilly dryly. 'Thanks for all you've done for me. I do appreciate it. I'll see you get what I owe you.'

The older woman nodded. 'I should think so, too.'

'Bye, Tilly, see you soon,' said Wendy, giving her a hug and whispering in her ear, 'Thanks for everything.'

'And you.' Tilly blinked back tears. What on earth was there for her to cry about? A chapter in her life was coming to an end and she was moving on to do what she really wanted. Even so, she felt more upset about leaving the Wright family's home than she would have believed. No doubt she would soon get over it because she would need to put all her emotions into her book.

When they reached the house, Tilly led the man round the back and he helped her to unload the cart. He was careful to avoiding the washing on the line. It gave her an odd feeling to see her father's clothes blowing in the breeze. As she paid the man she became aware that they were being watched. She waited until he had gone before going over to the wall and speaking to the woman, who was definitely getting bolder because she did not vanish out of sight as she was wont to do.

'What are you doing in the little house at the bottom?' asked the woman.

'I'm moving in,' said Tilly, smiling up at her. 'I'm going to write a book and look after Mr Bennett's garden for him.'

'What kind of book?'

'I don't know if I can put a label on it yet,' said Tilly, thoughtfully. 'But I hope it'll be exciting and keep readers turning the pages.'

'I like stories set in far lands and I like a love story weaved in there somewhere,' said the woman. 'My cousin and his wife left lots of books but most of them are too heavy. I liked those that belonged to his sister, Lily, but she ran away years ago and he cut her off when she got into trouble. I saw her, though, not so long ago.' The woman frowned. 'My, she had changed and had a foul mouth. There was another sister and she went to America and married and had a son, but both are dead now.'

She had no sooner stopped speaking than her eyes sharpened and she said, 'I must go now. He'll be cross if he knew I was talking to you.' She vanished out of sight.

Tilly could hear Fang barking and presumed Leonard had arrived home. She wondered what he would think when he knew that she'd moved in next door. One thing was for certain, his cousin had given her pause for thought.

Tilly walked back to her new home and made up the bed and put everything away. Her desk had been placed in front of the window overlooking the garden. She propped the photograph of herself and Don and her niece and nephews against her pencil holder on her desk. She gazed at it for several moments, wishing and hoping, before sitting down. Then she wrote three letters and in one of them she enquired after the Doyle children, thinking she must go and see them as soon as possible. Then she stuck stamps on the envelopes and went to the post box. She knew that she would need to watch her money until she saw the solicitor but hopefully it would not be long before he replied to her letter.

'Done much writing yet?' asked Joy, a few days later when Tilly dropped by at the house.

'Yes.' Tilly thought about the scene she had sketched out to do with the murder of an American soldier. She had clipped it to her notes, not sure yet whether she could work it into her novel. She was even considering having a flaxen haired American detective involved in solving the mystery. She did not doubt that having Don's lively eyes seemingly gazing into hers daily had something to do with it.

'There's a letter for you,' said Joy. 'I'll get it.'

For a moment Tilly wondered if it was from Don but decided that was highly unlikely; even so, she asked if there was an American stamp on the envelope.

'No,' said Joy, wiping her hands on her pinny. She went into the hall and returned with a long narrow envelope. 'It looks official,' she said, handing it to Tilly.

She opened it, read the letter enclosed and glanced up at

Joy. 'It's from the solicitor. He's asked me to see him on Friday. Is that OK with you?'

Joy nodded. 'I'll check with Mr Bennett but it should be fine.'

Tilly was glad about that and looked forward to getting the meeting over with.

The next couple of days passed swiftly and on Friday, she and Joy went into town and had the meeting with the solicitor. Everything went smoothly and he said he would arrange matters as she wished and get in touch with her sister about buying her shares when everything was sorted out. He offered to forward her some money to be going on with, which Tilly was relieved about.

Tilly and Joy parted at the tram stop in Dale Street as Joy wanted to buy some clothes, while Tilly was in a rush to get back and get on with her novel. It was another hot day but clouds had started to gather in the sky; she reckoned that the weather would break soon and there would be an almighty downpour. Suddenly she noticed Leonard with the dog and was tempted to pretend she had not seen him and to hurry into the house. Almost instantly, she realised it was too late for her to do that because he had spotted her and was striding towards her with Fang loping beside him.

He stopped a couple of feet away from her. 'What's this I hear about you living in the outhouse at the bottom of the garden?' he demanded without preamble.

The tone of his voice caused her to stiffen. 'It's true. I'm writing my novel.'

'But why there? I mean, it was the gardener's hut.'

'Why not? After all, he was my father and I feel close to him there.'

Leonard looked shocked. 'What the hell do you mean he was your father?'

'I mean he was my father,' said Tilly emphatically. 'Mr Bennett said I could live there rent free and in exchange I'll keep the garden tidy and have peace and quiet to get on with my writing.'

'I can't believe it! That crazy old man who found the body was *your* father?'

Tilly's eyes flashed. 'He wasn't crazy. He had been mentally ill due to having worked with lead but he was much better.'

Leonard continued to stare at her for several moments and then he turned away, muttering to the dog and dragging it towards his house.

Tilly felt a tightness in her throat and swallowed. Then she pushed open the gate and walked round the back of the house and down the garden. If she had not accepted earlier what Eudora had said about Leonard not being the right man for her, she certainly did now.

Tilly said much the same to Joy when she came down to the outhouse later with a plate of sliced boiled bacon, potatoes and cabbage. 'I thought you might have forgotten to eat,' she said. Tilly thanked her and waved her to a chair and told her about her encounter with Leonard. 'Mrs Bennett knew what she was talking about,' said Joy. 'She could read people in a way I never could. Best never to get married than marry the wrong man,' she added. 'By the way, I've booked a cruise for late spring for me, Mother and Mr Bennett.'

Tilly stared at her. 'Mr Bennett? Does he know about this?'

'Yes, I know it might seem odd the three of us going together but when I told him about my plan to take Mother away on holiday, he asked if he could tag along. He seems to think it will be just the medicine to cheer him up after the winter and his first Christmas without Mrs Bennett.'

'He's probably right,' said Tilly, a small smile playing round her mouth.

Joy flushed. 'He's almost the same age as Mother, you know. Although, the way she is, I find it hard to believe. He seems so much younger. Mrs Bennett used to say that it was an attitude of mind and a healthy body. Mr Bennett hasn't had to cope with much suffering in his life and maybe it's that which makes him optimistic about life. Just remember, Tilly, that too much misery gets people down, so I hope your novel is going to have a happy ending.'

Tilly said hastily, 'I like happy endings, too.'

'Good,' said Joy, 'then I'll buy it.' She got up. 'I'll leave you alone now to get on.'

After she had gone, Tilly thought about what Don had written to her in one of his letters about writing her novel. *You've got to give your characters obstacles to overcome but make sure they darn well overcome them by the end and they've developed as a person along the way.* She wondered if he had received Seb's letter about the button yet and what he had to say about the blonde in the photograph.

That night the weather broke; lightning flashed across the sky and thunder rolled. The rain poured down and was accepted by the thirsty earth. Tilly was kept awake by the noise and decided to light the oil lamp and get on with some work. Change was in the air again and she suspected that it was not only for the weather.

CHAPTER TWENTY-SIX

Tilly flexed her shoulders and rose from her chair. She went downstairs and out into the garden for some fresh air. October had been a strange old month, she thought, gazing about at the drooping, leafless shrubs and the sodden lawn. After the glorious summer had come the storms. The author Edward Porritt had drowned and his body had been washed up near Fleetwood. Ships had come to grief in the North Sea and, according to Mr Bennett, there had been daring rescues.

'There's something you could put in a book, Tilly,' he had said. 'It would make a good adventure story.'

'Perhaps another time, Mr Bennett,' she had said, thinking that her novel was not that kind of story.

Outside the Cunard building at the Pierhead, Lord Derby had unveiled a war memorial to the company dead. Tilly thought of Freddie, who had been a young sailor during the war, and how he could have easily been amongst those it commemorated. The war had changed so many lives. She thought of the uniform button and wished they would hear something from Don. He had not fought in the war but he could have so easily been killed, working as a journalist on the field of battle. Seb might never have been found and she would never have met Don. He was such a caring man and more worthy of her love than Leonard, whom she had not seen since she had told him about her father.

Suddenly there was a noise behind her and Tilly turned to see Grant Simpson, of all people. But it was his method of entry that gave her a shock for he appeared from up the side of the outhouse.

'Hello, Tilly,' he said. 'It's good to see you're taking a break.'

She had received a brief, businesslike letter from him that had acknowledged hers of resignation but she had not seen him for a while. Neither had she seen Wendy, who had been out the few times she had called in at the shop for a bag of sweets. 'How did you get in?'

'Surely you know there's a door in the wall behind your little house?' said Grant.

'Yes. Yes, of course I do,' said Tilly, puzzled as to why and how he had managed to come in that way. 'But I'd forgotten. What are you doing using it? I thought it was locked.'

'Well, it wasn't. I thought I'd try it. Do you know there's been a theft in one of the houses further along and I'm investigating the claim. I'm surprised you haven't heard about it,' said Grant.

Tilly frowned. 'I've been busy writing. If it was mentioned to me, it's gone in one ear and out the other.'

He smiled. 'Too wrapped up in writing your novel, hey?'

'You could say that. May I ask you a couple of questions?'

'Of course you can. But if the first one is about Wendy, I can tell you that her typing is improving and she's getting a dab hand at disguises. She has a real talent for this work.'

Tilly smiled. 'I'm glad I'm not missed.'

'I wouldn't say that,' said Grant, looking suddenly serious. 'But I'm not so slow on the uptake that I didn't realise my advances were unwelcome.'

'It's not that I don't like you,' said Tilly, her cheeks warm. 'I do. It's just that I'm fond of someone else.'

'Which one?' he asked. 'The American bloke that Wendy mentioned or him next door?' asked Grant with a jerk of his head in the direction of the dividing wall. 'You can't trust him, Tilly. I'll tell you now,' he said, lowering his voice. 'I think he's involved in some way in the thefts that have been going on.'

For a moment Tilly was silent and then she said, 'It's true I found him attractive but I accept he's not for me.' She hesitated. 'I saw him talking to Mrs Doyle's brother outside a pawnshop on Scotland Road months ago.'

Grant drew in his breath with a hiss. 'You obviously didn't think fit to tell me or the police – I'm surprised at you, Tilly.'

Tilly's cheeks burnt. 'At the time I thought that perhaps he worked for Leonard in his shipyard. We didn't know then that Patricia's uncle was our burglar. Even then, I didn't want to believe that Leonard could be involved in the robbery in any way. It just didn't make sense. He can't need the money. He owns a shipyard for heaven's sake!'

Grant's eyes glinted. 'Then you were mistaken. I think I'd better be on my way.'

'Wait!' cried Tilly, putting out a hand to stop him. 'Tell me what you're going to do.'

'You know the rules, Tilly,' he said, removing her hand from his sleeve. 'You no longer work for me. I suggest you go to the police with this information.' He disappeared round the back of the outhouse.

Tilly stood, staring after him, knowing she had been a fool. Grant was right and she was going to have to go to the police and tell them what she had just told him. She would ask to speak to Sergeant Jones and hope he would be sympathetic towards her.

'You never mentioned any of this to Mr Parker?' asked Sergeant Jones, after Tilly had unburdened herself in the interview room.

'No.' She wished she could sink through the floor. 'I'm sorry I didn't tell you earlier.'

He fixed her with a frown. 'I wish you had, Tilly. You could still be accused of being an accessory after the fact. But maybe you can make up for your mistake. D'you think you can remember which pawnshop it was?'

'Not the name but I could take you there,' said Tilly, brightening up.

The sergeant smiled. 'That'll do. I just have to make a couple of telephone calls and then you can lead the way.'

Tilly did just that, and within the hour, she was standing with the sergeant and a plainclothes detective in the exact spot where she had stood when she had seen Leonard and Patricia's uncle that day.

'Have you any idea where Mr Parker went next?' asked the detective.

'Yes. Because I followed him,' said Tilly.

'Good girl,' said Sergeant Jones. 'Can you lead the way?'

Tilly nodded. Unerringly, she took them to the yard she had seen Leonard enter. The men thanked her and told her to go home. Tilly did not have to be told twice and could only hope no charge of being an accessory after the fact would be brought against her. She wanted nothing more than to return to her typewriter and bury herself in her writing.

That evening, when Tilly came out of the outhouse to go to the lavatory, she heard a voice coming from the other side of the dividing wall.

'Guess what!' it said.

Tilly went over to the wall. 'What?' she asked, looking up at the woman.

'The police have been here. They asked me lots of questions about Leonard. I think they suspect him of being involved in the burglaries that have been taking place. They searched the house from top to bottom.'

'Did they find anything?' asked Tilly hesitantly.

'No, but they went round Leonard's bedroom, dusting for fingerprints.'

'Where is Leonard?'

'I don't know.'

'So they haven't arrested him?'

'No. They asked if I knew where he was and I told them that I presumed he was at the shipyard. They've left a plainclothes man watching the front of the house.'

'That makes sense,' said Tilly, squirming inside because she had allowed herself to be taken in by Leonard's handsome face and charming manner. She thought about poor Nanki Poo and Eudora's heart giving out and her father smashing the car into a tree and dying. These deaths could all be laid at Leonard's door if he turned out to be the Mr Big behind the robberies. Suddenly she hated him and wanted him brought to justice.

'I don't know what I'll do if they arrest him. This is his house. Where will I go?' asked the woman.

'Couldn't you just carry on living there? Perhaps you could take in a lodger or two to help with expenses,' suggested Tilly.

'Now there's a thought. I'll let you know if anything else happens,' she said, and disappeared.

Tilly remained where she was for a few moments and then carried on up the garden into the house. She knocked and went inside, expecting to find Joy in the kitchen but she was not there. Instead she heard the strains of a clarinet and realised that Robbie Bennett was either with Pete or one of his pupils. She decided to come back later and tell them what had happened. In the meantime she would do some shopping.

As she walked along West Derby Road, she could not help wondering what Leonard would do if he knew that she had given information about him to the police. Would he try to harm her? It was as she was returning to the house that she saw Wendy and Joy ahead of her, so, putting on a spurt, she caught up with them.

'I've something to tell you both,' she said.

'If it's about Leonard Parker being in league with our burglar,' said Joy, 'then you don't have to because Wendy's been telling me all about it.'

'She has?' asked Tilly, surprised.

'In fact, she believes he's the head of a gang of robbers and has been providing them with inside information about the homes he'd been invited to as a guest,' said Joy.

'Grant doesn't think he does any of the actual stealing himself but he's just as guilty as the rest of them in my opinion,' said Wendy.

Joy said, 'Your Aunt Eudora was right about him, wasn't she?'

'The police have searched his house,' said Tilly.

'Grant thinks they're not going to find him and that he's scarpered with what money and stolen goods he can get his hands on,' said Wendy.

'Well, if we've seen the back of him that's a relief,' said Joy. 'I'd rather he was punished but right now all I can say is good riddance to bad rubbish. I can't wait to tell Mr Bennett about all this.'

'Well, thank God he's gone, that's all I can say,' said Robbie when they told him the news. 'Although I hope they find him and he gets his just desserts. I know you had a fancy for him, Tilly, but Eudora always thought that he wasn't what he appeared.'

Tilly thought if anyone else repeated Eudora's words about Leonard to her then she would scream. She needed to be alone and excused herself, then went down the garden and let herself into her small refuge from the world. She unpacked her shopping and decided to indulge herself with fried bread, bacon and egg and a mug of cocoa. As she ate, she thought of Leonard, so that when she sat down at her typewriter, he and the burglaries were very much in her mind.

She could not remember dozing off but she woke suddenly and banged her face on the typewriter. Her hand caught her pencil holder and the photograph of Don, herself and the children slid beneath the typewriter.

'Hello, Tilly. I hope you don't mind me visiting you at this time of night?' said Leonard.

Tilly's heart seemed to jerk inside her breast and she blinked up at him in the lamplight. He was perched on the corner of her desk, holding her notes. For a moment she wondered if this was a dream. 'They said you'd disappeared,' she murmured. 'Now you're here in my dream.'

'No dream, Tilly,' he murmured. 'And even if I hadn't read this, I'd have had to vanish.' He waved the sheets of paper beneath her nose. 'How did you know I did it, Tilly?'

'I don't know what you're talking about,' said Tilly, ice seeming to trickle down her spine.

'Come off it!' His voice was sharp. 'The American soldier! How did you find out about him? Who's been talking? I thought I'd got away with it. Was it the old girl who lived here? I heard that Mrs Bennett was a medium, did she go and get in touch? She swore she'd keep quiet. She was fond of me, you know, had watched me grow up. She allowed me to kick a ball around in here, let me dig in her garden and gave me treats. I wasn't allowed to play in my own garden.' He frowned. 'Unless it was my bloody mother Mrs Bennett got in touch with.'

'You killed the soldier?'

'You know I did. It's all here in your notes!' He smacked the paper with his fist.

'But I made that up!'

'Don't try and kid me, Tilly.' He lowered his head, bringing his face close to hers, so that they almost touched. 'No one could make all this up. How did you know about my having been left on my uncle's doorstep in a basket and he and his wife adopting me as their son?'

'I didn't!' cried Tilly. 'Something similar happened to someone else. I admit that some of my story is based on fact, but the baby was not meant to be you, Leonard.'

He grabbed her shoulder. 'You're saying no one will

recognise me because you've turned me into a character in your book and given me a different name?'

'No!'

His face darkened. 'You're a liar. This character is a bloody murderer and a thief, gets blackmailed and is about to lose everything after falling in love with the heroine. Of course, it's bloody me! You even have an American detective who was the soldier's pal during the war.'

'I didn't intend him to be you,' said Tilly, her voice trembling. 'When you say you're a murderer, do you mean you deliberately killed the soldier?'

'No. My cousin's death was an accident. His mother had emigrated to America and he was born over there. My uncle and I had a falling out and he threatened to disown me and leave everything to this brave nephew of his who was going off to the Front to fight for England. He even went as far as telling him the truth – and that I was his illegitimate cousin. I knew the truth myself by then,' said Leonard in an undertone, as if to himself. 'My real mother, Lily, had turned up and introduced herself. She threatened to let the truth out if I didn't help her and her gang of thieves by getting information for them.' He paused. 'You even used the manner of her murder in the book. She was so confident she had me under her thumb but after accidentally killing my cousin when we both got drunk and had a fight, I found it easier to kill her later when she wanted to come and live with me. I couldn't have that! She soon realised her mistake.' He paused again and looked unseeingly out of the window. 'She didn't half make a splash when she went in.'

'The pawnbroker!' whispered Tilly.

Leonard dropped her notes on the desk and smiled. 'See,

you knew all the time.' He perched on the desk and stroked her hair. 'I'm not a killer by nature, Tilly,' he said seriously. 'I'd never have killed Nanki Poo. I like animals. But Brendan, now, he hated animals. I can't tell you how many he killed just for pleasure.'

Tilly quivered beneath his touch. 'So, so what are you going to do now? Why did you come here?'

Leonard gazed into her eyes. 'Do you really not know, Tilly? You're the heroine in my story.'

He took hold of her chin and brought her face close to his and kissed her. She was torn by a mixture of fear, repulsion and a peculiar sympathy for him, and knew she must not recoil.

When he broke off the kiss, he said, 'Come with me, Tilly. We can build a new life somewhere else.' She did not answer but could only look at him. Slowly, the light in his eyes died to be replaced by a harsh expression. 'The answer is no, isn't it?' She was too terrified to speak. 'You know what I'm going to have to do to you, Tilly, don't you?'

'Kill me,' she said through stiff lips.

He tutted. 'Don't you listen to a word I say? I'm not a killer. I'm going to have to tie you up until I get away from here.'

'You know there's a plainclothes policeman watching the front of the house?'

He laughed. 'Of course I do. But thanks for the warning. I came in by the back way. Don't ask me why they're not keeping an eye on that. You have some stockings?'

'Yes. In the chest of drawers.'

'Now, don't move because I don't want to hurt you,' warned Leonard.

Tilly did not want him to hurt her and, besides, she knew

that she'd never make it down the stairs before he caught up with her. She struggled when he tied her up with her best silk stockings and then he stood, gazing down at her. 'I'm sorry about this, Tilly, but I've got to do it.'

She watched in horror as he tore up her notes and the typewritten pages of her novel. 'You swine!' she cried.

He tutted. 'Not a nice name to call me, Tilly.' He bent over and kissed her. 'Goodbye.'

Tilly watched him walk away. 'Where are you going?' she called.

'Now, that's my secret, Tilly,' he said, and disappeared from her sight.

It was a long night for Tilly because however hard she struggled she could not free herself. She shouted until she was hoarse but no one came, and she was getting colder and thirstier and was desperate for the lavatory. She cursed Leonard Parker.

Joy found her the following morning when she came down the garden, carrying a letter. Tilly heard her climb the stairs and call out, 'Are you there, Tilly? We thought you might have called in for a cuppa by now.'

'Yes,' said Tilly huskily. 'Thank God you've come.'

Joy appeared at the top of the stairs and stared at the paper, torn small enough to appear like confetti, scattered all over the floor. Then she looked at Tilly. 'Oh, my God, what's happened?' She hurried over to her. 'Has Leonard Parker been here?'

'Yes! Untie me.'

As soon as Tilly was free, she bent over her desk and pulled open the bottom drawer. She took out the carbon copy of her novel so far and hugged it to her.

'Thank God he didn't kill you,' said Joy, staring at her.

Tilly nodded, moving away from her desk and stumbling across the floor, still holding the carbon copy. 'I don't think he suspected me of informing on him to the police. It was what I'd written in my notes for my book that caused him to do this.'

'At least he didn't harm you,' said Joy.

'No. But I'm going to have to retype everything I've done so far, although, having said that, I'm going to have to alter a few things.'

'Such as what?' asked Joy.

Tilly did not answer but hurried downstairs and outside to the lavatory.

Joy went and informed the plainclothes policeman about what had happened and within half an hour the detective inspector and Sergeant Jones arrived. They questioned Tilly about what had happened. She told them what had taken place, omitting that Leonard had kissed her and had wanted her to go away with him. They were obviously annoyed that they had not set a watch on the back door in the wall and that Leonard had eluded them. She guessed that a watch would be kept at the railway stations and the Pierhead, and at his shipyard.

As for Tilly, she bought some typing paper and typewriter ribbons, as well as a new pair of silk stockings.

'So what are you going to do next, Tilly?' asked Joy, following her out to the outhouse.

Tilly placed a sheet of paper in her typewriter. 'I'm going to retype the pages he destroyed,' she replied.

'Here?' asked Joy, glancing about the room. 'What if he comes back?'

'He won't,' said Tilly positively.

Joy sighed. 'I think he has enough nerve for anything. Why don't you go to Chester for a break? You'll be safe there.'

'No,' said Tilly, her eyes glinting with a determined light. 'I'm not going anywhere until I've finished my novel.'

Joy left her alone and Tilly placed the photograph of Don leaning against the car in Flanders against the pen holder. Lest we forget, she thought, remembering the encouragement, advice and affection that had filled his letters. She began to type.

CHAPTER TWENTY-SEVEN

Christmas was to come and go before Tilly eventually finished her novel and sent it off to a publisher. In all that time there had been no word of Leonard or Don. By then it was almost the end of February and she could take notice of the real world again. There was to be a royal wedding; the Princess Mary was marrying Lord Lascelles, son of the Earl and Countess of Harewood. There were photographs galore of the princess of when she was a baby and throughout her childhood. There were eight bridesmaids and the bride's bouquet was laid at the foot of the cenotaph. Among the pages of the *Liverpool Weekly Post*, Tilly discovered Ethel M Dell's latest arresting and remarkable romance, *The Obstacle Race*, in serial form. She decided to read it on her way to visit her family.

As it was a bright sunny day, she decided to travel by ferry to Birkenhead and to catch the train to Chester from there. She felt the sea breezes would help blow the cobwebs away and was quite excited at the thought of seeing her family again. Alice had mentioned finding a tiny shop that might be suitable for what she wanted in a recent letter but she had made no mention of Don having been in touch with Seb. Perhaps I will never see him again, thought Tilly sadly.

It was busy down at the landing stage because the Isle of Man boat was in and an ocean-going liner was discharging its passengers. At least there aren't many people queuing for the ferry, thought Tilly, watching the boat making its way across the Mersey. She did not have long to wait before it was tied up alongside the landing stage and the gangway was let down. Once aboard, Tilly climbed to the upper deck and leant on the rail, gazing down on the activity below. She mused that perhaps the next book she wrote should have a seafaring hero.

Suddenly Tilly froze, staring at a man leaning against the wall of the customs building. He was tall and lanky and carried a walking stick. There was a suitcase at his feet and a youth appeared to be talking earnestly to him. Tilly guessed the lad was one of those who hung around the Pierhead, hoping to earn a sixpence for carrying a passenger's luggage or obtaining a cab for them and directing them to lodgings. The man removed his hat to reveal a thatch of flaxen hair and took a handkerchief from the pocket of his long leather coat and mopped his brow. Was it Don or was it just someone who looked like him? Her heart began to thud.

She was tempted to try and attract his attention by calling his name. If he looked up, then she would know if it was him for certain. But would he be pleased to see her? As she watched, another man appeared, carrying a tripod and what looked like photographic equipment. A youth followed him, struggling with a suitcase. He stopped and spoke to the man she had been studying. Now she was certain it was Don. She did not believe that he could have a double who was also a photographer. Her heart was now beating so fast that she thought she might faint but she had to get off the boat.

Tilly made for the companionway and was halfway down the steps when she heard the gangway being hoisted up. She put on a spurt but was too late. Disappointed, she hurried to the side of the boat and leant over it. She called Don's name, only to have her voice drowned out by the noise of the engines. The expanse of water between boat and landing stage widened as the vessel manoeuvred into a position facing towards Birkenhead. She sprinted to the top deck and stood at the rail, gazing towards Liverpool, searching for the place where she had last seen Don. But he had vanished into the crowd.

Tilly seriously considered staying on the ferry and returning to Liverpool but decided that would be pointless. She had no idea where Don was staying and there was always the possibility that he would come to Chester to visit Seb. Perhaps he had even written to him. She looked up at the clock on the Liver Building and decided to call in at the motor repair yard on Canal Side before visiting Alice. It was possible that Seb would be there and might have news for her.

The journey seemed to take an age and it was a frustrated Tilly who burst into the office, without knocking. Kenny was there but not her brother-in-law. 'Where's Seb?' she demanded.

'And good morning to you, too,' said Kenny dryly.

Tilly flushed. 'Sorry. It's just that I need to speak to him urgently.' She went over and kissed her half-brother.

'So, what's so urgent?' asked Kenny, putting his arm about her waist and giving her a hug.

'I saw Don Pierce! At least, I'm pretty sure it was him.

There was a liner in and I was on the Birkenhead ferry when I caught sight of this man. He was leaning against the customs building and carried a walking stick. He took off his hat and he was fair-haired.' She paused for breath and added in an undertone, 'He's just as attractive as in his photograph.'

'And what happened next?' asked Kenny, his eyes fixed on her face.

'This bloke came up, carrying photographic equipment and spoke to him.' She met her half-brother's gaze. 'I can't see it being anyone else, can you?'

'It certainly sounds like it could be him,' said Kenny cautiously.

Tilly nodded. 'You know Seb wrote to him ages ago about a button Dad found in the garden?'

Kenny nodded. 'Surely Don wouldn't have come all this way just because of a button? Perhaps he's here in a professional capacity.'

Tilly stared at him and then moved away. 'Where's Seb? Somewhere I can telephone him?'

Kenny turned to the girl sitting at the other desk. 'Put the kettle on, Jacqueline. Then telephone the showroom to see if Mr Bennett is there.'

'You don't think it's possible that Don came to see me?'

Kenny shrugged. 'I don't know, love. But by the way you're behaving, I guess you'd like to see him.'

A sharp laugh escaped Tilly. 'Of course I'd like to see him. I hope we can meet and talk and get a few things sorted out.'

Kenny smiled. 'I hope you can. I liked Don.'

Tilly and Kenny were drinking tea when Seb telephoned. Kenny took the call and Tilly tried to grab the telephone from him but he held on to it. She had to make do with listening to a one-sided conversation. Then Kenny brought it to an end before she could ask to speak to Seb.

'He said he would see you at the house at lunchtime. You can talk then.'

Tilly frowned. 'Didn't he tell you anything about Don?'

'I told him what you said and he said that he would see you at lunchtime,' said Kenny firmly.

Tilly realised that she would have to be patient and, after drinking tea with him and telling him about having sent off her manuscript, she left to see her sister. There was an appetising smell of lentil soup when she entered the house. Alice was in the kitchen.

'I've missed your cooking,' Tilly told her sister.

'Then you should have come sooner,' said Alice.

'I couldn't,' said Tilly. 'I haven't stopped.'

'Sit down now then and I'll give you some soup.'

Tilly sat at the kitchen table and smiled at her sister as she placed bowls on the table and ladled out the soup. 'I thought Seb would have been in by now.'

'He'll walk through the door any minute,' said Alice. 'You can set the clock by him. We still have lunch together.'

'Has he given you the go-ahead for the shop?'

Alice nodded. 'Yes, since you bought my shares. I'm to have help in the house again. It's ages since those days when I had a cook and a maid. Not many girls want to go into service anymore and live-in, so it was a job finding one. She's an orphan.'

Alice's mention of an orphan reminded Tilly of the Doyles and she was filled with guilt. It was not that she had not thought of the children in all this time, rather that she had done so and then forgotten about them again.

'Seb and I will carry on having lunch together even when I have the shop because I'll shut up for lunch.' Alice smiled. 'Anyway, that's enough about me. Have you finished your novel?'

Tilly nodded. 'Finished and sent it off.'

'I must admit I never thought you'd manage it.'

Tilly raised her reddish eyebrows in a similar fashion to Kenny. 'Oh ye of little faith,' she said softly, only to add, 'To be honest, there were times when I had doubts myself. Especially after Leonard Parker tore up my work.'

'That was a bad business but at least he didn't harm you,' said Alice. 'So what next? Will you wait until you hear from the publisher?'

'No. I've already a germ of an idea for the next book – but that's all it is at the moment, a tiny germ. It's going to take time for me to work it all out.' Tilly dipped her spoon into the soup.

'You could come and live back here while you're thinking,' said Alice. 'Just having you here would be a help.'

'I'll think about it,' said Tilly.

There was the sound of footsteps outside and the door opened. 'You there, Alice? Has Tilly arrived?' asked Seb.

'Yes, we're both here,' said Alice. 'As you would see if you closed the door.'

Seb did as he was told and smiled at them both before first kissing Alice and then Tilly. 'It was Don you saw,' he said.

'What's this about Don?' asked the sharp-eared Alice.

'You knew he was coming, Seb?' asked Tilly.

'No. But I remembered the name of the hotel in Liverpool where he thought of staying last time he was here,' he replied. 'So I phoned the Adelphi.'

'And he was there,' said Tilly, her face alight with relief.

Seb smiled. 'He'd just booked in. I spoke to him.'

'Did you tell him I'd seen him but couldn't get off the boat?'

'What is this?' asked Alice.

'If you listen, love, you'll find out.' Seb reached out and patted her hand.

'So what's happening next?' asked Tilly.

'Don will pick you up from Robbie's house this evening. He's going to take you out for dinner,' said Seb.

Tilly felt a thrill of excitement and then her spirits plummeted and she was filled with fear. What if he wanted to tell her that he was married to the blonde?

Alice frowned. 'I was hoping Tilly would stay here for a few days.'

'Don wants to see the place where the body was found and hear Tilly's story from her own lips,' said Seb.

Tilly decided to put all thought of the blonde out of her mind. Even though she knew who the button had belonged to and who had killed the soldier she looked forward to telling Don her story. 'Was he able to tell you about the button, Seb?'

Seb looked chagrined. 'No. He said this was your mystery and he wanted to talk to you first.'

Alice looked put out.

Tilly smiled. 'I will be back but I'll have to go home early.'

Alice sighed. 'You said home. I thought you still thought of here as home.'

'I do in a way, but—'

'Hush, the pair of you,' said Seb. 'Don's bound to visit us and no doubt Tilly will come with him.' He glanced at Tilly and smiled. 'He said to put your glad rags on.'

Tilly grinned and decided to draw some money out of the

bank and buy something ready made from Dejong's in Bold Street before returning to Newsham Drive. She was going to ask Robbie if she could have the use of the bathroom and a bedroom for this special occasion.

'Tilly! There's a man downstairs who wants to see you,' called Joy, rapping her knuckles on the panel of the bedroom door.

Remembering that Joy had never met Don, Tilly said, 'Is he an American?'

'Definitely. Name of Don Pierce, so he's your man.'

'Tell him I'll be down in a few minutes,' said Tilly.

With hands that shook slightly she fixed a small hat that was a froth of net and ribbons on her red-gold hair. Then she stared at her reflection and wondered whether to apply lipstick or not. She smoothed the bronze velvet gown over her hips and decided not to keep him waiting. She picked up the matching jacket and her handbag before running downstairs. She was nervous, unsure whether Don would approve of the Tilly she was now, and could only hope for the best.

Her pulses were aflutter and they did not calm down as she entered the drawing room, where Don was talking to Robbie. She recalled that Mr Bennett had worked and lived in America for years and so the two men would be able to find common ground. Don stopped in mid-sentence and stared at Tilly and there was a look on his face that caused her to want to fling herself at him.

Their eyes held and he came to his feet with the aid of his stick. She went over to him with a hand outstretched, her gaze never shifting from his attractive features. She realised just how much she had needed to be in his presence once more. She wanted real kisses from him, not paper ones. He gripped her hand and held it tightly. Close up, his face was more lined than she remembered from three and a half years ago and she presumed that was due to his constant struggle with his war injury. Warmth and concern flooded her and she said, 'Where have you been? I was worried about you.'

'There was no need.' Don rested his stick against the chair and took hold of her other hand and brought both her hands against his chest. 'You look all grown up, Tilly. I think I'm going to have to give you a grown-up name and call you Matilda.'

She found herself unable to speak for a moment because it was so long since she had heard that American drawl of his and she just loved the sound of it. Pleasant tingles raced along her nerves. 'No one ever calls me Matilda,' she said in a breathy voice. 'I'm sorry I missed you last time you were in Liverpool, Don.'

'I guess it wasn't meant to be that we met then,' he murmured. 'We both had stuff that needed our attention. I've been in Russia and China, otherwise I would have been here sooner. If you'd seen some of the kids there it would have broken your heart. I had to bring their situation to the notice of the western world. But there wasn't a day that went by when I didn't think of you and wish you were by my side. It would have been too dangerous for you, though.'

'Liverpool has its dangers and there are children here, Don, who go barefooted and beg on the streets,' she said seriously.

His eyes narrowed. 'Are you saying I didn't have to go so far away to find signs of terrible depravation?'

'No. I wouldn't presume to tell you your job,' she hastened to add. 'Those countries are enormous so the suffering is on a larger scale, but I could have helped you if you'd stayed in

Liverpool a while and we wouldn't have been parted for so long.'

Don's features softened. 'You can have no idea how I felt when I eventually received Seb's letter, I fixed it to leave straight away and here I am. We have a lot to talk about, Tilly. '

'I agree that we won't be lost for words over dinner,' she said, her eyes gleaming.

He smiled. 'We have transport and a table is booked for two at the Silver Grill. Do you know it at all?'

'It's in Dale Street but I've never been there,' replied Tilly.

'I've heard good things about it. Excellent food and good music.'

Tilly gave him a sparkling glance. 'You've tempted me. I can't wait to get there. You mentioned transport – it wouldn't be a golden coach as in *Cinderella*?'

He grinned. 'I forgot my magic wand but Joe will see us all right.'

'Joe?'

'He's my right-hand man.' Don had been holding her hands all this time and now released one of them to pick up his stick. He turned to Robbie. 'I'll take good care of her, Mr Bennett, and have her back before the witching hour.'

'You take all the time you need,' said Robbie, smiling at them both. 'It's good to see Tilly looking happy. She's had a tough time.'

Don nodded and, with Tilly's arm linked through his, the pair made their way outside. When Tilly set eyes on the car waiting at the kerb, she knew the kind of money Don would have had to pay out to hire the American roadster. But there was so much more to him than money. Still, she decided better to be rich than poor. He must be doing OK despite his gammy foot. Often she had felt concern about how he would manage to continue in his chosen profession with such an injury, but obviously there had been no need for her to worry about him. He had courage and determination and that counted for much in her opinion.

He introduced her to Joe, saying, 'I couldn't do all I do without his help.'

The stocky young man with dark eyes and wavy brown hair smiled at Tilly. 'You take no notice of him, Miss Moran. Mr Pierce can do lots of stuff without my help.' He opened the rear car door for her and she seated herself on the soft leather seat. After all that had happened, it seemed unbelievable that at last she and Don were together.

Don sat beside her. 'Are you comfortable?' he asked, turning towards her.

'I'd have to be extremely choosy not to be,' she said, smiling.

There was an appreciative light in his eye. 'If you get to feel chilly you must say so and we'll put the top up.'

'No. I like the hood down. You can see so much more this way.'

'There's a rug if you need it,' he said. 'Let's go.'

They were silent as Joe drove along Newsham Drive and eventually out onto West Derby Road, where he had to cope with the traffic. Tilly was extremely conscious of Don's shoulder as it brushed against hers. He broke the silence. 'I was sorry to hear about your father, Til—Matilda. Seb told me how he died. It must have been a terrible shock. I know from your letters in the past how much he meant to you.'

'Yes. It was terrible. But at least he's at peace now. I only wish I'd got the chance to tell him the identity of the dead body he found.'

'That must have been quite a shock for both of you. I got to see plenty of dead bodies during the war but I never could get used to it.'

'I can certainly understand that,' murmured Tilly. 'One body was enough for me.'

Don reached for her hand and drew it through his arm. 'Shall we talk about the military button?'

'Let's.'

He grimaced. 'Difficult one. Buttons like it were worn by every infantry man that went to war. The eagle is the States insignia. There is no way I could trace it to any one man. Sorry.'

Tilly would have been filled with deep disappointment if she had not already known the identity of the soldier. 'I must admit I thought, with you coming all this way, you must have known who it belonged to.'

'Nope. But I did kinda get to thinking about the soldier who it might have belonged to. Here's an infantry man who went missing in Liverpool. Maybe he had few friends and his family back home were all dead – that's if his having gone missing other than on the battlefield hadn't been reported. But he could possibly have mentioned to his comrades about having relatives in Liverpool and being in two minds to look them up. Whether this was after hostilities ended and he was due to return to the States or that he never reached the Front, I don't know. What is for certain is that he never did return home.'

'I thought a lot about him myself and then I found out the truth. From what you've said I presume that Seb hasn't told you that I know the identity of the soldier.'

'Holy cow! How did you do that?'

'I'll tell you soon but first I'll tell you what I thought,' said Tilly.

Don gazed at her intently. 'Right. Spill the beans.'

She smiled. 'I wondered if he came to the Bennetts' house before they moved in to visit the old lady who used to live there and that *she* killed him. I even toyed with a similar idea for my book and wrote my thoughts down in my notes but decided against it.'

'Seb said you finished your novel. Satisfied with it?'

Tilly shrugged. 'I had to rewrite it several times. Once because the Bennetts' next door neighbour, Leonard Parker, tore it up.'

'What? Why would he do that?'

'Because he believed I had put him in my book and he was a thief and a murderer,' said Tilly casually. 'He's on the run from the police now.'

Don whistled through his teeth. 'He sounds a dangerous bloke.'

'He killed our soldier but he says it was an accident, then he confessed to me that he murdered his mother.'

Don swore and then begged her pardon. 'How did you escape being killed yourself?'

Tilly knew she could not tell him the truth. 'Sheer luck, I guess. Fortunately, he didn't get his hands on my carbon copy.'

Don stared at her and then hugged her against him. She rested her head on his shoulder and was filled with a sense of well-being.

They said no more after that until they were seated at a

table in the Silver Grill with drinks in front of them. Don ordered a steak while Tilly asked for chicken. As she sipped her cocktail, he said, 'Now tell me, have you sent your novel off to a publisher?'

Tilly nodded. 'Although the publishers might not like it.'

'You've got a copy?'

'Of course.'

'I'd like to read it, if I may?'

For a moment Tilly dithered. What if Don absolutely hated what she had written? He might say kind things but she'd know if he thought her story wasn't fit for publication. Yet at the same time she wanted him to read it and have his opinion.

She took a deep breath. 'OK! I'll give it to you when we get back to the house.'

His face split into a smile. 'I look forward to reading it.' He changed the subject, reaching across the table and taking her hand. 'I know I'm a bit of a crock, Matilda. But I still want to marry you. If you were to accept me then you must realise that your enjoyment of life might be curtailed somewhat. For instance, I'd really enjoy whirling you round a dance floor but if we danced it would be more of a hop and a skip.'

She was touched by his words and felt a deep urge to reassure him that she was no gadabout who only cared about her own happiness. 'Just because dancing has become all the rage it does not mean that we have to do it. We can have fun doing other things.'

His face softened. 'I'm glad you feel like that, but perhaps I'm rushing things. It's just so great seeing you again that I had to let you know how I feel.'

Tilly said seriously, 'You're still prepared to wait until I'm twenty-one?' she asked.

'I don't want to rush you.' He paused and said hesitantly, 'but Seb did say something about some other guy.'

'Yes, there's been a couple of men I fancied for a while.' She rested her chin in her hand. 'I wondered about the blonde in one of your magazine features.'

'Lisa,' he said instantly. 'She was a nursing sister in Flanders who lost her husband, poor kid.'

'You were on first name terms.'

'Yes, but...' He grinned suddenly. 'No need to be jealous. We were fellow compatriots in a foreign land, that's all. I didn't want to marry her.'

'Is that so?' She chuckled. 'Then I'll remind you that I'll be nineteen in July. Old enough, do you think to—'

His face lit up. 'Are you saying you'd marry me then?'

She winked. 'That depends on what you say about my book. I'll give you my answer then.'

Don looked as if he was about to say something more but their meal arrived and she changed the subject, telling him about the fun she'd had working for Grant Simpson, the great detective, and how he had fancied her but that while she had liked him, she had never wanted to marry him. 'Besides, Wendy loves him and I couldn't have spoilt her chances.'

'You're a thoughtful, kind person, Matilda Moran,' said Don, leaning across the table and planting a kiss on her mouth. 'But then I always knew that from the first moment we met.'

'I thought you were quite mad,' said Tilly, her lips tingling. She and Don had never kissed properly and she was now more than eager to discover what its full effect on her might be.

On the drive back to the house their conversation struck a lighter note and they discussed films and music. Tilly was in a dreamlike state after the cocktail and wine and enjoyed the feel of his arm around her.

When they arrived at the house, she told him to wait whilst she fetched the carbon copy of her manuscript. She was as quick as she could be and within ten minutes he had the precious pages in his grasp.

'Goodnight, Don. I hope you enjoy it,' she said tentatively. 'Some of it is based on real events. I thought *What if?* and made up the rest of it.'

'Thanks, Matilda. I'm sure I'll find it interesting.' Don brought her against him and kissed her long and deep. She melted into his arms and returned his kiss. She felt as if she was floating on air. Then he lifted his fair head and rubbed noses with her. 'I'll drop by in the morning.'

Tilly nodded. 'Thanks for dinner.' She said goodnight to Joe and hurried indoors.

Don made himself comfortable in the basket chair in his hotel bedroom and placed the carbon copy of Tilly's novel on the tray in front of him and began to read. When he finished, dawn was breaking over the Liverpool skyline. He was stiff and his eyes felt as if the were filled with grit. He had meant it when he had said to Tilly that he was sure he would find her book interesting but he had not really expected it to be so enthralling. After all, she was still only young and had seen little of the world. He found it incredible that her work showed so much perception about people. Despite what she had said about some of the story being based on real events, he had still half-expected it to be similar to the kind of romantic novels his mother and sisters read. He certainly had not expected it to be the page-turner it turned out to be.

He went to bed and slept for a few hours and when Joe woke him, the book was still playing over in Don's head.

Don could not wait to see Tilly so she could untangle fact from fiction for him and within no time at all he was knocking at Robbie Bennett's door.

Joy answered it. 'I know who you've come to see,' she said, smiling.

'Is that Don?' called Tilly, appearing at Joy's side a moment later.

'Sure is,' said Don, holding out her carbon copy to her. 'I couldn't put it down. I've been up all night reading it.'

Tilly put her hands to hot cheeks. 'You liked it?'

'Loved it! If the publisher doesn't take it – mind you, I'm sure he will – then I'll give you the name of a good American publisher.'

'Oh, Don!' Tilly dropped the carbon copy and flung herself at him, almost knocking him off balance.

'You'd best come in,' said Joy, gathering up the typewritten pages. 'I think I'll have a read of this myself.'

Tilly was about to say *No, wait for the book!* but stopped herself. She owed Joy a lot. 'You do that, but don't let anyone else know. They can wait for the book.' She grinned at Joy.

'It'll be our secret,' said Joy, hurrying ahead of them into the house.

Once they were seated on the sofa in front of the fire in the drawing room, which they had to themselves, Don said, 'So tell me what's true and what isn't. I can understand why Leonard Parker should tear up your partial manuscript if your villain was based on him. But am I to believe that there really was an American detective hired to find out whether the stolen property had been smuggled into America, where it was sold for a fortune to collectors?'

'No,' said Tilly, smiling. 'But I got to wondering where Leonard went when he went missing for weeks at a time. It was mentioned at one time that he had been to America, so I thought that perhaps that was where Eudora Bennett's antique Oriental vases disappeared to.'

Don smiled faintly. 'You hint that your heroine might marry the detective, Duggie Parsons.'

'Yes, I do,' murmured Tilly. 'I thought that maybe they'd get together and do some more detecting in another murder mystery.'

'Your mind is definitely darker than I ever imagined, Matilda.'

'Life is dark for many since the war,' said Tilly, a shadow in her eyes.

'I notice that you have your villain fighting with your detective hero aboard ship and the villain ends up falling overboard in the mid-Atlantic,' said Don, gazing at her intently. 'But you don't know what happened to Parker?'

Tilly had often wondered about that since Leonard had walked out after leaving her tied up. 'He owned a shipyard so maybe he managed to disguise himself and leave on a ship under an assumed name.'

'Going to America?' asked Don.

'Your guess is as good as mine.'

There was a long silence before Don said, 'This orphan gang who live on the streets. Their leader is quite a caring and spirited girl, who looks after the other kids. I'm glad they all end up being adopted by a rich childless couple.'

Tilly smiled. 'I did base her on someone I know. Although I can't see Patricia and her siblings really picking pockets and being forced to climb through pantry windows to let the burglars in by opening the back door.'

'So where are the real kids?' asked Don.

'In the Seamen's Orphanage,' said Tilly. 'I kept intending to go and visit them but I've been so busy, but now I have more times on my hands—' She let the words hang in the air.

'So there isn't really a rich couple who adopts them?'

Tilly sighed. 'I'm afraid not. They did stay here for a while but when Mrs Bennett died, Mr Bennett couldn't cope.'

Don was silent for several moments, and then he said, 'I'd like to meet her and her siblings. I'm sure there's rich folk in America who would be interested in their story. I'd take some pictures and they'd go in a magazine or newspapers.'

Tilly's face lit up. 'I'll telephone and see if I can arrange it,' she said.

She did so and it was agreed that they could visit the orphanage and Don could take some pictures.

The orphanage was a large sprawling building with two wings. The girls slept in one and the boys in the other, although they shared the dining facilities, as well as classrooms, the hospital and the adjoining chapel. The building backed on to a railway line and was not far from Tuebrook police station. Tilly could understand why Patricia had dreaded the thought of having to live there with her siblings because it was such a big place. The adults who looked after the children certainly did their best to take care of those in their charge, but what with its long, echoing corridors and large dormitories, the building lacked the cosy security of the small terraced house where the Doyle children had been reared.

It was playtime when they arrived and while Don spoke to someone in charge and Joe lugged his equipment about and took some shots of the building, Tilly asked one of the assistants if she could speak to Patricia Doyle. 'You'll have to be quick because the needlework class starts soon,' warned the woman.

Tilly went over to Don and told him what she was doing. He nodded and said he would come with her. They were shown into a yard where children were milling about and the noise level was deafening. She looked about for Patricia amongst the navy-clad children with sailor collars to their uniform and suddenly spotted her with Kathleen. Tilly hurried over to them, calling Patricia's name. Don followed more slowly.

Patricia's face lit up. 'Miss Moran! I thought yer'd forgotten about us,' she cried, clutching Tilly's hand.

'No! I should have come before now but so much has happened since I last saw you that I just haven't had time. I should have made time but—' Tilly gripped her hand tightly. 'No excuses! I'm sorry.'

'It doesn't matter. Yer here now. Have yer come to get us out? Has Mr Bennett changed his mind? I was never so happy as when I was living in his house. I was sorry when Mrs Bennett died,' she said earnestly. 'She really cared about us.'

'Yes, she did,' said Tilly. 'But I'm sorry, love, that's not why I'm here. I had hoped you and the others had settled down.'

Patricia's smile faded. 'No! One of the teachers treats me like I'm a fool because I'm behind with me reading and says me writing leaves much to be desired, as well. Some of the other girls skit the way me and me sisters talk. Then there's the baby—' Her voice trailed off and a muscle in her throat convulsed.

Tilly felt terrible and suddenly frightened. 'What about the baby? He's not—'

'No! He's not dead.' She pulled her hand out of Tilly's grasp. '*She* adopted him.'

'She?'

'That Mrs Nuttall who tap danced at the concert.'

Tilly was relieved. 'But isn't that a good thing? The Nuttalls are comfortably off. They'll look after him and give him a good life.'

'Yer don't understand!' cried Patricia. 'He won't be ours anymore. They'll turn him into one of them. They'll change his name to Nuttall. He won't be a Doyle anymore and he'll grow up not knowing us.'

Tilly understood. But what could she do? It had been simple in her book to provide a rich couple with a large house who could keep the family together, but real life was different. 'I'm sorry, Patricia. I never thought—'

'No. Most grown-ups don't. They forget what it was like to be a kid,' said Patricia in a dull voice. 'So why are yer here?'

Tilly told her.

The girl perked up and glanced at Don. 'American, hey? Is he your boyfriend?'

Tilly smiled. 'I suppose you could call him that. He has been asking me to marry him for quite some time.'

'And will you?'

'Probably.' Tilly looked up at Don and winked.

'I did notice that your hero's initials were the same as mine and that he had fair hair.' There was a twinkle in his eye.

'I always knew you were quick on the uptake,' said Tilly.

'So what's your answer?' asked Don, reaching out for her hand and grasping it firmly.

She raised her eyebrows. 'I think you can guess but I'm not going to say "Yes" here. I want somewhere more romantic,' she said in a dreamy voice.

Don chuckled. 'I suppose you want gypsy violins playing, red roses on the table and champagne?'

'That would do *me* for starters,' interrupted Patricia. 'I suppose I couldn't be one of yer bridesmaids?' she added eagerly.

Tilly glanced down at her and knew that here was something she could do for the girl. 'I don't see why not – you and your sisters – and my nieces. As well as Don's female relatives who would like to take part,' she added, looking up at him mischievously.

Patricia let out a whoop and flung her arms around her. 'Does this mean we'll all get new frocks?' Her voice was muffled against Tilly's coat.

'I should think so,' she answered, stroking the girl's hair. 'What d'you think, darling Don?' Tilly's eyes held his in a long look.

Don smiled. 'I think that's a great idea,' he said, lowering his flaxen head and sealing the agreement with a kiss.

Other titles available from
ALLISON & BUSBY
by June Francis

All Allison & Busby titles are available to order
through our website

www.allisonandbusby.com

You can also order by calling us on 0207 580 1080.
Please have your credit/debit card ready.

Alternatively, send a cheque made out to
Allison and Busby Ltd to:
Allison & Busby, 13 Charlotte Mews,
London, W1T 4EJ.

Postage and packaging is free of charge to
addresses in the UK.

Prices shown above were correct at the time of going to press.
Allison & Busby reserves the right to show new retail prices on
covers which may differ from those previously advertised in the
text or elsewhere.